A TED DANGER MYSTERY

Douglas Boatman

HOTWELL PRESS

Dayton, Ohio

USA

ISBN: 978-1-7339853-3-8 (paperback)
ISBN: 978-1-7339853-0-7 (ebook)

hotwellpress.com

Dayton, Ohio USA

Cover by eBook Cover Designs
Editing services by Refine Fiction

HOTWELL
P R E S S

To Dad, who drove all night

I happened to go to market, and bought a Spanish girl, ten or twelve years old. She cried as if her heart would break, and looked the picture of despair. It seemed strange, that at her age slavery should make such an impression on her.

—Alain René Le Sage,
The Adventures of Gil Blas of Santillane

A TED DANGER MYSTERY

Prologue

DOCTOR: YOU NEED TO remember that day.

    Patient: I was so young. It was chaos.

    Doctor: Take a step back. Make it a story about a different girl. See it through her eyes, but with the insight of an adult. Write it all down.

    So she wrote ...

SHE FELT THE EYES of the men on her body, today more than ever before, each glance as bold as the prickling sear of the sun, the teasing breath of the sea. She stayed by her father, watched his eyes, drew her calm from his. Nudity all around, on this secluded nook of beach, as common as the trampled sand and churning surf, and it was nothing new. She'd been here before, always with her father, and she knew the rules. (#1. Lots of penises but it's rude to stare).

    This time, something was different. She felt her own nakedness more sharply as its meaning changed. As she herself changed, and grew, and became someone else.

    Someone she didn't know.

    And she felt the eyes of the men.

    And she shivered. Chilled by a new bite in the air, a physical coldness. The sun no longer warmed her skin. Voices fell to silence. All eyes turned upward, only to the sky, to ratted clouds congealing in a roil of gray, reflecting, refracting the oily sea. A slick sickness of midday dusk, and a whirl, a swirl, viscous and heavy, sagging, drawing itself down, growing fat and turgid, a thick dirty rope dangling from the darkness above the dusky waters. A swollen tube, a pendulous mass, longer now, swaying and stretching, with a needle tip, slender and sharp. Down, downward, dropping, seeking, and she remembered the hot pale afternoon at the shabby zoo, the zebra's breath rasping in the heat, its listless stare from mucous eyes, the flies on its legs, and the black phallus dangling from its dusty haunches, nearly reaching the bone-dry earth, and from its charcoal tip a sudden startling jet in the dust, churning into gurgling yellow mud. And now the needle raked and stabbed the far waters and flung the broiling froth high, and as she stared the roiling multiplied in silence, wonderful and strange, and then she felt the throb and rumble deep inside, in her chest, in her feet, everywhere now, and she turned to her father and squeezed his hand, felt in her fingers the pain of his grip, and she followed his gaze back out to the sea. And the dark column swung and swayed with slow hypnotic grace, snapping its tip like a whip ...

—and now it's on them, too soon, too soon, and they run. Through the sudden amber chaos they run. Through the blast and howl and darkness they run. Through the thrash and lash that scours her skin, that stings her eyes, that gags her throat, they slip, they stumble, they run.

But it's too late to run.

She clings to her father's hand and his strength bends her bones. Then she sails through sand and sky, buried and flying and buried again.

That's all she remembers.

And later, when she wakes, and opens her eyes to the blinding sun, it's over.

SHE HEARS THE BREAKERS crest and roll, slow and steady and serene, as they foam the beach with creamy sheets.

Someone is crying.

Her father is gone.

1 Oedipal downpour

AUTUMN 2011

OUTSIDE MY OFFICE WINDOW, it was raining like a motherfucker.

September is usually tranquil in Ohio, weather-wise, day after day of low humidity and crystal sunshine bouncing off CGI clouds, as we start that long gradual slide through October and November and December, from summer's long days of mild malaise to winter's deep-freeze of full-blown melancholy, a few days of Indian summer along the way like gifts we wonder what we did to deserve.

But a tropical storm had blundered north from the Gulf of Mexico, flung its dying arms wide, and knocked us all out of whack. Record high temps all over the Midwest and now they were crashing—not cold, but crashing—and it was raining like a motherfucker.

I always liked that description of hard brutal rain—read it in a short story about a beach magician and a runaway—and when the rain comes howling down, slashing at the glass, sucking the light from the room, there it is, tip of the tongue, like the parrot-joke punch line I have to grit my teeth and grin to keep from shouting out loud when the cold wind buffets and blows—goes right *through* you, *damn* cold—and the parrot rocking in his cage spreads his outrageous wings and squawks to the unamused minister, *Ah*, he says. *Feel that fuckin' breeze!*

But it wasn't cold in my second-floor office—dim, damp, and drafty, sure, but still balmy on a rainy September afternoon in Dayton. I was standing by the window that overlooks Endgate Road, and my associate, Trudy Hart—aka Tru, or Ms. Hart, or anything but Gertrude, please—sat in the guest chair,

3

using the coffee table by the fainting couch as a desk for sorting and filing.

She glanced up from her invoices and ink pens, the glow of the goose-neck lamp smoothing her delicate features, and wanted to know, "What are you smiling about?"

I yawned. "Just daydreaming."

"Go take a nap, Ted."

She knows me well. "Tempting. Last night I—"

A DOUBLE TAP ON the office door cut my answer short.

A flicker from the window. A boom, a rumble, a growl.

What would bring someone out on a day like this?

THE DOOR OPENED, AND a woman of a certain age stepped inside, glistening with rain. She brought with her a trace of ozone and tropical spices, posh and elemental.

"Ted Danger?" she said. "Confidential Investigations?"

"Close enough," I said. "Come in."

She hesitated, and in fact, three's a crowd in my office. It's a renovated bedroom in a rezoned commercial strip crowded with sixty-year-old houses—homes once resting on ample lawns, safely buffered from a quiet avenue, now looming over a swollen thoroughfare.

Tru scooped up her paperwork and stood, a move that made her taller, but not by much. She smiled at our visitor.

"Please, take my seat," she said, turning her chair to face my desk. Then, to me: "I'll finish these in the annex." *Annex* is our code for the basement storeroom we share with two other tenants: a thin shady accountant and a thick vulgar broker.

"Thank you, Tru," I said.

She really is a lovely girl.

TRU CALLS HERSELF MY intern. I met her when she shadowed me for an undergrad criminology project, which led to an internship and a summer job. Now she's a fixture. Last fall she graduated *cum laude* with a BA in Law Enforcement. Her prospects are good, but she still hangs around this dive. Lord knows why.

Tru's adoptive mother-to-be, an English professor, had fallen hard for a grad student with whom she shared a Gertrude Stein infatuation. The prof was in her forties, never married, and her student paramour—divorced and back in school to finish his master's—wasn't much younger. They married, adopted Tru as an infant, and promptly christened her Gertrude, a name she'll answer to, but grudgingly. ("Why didn't they name me Alice B.?" she once complained.)

Her dad died when Tru was a child, she told me, and her mom withdrew from life. She doesn't say so, but that would explain the casework that intrigues her. Tracking down estranged relatives, birth parents, and children given up for adoption. Bringing families together.

She talks about setting up her own PI shop but wonders if she has the gravitas clients expect, and I see her point. Even after working with her for months, I still think of her as a child.

"I'M NICOLE VAVUL." MY rainy-day visitor delivered a firm enough handshake and took a seat in my client chair.

"What can I do for you?" I eased into the creaky leather swivel behind my desk.

She shrugged out of a washed leather trench coat but kept her massive snakehide bag on her lap. *A bag like that can hold a lot of secrets, but I'm getting ahead of myself.* Her fall frock was short and chic, black suede with a splash of bittersweet. When she leaned forward and crossed her long legs I glimpsed her chunky leather ankle boots. *This woman is showing a lot of skin: bovine, ovine, reptilian, and human.*

"I'm told you perform confidential investigations," she said.

"Hence the name."

"Danger?" Her makeup, deft and understated, couldn't veil the fine lines around her eyes. Dark eyes shadowed with distress.

"Not much, usually," I said. "And really, there's no guarantee of confidentiality. Once you start investigating, people find out."

"Well, you're not trying to snow me," she said. "That's a bonus."

The storm slapped the window, rattled the panes.

"Who referred you to me, Ms. Vavul?"

"Nicki," she said.

"Nicky who?"

"Please, call me Nicki." The raindrops in her hair were stars fading at dawn.

"Okay. And I'm Ted. Who referred you to me, Nicki?"

"Nobody. I picked you out of a phone book."

"Not many people use those anymore."

She shrugged. "I do. I like them."

I nodded. "Me too." I was beginning to like this woman.

SHE SEEMED IN NO hurry to get to the point. "What kind of a name is Danger for a private eye, Ted? Isn't that a bit camp? It's like ... Max Gamble. Or Johnny Action."

"Actually, it rhymes with *banger*," I said. "Ted *Dang*-er."

Her laugh surprised me—loud and unaffected, with lots of teeth. "Ted *Dang*-er, Private Eye." Her grin looked forced. "Dang. Is that legit, or an affectation?"

I flattened my hands on my desk. "My secret. And you're not here to talk about me."

She took a breath and the mirth fell from her face. From the big articulated jaws of her bag she drew a bulky manila envelope and placed it on my desk.

"Right," she said. "I want you to find someone."

"Okay, a missing persons case."

"Well ..." She set her bag on the floor and slid her palms down her thighs, smoothing her dress. "Not exactly."

2 Lights out

I OPENED THE FLAP and dumped the contents onto my desk pad: tidy bales of one-hundred-dollar bills in butterfly clips and rubber bands, plus a big photocopy of a black-and-white snapshot on a sheet of copy paper.

The money, I slipped back into the envelope. This client got better every minute. I picked up the copy paper and took a good hard look at the snapshot.

A man and a young girl stand on a beach, facing the camera, the ocean behind them. The girl leans on the man, one arm wrapped behind his waist, her other hand on her hip, elbow jutting forward, a defiant toothy grin on her face. The man smiles. His hands rest on the girl's shoulders, one palm against her neck, a finger hooked casually in her ear.

I swung the lamp over the photo.

In the background, sand and ocean and sky and nebulous shapes at the horizon, low-res and unfocused. The man's hair is on the shaggy side of average, and the girl's might be longer, but it's hard to tell—it falls behind her and clings to her head as if she's been swimming.

As for their clothing, there isn't any. Nothing blurred or hazy here, their bodies in crystal focus and sharp relief, revealing every line and every lesion. Every crest and every cleft.

Every patch of thatch, you might say, and every surface of epidermis.

"How long has she been missing?" I said.

Nicki smiled, but her eyes flashed pain. "She isn't. I want you to find the man."

"Okay. Tell me about it."

SHE LOOKED DOWN AND said nothing.

"Start anywhere," I said.

"I don't know how to start." Her head tilted a fraction.

"Start with the photo. Where it came from. Who the people are."

"The girl is my daughter Haley."

I studied the girl's face. "I see the resemblance."

"She's fifteen now. She was eleven in the picture."

"Eleven?" I looked again. "I don't have kids, but I'd have guessed older."

"You a steak lover, Ted? A carnivore?"

"Sure."

"Hormones in the cattle feed. More beef for the buck, and schoolgirls get to bleed in second grade. Little women. By twelve they're all grown up. God bless America."

I didn't have an answer for that. "Who's the man?"

"I don't know."

"Your daughter's naked with him and smiling."

Her hands curled into fists. "I know, Ted. It doesn't make sense."

"She doesn't remember him?"

"No," she said quickly. "I mean, I haven't asked her."

"Why not?"

"She's ... she was so young." She put her palms to her temples and closed her eyes. "I don't know. Maybe it's better for her not to remember."

"Your call, I guess. So where did you get the photo?"

THE WINDOW STROBED WITH a thousand suns.

"What the—" I started to say, when a thunderclap punched a shock wave through the room.

Lamps flared and went dark, leaving me blind.

RAIN LASHED THE WINDOW, drummed the shutters, pelted the roof. The building thrummed. Then a keening pierced the din. A scream choked with fear.

Nicki faded in, curled in her chair. Her wails fell into whimpers as I groped my way around the desk and knelt beside her. She sobbed and turned away.

"We're safe." I patted her shoulder. "It missed us."

"I hate storms." Her voice quavered. She pulled a tissue from the box on my desk and dabbed her face. "Hate them."

"I figured," I said. "But I'm a trained observer."

Nicki gave me a look and blew her nose and sighed. We stared at the window without talking. Rain layered the panes like rippled glass, warping the outside world and sealing us in our secret sanctuary, a shelter dim and shimmering.

She shook her head. "It's raining like a motherfucker," she said, and I almost fell in love.

3 Rainy-day money

TRU BURST THROUGH THE doorway. "Christ, are you guys all right?"

"More or less," I said. "What about you?"

"Nothing a fresh pair of panties won't fix." She looked at Nicki, a double-take. "You've been crying."

Nicki made a noise in her throat. "I almost didn't go out today. Storms scare the hell out of me."

"So why did you?" Tru picked up the photo and dropped into my chair.

"Nicki," I said, "this is Trudy Hart, my associate. Tru, Nicole Vavul."

Tru stared at the picture. "Oh, my goodness. This looks dubious."

Nicki snatched the photo from her hands. "You get your associates from the Girl Scouts, Ted?"

Tru looked sideways at me. Rain pounded the roof.

It's a fact: Tru is not a big person. She's a head shorter than me, a hundred pounds lighter, and a quarter century younger. She's twenty-three but with her slight frame and ingenuous face she could pass for anything from thirteen to thirty.

I CLEARED MY THROAT. "Nicki, Ms. Hart is a valuable member of the firm. Her youthful appearance and outstanding skills have proven a distinct advantage in many of our investigations."

"Ms. Vavul," Tru said, "I apologize for being flippant about the photo."

"Apology accepted," Nicki said. "I suppose I ..." She dabbed at her eyes. "I'm very tired."

We all made nice for a while. I leaned back on the fainting

couch and let Tru stay at my desk.

Nicki blew her nose again, and her story began.

FOUR YEARS AGO (NICKI told us) her husband, a medical software VP, was invited to a business convention in Spain. She went along. They mixed business with pleasure in Europe, while their daughter Haley, eleven years old at the time, stayed with Nicki's parents in Florida.

Haley was their only child.

"How was she when you got back to the US?" I said.

"Fine. Happy to see us. Sad to leave her grandparents."

"Not moody? Secretive?"

"Not at all. In fact, she seemed more outgoing."

In fact, Haley had been begging to go back (we learned), and the family was planning a Thanksgiving vacation to Florida. And Nicki had been organizing the luggage.

"Haley's suitcase was on the closet shelf where I'd stored it four years ago, after her Florida trip. I dropped it and the picture fell out, face down. I turned it over and ..."

We all stared at the copy centered on my desk.

"And no one had used the suitcase since Haley?" Tru said.

"No. It's too small for Ben to use, and it's pretty old. I think Haley—"

"Ben's your husband?" I said. "Benjamin?"

"Yes, but it's Bentley. I think Haley must have put the picture in a suitcase pocket and forgotten it when she unpacked."

"Do you have the original with you?" I said.

"No, I made this enlargement on our printer. I—"

"On your printer? I thought the original was a hard copy."

Nicki frowned and Tru shook her head.

"Ted, most printers are copiers too," she said. "Welcome to the twenty-first century."

"Okay," I said. "Yeah, I knew that."

"I put the original in a safe place," Nicki said. "Where Bentley and Haley won't find it."

"How long ago?" Tru said.

"When I found the picture? About a month."

"Why wait so long to come to us?"

She bit her lip and looked out the window. "Ben's out of town. Philadelphia. I want to do this while he's gone."

"He doesn't know you're here?"

"My husband monitors all my accounts. So I brought cash, from our safety deposit box. He won't notice right away."

"Your rainy-day money," I said. "Ha ha."

No one spoke. Tru looked at me through slack eyes.

"Because it's raining outside," I said. "It's like a pun."

She shook her head and turned to Nicki. "You don't trust your husband."

"I wouldn't say that. I'd say ... he doesn't trust me."

"Why not?" I said.

"Well," Nicki said. "It's kind of embarrassing."

Tru reached out and touched her hand. "Tell us."

Nicki looked at me and I nodded but kept my mouth shut.

She sighed. "I'm afraid he thinks I'm a little bit crazy."

IT TURNED OUT NICKI suffered from periods of insomnia and depression. She'd always been moody, she told us, but her symptoms escalated when she got pregnant with Haley. During her spells, she'd go on shopping sprees and forget things. Important things. Like coming home.

Lately, she'd improved. And her husband called daily to make sure she stayed that way.

"Are you ever, uh, delusional?" I said.

"I don't think so."

TRU AND I WALKED her through her story again.

"You don't seem crazy to me," I said. "You're rational. And you're telling us the truth."

"And I know one thing for certain." Her finger traced a circle around the nude couple. "I'm not imagining this."

I AGREED TO TAKE the case. Nicki would call her parents in Florida that evening and tell them I'd arrive in two days to discuss a family matter. Tomorrow I'd drop by her house to see the original photo and examine the suitcase. And meet Haley, I hoped. Nicki still wasn't sure how much she wanted Haley to know.

EVEN IN THE GLOOM of late afternoon, Nicki's wedding set gleamed and flashed as she signed my standard contract. The diamond wasn't as big as the Ritz, but it was big—plenty big enough to symbolize the lasting bond between two people in love. *Mostly I don't mind being alone, without a wife and a family. But sometimes a case like this comes along and I miss having someone who gives a damn.*

She caught me staring. "What are you looking at?"

"Your husband's a lucky man."

"Yikes," Tru said. "Let's focus, okay?"

"Thank you, Ted," Nicki said. A flush tinted her face. "I'm lucky to have him."

"Okay," I said. And it was.

4 Scratching the scar

THE COLD FRONT ROLLED into Dayton overnight, record cold, but it wasn't my problem. By six a.m. I was five miles high and bound for the Sunshine State. I'd barely slept the night before, up late going over my interview notes, doing web research—Tru's the internet whiz but I can Google—paying bills, etc.; then rising early to negotiate airport security drama-free. Not difficult, since I left my handgun at home. *Shouldn't need one to investigate naked people, right?*

I'd planned to wait another day before leaving, but Tru and I decided she would handle things in Dayton—nothing much on tap—and I could grab an early flight. So I did.

WE HADN'T PARTED ON good terms.

When she urged me to leave the business in her care, I made the mistake of telling her to keep her damn boyfriend out of the office. I'd caught them one Saturday in my visitor's chair, not exactly hooking up but on the way. Naked from the waist up, sort of straddling—and when I saw Tru's small breasts and rosy nipples I remembered the time I walked in on my mom sitting in the tub when I was a kid and wondered why she wasn't happy to see me. But I didn't mention that last night.

"You never liked Jason, did you?" she'd said. We were wrapping things up at the office long after Nicki had gone. The power was back but most lights were off.

"He's a jerk. You can do better."

"You don't even know him."

"Sure I do. I used to be his age."

"He's a decent guy. And I can help him find his birth parents."

14

"Never fall for a client, Tru."

Her expression darkened. "Maybe I should be like you. The lonely private eye."

She had a point. "You're an adult. Do what you want. Just keep things professional." I glanced at the visitor chair, the scene of the crime, and shook my head.

When I looked back, she was glaring.

"Hey," I said. "What do you say we get ice cream?"

"Ice cream. Oh. My. God. Can we ride ponies too?"

"Fine. Forget it."

She smiled and the room got brighter, or seemed to.

"The hell with ice cream," she said. "Let me buy you a drink."

WE ENDED UP WITH ice cream after all. We drove separately to Eaty's Bistro and Tru ordered us mudslides—premium vanilla with Bailey's and Kahlua and who knows what else. Vodka? The bartender checked her ID twice and still frowned. I gave him my tough-guy stare and got a smirk in return. But he served her, and my god, the drinks were good.

"So you've never been married, right?" she said.

We'd picked a booth near the back. The place was nearly empty: three young guys at the bar, two women eating wings at a table by the window.

"No. You know that."

"Not really," she said. "There are lots of things we don't know about each other. Deep dark secrets."

"It's possible. But I've definitely never been married."

She slurped the ice cream melting at the rim of her glass. "Not even close?"

I remembered sitting across from a beautiful woman about Tru's age. "Maybe. I was in love."

Her shoulders went up. "And?"

"I guess I didn't love her enough." The booze was unwinding my mind. "We'd been getting serious. Then I ran into this girl in a bar one night. Real cute. Laughed at my

15

jokes." I tasted my drink and it wasn't as sweet. "We ended up in bed and Hope caught us. *In flagrante delicto*, as we say in the business."

She held her drink near her face. "Hope? Was that her name?"

I shook my head. "Let's not talk about her."

"Why not?"

"Why not? It makes me sad, that's why not."

"Poor Ted," she said. "What happened?"

"That face. She looked at me and said *What have you done?*" The words choked me. "Then she walked out. I never saw her again."

"Why don't you track her down?"

"Why do you want to know all this ancient history?"

She touched my arm with cold fingers. "Tell me, Ted. Maybe I can learn something."

I hadn't scratched that scar in a while. "We'd been getting along great. Then she changed. Got spooky on me. We argued, then she caught me with this girl and, like I said, Hope wanted nothing more to do with me. And I get it. I respect that."

"Maybe she needed you to go after her—"

"No."

"—and bring her home."

"You're wrong."

A YOUNG GUY IN a Bengals jersey and torn jeans walked up to our table, focused on Tru. "Hey, aren't you that girl in the ads? For like clothes and stuff? That model?"

We both stared at him.

"I'm Dom." He held out his hand and Tru shook it.

"I'm not up for meeting anyone tonight," she said.

"That's cool. My friends and me wondered, like, you look familiar." He nodded at the two nitwits at the bar. "Like how old you are, you know?"

She smiled. "Old enough." She touched my hand. "Right, big guy?"

I was tired of this pick-up artist, and of Tru too. "She said get lost."

Dom took a step back. "Yeah, sure." He threw Tru a look. "Nice to ... uh, see you later."

When he was back with his buddies I told Tru, "That wasn't funny."

She exhaled through tight lips, blowing me off. "Not a bad approach. For a kid. Pretty smooth, really."

"Let's go. I've got things to do."

"Go ahead. I'm not leaving until I finish my drink."

"And I'm not leaving you here with those hooligans."

She tapped the table with a straight finger. "Maybe if you'd been like this with Hope, more protective, she wouldn't have—"

"Stop right there. We're done talking about Hope."

We glared at each other and finished our melting drinks. When she stormed out, I followed to make sure the three amigos weren't planning to complicate her evening. She drove off and I tailed her to her place, keeping my distance, and then drove home. Brain lightning flashed images in my head. *Nicki. Hope. Tru. Mom.* I hadn't told Tru, but she reminded me a lot of Hope. Her toughness, her sense of humor. But Hope had been tall, I could look her in the eye when we danced, when we made love; a woman and a half, from the Amazon tribe. Tru was more the prom girl, the full-grown child: small but mighty, like my mother. Mom. *Scenes and pictures in my mind. Swirling, with full narration and subtitles.*

Making love to an Amazon ... Tru, the small-breasted woman-child ... Mom in the bathtub ... and a girl on a beach, wearing nothing but a smile.

God, these voices in my head.

How much vodka was in that mudslide anyway?

5 Contraband coffee

THE ENDLESS DRONE OF the engines and the muted jostle of the cabin—not to mention my lack of sleep the night before—worked like a narcotic, a big slug of codeine, as our jet devoured the stormy miles. I woke up on the descent into Miami International feeling sticky and gritty, a stream of spittle cooling on my chin.

Air travel on TV: Beautiful people lazing in a spacious cabin, the soft-lit silence ruffled with quiet conversation. The reality: A human horde trapped in a dingy lair of noxious air, a big tin can that quakes through the night, and beneath the constant din, the whispered threat of sudden savage death.

But this time I'd slept through most of it, and when I woke up my ears barely ached.

IT WAS STILL MORNING by the time I negotiated the MIA baggage claim and picked up my rental—a compact SUV, red—and headed north to Pompano Beach. The sun was hot through the glass and I buzzed the windows down to cut the smell of fast food, body spray, and BO wafting from the seats. My route took me close enough to the Atlantic to catch the glint of sun on water and to imagine the churn of the surf and the smell of seaweed.

After a few wrong turns I tried launching my rental's GPS. No luck. So I called Nicki's mother, who guided me north to their address, several blocks inland. I pulled into the weedy shell driveway and straddled a puddle. Morning sunlight through hanging moss painted the property in streaks of shadow. A clothesline in the side yard sagged with pale laundry. An elderly woman waited at the door.

18

"Mrs. Landis?" I said. "I'm Ted Danger. I hope I'm not calling too early."

"Heavens no," she said. "I already washed clothes this morning and Wally's driven to the beach. To exercise, he says. I'm Reva, by the way. Come right in."

WE SETTLED IN A bright sitting room that smelled of fresh Pledge, stale breakfast, and good coffee. The narrow sofa was as hard as it looked, but the coffee made up for it. Rich and dark and hot. As I was burning my tongue, Reva lowered herself into a wooden rocker with corduroy cushions. Her thin hair might have been auburn once, and her rheumy eyes, pale blue, stared at the window over my shoulder.

"So Nicole sent you," she said. "Something about Haley?"

"This is good coffee. I needed this."

"It's from Cuba, but that's a secret. Wally gets it somehow."

"Does Wally have a lot of secrets, Mrs. Landis?"

From the end table she picked up a framed photo—a girl painting at an easel—and ran her hand across the glass. "I'm not much for intrigue, Mr. Danger. Tell me why you've come."

"Is that Haley?" I said.

She slid her fingers into each corner of the narrow gold frame. "No, this is our daughter when she was about Haley's age."

"Nicki?"

Reva had closed her eyes. I drank more coffee and waited.

"Mrs. Landis?" I said.

Her head jerked and she opened her eyes. "Yes, what is it?"

"May I see it? The picture?"

THE PHOTO HAD CAPTURED the girl's focus as she held the palette in her left hand and painted with her right. I had to work to see her resemblance to the woman in my office the day before. Nicki had changed a lot in a quarter century. Who hadn't?

No point putting it off.

"I have a nude photo of Haley with an older man at the

beach," I said. "It's nothing overtly sexual. Nicole just wants to find out where it came from."

"What could that possibly have to do with Wally and me?"

"The only time Haley's been near the ocean was four years ago when she was staying with you and Wally."

Reva sat motionless in the rocker. "I'm speechless."

"Tell me, are you and your husband naturists?"

"Naturists? What do you mean?"

"Nudists. Do you enjoy nude sunbathing with other likeminded people?"

"Excuse me?"

"Skinny-dipping?"

She coughed. Choked. I waited.

"I'm sorry, Mr. Danger. Perhaps you're serious."

"May I show you the photo?"

"You may certainly try." She waved a hand in front of her face. "I'm all but blind."

So much for my detective skills. "I didn't notice."

"I playact well enough in my own home. But frankly, the daylight in the window is just a square of darkness to me, not quite as dark as everything else. Go talk to my husband. I need to take the laundry in." She leaned forward and pushed herself upright. "It's going to rain."

I downed the last of my coffee. "How can you tell, Mrs. Landis?"

"Ted," she said. "It's always going to rain."

6 PhotoCrapped

I FOUND WALLY LANDIS right where Reva said he'd be, watching the girls go by from a concrete beach table outside Vic's Seaside Café. He wore running shoes, no socks, ragged cargo shorts, and a faded Miami-Dade Fire/Rescue sweatshirt with the sleeves ripped off. A haze of white hair sprouted from his lanky limbs and bony shoulders, but his head was smooth and gleaming. I knew he was almost eighty but wouldn't have guessed it.

"Mr. Landis?"

He squinted up at me. Eyes the color of deep seawater, sunken cheeks with knife-edge bones, and a thin smile that was forty-nine percent sneer.

"Okay, paleface, let me guess," he said. "No sunscreen, overdressed. Snowbird. You're Ted Danger, Private Dick. Take a load off."

"Thanks." I sat with the table at my back, like him, facing the ocean, resting on my elbows.

"So you must have gone to the house and met my bride, and she sent you here. Quite a gal, isn't she?"

"Makes a damn fine cup of coffee."

"Buddy ships it up from Little Havana." He leaned in my direction without turning his head. "Likes to pretend it's Cuban, but who knows?"

A middle-aged couple in swimsuits too young for them strolled the wet margin between land and sea, leaving footprints that vanished before our eyes.

"This is a great spot," I said. "Relaxing."

"Eh. Not really."

"Why not?"

"I was a lifeguard for a good bit. Did Reva tell you?"

"No."

"It stays with you. You can't really relax. Ever. One minute it's calm, life goes on. Then *bang*. Somebody's in trouble, life-and-death." He ran a hand across his scalp. "You think it's just another morning. By nightfall, everything's different."

"Especially if you're the one who drowns," I said.

A MUSCLE TENSED IN his jaw.

"You ever have to rescue someone?" I asked him.

He glanced up and down the beach. "Somebody's drowning right now. Somewhere."

I dug my shoe into the sand. "You jog in this stuff?"

"Walk a ways, now and again. Mostly sit and watch the ladies."

"Nice," I said. "Any nude beaches around here?"

He met my eye for a beat or two. Then he nodded and turned back to the ocean. A gaggle of girls crossed our line of sight in fits and starts, laughing and splashing and circling into the water, with swimsuits that didn't hide much.

"Down Miami way there's one," he said. "Haulover Beach."

"All Over? Like an all-over tan?"

"Haulover. With an H."

"Ever take Haley down there?"

HE CLACKED HIS TEETH. "Now we're getting to it, aren't we? Did you ask Reva that?"

"I asked her if you were nudists, yes."

"What'd she say?"

"She laughed and kicked me out."

"That's my girl."

Something warm and wet touched my face. "And she said it was going to rain."

"She was right."

The sky had darkened when I wasn't paying attention and the rain slapped down in earnest. The beach walkers scattered.

"Come on," he said. "You got a car here?"

We ran to my rental and climbed inside, both of us half soaked and out of breath—me more than him.

"You want to tell me what's going on, Ted?"

Over the din of the rain, I told him.

HE HANDED THE PICTURE back. "Somebody's jerking you around, Ted."

"How do you explain the photo?"

"Dirty marks on clean paper, that's all. It's not even Haley."

"Nicki doesn't know her own daughter?"

"Well, that's debatable." He leaned over and studied the picture again. "This girl's too old. Haley was only ten or eleven when she was down here."

"You give her a bath? Check her out?"

"Stop it, Ted. I'm trying to help here." He shook his head. "For Christ sakes."

He was honestly offended. Or a damn good actor.

"No," he said. "I didn't give her a bath. No, I didn't take her to a nudist beach. No, I don't know the fella in the picture." He snapped the paper with a fingernail. "This thing could be, what the hell, PhotoCrapped, or Cropped, or whatever you call it."

THE RAIN STOPPED AS abruptly as it started, and the car got hot in a hurry. I twisted the key and powered down the windows.

"The guy looks a little like you, in fact," I said. "When did you start shaving your head?"

"Give me that." He glared at the photo. "Yeah, it's me, all right, if I was six inches shorter, thirty years younger, fifty pounds heavier, and had a tiny little pecker. Christ, my wife's clit's bigger than that."

"Okay, okay. It's not you. But the girl—"

"Here's what happened, Ted. These kids, they surf the internet, they're curious. One of Haley's little friends sees this picture. *Hey, this girl kinda looks like Haley.* So she prints it off as a joke. *Haley, who's your boyfriend?*"

"Nice theory, but this is a photocopy. The original is an actual photo, not a computer printout."

He made a noise with his tongue against his teeth. "Guess what? I'm eighty years old and even I know people print real photographs, on real photograph paper, right off their computers. Have you even seen the original?"

"No, I—"

"Not much of a detective, are you?"

"Mr. Landis—"

"Why don't you call me Wally, all right? After all we've meant to each other." He looked like he bit into something vile.

"Look," I said. "Your daughter isn't accusing you of anything, and neither am I. But Haley brought this picture back from her visit with you."

"I can't help you, Ted."

"Think about it," I said. "Call me."

"All right, I'll think about it," he said—to get rid of me, no doubt. "Give me your telephone number. I'll talk to Reva and call you if we come up with anything."

"Call me either way."

He took my card and left without shaking hands. I watched him scoot off in a little orange car with black trim that would fit sideways in the back of my rental. It looked like a toy, but maybe it worked for a retired couple who weren't cruising swingers' clubs and nude beaches.

7 El Toro y la vaca

THE SUB-TROPICAL PANORAMA blazed with Florida sunshine. I squinted behind my sunglasses and steered my rental down A1A, following the coast, staying between the lines. Trying to keep my eyes open, my head off my chest.

After a long night of little rest, my body craved sleep.

Reva's contraband coffee was wearing off fast. The coastal road changed from A1A to something else at least twice before I found my oasis: a palm-garnished two-story on the beach. The name, painted in bold script on burnt-orange stucco: *El Toro*. The sputtering vacancy sign read VACA.

Toro, the bull. *Vaca*, the cow. The bovine symmetry was a good omen. Or I was just punchy.

I get that way.

THE LATINO GUY WHO checked me in after I *ding-ding*ed the call bell had been lounging on a sofa in an alcove behind the front desk, watching a soap opera in Spanish on a big-screen TV. He was broad but not buff, with even teeth and heavy-lidded eyes that looked cynical and suspicious. Or tired and bored. Or bemused. *What do I know? Why do I care? Just let me sleep.* He grabbed my bag and showed me to my new digs—second floor, south corner, ocean view—reached from an open-air stairway by a spiffy courtyard with a sparkling pool. My room smelled of Pine-Sol and ocean and fruity shampoo. I tipped the motel guy and don't remember anything else until I woke up from a cryptic dream. Something about ...

Something. The room was dark, the ocean loud through the jalousies, closer, heavy with the musk of seaweed.

I SAT UP IN bed and tried to remember. Dreams tell me things.

A hairless woman hands me a photograph, but the image is a black rectangle. Then a child fades in. A girl. She points at me with both hands. I tell her, "That's rude."

Her laughter is the murmur of ocean waves.

I turned on the feeble room light and splashed my face in the bathroom sink. The water from the cold tap wasn't cold, but I was thirsty and didn't have the energy to find an ice machine. I cupped my hand under the flow, drank deep, and crawled back into bed.

8 Haulover all-over

THE THREAT OF THUNDERSTORMS didn't keep the naked people away.

In the morning I'd hiked to an Atlantic Boulevard café where I ate like a starving man. The walk back was hotter, but overcast. At El Toro, I paid for another night, then found A1A and drove south toward Miami, which kept the ocean on my left. I had packed a swimsuit and my old flip-flops (I used to call them *thongs*, but not anymore), and a towel I borrowed from the motel. The drive down the Gold Coast was nice enough, but after an hour I'd seen enough of A1A to last me a decade or two.

Haulover Beach was to the left of the highway—called Collins Boulevard along that stretch—with parking on the right. In the pedestrian underpass, the sound of the surf grew stronger, and another sound, nearly subsonic, buzzed my feet through my flip-flops, a resonance powered by the endless megaton waves lashing the Florida shore. Or was it the rattle of traffic on Collins?

A SIGN ALONG THE path warned of nudity ahead.

It wasn't the worst task I'd taken on. I claimed a spot in the sand not too close to anyone else and sat and stared at the surf. People drifted in and out of my gaze, some nude, and the effect was unremarkable. Male genitals don't intrigue me and the female bits are pretty much out of sight. And boobs—well, I'm no authority but they weren't great that day, not that the men were prime specimens either.

One barefoot beauty reminded me of the old punch line. *Wow, she'd look great in a bikini.*

After a while I slipped out of my suit to feel less like a voyeur. The broken cloud cover slip-slid across the sky, a steady strobe of shade and sun. The cycle of dim and bright, the breeze, the endless susurration of breaking waves, lulled me into a strange mental space and I saw time passing, not into the future, but flowing in reverse, across the eons.

And I see Africa approaching, looming between sea and sky, as the Mid-Atlantic Ridge sucks magma into the earth's core, dragging the land masses closer, continental plates gliding on deep molten pools. Nearer still, until an ancient river separates the continents, then a stream, a brook, a trickle. And my great-great granddaddy, a billion times removed, extends a scaly claw and lurches across the vanishing boundary.

THE BUZZ OF MY phone brought me back. Tru wanted an update. Kids played in the surf to my right, toward the slat fence boundary to the non-nude stretch of beach.

"Hold on," I said. I pulled on my trunks. I was okay being naked with strangers, but not with Tru on the line. "Okay. I'm here."

"Where?" she said. "The beach?"

I guess she heard the breeze, and the kids shouting.

"Yeah. It's called Haulover Beach."

"Is that the scene of the photo?"

"No way to tell. But it doesn't feel right."

"Why not?"

"I'm not sure. It's ... I don't know."

"Well, are there naked people?"

I didn't answer fast enough.

"There are, aren't there? My god. Here I am, stuck in the office, murky and cold outside, and you're on a nude beach soaking up the rays."

I squinted at the sky. "It might rain here."

"*It might rain here,*" she said. "Poor Teddy." Her voice dropped. "What are you wearing?"

"Stop it, Tru."

She laughed. "Trust me. I really don't want to know."

I told her about my talks with Reva and Wally Landis.

"Is Wally the guy in the picture?"

"Ninety-nine percent, no," I said. "But something's going on. He's too quick to steer me away."

"So what next? After you recharge your skin vitamins."

"I'll talk to the lifeguards here. See what they can tell me."

"That's a long shot."

"They might know someone who knows someone. Six degrees and all that."

"Hey, Ted. How long have you been on the beach?"

"A while. I dozed off. Dreamed about time and generations, stretching back to dinosaur days. Strange."

"You dozed off."

"Yeah. Power nap."

"What kind of sunscreen are you using?"

"Sunscreen?" I said.

She laughed. "Ouch."

I SHUFFLED BACK TO my rental for the photo of Haley with her mystery man. Found no Walther under the seat—I'd left it in Ohio. *Right. If a bully kicks sand in my face I'll just growl.*

The first guard I spoke with barely glanced at the photo and had no advice.

The second guard asked, "She missing?" Above her zinc-white nose, my face stared back from mirrored sunglasses.

"No, she's okay," I said. "I'm tracking down the guy."

She flipped the picture over as if his data might be written on the back. It wasn't, or I'd have felt pretty stupid.

"Come with me," she said.

She led me to the shady side of a guard tower, a complicated tree house on fat stilts, painted in hot pastels. I leaned on a support and closed my eyes. The sound of the surf blurred the voices of the beachgoers, like static on an old radio. Time passed and I realized she'd gone and come back again.

"Here," she said. "Drink this."

I twisted the top off the water bottle and downed half of it. "It's warm," I said.

"Better for you, *mi cuate*."

"You're Latina. *Tú eres latina*."

"Drink," she said.

I finished the water. A murmur of nausea twisted my gut and melted away. "I needed that."

"You also need to stay out of the sun."

"You know a guy named Landis?" I said. "Wally Landis? Used to be a lifeguard?"

"Go now," she said. "I'm working."

"What about the guy in the picture?"

"Keep hydrated, stay cool. Rest."

Her face turned to the ocean, where the children had wandered into deeper waters.

9 Can't see what isn't there

THE CAMERA SHOP ON Flagler Street was narrow and deep. Little daylight filtered in from the canopied sidewalk. The guy behind the scuffed glass counter studied the photo and shrugged. His name tag said *Jeter,* and he shrugged a lot, and blinked, and shook his head continuously, a fraction of an inch each way.

"Not much black-and-white photography anymore," he said. "Art stuff. Could be this is a black-and-white copy of a color shot."

"No. I was told the original is black and white."

"This is enlarged, right?"

"Yes."

"I can tell. How much?"

"Don't know."

He nodded and shook his head again. In his fifties, but with the hair of a teenager. Thick, gleaming, black—had to be a rug. I pictured it slipping, bit by bit, with each head shake.

"If you had the original," he said. "Yeah. That would help."

"How?"

"Format. Um, resolution." He held the picture up to the overhead light. "You know, blowing up a hard copy to see more detail only works on TV. Here's a trick." He turned and slid the photo onto a copier and closed the lid. I studied his wig from the back and remembered seeing a picture of myself from that angle, being surprised at the glint of scalp shining through. And that was a while ago.

I wonder how much a good wig costs.

Jeter aligned the two images on the counter. "Reduced twenty-five percent. It's crude, but you kinda see, it's a tad sharper. Scan it on a computer and there's programs to

31

sharpen it." He shrugged. "But you can't see what isn't there."

I thanked him but didn't see much difference. "Anybody else I could talk to?"

"Oh, sure. Come back tomorrow when Pop's here. After lunch. It's his store, but he's mostly retired. Bring the original. He'll tell you whatever you want to know."

"Great." I kept looking at the copy he'd made. "What do I owe you for this?"

His head shake intensified. I thanked him and left.

ON THE WALK TO the parking garage, I called Tru and asked her to get the original photo from Nicki and overnight it to El Toro. I kept staring at the smaller copy and remembering my fantasy on the beach. The continents riding on tectonic plates. Africa bulging on the horizon. And the ragged claws of ancient ancestors.

It seemed important, but I didn't know why.

10 Go home, Ted

I STUCK WITH I-95 on the drive back to Pompano and cut my travel time in half. The nausea returned and I adjusted the rental's AC—didn't help. Stopped at a drugstore for aloe vera gel, aspirin, and a half gallon of cold OJ. Back at El Toro I took a shower (warm, even with the hot valve shut tight), chased a fistful of aspirin with a quart of juice, slathered the gel, and eased into bed.

I was plunging into oblivion when my phone rang.

"Ted, it's Wally. Wally Landis."

I made a noise into the phone.

"Ted. You there? You okay?"

"Too much sun today. Wiped out."

"Haulover?"

"All over."

He clicked his teeth. "Snowbirds."

I had no response to that.

"Okay," he said. "You said to call—I'm calling. Reva and I talked. There's nothing there. You should drop it. Go home. Nicki's fine, Haley's fine. We're all fine."

"I hear you, Wally."

He waited for more, but I was out of gas. "So," he said. "Any idea when you'll head north?"

"Not soon. Rest up a while first."

Silence on the line disapproved. "Get out of the tropics, Ted. You'll feel better."

"Thanks." I hung up. And before I fell asleep, or just after, I thought of Reva, darkness, and pictures.

And kids, and the adults they grow into.

THIS TIME THE PHONE rang in darkness.

"You need to understand about Nicki." It was Reva.

"Can you speak up, Mrs. Landis?"

"No. Wally's in the garage. He mustn't hear."

I staggered out of bed and closed the jalousies to dampen the roil of the surf. My nausea was gone but I was still freezing. And broiling. "He doesn't want you to talk to me?"

"Nicki changed when she was a teenager. She wasn't the same girl."

"It happens," I said.

"I knew who could help. We took her to my friend."

"Mrs. Landis, did Wally give you my number?"

"I heard him tell you that Nicki and Haley are all right."

"Aren't they?"

"We should tell you about Nicki, but Wally says no."

"But he gave you my number?"

"No. But I know how to press Redial."

"What is it you want me to know?" I eased back into bed, cold sheets full of hot needles.

"She wasn't—Wally's coming."

"Can I stop by tomorrow?"

"No. Talk to Madam Fernando. I must go."

"Madam Fernando?" I said.

But Reva was gone.

THE ROOM WAS CLOSING in, so I pulled on my trunks and flip-flops and took the stairs to the courtyard, turned right at the pool, and strolled to the beach. Darkness enveloped the sky and sea, dimming the white foam that crested and washed ashore.

Darkness punctuated by the sweeping beam of a lighthouse to the north.

I sat on the sand and pondered my dream about the photograph. It was the photo Reva had shown me of her daughter sitting at her canvas, painting.

But in my dream the girl laughs and points with an artist brush in her right hand, a pen in her left. Like pistols. Firing pulses of light.

Light from the glittering diamond on the left hand. And the girl's face blurs into two faces, drifting apart. To the right, Reva's daughter, the right-handed child artist. To the left, grown-up Nicki signing the contract in my office. With her left hand.

I know what the dream is telling me.

And Reva's call had confirmed it.

"Nicki changed when she was a teenager," she said. "She wasn't the same girl."

11 No comprendo nada

THE LOBBY WAS DESERTED the next morning except for the desk clerk, whose name tag read *José María*. He grinned and shook his head. "How you liking the Sunshine State, Mr. Danger?"

I felt my face burning. Hell, I was burning all over. And starting to itch. "Call me Ted."

The desk phone rang, he answered, and I headed for the *Free Continental Breakfast Bar*.

Today would not be a good day for undercover work. My skin was a molten mirage, shimmering with heat.

I sat at one of the wrought-iron tables wedged into El Toro's small lobby, and enjoyed a bowl of stale cornflakes with tangy milk from a plastic pitcher. The bar also offered a vivid orange drink (the color, not the fruit) and bagel specimens of unknown ancestry, with your choice of flavored spreads, in convenient plastic packets with lots of corn syrup and chemicals.

The patio offered seating al fresco, with an ocean view. But the sun was out there.

I wanted to talk to José María, who had disappeared, so I sat and made notes about the case. The coffee was hot, wet, and caffeinated—the key essentials. I had another cup to shake loose an idea or two.

DREAMS CAN REVEAL THINGS. My dream about Reva's photo had told me Reva's right-handed paintbrush girl was not the left-handed woman who hired me. But what about the continents surfing on tectonic plates? Africa on the horizon, and generations passing, as if—

The desk bell pinged José María's return. "Ladies and

gentlemen, boys and girls. The complimentary breakfast bar closes in five minutes."

Comedian. I was his only customer.

I downed my coffee and disposed my disposables.

José nodded my way and said, "How are you today, Ted?"

"*Lo mismo como siempre,*" I said.

He answered in rapid-fire Spanish, reminding me that a few phrases didn't make me bilingual.

"*Lo siento, amigo,*" I said. "*Hablo un poco, pero no comprendo nada.*"

He pushed air through his nose. "Okay, you plan to get a little sun today?" He began clearing leftovers from the bar.

"You can throw that milk out."

He sniffed the pitcher. "Tomorrow's special. Buttermilk."

"Let me ask you, José. You ever heard of a Madam Fernando?"

He raised an eyebrow. "*Por supuesto que sí.* Madam Fernando. The reader."

"Reader? What does she read?"

"The psychic. She reads your brains, *amigo.*" He grinned but his teeth looked dangerous. "You go to Madam Fernando, you got no more secrets."

12   Reva sent me

THE CUTE-AS-A-KUMQUAT bumper car stayed three cars back as it tailed me down I-95 to Miami. Wally's surveillance vehicle could hide behind anything, and turn on a dime. On the other hand, it was about as subtle as a bloody nose. *Why would he care about my itinerary anyway?*

IT WAS TOO EARLY to see Jeter's pop at the camera shop, so I was headed for Madam Fernando's hideaway. José had called his cousin Carlos, a theater manager in Miami, who didn't know (but knew someone who knew someone who knew someone who knew) where the Madam's husband, stage hypnotist Derish Flin, had landed in retirement—a quiet little chateau in Miami's chic Coco Brisa bailiwick. By mid-morning, I had the street address, written directions, and an aerial photo of the property (a pool *and* a gazebo—nice). Also, the *Nude Man with Child* photo Ms. Gertrude Hart overnighted from Dayton had arrived, and all was right with the world.

Except for Wally in his pumpkin minicar behind me.

He got closer coming out of a long bend, a giant in his junior jalopy. At least he hadn't dragged Reva along. In a garage near Flagler, I cut the string. Drove in one side and out the other. Left Wally to circle the levels, scanning for my rental and not finding it.

To make sure I'd lost him, I backtracked two blocks, turned at random, took Calle Ocho toward Coral Gables, and pulled in at a funeral home near a Cuban coffee stand to wait and watch. The *café cubano* was small, sweet, and strong. I savored every drop and put Wally Landis out of my mind.

Coco Brisa, here I come.

38

I WAS OFF ROUTE so my written directions broke down, but I pulled over and decrypted my rental's GPS, which guided me nimbly to the Flin place. And what a place it was. In the tonier neighborhoods, even the clouds are creamier.

Nature herself smiles down on the rich.

No rutted parking zone, no sagging clotheslines. A red paver drive in a herringbone pattern and orderly grounds, what I saw of them. A stone privacy fence, vine-covered and guarded by a gargoyle, hid the pool glimmering somewhere back there.

NO ONE ANSWERED THE bell right away. In the opulent shade of the arched portico, the massive door with its elaborate hardware whispered of treasures on the other side. Now if only my skin would cool off and stop itching.

All things come to those who wait. Not true, of course, but a nice sentiment.

When at last the door swung silently inward, the man on the other side fit the setting. His golden hair, thin but bouffant, deepened his deepwater tan. Sharp features, bold nose and chin, and dark bottomless eyes whose subtle gleam echoed the sheen of his dressing gown. A savory blue, or green, or black.

"Good morning," he said. He projected. He articulated. I liked him instantly.

"I'm Ted Danger. I'd very much like to speak with Madam Fernando."

His eyes. It was hard to look away.

"It's likely," he said, pausing a beat, "*you have the wrong house.*"

And I wanted to believe him. But I resisted. "It could be quite important."

"There is no one here by that name."

"Mr. Flin? Derish Flin?"

He shook his head. "We're retired. Whatever it is, we're not interested."

"I'm a private investigator." I held out my card. He didn't reach for it.

"Good day," he said. The door began to close.

"Reva sent me. Reva Landis."

Somewhere in the neighborhood, the pulse and stutter of a lawn sprinkler.

"It's about Nicki," I said.

He opened the door, but slowly. "Little Nicki Landis," he said. "Well, Mr. Danger. I suppose you'd better come in."

13 I love doubters

INSIDE THE HOUSE, AN ambiance of order and tranquility. He led me through dim rooms with high ceilings and cornices. Carpets like tapestries softened the stone flooring. We wandered past burnished tables with inlaid designs, and grand vases lush with color. Over a stone-mantled fireplace, a handsome bas-relief sculpture caught my eye. People cavorting in togas. Or naked.

"What's this?"

He turned and smiled. "A scene from a Grecian urn. It's a beauty, isn't it?"

"That's the truth."

We continued to a spacious sunroom, where he cleared a few tasseled pillows from a stout sofa with thick cushions.

Which is where he parked my ass.

"Excuse my attire." He smoothed the lapels of his lustrous robe and slid into a leather recliner. At the touch of a button, a servo hummed, tilting the back and extending a footrest. "I was about to swim when you rang."

A bank of tinted windows framed the terrace and pool, waters glistening, and just beyond, a latticed gazebo. French doors stood open, admitting a tang of chlorine. I liked it.

"So," I said. "Is Madam Fernando in?"

"No, but I expect her soon." He twisted in his chair and stood suddenly, without lowering the footrest. "Can I get you ·something? Coffee? I'm having a cup myself."

I hadn't smelled any coffee and soon found out why. It was instant.

"YOU ARE DERISH FLIN, right?" I said. "The hypnotist?"

"Yes, of course. Sorry. *Derish Flin. Take the Dare!*"

"What?"

"Never mind."

"How do you know Reva Landis, and her daughter Nicole?"

He tented his fingers. "Well, Reva and Maddy were friends long ago, before I knew them."

"Maddy?"

"Madeline. Madam Fernando is her professional name."

"So Fernando is her last name? I thought it sounded too masculine. Like Madam Fred."

His mouth opened and then shut again.

"What is it?" I said.

"Funny you should ... It doesn't matter."

So I plowed ahead. "What's the story with Nicki?"

"Why don't we wait for Madeline?" His black eyes looked through me. "She'll be back soon."

We sipped our coffee in silence.

A PLATE OF GOLDEN pastries rested on a marble counter-top near a vase of fresh-cut pansies. The growl of my stomach was too loud to ignore.

My host nodded. "I won't offer you a blondie," he said, "but I'm not being rude. They're actually Maddy's. She bakes with particular herbs, to enhance her psychic connection to the superconscious, or whatever. And to help the rest of us do the same. So beware."

"Thanks for the warning."

"You're quite welcome." He showed his teeth in a quick grin. *Wolfish.* "Say, Ted. May I call you Ted? Have you ever been hypnotized?"

"No. I took a seminar once. *Hypnosis for Private Eyes.* I'm one of those that can't go under."

"Interesting."

"You must run into that a lot."

"No, not really. In fact, I'd love to meet someone I can't hypnotize."

"You're saying you can hypnotize anybody?"

He pursed his lips. "Well, some faster than others. But we all have the same apparati." He tapped his forehead. "We all sleep and wake up. Daydream and fantasize. It's just brain physiology."

My skepticism must have shown.

"It's true." He aimed a finger at me. "And here's my favorite myth. *You can do nothing against your will under hypnosis.* Complete rubbish."

"I doubt that."

He smiled. "I love doubters. I'm glad you showed up today, Ted."

"That sounds ominous."

"Not at all. Retirement simply bores the bejeebers out of me." He tilted his head. "Let me ask you, is that sunburn painful?"

"Sure. Itches too."

"I can fix that. I'll have you down and back before you can change your mind." He snapped his fingers. *Snap.* "Just like that." *Snap.* "May I?"

Tempting, but that's not why I was there. "No. Not today."

Derish nodded. "That's fine." *Snap.* "I'll be happy to do it." *Snap snap.*

So I changed my mind. Don't know why. "Okay. But I still have my doubts."

"Thanks, Ted. Shake."

He stood and held out his hand, so I stood too. The last thing I remember is the odd way he turned my arm and tugged it as he spoke the word *sleep*.

I WOKE UP LYING on the sofa. Pain-free and itch-free. "How did you do that?"

"You're easy, Ted. You went down so fast I had to catch you. Nearly cracked your skull."

"I feel great."

"Of course you do. You're still burnt, though. Even if your mind thinks otherwise."

A door closed.

Derish's dark eyes gleamed. "Good. Maddy's home."

I STOOD AS SHE walked into the room. When our eyes met, a liquid weakness flowed from my chest to my arms and legs and my pulse pounded in my ears. My throat thickened and I couldn't breathe. I sank onto the sofa and stared.

She turned to Derish. "What have you done this time, Flin?" she said.

THE FACE. THE HAIR. The walk. The voice.

She hadn't changed in over twenty years.

It was Hope.

14 Bad boy Derish

"WHAT HAVE YOU DONE?"

"Nothing, Maddy," he said. "It was nothing."

No. Hope couldn't be here. She *could not* be here, staring with tight-lipped sadness, the same expression—and god help me, even the words were the same, the last words she ever spoke to me. *What have you done?*

The moaning I heard came from my own throat.

"Help him, Flin," she said.

"This wasn't me. I did not do this." But he held up his palm and lowered it in front of my face. "Sleep," he said.

And I slept.

WHEN I CAME OUT of it, Hope was gone. The sun streamed at a different angle. Derish stood by the french doors, arms crossed, gazing across the grounds. His robe shimmered in the breeze like a conjurer's cloak. I was slumped on the sofa, looking into a face of perfect tranquility. She was old enough to be my mother. Older, in fact, and bigger too. But stunningly beautiful.

"I'm Madam Fernando," she said. "I must apologize for my husband."

Flin kept his back to us.

"Where's Hope?" I said.

"Tell me about Hope," she said.

"Don't play dumb. Where is she?" My anger rolled off Madam Fernando and dissolved in the shimmering reflections that painted the walls. I leaned forward and tried again. "Look, I want answers—"

Derish turned and raised his palm. I flinched.

"Easy, Ted," he said. "Maddy, would you like me to—"

45

"Flin, please," she said.

"I'll scrub his memory. He'll forget he ever heard your name."

"Flin!"

"Please," I said. "Don't do that."

Derish showed his teeth. "So now you're a believer, eh Ted? That's what I like to hear."

Madam Fernando turned to her husband. "You're a bad boy, Derish Flin. But I love you anyway. Take your swim and let me talk with Mr. Danger alone."

He winked at her. Out through the doorway, he unbelted his robe and flung it onto a sleek chaise by the pool. Holding the chrome railing, he descended step by step until his bare brown derriere slipped under the water.

"Ted," she said, touching my arm, "I'll tell you everything you want to know. But first, tell me about Hope."

15 Men and women

MADAM FERNANDO WAS THE anti-Derish. Where his eyes were probing, midnight black, hers were as wide and green as a summer forest at noon. She knew me already. But my mind wasn't a vault she had cracked. It was a book I opened freely.

"Hope is a girl I knew," I said. "A woman. She's been out of my life for a long time."

Madam Fernando was shaking her head. *Like Jeter at the camera store.* But no, she was nothing like him. Well, her hair was black. And long and straight. And maybe dyed. But it wasn't a wig. *Or was it?*

"Give me your hand, Ted." She held my palm and traced the lines. With each movement, bangles on her wrist tapped muted tones.

"What do you see?"

"Hope. Not just a name from the past. You have a powerful link to Hope."

"No. There's nothing between us but time and distance."

"In your mind," she said, "you have created a mythology around her."

I told her about the friendly girl I'd met at the bar. About Hope finding us in bed together and leaving me.

"And you never went after her?"

"Wait. That's what Tru asked me. Trudy Hart."

"Trudy Hart." Her grip tightened. "Ted, why didn't you try to find Hope?"

SHE WAITED, HER FINGERS on my palm, thawing my disquiet with her eyes.

"I guess I didn't love her enough to stay true to her. After that, I didn't deserve her."

"What an epic tragedy, and you're the star scoundrel. Because of your grievous sin."

"She could never get past that."

"How do you know?"

"Because she disappeared. She never got in touch."

"Ted. Let me tell you about men and women."

"Oh, great."

"Men should be faithful, and not squander their sexual energy. But it's hard for men, when pretty girls offer warm diversions. They *can* resist, and *should*. But it's hard. Harder than a woman can imagine."

"How would you know what it's like to be a man?"

She stared, and I felt her pulse across our fingertips.

"There's something equally difficult for a woman to do," she said. "Harder than a man can imagine." Her face didn't change but I felt her sadness.

"What is it?" I said.

"You needed it from Hope, and she couldn't give it."

"No. She owes me nothing."

"She's the star of her own tragic story. The flawed heroine who kept from her lover the one gift that would save him."

"It was my fault. All mine."

"That's your ego talking, Ted. *Look at me. Look at the depth of my transgressions!*" Her eyes swam with tears.

"Why are you crying?"

"It's Derish. Do you know how many women he's been with? Can you even—"

"Maddy, look. I'm sorry. Just tell me about Hope. Where is she?"

SHE MANAGED A SMILE. "Derish has this thing he does. It embarrasses me."

"Has he done something with Hope?"

"A woman wants to feel attractive. It's more difficult as you get older. By the time you're my age …"

"Maddy, pardon my brass, but you're very beautiful."

"Oh, Ted. I know you think so. That's what I'm trying to tell you."

"For the love of god, just say it."

"Derish gives a suggestion to the men he hypnotizes. When they see Madam Fernando, she is the most beautiful woman they can imagine."

I shook my head. "No."

"Yes. Most often they see me as Maddy, but so, so beautiful." She bit her lips and her tears spilled over. "You saw me as someone else."

"I saw Hope."

"But she was never here."

I pulled away and stood. The room tilted and I sat again. "No. How can I trust anything, if Hope wasn't real?"

She dabbed her tears with her fingertips. "You can't, Ted. Not with Derish Flin around."

DERISH. I DIDN'T SEE him by the french doors until he spoke.

"It's time for Mr. Danger to leave."

Maddy bowed her head as if to pray, and spoke a single word. "Forgiveness," she said.

Forgiveness? What's that supposed to mean?

Just one of a thousand questions I wanted to ask. But the answers would mean nothing if Derish wiped my memory clean.

His eyes told me he could do it. And would.

So I chose the greater part of valor and got the hell out.

16   Back from the brink

S EX.

There, I said it.

I'd been denying and repressing, but I couldn't any longer.

It was catching up to me, the sexuality, blatant and implied, everywhere I looked. At Haulover Beach, I coldly critiqued the imperfect breasts, bored with bared genitalia. And Wally, speaking with love of his eighty-year-old bride, with sudden crude allusions to her mega-pudenda and his own hefty phallus. Maddy, too. So old, so beautiful, with her psychic link to my long lost lover, Hope. Even Tru, *my god*, cute and sexy and in her prime—but no. Too close to home. *Way too close.* I shut it all down, intellectually. But my body told me otherwise.

On the drive back to Pompano—I-95 again—the thrum of tires on pavement pulsed a persistent quiver through the car seat. Almost ... stimulating.

The radio delivered the 1960s. British invasion stuff, plaintive pleas—*come on!*—for love and satisfaction, begging and building and bursting with crescendos.

T HAT EVENING I HIKED to the café on Atlantic, and everything in sight made me hornier. It got to be funny after a while. A woman blissfully masticating a hoagie two booths over, a dollop of creamy condiment on her chin. A gaggle of girls strolling the sidewalk—legs extra long and shorts extra short, just old enough to ogle without feeling grimy—enjoying the hell out of their ice cream cones. At the motel, climbing the outdoor staircase, I glanced into the courtyard where a woman on a chaise by the pool casually opened her blouse and exposed a turgid breast. She squeezed the nipple between two fingers and guided it to the face of the infant in her arms who turned its head side to side, sensing sweet nectar and latching on.

Back in my room I wasn't sure what to do next. So I found my notepad and brainstormed for answers. Connections always emerged. Parallels, links that led to solutions. Or blind alleys.

I remembered the beach where I sat with Wally, the children playing in the surf, the adults in risqué swimwear. Then Haulover, more kids, but this time as naked as slugs, and adults too, in nothing but sunscreen. Another beach, the one in the photograph, more casual nudity, smiles all around. Jeter, looking at the photo, shaking his head like a suckling babe that seeks the nub of its mother's breast, the channel of flesh through which it saps her body to satisfy its own.

I TORE THE PAGE from the pad, crushed it to a wad, and flung it at the oval rim of the circular file. It fell short, bounced, and rolled to the baseboard.

There was no point in going on in the state I was in.

I cleaned my teeth and finished my ablutions, not feeling much absolved. From the basket of free soaps, shampoos, and lotions, I chose a tube of hand cream and placed it on the bedside table by a box of those thin scratchy tissues all motels get from somewhere. The thin scratchy tissue store, maybe.

THE ROOM WAS WARM and so were the sheets as I lay on top of them. From the window, the sultry breath of the sea played across my skin. I closed my eyes and my body took my mind to a clothing-optional world of friendly people, couples young and old, hand in hand, arm in arm. I reflected on things I had seen or imagined, waking or dreaming, wicked or wise, bits and pieces swirling in the melancholy music of fantasy. The melody sharpened—the sounds, the shapes, the taste, the touch.

The touch. *And now the tempo rises.*
The touch. *And now the chorus builds.*
The touch. *And now crescendos loom.*
The touch. *And now—*

A KNOCK AT THE door, and the music fled. Signal lost, plug pulled. On my tongue, the taste of mother's-milk ice cream, so sweet and so cold, thawed into warm saliva.

"What—" I croaked. I cleared my throat. "Who is it?"

"Ted, you want to open the door now?" It was José María.

"Just a minute." I reached for my clothes but remembered the lotion on my hand so I grabbed the tissues. The first few shredded, but a dozen did the job and I pulled on my pants. I grabbed my phone to check the time, and scooped up my shirt just as José María knocked again. "Yeah, yeah," I said. I tossed the shirt on the chair and opened the door.

He stood with arms crossed, glaring through heavy lids.

"I was asleep." I scratched my chest and faked a yawn.

"Is time for you to wake up," he said.

HE STEPPED ASIDE TO reveal a slouching schoolgirl with a ratty rucksack across one shoulder, a battered valise at her feet. Messy tresses masked her face, but I got the sense of bloodshot eyes in a fresh field of pimples.

Something familiar about her.

"Who's this?" I said. My phone rang in my hand. I recognized the number. "Hang on. What is it, Nicki?"

She breathed static in my ear. "Ted? Is this Ted Danger?"

"Yes, Nicki, it's me. What do you want?"

José María said "Ahem" into his fist.

I held up one finger.

The static ended. "Ted, it's about Haley." A deep breath. "I can't find her. She's run away."

"Hold on." I studied the girl and saw Nicki in the shape of her mouth, the delicate bones of her face.

"What are you staring at?" she said.

I held out the phone. "It's for you."

She made no move to take it.

17 Stop talking about me

AFTER I DROPPED OFF Haley with her grandparents the next morning, I headed back to Miami to talk with Pop, Jeter's dad. I was glad to be rid of Haley. The ride over to the Landis's in my rental had been pretty quiet. Just the muffled buzz of the four-cylinder motor, the buffeting of balmy air through the windows, and country/Latino music low on the radio, with too damn many accordions.

Haley had been pissed, but why? Maybe she was just tired.

IT HAD TAKEN A half hour to sort things out the night before.

She'd finally agreed to come inside and speak with her mom on the phone. José and I sparred near the doorway and eavesdropped at the same time.

"Mom, I told you, I'm all right." Pause. "I don't know. I just—"

José: "What are your plans for this child, Ted?"

Me: "Christ, José, I don't know. Her grandparents live here in Pompano. I guess take her over there."

José: "It is not good that she remain here with you. You know this."

Me: "Tell me about it."

Haley: [drops her arm to her side] "Stop talking about me."

Me: "What?"

José: "¿Qué?"

Haley: "I just want to take a bath!" [starts crying]

Me: "My god."

José: "Dios mío."

The woman from the next room over showed up, the one breastfeeding her baby by the pool earlier. Tonight, though, her

53

breasts were covered by an oversize T-shirt with a grinning sponge character, wearing pants. But she wasn't. Wearing pants. Or grinning.

"My baby's sleeping," she said. She told us her name, Kendria Spitler, which José knew already.

I started to introduce myself, but she'd spotted Haley motionless by my unmade bed, holding my phone by her side, face blotted with tears, staring at the desk where I'd left the enlarged photocopy of the happy nude couple. I never imagined the photo and its star subject would cross paths tonight.

In three or four long strides, Kendria was across the room.

"What the hell?" She snatched up the photo, then studied Haley's face. No one moved.

"Is this you, child?" she said quietly.

"No ... I don't know. I'm so tired."

Kendria dropped the photo as if it were toxic. She put her arm around Haley's shoulder, and the girl rolled into her embrace. Silence. Until a voice squeaked from my phone. Nicki.

And then another woman crashed the party, her ebony eyes seething fire. Jean shorts and a poncho shirt with an Aztec design. *Or Mayan?* She blew past José and me and scanned the room, hands on her hips. She glared at the lotion and shredded tissues by the bed, and when she looked up, scowling, I prayed she wouldn't glance toward the desk.

She glanced toward the desk.

Damn. Why hadn't I filed that damn picture face down in a drawer somewhere?

She turned to Haley and Kendria. "What in the hell goes on here?"

Haley kept her head buried in Kendria's shoulder. Kendria tilted her head toward José and me, shooting us a wicked glare. I wished I had a shirt on. And a jacket.

A flak jacket.

JOSÉ LEANED MY WAY. "*Mi hermana*, Yesi. El Toro is our motel, hers and mine."

"Tell her nothing bad is happening." I retrieved my shirt and pulled it on. Nonchalantly. Not easy with everybody staring. "We're all innocent parties here."

"How do I know what you say is true, Ted?" he said. "No, *cabrón*. Speak to her your own self, if you dare."

The raven-haired sister spoke up. "Prove it to me why I should not call the *policía*. You have one minute."

"Yesi," I said. "*Calmate, por favor.*"

The furrow above her nose deepened, drawing her dark brows closer.

"The girl's name is Haley," I said quickly. "I'm a private investigator working for her mother, Nicki Vavul, who is on the phone right now." I pointed to the cell hanging in Haley's hand. "Talk to her. Tell her we've found Haley. She's safe now."

Haley lifted her blotchy forehead. "Stop talking about me!"

"Hush, baby," Kendria said. She took my phone and gave it to Yesi.

"Miss Babble?" Yesi said.

"Vavul," I said.

She showed me her palm, frowned, and listened.

Somewhere, a baby cried.

18 Verge of hysterics

WE STRAIGHTENED THINGS OUT without police assistance.

Haley was exhausted and grimy from a day and a half of riding a bus, eating junk food, and watching her back. She demanded an immediate shower and a bed and was on the verge of hysterics until we agreed. She absolutely did not want to face her grandparents and further drama.

Her story wasn't complicated.

SHE'D BEEN SNOOPING IN her mother's diary, email, desk drawers, and files. Eavesdropping, too. Necessary actions, she told us, when living with someone a little bit crazy like Nicki. She found my Pompano Beach address and enough about the case to know her mother was hiding something big.

With her curiosity more than she could bear, she liberated a few crisp hundreds from her mother's lingerie drawer, and contrived a story about spending the night with her friend Emily. Instead, she called an older boy from school for a ride to the bus station, where she met a frazzled woman with two little kids waiting for the southbound, their belongings stowed in one battered suitcase and a matching set of garbage bags. They struck a deal. For one of Nicki's hundreds, Haley became kid three—big sister and babysitter—a role that carried her all the way to Valdosta. By then she'd fallen in with a woman traveling alone who got her to Fort Lauderdale without harassment.

From there, she grabbed a taxi to ... well, she had her grandparents' address, and mine. She chose mine, thinking I might answer more of her questions.

But now that she was here, she didn't want to talk about it. Not yet. All she wanted was a hot shower and a real night's sleep, in a real bed. Not a grungy bus seat.

So she stayed overnight in my unit, with Yesi, while I slept on a sofa behind the lobby. The ice machine punctuated the night with cubes tumbling into the bin.

THE NEXT MORNING WALLY phoned, early, saying Nicki had called, and they'd agreed that Haley could stay with them in Pompano Beach until things resolved. He and Reva would be home all morning waiting for me to haul her over.

I went back to my room and surprised Haley as she was coming out of the bathroom, already dressed in a modest (by today's standards, anyway) two-piece swimsuit in rich scarlet. It showed off the smooth lines of her collarbones, her crazy-long adolescent legs, and her flawless boyish torso, made more flawless by four moles defining a graceful arc from her left breast to her navel. In spite of myself, I found my mind making comparisons between the girl in front of me—whose ears glowed red as she snatched a cover-up and dashed back to the bathroom—and the child in the photo.

I saw the resemblance, but ...

I guess kids change a lot in four years.

LIKE I SAID, HALEY and I didn't talk much on the way to the Landis's, where more laundry was drying in the humid morning air. Or maybe it was the laundry from three days ago.

Wally waited in the doorway, Reva a shadow behind him. Haley hopped out and slammed the door without saying goodbye.

I headed for Miami.

BEFORE I JUMPED ONTO I-95, I pulled over and called Nicki.

"Hello?" She sounded far away, which I suppose she was.

"It's Ted," I said. "Haley's with her grandparents."

"I know. They just called. How does she seem to you?"

"Tired. That was pretty ballsy, hauling herself down here on her own."

"She's strong. She gets it from her father."

"Hang in there, Nicki. You're doing all right."

"It doesn't feel like it," she said. "Ted, what should I do? Should I come down there?"

"Give me a couple of days. If I need help, I'll let you know."

"Are you any closer to knowing who he is? The man in the picture?"

"Not really, but yes, if that makes sense. Look, I need to keep moving. I'll talk to you later."

She cut the connection without a word. Just as well. I had damn little to report.

19 Go see old Hard-On

POP, WHOSE ACTUAL NAME was Percival—"But call me Pop, everybody does"—ran a knobby thumb across a corner of the picture. He flexed the paper, turned it over. Handed it back.

"Haven't seen one of those in a while," he said.

"What can you tell me about it?"

"Polaroid," he said. "Land camera. Used to, I could tell you what model."

"Land camera. That's instant, right?"

He kept staring at the photo so I passed it back to him.

"Haven't seen one of these in a while," he said.

"You already said that, Pop." Jeter was hovering.

"It's a fact," Pop said. "Black and white too. Now you're going back a piece."

Pop squirmed on his stool, a chrome job with duct-tape repairs to the red plastic seat. I perched on the customer side of the counter. My stool had one short leg, and I caught myself rocking in time with Jeter's head shake.

"How far back is _a piece_?" I said. "My client believes this was taken about four years ago."

Jeter shook his head.

"You don't think so?" I looked at Jeter, but Pop answered.

"Now, I didn't say that."

Outside the windows, plenty of traffic on Flagler, vehicle and pedestrian. But no one stopped in to chat.

"So what are you saying, Pop?" Like pulling teeth, getting an answer from this guy. If he had any left to pull. His super-white choppers looked as fishy as Jeter's jet black toupee.

"Anything's possible," he said. "But the film's expensive. Digital's a dern sight cheaper. Cost you nothing to take all the shots you want. Then print the best ones. Or just look at them on your portable telephone."

"So how old is this picture? Your best guess."

"Thirty, forty years old."

"Are you sure?"

HE SIGHED. "SON, YOU'RE not listening. No, I'm not sure. My point is, every shot costs you real dollar bills, no matter who blinked or didn't say *cheese*. Nobody pays that kind of money nowadays without a damn good reason."

"Like taking naked pictures of children that won't show up on a database somewhere?" I said.

"Well, you've got a suspicious mind, but I can't fault your reasoning."

"So this photo could be four years old, right?"

"That's right," he said. "In my professional opinion, however, it's much older."

I shifted in my stool, and the short leg rocked me back. "Tell me why you say that."

"Instinct," he said. "Heft of the paper. The feel, the edges. Hell, I don't know. The smell. Four years old? Closer to forty."

I HELD THE PICTURE to my nose and sniffed. No ideas popped into my head.

"Fair enough," I said. "So all I need to do is track down someone who took one particular photograph on some unknown beach forty, fifty years ago—"

"Maybe thirty," Pop said.

"—maybe thirty years ago, near Miami or somewhere else in Florida or the U.S.A., or maybe in the Caribbean, or the east coast of Australia, or on the French fricking Riviera. But somewhere on planet Earth, that's probably a given." I felt like spitting. "I'm going to the movies."

"You give up too easy," Pop said.

"Is there something you're not telling me?"

"I've seen pictures like this before." He tapped the side of his nose. "Ask around, Ted. Ask folks who been here a while."

"Like who?"

He wiped his glasses with a purple rag that looked unqualified for the job. "Jeter, what's that fella's name with the petting zoo? Took nudie pictures of tourist ladies with the monkeys, down Homestead way."

Jeter swallowed. "Um, I heard about him. Crankshaft?"

"Axelrod," Pop said. "Hardy Axelrod."

"Hardwick," Jeter said.

Pop's teeth gleamed in the semi-gloom. "Although he goes by Hard-On, as I recall."

"Hardwick?" I said. "Hardwick Axelrod?"

"Go see old Hard-On, Ted." Pop let loose a laugh with phlegm in it. "Get yourself a nice picture with the orangutans."

20 Rytt and the runaway

RYTT SLAVEN. I'D BEEN thinking about her since the first mention of Florida.

She's a Miami PI who tracked a runaway to Dayton two years ago. Seems a young Latino, with the help of a sympathetic adult male he met online, left his home and his family to escape stepdaddy abuse. Only to end up repaying his benefactor by doing hard time in a blue-collar brothel.

The kid didn't like it.

So he fled his Fairy Godpimp and ran home—briefly, when the house was empty—to disencumber his callous-handed *padre* of a stash of cash and semi-precious heirlooms. The boy skedaddled northward. Meanwhile, the kid's grandparents on the mother's side hired Rytt to find him.

When she traced the kid to Dayton, Rytt needed someone with local contacts. And hired me.

We tracked the boy down through the items he pawned around town, including a gold Libertad with a drilled hole and a Castro/Nixon photo reprint signed by the photographer.

Rytt was a dish and smart and funny, but her shields engaged whenever things got personal.

At least that's how I remember things.

She'd wrapped up her case and gone back to Miami. I don't know what happened to the kid.

NO ONE HAD ROLLED out the red carpet.

When I entered her fourth-floor PI digs off Flagler Street I didn't see any sign of Rytt. A woman I didn't know strolled into the reception area from a private office. She held a large black stapler.

"How may I help you?" she said. A Latina accent, but her coloring was fair. Athletically lean, and tall enough to look me straight in the eye.

"I'm Ted Danger. I called earlier to meet with Rytt."

"Mr. Danger. Of course. I'm Navi Bustamante, Ms. Slaven's partner."

She dropped the stapler onto the unoccupied reception desk and extended her hand. Her grip was dry and assertive.

"I didn't know Rytt had a partner."

From a crystal holder on the desk, she plucked a business card that read *Slaven and Bustamante Investigations*.

"Ms. Slaven was called away," she said, "but expects to rapidly return. She anticipates you will wait."

"Thank you, Navi. I will."

"Please, you may call me Ms. Bustamante. Perhaps later, when I have made up my mind about you, we use the first names."

"Of course, Ms. Bustamante," I said. "Perhaps I'll wait out here for Ms. Slaven's rapid return, as you continue your stapling."

HER SMILE DID NOT reach her eyes. Eyes profoundly calm and blue, like the blue of her slim jacket and just-short-enough skirt. The neckline of her coral blouse yielded not a trace of cleavage above her compact breasts, not that I notice things like that.

"Rytt was correct about you," she said.

She turned and I admired the departing view of her gold-kindled hair in its elegant bun, her slender neck, her straight back, her trim butt, and those long lithe legs. But her heels on the burnished floor tapped an indifferent rebuke.

I tried not to take it personally.

21 Pneumatic splendor

I DIDN'T SIT.

Instead, I squinted through an east window to admire the ocean view, a slice of surf between a high-rise and a parking garage. And from this angle, I could keep an oblique eye on Navi—that is, Ms. Bustamante—seated at her desk with a file open in front of her.

I gave her a nod and my we're-in-this-together smile and she smiled back, but tight-lipped, with eyes half closed. As if weighing options.

THE OUTER DOOR OPENED, and Navi's smile bloomed. Rytt flowed in like the tide.

"Rytt," I said. "So good to see you again."

"Ted Danger," she said. "Hang on."

She sailed into Navi's office and closed the door.

Voices. Laughter. Silence.

The door opened and Rytt swayed on over. Where Navi was pale sunlight and severe, Rytt was sensual, the colors of dusk. A placid smile and the scent of the sea. Flyaway hair, flamboyant hips, and big fucking hooters.

Her shirt was sheer and blowzy, a saltwater blue that rippled with each motion, above which floated in pneumatic splendor her miraculous cleavage, a life preserver for a drowning man to embrace in endless bliss.

"Hello, Ted." She guided me to a loveseat and pulled up a chair for herself.

"Rytt, it's so good to see you again."

"You're lucky to catch us here," she said. "Our lease ended and we're moving farther west."

"It's great to see you again, Rytt."

"You've said that already." She shook her head. "Look, thanks for helping with my runaway case. You were amply compensated."

"Sure. Yes. You're welcome. Thank you."

"You know, the more I thought about you later, the less I actually liked you."

"You—what?"

"You're a bit of a pussy, Ted. Maybe you were born that way. Or suffered an early trauma."

"Goodness," I said.

"Perfect example. You think you're funny, ironic. Who says *goodness*? My delicate ears can't handle *what the fuck*?"

"What the fuck?"

"You're a follower, passive, a bit slow."

"A deep thinker," I said.

"Sure. How do you solve your casework with such low initiative?"

I played along. "I have my methods."

"Do tell." She yawned.

"I contemplate. Ask questions. Answers come to me in—"

"And why didn't you make a pass when we worked together in Dayton?"

"That's what this is about? I sensed you wouldn't have been receptive."

"You sensed I wouldn't have been receptive."

"Are you saying I was wrong?"

"Am I saying you were wrong?"

"Well, are you?"

"No," she said. "I'd have told you to go to hell."

"Look, is this something *Ms. Bustamante* put you up to?"

"Navidad? Not exactly. But you're on the right track."

"Navidad?"

"Navi."

"Okay, fine. Listen, Rytt. I need local support, and I'll pay for it. But I wanted to see you personally too."

"Be still my trembling heart."

"However, based on how things are going, could you refer me to another PI?"

Navi chose that moment to join us. "Ted. May I call you Ted? You may call me Navi, or Navidad if you like. I hope Rytt has not been too heavy-handed on you. She is really quite sweet." She touched Rytt's arm and leaned in.

WHEN THEIR LIPS MET, and stayed that way, things began to make sense. But then they didn't. My brain went buggy. All the blood rushed somewhere else.

"Of course you may call me Ted," I suavely responded.

But the words came out like "Urk. Urk. Urk-urk."

22 Ted the sex toy

THE KISS EVENTUALLY ENDED. Rytt sighed and wedged her plush bottom onto the loveseat on my right. Navi's narrow hips squeezed in on my left. They held my hands and I became the semiconductor between two high-voltage poles: Rytt's hot surging positive and Navi's cool sultry negative. Their current rippled like rays of joy through my body.

"As I told you," Navi said. "We are partners."

"Who really like each other," Rytt said.

"That is certainly true," Navi said.

"And we like new things in the mix."

"For the levity and pleasure."

"I understand completely," I said. But this time it sounded like "Gah. Gah-gah."

"A toy," Navi said. "With man parts."

"So," Rytt said, "if you're healthy and uncommitted at the moment ..."

Navi's hand fell to my thigh. "You will be our sex toy for a time. You are able to do this?"

I knew the phrase *creamed my jeans*, but had never been this close.

"Navi," I said, "first tell me why Rytt is so rude to me."

"She is testing you, Ted. If you give hostility, we do not invite. Now answer, *sí o no*."

"*Por supuesto que sí*," I told her. "Yes, of course."

I WAS PARKED IN a beach lot facing the broad Atlantic, eating a Cuban sandwich from a food truck and drinking a Diet Coke when Tru returned the call I'd placed earlier.

"What's going on?" she said.

"Couple of things heating up here."

"Like what?"

"Got a lead on a guy who takes nude photos of tourists."

"What's his name?"

"Hardy, um, Axelrod."

"Hold on," she said. "Um, Axelrod ... photos ... nudity ... Florida." Silence. "Uh oh."

"What?" I said.

"I Googled him. First name was Hardwick."

"Was?"

"He's dead, according to this."

"Well, if it's on the internet, it must be true."

"Ermahgerd, Ted, I'm trying to help."

"Yeah, sorry. I'll check it out."

"And I'll keep researching. Wait, what? It says here he called himself *Hard-On*."

"Nice."

"Enough of that," she said. "What else is heating up?"

"Yeah, well, I'm developing a couple of other local sources I'll be, uh, pumping for information."

"Any way I can help? I'm bored."

"Nah. It's more of a hands-on consultation. And, uh, I'll probably have my cell phone off, so I can focus, you know, on the interview. In depth."

"If you say so."

"Yeah. Thanks. I just, it's, I don't want to be interrupted at a sensitive moment."

"You're overexplaining, Ted. Is everything okay? If you're being held at gunpoint, use our safe word."

"Stop it. Everything's great, Tru. Absolutely could not be better."

NEXT I CALLED NICKI and gave her the same spiel. I wanted her calm and satisfied, not trying to reach me in the next several hours.

I finished my sandwich and Coke and pushed the trash into

an overfilled receptacle near my parking spot. Rytt and Navi had already made dinner plans, which most definitely did not include me. I was simply a tool they would use for after-dinner diversion, intimate but impersonal, and I had no more place on their dinner date than an anal-bead necklace.

Fine with me.

So I drove to a drugstore and picked up the supplies Navi and Rytt had specified—lubricants and warming gels and two kinds of condoms—and a vibrating gizmo that caught my eye. Bizarre, the tackle available at the corner store these days. The checkout guy rang me out and said "Have a nice evening" without a trace of irony.

Then I drove off for my interview, assignment, assignation—whatever.

Hard-On Axelrod could wait until tomorrow.

Dead or alive.

23 Take the Dare!

ON THE WAY TO Homestead the next morning, I drove like an old man in a Buick. Short guy, with a hat. Leaves his signal on. Five miles an hour below the speed limit.

I was cruising slowly, savoring life, my sex drive lower than the day I was born. Than before my ancestors were born.

God, those women.

THEY MURDERED ME. COLDLY. Hotly. An execution. Or, what the hell, assisted suicide.

I ached. All over. Especially there. And there. And, yes, there too.

But it was a good ache.

Every time they finished me off—*ino más!*—that urgent pulse warmed again. Improbably. Impossibly.

They knew what they were doing, but there was other magic at work. Love potions. No exotic ingredients—powdered horn or virgins' tears—just common ED meds they fed me to keep the batteries charged in their sex toy.

But even the chemicals finally wore off.

We slept.

And barely spoke this morning. It could have been awkward, but I was too wiped out to care. Besides, from what I remembered, I held up my end like a boss.

Breakfast was cold éclairs and hot coffee, dark and rich.

I drank a cup there and took one to go, in a hefty china mug that fit nice and snug in my rental's cup holder. Slid right in there.

Yep, like a boss.

SO, HOMESTEAD.

I took my time along the way, letting the GPS choose the route. In Perrine, I pulled over to top off the tank and take a restroom break. No blood in my urine, luckily. A relief, after last night's rampage.

My cell rang as I was pulling onto Dixie Highway, so I spun back into the lot and parked in a shaded slot near the pump canopy.

"Ted Danger."

"It's Derish Flin."

"*Take the Dare!*" I said.

"Right. How are you this morning, Ted?"

"Great. Nearly perfect, in fact."

"What happened, you get laid last night?"

"You don't know the half of it, my man." Okay, it's rude to brag about your sexual conquests (or capitulations, in this case), but, okay, I'm rude sometimes.

"I'm happy for you," he said, surprising me by not asking for details. "And I have more good news."

"I'm listening."

"Maddy and I are half-convinced we should tell you the whole story about what happened to, uh, the person you were asking about."

"You mean—"

"No names on the phone."

"Why not?"

"You'll understand when we tell you about it."

"When can we meet? I'm headed south. My morning's booked."

"After dinner this evening? Around seven at our place."

"That works."

"Do something for us, first. This afternoon, if you have time."

"Sure."

"Are you driving, right now?"

"No. I'm parked at a gas station. Why?"

"It's important." *Snap*. "I'm going to tell you why." *Snap snap*.

The sound of his voice conjured his eyes, their intensity.

MY ARM WAS TIRED from holding the phone.

"Good, Ted. We'll see you tonight."

"Wait. What were you going to tell me?"

"I already did. We're all set."

And the sun was in my face. Somehow the shade had vanished in the last few seconds.

That doesn't make sense. Unless—

"What the hell," I said. "You did it again, didn't you? You put me under!"

"Ted, you're too easy. I can't resist."

"What did you do this time?"

"I told you what Maddy and I want you to do. You don't even have to write it down."

"I don't fucking believe it."

"Oh, and I satisfied my curiosity about your good mood."

"Oh, lord," I said. "What did I tell you?"

"Sounds like you enjoyed yourself."

"Anything salacious?"

"Want me to tell you your safe word?" I felt his smirk over the phone.

"We argued about that one. I wanted *flaccid*."

He laughed. "Whose idea was *priapism*?"

"I'm not saying."

"Had to be Ms. Top Bun or Ms. Bottom Bun."

"What?"

"Oh, yes, you told me about the Rytt-and-Navi sandwich."

"I'm going to hang up now." I cut him off mid-laugh.

24 They're all gone

A BILLBOARD GORILLA URGED me to *TURN HERE FOR MONKEYS* but my GPS made no comment so I forged ahead. Hardy Axelrod's place was farther south and west, down where the street and avenue names hit triple digits.

As I drove on, I picked up an Everglades vibe. My lizard brain nudging: *stay alert.*

WEEDS AND MUD CAMOUFLAGED the gravel drive. I drove past it and had to backtrack.

From the street, I could make out ramshackle structures off to the right, obscured by overgrowth. I pulled in and stopped at a lopsided gate. Just beyond, a dusty irregular tract might have once held parking for a dozen cars. No real security—a loop of wire held the gate closed—so I left the rental in the drive and let myself in.

A weedy concrete walkway led me to a somber cottage. It was small, with a dormer near the peak—just one, with thin curtains and a cracked windowpane. I thought a face stared down at me but when I looked again it was gone.

On the porch, dead plants spilled from plastic flowerpots. Latticework sagged.

I rang the bell. Nothing. Knocked on the weathered door and waited.

A curtain shuddered behind the window.

I knocked again.

SOUNDS FROM INSIDE THE house. A raised voice and a reply. A muffled slam. *Who's escaping out the back?*

Then the door opened. Only far enough for two dark eyes

to peer from a sallow face framed in wisps of pale hair.

"What is it." A woman's voice, tired, her question spoken like a statement, without curiosity.

"I'm looking for Hardy Axelrod."

SHE OPENED THE DOOR another inch and leaned on the doorjamb. "Too late. Hardy's gone. Bonobos too. They're all gone."

Her face sagged with gravity and a sorrow I could feel. She might have been fifty, or a battered thirty. In her eyes I saw the beautiful woman she must have been before the wounds of time and sadness.

"It's important that I speak with him. Can you tell me where he went?"

"He's dead. Is that plain enough for you?"

"I'm sorry to hear that."

"You and me both," she said. "Not that he was the easiest man to live with. But you don't need to know about that."

"Maybe I do. Look, my name's Ted. Ted Danger. I'm a private investigator, and I'm working for a woman who is concerned about her daughter."

I offered my card, and as she reached for it, the square collar of her shirt framed her delicate collarbones. It was a graceful detail that clashed with the decrepit surroundings. I went with my instinct.

"You know," I said, "it's after eleven and I've barely eaten today. Let's go somewhere nice for lunch and we'll talk about Hardy's work. My treat." I cranked up my charm to ten and a half. Eleven's too dangerous. "Nothing tedious, I promise."

"You want to take me to lunch?"

"What's your name?"

"Jenny. Jennifer Axelrod."

"Mrs. Hardwick Axelrod?"

"That's right."

"Jennifer, would you do me the honor of joining me for lunch today?"

She scanned me up and down. One corner of her mouth lifted. "All right. Yes. I'd love to. I need a few minutes." She glanced into the house. "You can't come in."

"That's fine. I'll look around out here."

The grooves between her brows deepened. "Pull your car into the lot, will you? And I ..."

"Yes?"

"Just move your car. Twenty minutes, okay?"

"Twenty minutes."

THERE WERE NO LINES painted on the dirt, so I parked my rental in a blotch of shade under a strangely bushy palm.

Twenty minutes was plenty of time to tour the compound. The main path circled out from the lot and passed by a leaning barn and a concrete block building with *RestRoom* hand-lettered on the side. A pitted doorknob wobbled but didn't turn and the *RestRoom* door held tight.

The barn door hung wide open from rusted rollers. Inside, gaps in the roof laid stripes of sunlight across the dirt floor and animal pens, empty and silent.

It didn't take long to stroll every path. Nothing much to see. Snarls of chain link littered the animal enclosures. Shingles and tar paper. Empty compost bags. Weeds, dead and alive.

"Not much left." I hadn't heard Jennifer come up behind me. "I sold everything I could after Hardy died, animals included."

"So this was your zoo?"

"That's being generous." She glanced around. "Yeah, we had critters."

"What happened?"

"Always something. Neighbor complaints. Insurance hassles. Permit issues." She shook her head. "Disease. That was a big one. Hardy had a brown thumb for animals. Like an animal hospice around here."

We walked the overgrown path to the parking lot.

"And money, of course," she said. "Expenses higher than

we planned, income lower. Plus it was crazy hard work. It beat me down. Believe it or not, Ted, I used to be pretty. Really pretty."

I waited too long, but I said it: "You still are, Jenny."

We reached my rental and I opened her door.

"You're sweet, Ted," she said. "Now let's get the fuck out of here."

25 Love your shoes

FOR OUR LUNCHEON VENUE, Jenny proposed the Sea Knight Brazier near Leisure City. She pointed me in the right direction and I wheeled the rental into the street.

"You'll like the Sea Knight," she said. "Good wine, warm bread, cloth napkins. Real china and flatware. You don't suck your drink through a plastic lid and a bendy straw, for Christ sake. Good coffee with dessert."

I glanced over. She sat straight but restless in her seat. She'd fixed her face and hair. And wore a simple black dress, a thin bracelet, nylons, and low heals.

"Love your shoes," I said. That's the best thing to tell a woman, I read somewhere.

"You read that somewhere," she said.

"Guilty. But you do look great, Jenny."

Getting away from that dead-animal park stripped years from her face.

"Matter of fact," she said, "I believe you. I used to feel like this all the time. Out with a good-looking guy, spending his money."

She touched my arm and her neck bloomed red. Another day I might have been tempted, but Rytt and Navi had ruined me.

"And it's my pleasure to be with a lovely woman like you," I said. "But ..."

"But I'm not as attractive as I feel, is that it?"

"That's not it, Jenny. If I were, uh, so inclined, I'd find you very appealing."

"That sounds like a challenge."

"Take it that way, if you want. But women aren't my thing

right now."

"Ah. Gay. I should have guessed when you noticed my shoes. Well, thanks for telling me before a gal gets her hopes up." She sighed dramatically. "You know what? That's one less thing to worry about, right? We'll just enjoy a nice dinner."

"And talk about the case too. You need to tell me about Hardy's little sideline. The photographs."

"So, here we are at last."

"Yes, I want to know if Hardy—"

"No, *here we are*. The restaurant."

THE SEA KNIGHT BRAZIER: a one-story building, flat black. Two chess knights—five-foot silhouettes with a silvery coating—flanked the entry. Knights with narrow snouts, like seahorses.

We crossed the heat-rippling pavement and stepped into refrigerated darkness. The aromas of warm bread, and garlic, and something baked in butter welcomed us. Ice jingled in a highball glass.

Jenny took my hand. "Ah," she said. "Honey, I'm home."

26 Cheesecake

JENNY AXELROD'S REVIVAL CONTINUED. The sad woman in the shabby doorway had vanished.

"We'll have the bloody marys," she told our waiter. He had emerged from the shadows moments after the hostess dropped us at a quiet booth near the back. He didn't tell us his name. Or call us *you guys*. Gold piping and brass buttons on his vest gave him a nautical look, and his pearly buccaneer sleeves kept him visible in the dark chill.

The dark chill warmed with gilded candlelight.

Yeah, that kind of place.

THE CANDLELIGHT DID WONDERS for Jenny's face. A sparkle lit her ebony eyes.

She stroked the tablecloth and smiled. "This is satin."

I wanted to talk about Hardy, but first the drinks came. Then demi-bowls of chowder, compliments of the chef. Then breads, salads, pasta, and lots of fish.

And wine. Jenny's smile had faltered when I specified "Nothing too expensive," but our server betrayed not a hint of disdain—"Of course, sir," he said—and we agreed on a *zesty but discreetly sweet* white that set me back less than twenty bucks.

"OKAY, LET'S TALK ABOUT Hardy," I said. We'd taken the edge off our appetites, and the booze made life good.

"Mmm," she said. She stabbed a morsel of broiled sea creature, chewed languidly, and sipped from her wineglass. Raised her napkin and dabbed her lips.

"Good old Hard-On," she said. "He liked to be called that."

"So I've heard."

79

"Not that he was gifted."

"I doubt that's relevant."

"It's just that he was always interested. Like one of his damn bonobos."

"Tell me about the photographs."

She strummed her nails on the tabletop. "Okay, he had a place by the barn, screened off. He was a charming guy, lord knows. And the women showed up. Heard about this animal guy and the pictures. Just curious, they'd say. Five minutes later they're shedding their clothes, nothing but a smile and a hat, or feather boa. Or they'd hold an animal—a baby, usually. But that got dangerous."

"How did you feel about that side of the business?"

"I didn't like it, when I was young and in love. After a while it didn't matter. It brought people in. They bought snacks. Trinkets. Tickets to see the animals."

"And these nudes were women only? Did he ever include men? Families? Kids?"

"Hardy liked adult females. Period. Not saying he never shot a man, or a married couple, whatever. But no kids, for sure. We had enough legal problems without going there."

"Legal problems?"

"Technicalities, like I told you. Licenses, taxes. Not real crime. Not Hardy."

"But money was tight," I said. "So he takes a few tasteful shots. Innocent poses, with young subjects. Appealing to the right audience, but plausibly deniable."

"Nah. Not Hardy."

OVER COFFEE AND DESSERT—cheesecake with berry compote—I slid Jenny the original photo of Haley at the beach with the older man.

She looked without touching. "This isn't Hardy's work. No way." She pushed aside her half-eaten dessert. "I've had enough."

"Tell me about this picture," I said.

"No. I don't know a thing about that." Her eyes held mine, too long.

"You're lying, Mrs. Axelrod."

She looked away.

"Who's living in the house with you?" I said.

"Nobody. Only me."

"What's going on?" I leaned forward. "What are you hiding, Jenny?"

"I live alone. My husband's dead. That's all. If you don't believe me, boo-boppity-hoo."

"I saw a face. Upstairs window."

"It was me."

"It wasn't you. And when I knocked, you shouted. Someone answered."

"Okay, look. Forget that. It has nothing to do with the stuff you're asking about."

"Let me decide."

SHE RAN HER FINGERS across the table and brushed a crumb to the floor. "Okay. Why not? It was Boyce. Hardy's favorite. We raised him like our own."

"He's adopted? A foster child?"

She snorted. "Boy? Hardly." She lifted her coffee but put it back without drinking. "He's the last of the bonobos."

27 Almost human

THE BLOWERS IN THE rental baked us like a convection oven. The AC eventually tempered the heat. But the roar of the fan put a damper on conversation, and neither of us seemed to care.

Food, booze, caffeine, and lies. Lunchtime in Florida.

WE WERE PULLING INTO Jenny's driveway when she spoke.

"He didn't take that picture. I wasn't lying."

"But you know about it."

She sighed.

I parked under the weird palm tree again.

"It was ... a good lunch, wasn't it?" she said.

"The best."

She slumped out of the rental, and left the door open. The midday sun through the fronds was unkind to her face, as the neon cosmopolite from the restaurant faded into sepia tones.

"Come in and look through Hardy's papers if you want," she said. "There might be something you can use."

I secured the rental and followed her to the house.

"Wait out here," she said. "I'll put Boyce in the back. He's not ... great with strangers."

THE DOOR CLOSED AND I leaned my back against it, shrinking from the sun. Two minutes out of the AC and sweat trickled from my pits, prickling my ribs.

Jenny's voice through the door, indistinct, cajoling. *Something-something-Boy*. Then a response. Like *What? What. What!*

Almost human.

I shivered in the heat.

28   Monkey bed

"THE MAID HASN'T CLEANED this week," Jenny told me.

Is she kidding?

"I'm kidding," she said.

Nothing in the house sat square. The chairs, the sofa, the rugs. Even the pictures on the walls were skewed. A curious smell stood my hair on end.

She led me down a narrow hallway to a ten-by-ten bedroom with a sagging single bed, a shallow closet, and a vintage dresser with a round mirror. Plus a four-drawer filing cabinet and a fiberboard desk with a big beige computer. With two of us in the room, space was tight and I could tell what she had for lunch.

Fish and garlic.

"This is Hardy's room," she said. "Was. And his office."

I didn't comment, but she explained anyway.

"We slept in separate rooms. He put on weight and snored like a fucking alligator. He'd go completely silent, I mean like he died, then he'd jerk and choke and start snoring again. Sorry. Too much information."

"No, it's okay."

"Anyway, his files are in these drawers. You won't find anything shady, but look if you want to. Check the closet too."

"Got it. Thanks."

"Bathroom's across the hall, if you need it. Don't open the door at the back. That's Boy's room."

"I don't get to meet him?" I smiled but she didn't.

"Maybe later." She leaned in and kissed me on the mouth.

I wasn't expecting it, but I managed not to dive for cover.

"Not feeling it?" she said.

I shrugged. "Like I said, not my thing right now."

Her eyes narrowed. Then she nodded and walked out, and I got busy.

IN THE DESK DRAWERS I found the usual jumble of office paraphernalia: pens, pencils, scissors, rulers, sticky notes, paper clips, a multi-tip screwdriver, tape, and a glue stick—for starters.

A wallet with dozens of business cards in clear sleeves—electrician, plumber, landscaper, vet. Some with *GOOD* written in the upper right corner, others *NG*. For *Not Good*, my detective instincts told me. A pack of thumbtacks, unopened. Two pencil sharpeners and a fat eraser for graphite and ink.

Next, the file cabinet. The guy saved everything. Decades of invoices, receipts, and bills. Even his high school report cards. I found no clues.

The bloody marys, cheesecake, and *discreetly sweet* wine had dulled my senses more than my after-dinner coffee sharpened them. I pulled out a folder labeled *Miscellaneous* and sat on the bed to leaf through it. From the patterned bedspread, a hundred monkey faces grinned up at me—somebody had a sense of humor—and I thought, *I'll rest my eyes for a minute.*

TIME PASSED—I DON'T know how much—and when I woke up I wasn't sure where I was. But there was a woman sitting on the bed next to me. She had my penis in her hand. It was Jenny.

29 Pleasure and pain

SHE WORE A MAN'S long-sleeve shirt. Unbuttoned. Nothing beneath it.

"Challenge accepted," she said.

"What?"

"I haven't seen one of these in a while. Not human, anyway." She squeezed. "It likes me."

If my half-way impressed her, she really *hadn't* seen one in a while.

She had my pants around my thighs, limiting my mobility. That's my excuse for what happened next.

SHE SWUNG A LEG over and slid me into a warm lubey spot. Her shirt vanished and she gripped my shoulders and got to work. My half-way woke up and took notice. Jenny's breathing went ragged, and little moans and cries fell from her throat. I'm sure her expression was erotic as hell, but I'll never know because I couldn't tear my eyes from those stunning breasts, swaying inches from my face. Their size was average but the nipples were darker than I expected, and bigger, and turgid to the bursting point.

I covered them with my palms and squeezed.

Jenny groaned and picked up the pace. "You like those, gay boy?"

I pushed harder, and sent her over the edge. She shouted something nasty and ground her groin into mine, and I felt a grip and quiver that should have taken me with her, but didn't.

After a time she climbed off and slipped into her shirt. Or Hardy's.

"You're not so gay after all, are you?" she said. She was

looking at my penis, still standing proudly.

"I need the bathroom." I swung out of bed and adjusted my pants and stumbled across the floor. In the bathroom, my tumescence slowed things down. Eventually I managed in dribs and drabs to relieve my bladder, but my erection wasn't going anywhere. *An ED drug aftereffect?*

Jenny knocked. "You okay in there?"

"No." I opened the door and she made a quick diagnosis.

"You didn't come."

"You couldn't tell?"

"I was kinda busy." She reached out and touched. *This woman isn't shy.* "It's dangerous to go around like that."

"So they say."

"Come back to bed," she said. She literally rubbed her hands together. "Challenge accepted, part two."

I HADN'T LEARNED MUCH about Hard-On Axelrod, but I was learning all there was to know about his grieving widow. She was triple-threat tenacious and prolific as hell, I'll give her that. She didn't quit until she had a fistful of my fluids, and it wasn't pretty.

"You've got blood in your come," she said.

I heard her but I had more urgent problems. Someone had plunged a phantom ice pick deep into my brain. I covered my face with my hands and pushed, to force out the fire.

"Ted, what's wrong?"

I choked out a word. "Hurts."

"Your head?"

"Ow." I staggered to the bathroom, twisted the cold tap and wedged my head under the flow. No relief, but at least I was doing something. Then the pain faded, and faded faster. Almost gone. Gone.

I pulled a towel from the rack and dried off. Jenny was watching.

"Whatever that was," I said, "it sure took the joy out of sex."

"Headache? Right when you came?"

"Yeah."

"Hardy used to get those, from his blood pressure. You got BP problems?"

"It's the meds I'm on," I said. "*Was* on. Never again."

"Maybe it's my technique." She put a finger to her cheek. "I could move the triple nimbus to a later slot in the program. Give you a fighting chance."

Her grin annoyed me. "Stop. It's not funny."

"You're right. Look at this." She wiped her palm with a handful of TP. "It's blood in there."

"That's mine?"

"You see anybody else ejaculate around here? Don't answer that." She flushed the tissue and washed her hands with hot water and soap.

IT WASN'T THE HAPPIEST ending to a sexual interlude, but we got dressed and got over it. And I had a grim thought: *I never want to have sex again.*

Ever.

30 Nature Beach Angels

"SO DID YOU FIND anything useful?" Jenny was back in her square-neck top and khakis.

"No," I said. "I didn't."

"What did you think of Hardy's pictures?"

"Pictures?"

"The nudes. In the closet. You didn't check the closet?"

So I checked the closet and found a box with folders of portraits. Sorted through them at the kitchen table.

The women were mostly in their thirties, I figured, or forties. In swimwear, or topless, or nude, or in outfits that concealed and revealed. Props too. Hats and guns and feathers. In various pictures, the same florid guy with the crooked smile posed with the woman, an arm or two wrapped around her, or holding her on his lap. He was fully dressed, his open shirt Western or Hawaiian.

Grins and good times.

"That's Hardy," Jenny told me.

"You take those?"

"Not me. Timer. I stayed away from that."

"Was he intimate with these women?"

"What difference does it make?"

SOME INTERVIEWS ARE LIKE that. All silt in the pan, and nary a gleam of gold. Not even fool's gold.

I browsed random folders and found more undressed women. Meh. I hadn't felt this blasé about female nudity since ... since ever.

"I've had it," I said.

"What does that mean?"

"Enough already. I give up."

"Poor Ted."

"I'm sorry I bothered you."

"Don't be. Today was kickass."

I stood. *Will she expect a goodbye kiss?*

"Sit down, Ted. You haven't seen this yet." She pulled a manila envelope from the back of the box.

"What is it?"

She bent back the metal clasp and slid the contents onto the table. Déjà vu. A week ago a woman had brought a similar envelope to my office. It contained a picture of a naked man and girl. And thousands of dollars in cash.

This one offered no cash. But there were plenty of naked girls.

THE PICTURES WERE PRINTED in a comb-bound notebook, maybe eight by ten inches, the kind of thing you throw together on a kitchen table. The cover was buff card stock, uncoated and hand-lettered: *Nature Beach Angels.*

A wonky halo crowned the *A* in *Angels.*

Inside were a dozen pages of photos like the one in my pocket. Black and white, same size, as if they'd been printed on a photocopier without adjustment. Every photo included a girl or two. Frolicking with other kids, or standing around with adults, everybody naked.

Well, not entirely. If you count hats, glasses, and sandals.

Some girls appeared in multiple shots. The most photogenic, maybe, or extroverted, or accessible. Some were very young, chests like boys. Others, a little older, with starter breasts, and a few were shaped like little women. And always the beach, the ocean.

The background reminded me of another photo: the one of Haley and the naked man.

I TURNED THE LAST page and there they were.

There they were.

Enlarged, filling two-thirds of the page. And crooked, like the pictures on the walls all around me.

"There they are," I said.

"Yeah. I recognized the picture at lunch."

"Why didn't you show me this sooner?"

"I thought it'd be nice to keep you around a while." She peered through her eyelashes. "And it kinda was."

"Christ, Jenny. You're ... never mind. Where did this book come from?"

"Originally? That's the big question, isn't it?"

"Hardy put this together, didn't he."

"No." She slapped the table. "Dammit, Ted. Hardy had nothing to do with this. I told you already. I told you and told you."

I checked the back cover. Across the bottom, in typewriter font: *Kolaca Publications*.

No address or contact information.

"Kolaca Publications," I said. "Who's that?"

"I don't know. But I know how we got this thing."

31 Brainstorm

"A GUY SHOWED UP," Jenny said. "I don't know his name. He'd heard of Hardy's work, his nudes, and thought we could move his *Beach Angel* books. We could buy them outright or sell on consignment."

"Which did you do?"

"Neither. Hardy sent the guy packing."

I held up the book. "So how did you end up with this?"

"The guy left it, with his contact information in the back, in case Hardy changed his mind."

A paper clip clung to the back cover, shadowed by a trace of rust.

"I need to track down this Kolaca Publications guy. What did he look like?"

"An average white dude with an ordinary car."

"That's it?"

"Look, if he was a genie with a jetpack, I'd say so."

SHE AMBLED BACK INTO Hardy's bedroom to boot the computer and I followed, leafing through the pages. Searching for clues in the pictures. A city limits sign in the background, the photographer's face in somebody's Ray-Bans. Or an overlooked appendix, listing the name, address, and star sign of everyone on both sides of the camera.

No joy.

JENNY TAPPED THE KEYBOARD. "I'll Google *Kolaca* and see what we get."

"Yeah, I know about the Google," I said. "Does your computer always chirp like that?"

"You *know about the Google*?"

"Sure."

"And no, the chirping is new. It's the hard drive." She whacked the case with her palm, and a results window staggered into view.

"Not many hits on Kolaca." She scrolled down. "Nothing about pictures or publishers."

"What's this about koala bears?"

"The internet thinks I can't spell."

"Okay." I ruffled the *Nature Beach Angels* pages. "Can I borrow this? Somebody might recognize the beach or the publisher. Or one of the naked people."

"Ted, I never want to see that book again."

"Right. And if you remember anything else, you've got my—" *Wait a minute. Brainstorm.*

I wrenched open the desk drawer. There. The business card wallet. My fingers flicked through the sleeves.

No. No. Nope. And then ...

Yes. This one: *Kolaca Publications. Miami.* I slid the card out. An address across the bottom, a suite number in Miami Springs. In the upper right corner, *NG.* Hardy Axelrod's verdict: *Not Good.*

And on the back—jackpot.

In pale green ink, a name: *Ronnie Panko.*

THE AFTERNOON WAS BLEEDING out.

Jenny didn't walk me to my rental, but watched from the porch as I started the engine, buzzed down the windows, and cranked the AC to *Witch's Tit.* Blasting out the heat.

We'd said our goodbyes at her front door. She'd keyed her number into my cell phone and told me to get my ass to a doctor about my climax headache—"Could be a mini-stroke," she said—and the blood in my semen. But I'd already settled on the source of my ills: a certain trio of she-devils, and the salacious joyride they'd put me through.

A man's not meant for that much sex in twenty-four hours.

I SCANNED THE DASH gauges, buzzed up the windows, and snapped my seat belt. When I glanced at the house, Jenny was gone, but a stirring in the upstairs window caught my eye. The face behind the sheer curtain was not hers.

I put the transmission in gear, ready to drive away and never look back.

But the movement in the dormer reminded me of Boyce the bonobo—Boy, Jenny called him. I couldn't leave without a glimpse of that specimen.

A decision that would change everything.

32 Can I trust you?

SHE CRACKED THE DOOR before I could knock.

"Forget something?"

"Yes. Boyce."

"What about him?"

"I want to meet him, Jenny."

"Why?"

"The poor guy was stuck in his room the whole time I was here. He must be glad to be free."

"That's not an answer."

I said nothing. Sometimes that's the best argument.

"Can I trust you, Ted?"

NOT WHAT I EXPECTED to hear. But after our bizarre intimacy, all I could say was *yes*. "Yes."

"All right." She checked over her shoulder and opened up. "Don't let him out."

He wasn't even in the room. She locked the door and pocketed the key.

"Boyce! We have company!" To me: "Sit down, Ted. Let me tell you about bonobos."

"They're hyper-sexual, right?" I settled into the sofa. "And non-violent."

"Not as violent as chimps, no. But they aren't sheep." She sat on a footstool by the window. "I'm staying over here, Ted. He might get jealous." Calling up the stairway: "Boyce! Do you hear me?"

Voice from upstairs: [bark-like] "What."

Jenny: "Come downstairs. Now."

"It sounded like he said *what*," I said. "Like I was

94

talking."

She looked at me without blinking. "He can talk, Ted."

"Like ASL? Sign language?"

She shook her head, and a shadow fell across the stair.

"No," she said. "Not like that."

33 Boyce the bonobo

THE CREATURE DESCENDED THE staircase, walking roughly upright, dressed in a black vest and nothing else. His skin was the color of coffee with cream, the hair above his blunt forehead two shades darker, with a middle part. Over the rest of his body, his gleaming coat was sparse, highlighting his nakedness.

He stopped at the bottom of the steps and stared at me with black amber eyes in bony sockets. Below his slender nose, his broad mouth ticced up on one side in a half smirk.

"Boyce," Jenny said. "Look at me."

He faced her, swinging arms that reached his knees.

"What," he said.

His pronunciation was imperfect—heavy on the glottal stop—but he spoke.

Jenny pointed. "Boy, you forgot your pants."

He looked down and used an overhand grip to sheathe his slender penis, stroking it absently. He shook his head and grunted.

"Use your words, Boy."

"Too hot," he said.

"Boy, this is Ted. A friend. He wants to meet you."

"What."

"Say hello to Ted, Boy. Don't be shy."

He turned with a bowlegged pivot, released his sleek phallus, and thrust a muscled arm my way.

"Hello," he said.

WHEN I DIDN'T OFFER to shake, he thumped his chest.

"I Boy," he said, and after he spoke, his lips moved in a

silent repeated pattern. His eyes locked onto mine.

"I Boy," he said again, tapping his chest and reaching for my hand. His mouth continued its action, slow and explicit, releasing a breath like a whisper.

I took his hand. He didn't shake mine, but gave it a docile squeeze.

"Pleased to meet you, Boyce," I said.

"What," he said.

I spoke louder. "Pleased to meet you."

"He heard you," Jenny said. "*What* is his go-to word. First one he learned."

"What," he said.

"Boyce," she said. "Say *pleased to meet you.*"

"Please," he said. "Please." Then his lips mimed the same pattern as before.

"That'll do," Jenny said. "Go back upstairs while Ted and I talk."

He held eye contact for a heartbeat, then turned and bounded up the stairs in three leaps of knuckles and feet. Gone.

A SURREAL DREAM.

"I don't believe what I just saw," I said. "He's brilliant. Why isn't he being studied by every anthropologist on the planet?"

"They're not aware of him, Ted. I haven't told anyone except his doctor. And you."

"Why the hell not?"

"Selfish reasons, I suppose. I don't think it's strictly legal, me keeping him here."

"What are you afraid of? A fine?"

"Well, I'm broke, that's true. But I'm afraid they'll take him away. He's all I have left of Hardy."

"Boy does remind me of Hardy," I said, recalling his photos with the nude women. "Around the mouth. They say kids start to resemble their adoptive parents after a while."

Jenny sat very still. "He's not adopted."

"Sure. But you know what I mean. And anyway, you and

Hardy weren't close for a while. So why do you want Boy around as a reminder?"

She stared into her lap. "He reminds me of the good times with Hardy." She rose and walked to the window. "But he's an adolescent now. More aggressive, sexually." Fingers spread, she touched the glass. Outside, the property baked in the brutal heat. "He's always been sexual. Touching, mounting behavior, that kind of thing. It's his bonobo blood. Lately he's more insistent. He wants to mate."

"Insistent how?"

"Intrusive. Urgent. In my personal space. I'm not going to draw you a picture."

"You just did."

Her back shuddered. "What am I going to do, Ted?"

"You want a solution, or just someone to listen?"

"I want a goddamn solution."

"Get yourself a publicist. Cash in. An animal like that's a gold mine. Use the profits to get Boy into a natural environment, with other bonobos, where he fits in."

She sat next to me and took my hand. I waited.

"He's not an animal, Ted. And he'll never fit in with other bonobos."

SHE WOULDN'T MEET MY eyes, and my gut twinged. Queasy. *Not adopted. Not an animal.*

Pieces fell together in unwelcome ways. *Nuh-uh.* No, I didn't want her to say it. *Don't say it.*

She said it.

"He's genetically half human," she whispered. "He's like a son to Hardy and me."

JESUS CHRIST.

Half human. *Like a son.*

"So, his parents," I said. "One human. One bonobo."

She nodded.

"Is his bonobo parent," I said, "a male or a female?"

She gave me a blank look. Then her nostrils flared.

"My god," she said. "You don't think—"

"I don't know what to think, okay?"

"His mother is bonobo," she said. "He's Hardy's biological son. *His* boy." She shook her head. "My god."

"How does that even happen?" I said. "No, don't tell me." I couldn't think of what to say. "You need more help than I can give you, Jenny."

She was crying. "What am I going to do?"

This time I didn't have a solution.

I LEFT HER SOME money, which wouldn't solve her Boyce problem, but couldn't hurt. And it eased my conscience enough to get the hell out, pronto. I scurried to my rental and didn't waste time checking the gauges or cooling the interior.

But just before I floored the gas and fled the insanity, I saw Boy slide a sheet of paper against the second-floor window. Big snaky letters in black marker.

So the boy writes too.

Two words, a short one above a shorter one. Almost legible. Then it clicked ... the pattern Boy's lips had repeated in silence, mouthing the sounds.

Now they rang clear, revealed in the sad sorry sign he'd scrawled for the passing stranger.

HELP
ME

34 Groovy Toovy

I FOLLOWED THE RICKENBACKER Causeway onto Virginia Key and hung a left on Arthur Lamb. The beach I wanted blazed across my brain in living color, like a fresh memory. Derish's hypnotic directions led me along a dirt track by a chain-link fence. Next to a sewage plant.

This can't be right.

A paved road veered right, and carried me after a block or so to the beach parking lot, every space vacant. *Odd.*

The beach was deserted. From the sand, I looked out to an empty sea and sky.

Until a sleek catamaran motored in from the right, dead slow, toward a cluster of oceanfront high-rises to the left—Miami Beach, most likely—across a far expanse of water.

In the other direction crouched Key Biscayne, like clouds hugging the horizon. *This looks familiar. I'm where Derish wants me. Or very near.*

I bared my feet and rolled my pants and walked. The Axelrod weirdness faded with the sigh of the surf, gentle today, going about its business.

As the coastline curved right, Miami Beach receded behind me. Ahead, the Rickenbacker Causeway slid into sight—the stretch linking Virginia Key to Key Biscayne.

THE MAN ON THE fronds sat languid in the sand. Invisible, somehow, until I stumbled into him.

"Greetings," he said.

"Same to you."

His mane, tangled as seaweed, trembled in the ocean breeze. "Have you a moment for conversation?"

This is the place. "Yes," I said.

His rugged face disguised his age, and he wore something leathery around his hips, the detail lost in his bed of fronds.

He gazed out to sea, eyes tranquil. "One can sit in this place and exist in any era humankind has walked the earth."

As I could neither confirm nor deny, I said nothing.

THE SUN CREPT LOWER behind us, nudging our shadows to the water's edge. The catamaran stayed its lazy course northward.

"Close your eyes," he said.

I closed them. A pressure change in my ears. A smell—ozone before a storm.

"Open your eyes."

"What happened?" I said. "Where's the motorboat?"

He said nothing. The sinking sun ripened the colors of the sky, clouds, and sea, and set the vegetation glowing.

"What am I doing here?" I said.

He surprised me with a grin. "What is this all about, Alfie?" Almost a song title.

"What's the frequency, Daniel?" I countered. *Pretty sure that's a song too.*

"Is that all that there is?" he said.

Okay. I know that one. Game on, my friend.

We mixed and matched nihilistic lyrics until the music in our heads faded.

WE SAT. TIME EBBED and flowed.

"What's your name?" I asked him.

His eyes were closed and he didn't answer.

My gaze wandered southward and I saw no Rickenbacker. Only open water. I nudged the nameless guy. "Hey. The causeway to Key Biscayne. Why can't we see it?"

He opened his eyes. "The bridge?"

"Yes."

"What is your name?" he said.

"Ted. What's yours?"

"It is Ted also."

"That's unlikely," I said.

"Many things are unlikely. Most things, perhaps."

"Like a bridge disappearing?"

"Close your eyes, Ted."

"Again?" I closed them.

"Now tell me why there is no bridge," he said.

"Beats me."

"Why is there no bridge?"

"Because there are no people to cross the bridge."

"Another answer," he said.

"Because there is no island to cross to."

"Another."

"Because there is no water to cross."

The temperature cooled.

"Open your eyes, Ted."

I LOOKED AGAIN. THERE was no water to cross. A solid land mass distended from Virginia Key, curving in unbroken tranquility to the east.

"A magic trick," I said. "An illusion."

"Hocus pocus," he said. "Conjuring."

"I've been hypnotized."

"Delusions, then." He stretched onto his back, fingers laced behind his neck. Closed his eyes.

"Or time travel," I said.

"In your words: *That's unlikely.*"

"In your words: *Most things are.*"

He didn't answer.

"If this is time travel," I said, "then ..."

"Then what?"

"Well, what's the point? Why?"

"Why not?" he said. "Because it's there."

"No, because it's *then*." I laughed at my own joke.

He didn't. "Because of what it teaches."

"What does it teach?"

"You tell me."

"Okay. Don't kill your grandfather before your father is born." I had more. "A billion parallel universes exist simultaneously."

"Those are intellectual conundra. What does one learn?"

"About what?"

"Oneself," he said. "One's place in history. In eternity."

"I don't know."

He nodded but did not open his eyes.

THE CATAMARAN I'D SEEN earlier approached on the opposite bearing. Heading for the causeway between Virginia Key and Key Biscayne. The air stank.

"Ted," I said. "The bridge is back."

He sat up. "What?" He rubbed his eyes with the heels of his hands.

I pointed. "The causeway."

"Rickenbacker," he said. He rolled his head and his neck popped. "Spare me five bucks? I'll definitely pay it forward."

I stared at him.

"When I'm in a better fiscal space," he said. The hair was the same but the eyes were anxious.

"Is your name Ted?" I asked him.

"No, man. It's Toovy. Is your name Ted?"

"Yes, in fact."

Toovy: "Groovy, Ted."

Me: "Groovy, Toovy."

I donated a C-note, grabbed my shoes, and fled.

35 Coco Brisa break-in

BACK AT MY RENTAL, I pulled on my socks and shoes and checked my phone. One voice message—from Derish.

"Change of plan, Ted. We have to cancel tonight."

I lowered the windows but didn't hit the starter. Afternoon was drifting into evening, and the breeze across the key invited me to stay a while.

Why had Derish and Maddy canceled? *And what was so damn important about this post-hypnotic side trip to Virginia Key?*

My finger hovered over the phone.

But I didn't trust Derish. He could zap me to zombieland— as he'd proven—and I'd still be sitting here when the morning sun slapped me in the face.

I tossed the phone into a cupholder and started the engine.

MY ROUTE LEAVING VIRGINIA Key avoided the sewage plant. Better aesthetics.

Once I hit the Rickenbacker, a twenty-minute jaunt down Dixie Highway took me to the Coco Brisa turnoff, and I eased into stealth mode.

THE FLINS LIVED ON a cul-de-sac, called a court in Coco Brisa. I parked near the sac end, on a gravelly berm under shaggy but chic greenery. The fading daylight helped camouflage my rental, but anyone could call the cops at any time in a posh neighborhood like this.

So I didn't dawdle.

I hopped out, locked the doors, and strolled to the Flin property like I belonged. Resisting the urge to slink, I ambled up the drive, dodged the double garage, and tested the garden door. Locked. Without overthinking things, I took a boost from a stoic stone gargoyle and crossed into the private grounds.

I sidestepped the pool and dashed to the gazebo. Inside the house, lights blazed behind the broad sunroom windows and tall french doors, so I felt concealed behind the latticework in the gathering dusk.

Derish and Maddy hustled through the bright tableau, stacking luggage near an opened door that framed a slice of dark automobile and a wall of garage gear. At one point they argued, apparently about a big manila envelope balanced on a suitcase.

Their voices drifted through a set of jalousies cracked open between an AC unit and a storage bin.

When they both turned away, I scampered to the bin and knelt behind it. At that instant, low-watt lighting flowed over the pool and grounds. I froze as Maddy glanced outside, but Derish jabbed her shoulder and she turned away.

Did my motion trigger the lights? I took a silent breath and inched closer to the window.

Their conversation got clearer by the second.

Maddy: "I think you're being—"

The AC compressor kicked in. Buzz and whir drowned every voice.

THEY ARGUED INAUDIBLY. IN frustration, I switched to lip-reading. *"Pee Wee slow cooker,"* Derish insisted. *"Dry socket paddle frost,"* Maddy countered.

Or not. Probably not.

Tempers rose. Toe-to-toe, Maddy stood nearly as tall as Derish. Voices louder now, something about a phone call? A threat?

At last, the howling AC fell into silence. And the confrontation ended. *Damn.*

Derish exited stage right. Maddy glanced around, then slipped the envelope onto a glass shelf, behind an antique map of the Gulf of Mexico. On which Florida was a gimpy digit drooping from the fist of North America. Thumbs down.

Maddy exited stage right, following Derish.

Fuck it.

In two beats I reached the patio door. *Unlocked.* I angled it open and stole across the floor. At the shelves, I tilted the map and liberated the envelope. A name on the front. *Ted Danger.*

A shadow hovered on the wall. My breathing slowed. I froze.

Maddy: [distant] "Derish. Have you seen my readers?"

Derish: [under his breath] "Good lord." [louder] "Coming, dear. Have you looked on the dresser?"

The shadow faded. I glided away and vanished into the night. *Ted Danger, Ninja Detective.*

SECONDS LATER I WAS over the wall, across the drive, down the court, and in my vehicle. Which was neither surrounded by light-pulsing police cruisers nor being winched onto a tow truck by a surly dude with an untidy beard.

I tossed the envelope onto the passenger seat, buckled up, and cranked the engine. Time to go. Then two windows went dark in the Flin home. I crept the car forward, lights off, to a shadowy spot near a stucco wall where I could surveil the garage doors.

Killed the engine. Waited. Not for long.

The left garage door, a one-piece model, angled out and up with the purr of the opener, revealing a small BMW. Gleaming black, or charcoal.

The trunk popped, and Derish appeared from deeper in the garage with three matching bags, which he precisely stowed. He retreated into the house for a minute. Or two. Or five. Which seems like an hour when you're waiting for the police to scream around the corner and ruin your evening.

WITH MADDY RIGHT BEHIND him, Derish marched into the garage carrying a garment bag, which he tossed onto the other luggage. Maddy slid into the passenger seat as Derish slammed the deck and skirted the back fender. Seconds later, brake lights flared, then backup lamps.

I slouched in my rental.

The BMW backed into the street as the garage door pivoted down.

I let them get to the end of the court, stop completely, and hang a sedate left—properly signaled—before I started my engine, hit the lights, and discreetly followed.

36 Hideout

THEY APPARENTLY WEREN'T GOING far.

I followed the BMW north, up US 1. My mirrors revealed no vehicles tailing us. But a good tail is hard to spot. And I couldn't take evasive action without losing the BMW.

Not far out of Miami, Derish turned in at a brick one-story motel with parking off the cross street. Guests' cars angled toward the main drag, license plates on display.

Not a great place to hide.

A lounge next door provided space for me to pull over. But before I'd shut off the engine, the BMW slid by again, continuing north.

In less than a block, it pulled off at the Rey-Day Inn, a stucco two-story. I parked my rental catty-corner, at a diner with big windows. When the aromas ambushed me, my stomach let out a growl and I swiped the back of my hand across my mouth. I hadn't eaten since my lunch with Crazy Jenny, Boy the bonobo's stepmom. Which seemed like days ago.

But first things first. I locked the rental, crossed the street, and strolled down the block past the Rey-Day.

THE BMW WAS PARKED in front of the office. Through the lobby door I saw Derish chatting with the desk clerk, a young woman with an olive complexion and a mannish haircut. Maddy remained in the car, behind dark windows that mirrored the night signage along US 1. In the office, the clerk was nodding. Derish passed her some bills and she smiled in a way I'm sure he was used to.

I ambled down the cross street, hiding my face with my

phone. Keeping an eye on the BMW. Derish slid into the driver's seat and drove to the back of the Rey-Day where five parking slots faced three ground-floor units.

Good thinking, Derish. Pay in cash and park in the back.

The trunk popped open and so did the doors, and Derish and Maddy stepped into the night. I slowed my pace as they both grabbed a couple of bags and headed for the leftmost room. Derish paused to deal with the key, but my focus was on Maddy.

She had rested her bags on the pavement and stood with her arms at her sides, palms forward, gazing skyward. Maybe a cosmic blessing spiritualists do for a new hideout. Lord knows.

"Maddy," I heard Derish say.

When I peeked over my phone, her gaze swung my way. After a beat, she hefted her bags and followed Derish into the unit.

I kept walking.

37 Alias James Dare

THE DINER SERVED BREAKFAST all day, so I ordered orange juice, a fruit bowl, a stack of whole-wheat blueberry pancakes—with real maple syrup (a nice bonus)—and, to cut the sweet, a rasher of thick-sliced bacon, two eggs over easy, and black coffee.

The waitress—her name was Christelle and she told me she was from Haiti—brought me a sweaty tumbler of ice water, a miniature orange juice ("A single orange we have juiced for you," she said), and my personal pot of coffee in an insulated carafe.

I downed my OJ shot and ordered another. It was a good start.

While I waited for my food, I opened my purloined envelope and discreetly removed the contents. The way this case was going, I half expected pictures of naked kids to spill out.

But not this time. I ruffled the stack of 8.5 by 11 sheets, organized with plastic clips of green, yellow, red, and blue.

The first section, regarding Virginia Key, included photocopied news stories, a couple of internet articles, and a double-spaced academic report. With key points highlighted in classic yellow for my convenience.

I'D JUST STARTED READING about Virginia Key's designation as a segregated beach (or *colored only*, on a beach sign) in the mid-1940s when Christelle arrived bearing breakfast.

Perfect timing. Through the window, Derish Flin was crossing US 1, headed my way.

"Christelle, where can I wash my hands?"

She aimed me toward a back hallway and I scooped up my

110

documents and bolted. After rounding the corner, I looked back by exposing just enough of my face to observe my target with one eye.

It's the first trick they teach you in detective school.

Christelle looked at me, head tilted.

Behind her, Derish entered the diner. "Carry-out order for James Dare," he told the cashier.

Using what we in the detective racket call a *false name*.

BEYOND THE MEN'S ROOM, an exit sign warned *ALARM WILL SOUND IF DOOR IS OPENED*. However, the door was propped wide with a plastic carton, and no alarms sounded. So I zipped out and hustled around the building until I found a spot near a concrete planter where I could spy on Derish undetected.

The Rey-Day Inn sign, visible from my stakeout, provided the motel phone number. Which I punched into my cell. Leaning out, I watched the Rey-Day clerk through the motel door as she picked up the phone. Her lips moved a half second before her voice reached my ear.

"Rey-Day Inn."

"Connect me with, uh, James Dare's room, please."

Maddy answered on the fifth ring.

"Hello, Ted."

How does she know it's me? "Hello, Maddy. How are you?"

"We're avoiding you," she said. "But I felt you were near."

"Felt?"

"You have an unsettled aura."

"Sure, that's me. Look, Maddy. What's going on? Why did you guys cancel our meeting tonight?"

A northbound police cruiser shrieked by in out-of-my-way mode. Inside the diner, Derish dug through two carry-out bags.

"What did you say, Maddy?"

"I said nothing."

"Has someone threatened you? Warned you not to talk to me?"

111

"That's a remarkable inference, Ted. But Derish and I ... you need to speak with both of us."

"So he's the one who's afraid to talk to me?"

Silence on the phone. Derish collected his bags and two hefty drinks and exited the diner with deliberate movements, balancing his cargo. I pressed deeper into my dark niche.

Maddy finally spoke. "I'm not saying anything else. And I'll tell Derish of your call. I'm keeping no secrets from him."

My food was getting cold. "You're a sweetheart, Maddy."

AS DERISH CROSSED THE street, I put my head down and took the shortest route to my table, through the front door.

The cashier barely glanced up and Christelle wasn't around. And my food was still warm.

Here's to small victories. I toasted myself with a sip of hot coffee and dug in.

MY PHONE RANG HALFWAY through my meal, and it wasn't good news.

"Ted, listen." It was Tru. "Nicki's disappeared. Her husband's out for blood."

The signal faltered, dropping syllables.

"Her husband? What's his problem? He didn't even know about this."

"When he came back from his conference, Nicki was gone. Haley too, of course." Her voice shook.

"Relax, Tru. I'll talk to him—Benjamin, right? And—"

"He found the ... threatening to sue us, Ted." She was talking fast through the signal problems. "... that we knew ... unstable and we took advantage ..."

"Tru, stop. Breathe."

She sighed over the phone.

"I'll talk to him," I said. "This could work to our advantage."

"How?"

"Look, first tell me exactly what happened. How did you

find out what's-his-name, Benji, was—"

"Bentley," she said. Followed by word fragments.

"Tru, you're breaking up. I'll call you later. Meantime, relax. Don't worry."

We spoke no more. My phone was dead.

38 Burnout mode

ME TOO. DEAD.

Exhaustion blindsided me. The Möbius road to Pompano laughed at my fatigue. Only the caffeine I'd downed at the diner kept me between the lines. The boozy lunch, the punishing afternoon sex, the miserable *HELP ME* wretch in the dormer window, the Virginia Key weirdness, the Coco Brisa burglary—it was too much for one day.

Not to mention the debauchery marathon the night before.

And now Nicki is missing, and big Ben is sounding off.

My brain shifted into burnout mode, and my body had no strength to fight it.

And the darkness moved in.

It's not worth the trouble sometimes. This job. Maybe life itself, come to think of it.

Life. It's sad. So sad, and then you die. Or you don't die. You just get sadder.

When I get like this—and it happens too often—my systems shut down. Sleep is the cure.

Sleep. The tires thrummed and the warm Florida night blurred past my windows. I needed sleep.

But Tru needed me. I'd promised to call her.

But I need sleep. But Tru needs me.

Sleep. Tru. Sleep. Tru.

Voices bickering in my head. Madness.

But the voices kept me company as I flogged my rental northward, foot heavy on the gas.

And then, at last, Pompano Beach. El Toro.

I lurched up the stairs, each step an argument (*Tru, sleep, Tru, sleep*), and slid my key into the door on the second stab.

HALEY AND WALLY WERE inside, Haley's phone ghosting her face in the semi-gloom as she sprawled on a loveseat by the window. Wally slept on the bed, hands folded across his gut. Like a corpse.

Haley swiped her screen and glanced up.

"Ted Danger," she said. "Private Eye."

"Haley. What are you doing here? And Wally."

"The guy let us in. José. With a girl's name."

"Yeah. Okay. What are you guys doing here?"

"Dad called. He can't find Mom. Grandpa freaked and said it's your fault. Grandma cried. Grandpa called you but your phone's not working."

"Dead battery. And so you're here because ..." *Wait. Didn't I already ask that?*

"Grandpa's here to kick your ass." She looked at Wally. Each time he exhaled, his lips quivered. "Can't you tell?"

I put my head in my hands. *I'm falling asleep standing up, standing right here, like this. Just like this ...* I shook it off. But some of it stuck to me. "And you're here because ..."

"I'd rather watch Grandpa kick your ass than listen to Grandma piss and moan."

"Is Grandma okay? I mean, Reva? By herself?"

"She's fine. She told me to stick with Grandpa, so he won't do anything stupid."

"Okay. Okay. Look, I've got to call my Trudy. Uh. My assistant, Trudy. And I've got to sleep for about two days." I pawed through my travel bag and scooped up the phone charger.

"Whatever." Haley looked down at her phone. Her voice softened. "Do you know where my mom is?"

I closed my bag and deployed my reassurance face. "Shit, I'm sorry. I mean, shoot. Your mom. Of course you're concerned about your mom. No, I haven't heard from her. But we'll find her. I'm sure she's okay. She's fine, I'm sure." *There. That made sense. I'll be fine too. Hang in there, Ted.*

"You're sure," she said. "Right. I hate it when people say

that shit. You don't know where she is or what happened, so there's no freaking way you know she's okay, okay? Fuck that."

A PERSUASIVE ARGUMENT.

"You're right, I hate that too. Patronizing. Sorry. But listen." I sorted my thoughts. Found the right words in my mind. *Based on my intuition and my knowledge of your mother, I'm convinced the chances of her being okay are good. And that's the truth.*

There. Perfect.

"I'm listening," she said.

"What?"

"You said listen. I'm listening."

Okay. "Okay." *Maybe I wasn't talking out loud.* "Maybe I wasn't talking out loud." *I'll try again.* "I'll try again."

"Okay," she said.

"Okay." *Okay.* "Like this: Based on my experience and my intuition about your mother, I'm convinced she's okay. Chances are good. And that's the truth."

She nodded. "Okay."

I plugged my phone into an outlet near a chair. "Now," I said to Haley. "You need ... you need to ..."

"What?"

My phone sprang to life. I had two missed calls from Wally. Nothing from Nicki. Nothing from Benji or whatever.

"What do I need to do?" Haley said. "You started to tell me."

"I don't know," I said. I scrolled to Tru's number and made the call. "I don't remember."

"Hi, Ted," Tru said.

"My phone tried before," I said. *So sleepy. So sleepy.* "Died, I mean. Before. How are you?"

"Okay. Calmer now. Or faking it."

"Have you heard from Tru? I mean, Nicki? From Nicki?"

"No. Ben Vavul called back, though."

"Ben. Bengali. Ben ... been there done that."

"What?"

"Ben-Hur. Ben Dover. Ben-Anna. Banana."

"Ted, are you all right?"

"Banana. Met this guy today, Tru. Likes bananas. Banana banana bonobo. Orange. Orange you glad I didn't say banana?"

"Ted. Ted."

"You like boys? You like Boyce? Strong silent type." The room swayed, but I shifted my weight and stayed upright. Easily. Easily-peasily. "Athletic. Doesn't say much. What. What. Loves his mother. Really really loves his mother." I laughed. As the floor steepened, I staggered.

Yesi took the phone from my hand. *Yesi? José María's sister. Yesi. Where the hell did she come from?*

"Hello, this is Yesi," she said into the phone. "Ted needs to rest now."

I SAW HER HOLDING the phone, listening, and then she talked some more, but she faded in and out. *Is her battery dying? It happens. She needs to be plugged in and recharged. That's funny. Like sex. Plugging in. Get it? I should tell her, she'll laugh like, "That's so funny, Ted!" She'll laugh. But if we have sex my penis will bleed and oh my head! Ow! That's not funny. It's sad. Like poor sad Boyce. Bounding up the stairs on his knuckles but we're stepping down, not up, and I'm stumbling, and Yesi holds my arm. "Be careful," she says, and I say "No charge!" because I can't plug her in and no sex no-no sex and then I'm on the office sofa again, the short one near the ice maker, and she puts a blanket around me and stuffs a pillow under my head and the ice falls and crashes in the big aluminum box and when I close my eyes the noise is like a hundred people clapping for TED DANGER, PRIVATE EYE and maybe life's not so sad after all ...*

39   Resurrection

THE NEXT MORNING YESI woke me with a cup of Cuban coffee in one of those little mugs. I sat up on the couch and choked it down.

I had a lot to do, too much, and didn't know where to start. Or feel much like starting.

One of those mornings.

Maybe if I sleep a while longer. Or vomit.

"Now this," Yesi said.

It looked like a bloody mary but tasted like fire and ice. She gave me two pills—a big one and a bigger one—and watched as I swallowed them with another slug of her magic cocktail. My stomach roiled, but without conviction.

WHEN YESI REACHED FOR my glass, the collar of her denim shirt fell open, framing a simple gold cross on a slender chain, floating in the hollow of her throat.

My savior.

"Yesi," I said. "Why are you helping me? Why did you come to my room last night?"

"My brother should not have allowed those two into your room without your permission. When he told me of this, I came promptly and saw that you needed help."

"But why are you helping me now?"

She tucked a stray curl behind her ear and didn't answer. She wore her hair in a loose knot today, low in the back, a wooden stick angled through the whorl. Smooth wood, gleaming and dark, like the hair it pierced, but a shade lighter. And another image invaded, the phantom of Boyce, standing naked before me, his slender penis sprouting from a tangle of pubes like a pornographic hairstick.

I forced the picture out of my head.

The brain makes too many connections that aren't really connected at all, complicating a reality that's already too damn messy to make any sense. It's too much, really, to ever figure out. Ever. Pretty much hopeless, in fact.

Yeah, one of those mornings.

"Finish this," Yesi said. She put the drink back in my hand. "Sit for ten minutes. *Tranquilamente.*"

"With tranquility."

"*Sí. Con calma.*"

She left me, and I did as I was told.

IT TOOK CLOSER TO twenty minutes. Then my resurrection began. Breath deepened. Heart thumped and pumped, driving fuel and oxygen to all sectors.

Life made sense again.

You have things you need to do. So you do them. One after the other until they're done. It's not that fucking complicated.

I pushed myself off the couch and a quick throb in my head tried to knock me down. It failed, by god.

I was on my way.

BACK IN MY ROOM, a bad smell caught my throat. It was me. Haley and Wally were gone.

My phone rang while I showered and again as I pulled on fresh clothes. "Ted Danger."

"Mr. Danger, this is Bentley Vavul. Nicki's husband."

"I'm glad you called. Have you heard from Nicki?"

He paused. "No. I hoped you had."

"Did she leave any—"

"Hold on, Danger. You've got questions for me. I've got questions for you. Let's—"

The phone fell from my shoulder as I pulled on my shoes. "What?" I said. "I missed that."

"We should meet face to face."

"You're in Pompano?"

"More or less," he said. "My team is integrating our software into a virtual meeting room ten minutes from you. For a plastic surgery practice. How soon can you leave your motel?"

"Five minutes."

He gave me the address and told me to bring all my case documents. I didn't mention that I wasn't inclined to share.

I'D RINSED AND SPIT my morning fluoride when Wally and Haley let themselves into the motel room.

Wally got right to the point. "Ted, I've got a bone to pick with you."

"Hello, Haley. Everything all right?"

"Sure." She rolled her eyes, but smiled.

I sidestepped Wally. "I'm meeting your son-in-law in ten minutes," I told him. "Want to come?"

"What?" he said.

"Dad's here?"

"Virtual meeting room." I scribbled the location in my notepad and ripped out the page. "Follow me, but here's the address if you can't pedal fast enough."

Wally glared.

But Haley said, "Good one, Ted."

40   Back to badinage

ON THE DRIVE OVER I considered my next moves.

Mr. and Mrs. Yin and Yang (the evil Derish Flin and his kindly spouse Madam Fernando) held the key. Without delay, I had to review the packet they had prepared, and I had pilfered. Then I had to find a way to interview them without Derish the Nefarious setting my clock back to zero with post-hypnotic duplicity.

And I needed to track down Ronnie Panko of Kolaca Publications to find out where these problematic pictures were coming from.

I also called Nicki's number, but she didn't pick up.

I left a message.

THE PHYSICIANS' OFFICE BUILDING was an older two-story choked by dense shrubs with glossy leaves. I parked by the main doors near a couple of trees—palms, of course. Tall ones, that didn't provide much shade. I'd lost Wally and Haley at a yellow light after a guy in a Jetta slid between us. The Jetta followed me through, but Wally made the wiser choice.

So. Even jacked up on Yesi's get-it-done pills—*I'm sure they're just vitamins, right?*—I still hesitated to select the next number.

Fuck it. I called her. Rytt Slaven, of Slaven and Bustamante.

"How are you, Ted? Back to normal yet?"

"Would it surprise you if I said yes?"

Her voice dropped an octave. "Ready for a replay?" I imagined her eyelids at half-mast. The Rytt I knew and loved.

"Not yet," I said. "In a lustrum or two."

"You'd wait a lustrum for lust?"

"Or a decade for decadence."

She didn't laugh. "Oh, god, Ted, this is painful. Let's stop."

"Good, because I need your help with a couple things."

"Just a minute." Her voice went from creamy to crisp. "Okay, shoot."

"First, find me a hypnotist," I said. "A good one, who can see me right away. Today."

"You're still in Pompano Beach?"

"Yes, but I'm driving to Miami later. The main thing is, I need someone skilled, and available now."

"That's ... That shouldn't be a problem. What else?"

"Okay, I have a booklet. Amateur, with a plastic binding. Full of black-and-white snapshots, photocopied. People on a nude beach. Kids, mostly. Girls."

"Lovely."

"Yeah. It's called *Nature Beach Angels*, put out by Kolaca Publications." I spelled it for her. "The guy touting it calls himself Ronnie Panko. No phone number, but there's a Miami Springs address." Which I gave her.

"So what exactly do you need from Slaven and Bustamante?"

"See if you can track down Panko, and this Kolaca outfit. If they're still in business. Ultimately, I need to know where the *Beach Angels* photos came from."

"Can we get a look at this booklet?"

"Yeah, I've got a meeting in about, uh, five minutes ago, but I'll drop it off afterward. Or send a courier if I get sidetracked."

"Understood. Do you want us to question this Panko when we find him?"

When, not *if*. Nice.

"I'll do it. Call me, and keep track of him till I get there."

Wally's toy car bounced into the parking lot.

"Or we could feed him ED meds," Rytt said, "and put things in his butt."

Okay. We were back to badinage.

"Surely you would never do that," I said.

"It's entirely possible," she said. "As you well know."

"And?" I prompted.

She sighed. "And don't call me Shirley."

41 Mother's not crazy

A MASSIVE VIDEO DISPLAY—actually nine big-screen monitors in a three-by-three grid—dominated an entire wall of the upscale meeting room. The composite image represented a continuation of the brick-and-mortar room we stood in. Even our conference table—fine grained and glossy—flowed seamlessly into the virtual space, as if both ends were hewn from the same hunk of mahogany.

The room tech was a red-haired dude in olive cargo pants and an Ellie May T-shirt. His stone-gray vest bulged with esoteric tools. An aluminum receiver sprouted from one ear.

He said his name was Cody.

"You're Mr. Danger, right?" He ignored Wally, but gave Haley a glance that lingered into leer territory. "Take a seat anywhere, or stand. Like you were in a conventional conference room."

"A conventional conference room?"

"But don't sit near the screens. The effect's better farther back, and I might need to make adjustments."

"You're staying?"

"Just to monitor the process, you know, at the meta-data level. Don't worry, we're not mining the content."

Wally spoke up. "Whatever the hell that means."

A DOOR OPENED IN the virtual end of the room, and a dark-haired guy in a charcoal jacket—he was broad but not tall—entered the image. His starched white shirt, open at the top, showed off a tuft of graying chest hair.

"You must be Ted Danger," he said. He looked me in the eye, as if I were holding the camera shooting him.

"And you're Ben Vavul."

He nodded and looked past me. "Hello, Haley. I didn't expect to see you here."

"Hi, Dad."

His eyes shifted and his mouth tightened. "Wally," he said.

"Ben," Wally said.

The technician, Cody, sat against the wall, his chair back on two legs. His Starbucks cup rested on the floor as he poked a handheld screen and touched the device in his ear.

"So why are we here, Mr. Vavul?" I said. "What can't you tell me on the phone?"

"Please, call me Ben." He draped his jacket over a chair. "You know, Ted, human communication is mostly non-verbal. Ninety percent." He stepped closer, his open palms supporting his point. "I wanted to get a sense of who you are, and vice versa."

I stepped around our end of the table and his eyes followed me. "Fair enough. Have you heard from Nicki since we talked earlier?"

I sat near the screen, opposite Ben's position. His forehead gleamed. Distortion was minor.

"No." He dropped into his chair. "She's just gone."

"What about her friends? Someone she might—"

"Ted, you need to understand about Nicki. She's ..." He glanced at Wally and Haley, side by side in high-back leather swivels. "Look, this must relate to the matter she hired you for. Let's talk about that." He paused. "If it's appropriate."

Haley leaned forward. "I want to hear about it too."

"The whole thing's ridiculous," Wally said.

I turned to Ben. "Not much I can say. Nicki's my client, and our communications are privileged."

"I'm her husband."

"I believe you. Also, you're not my client."

NO ONE SPOKE. A nearly subsonic hum leaked from the monitor wall.

"Cody," I said, "is it supposed to make that noise? Like a buzz?"

He swiped his screen and tapped his earpiece. "It's within tolerances. I think." He drew a slender meter from his vest.

"Wait," Ben said. "Is this about me? Did she ask you to investigate me?"

Wally snorted. "It's all about Bentley."

Bentley ignored him. "Because that's crazy."

"Like Mom," Haley said.

"Haley, don't," Bentley said. "Your mother's not crazy."

"What is she, then?"

He stood up. "Ted, you and I need a come-to-Jesus. Wally, take Haley back to your place. We'll speak later."

Wally muttered "Can't hardly wait" and stood to leave.

"Wait a minute," Haley said. "Grandpa was going to kick Ted's ass."

"Maybe tomorrow," I said.

"Don't think I can't, gumshoe."

"Mr. Landis," I said. "I—"

"You too, Cody," Bentley said. "You can take off for now."

Cody leaned his chair forward and stood as Haley and Wally left the room.

"Hold it, Cody," Bentley said. "Before you go, check the roof dish, will you? Doc saw a cable hanging loose."

"Will do." He picked up his coffee and scrammed.

BENTLEY SPRAWLED IN HIS chair. "He won't find a problem. I made it up."

"Why?"

"Cody's a fucking cock hound. The crap he brags about ... I don't want him walking out with Haley. She's only fourteen, but she—"

"Fifteen," I said.

"Fifteen? Are you sure? And how would you even know that?"

"She must have mentioned it."

He was studying my face. "You're not a great liar, Ted." His eyes widened. "Christ, this whole thing is about Haley, isn't it?"

"I'm not saying one way or the other," I said. "But yeah, it's about Haley."

42 Spoiler alert

BEN TOYED WITH HIS wedding band, turning it in a gesture that looked habitual. "All right. What's it about, Ted?" He leaned forward on his elbows. "I'm asking as a father."

"And I'm telling you, I don't know how far to trust you."

He whacked both palms on the conference table and I swear I felt the vibration a thousand miles away.

"Why the hell not?" he said.

"Ask yourself, Bentley. Why did Nicki wait for you to leave town before she hired a private eye?"

He didn't answer.

"Can't she trust you? Is she afraid of you? You knock her around when she gets out of line?"

"Maybe it was just a coincidence."

"Jeepers, why didn't I think of that?"

He scowled. "How is she even going to pay you? Her credit limit's a joke and her checking account is chump change."

"You keep her on a tight leash, moneywise, is that it?"

"Let's just say if you want to get paid, you'll have to deal with me."

"Why didn't you say so? It's all about the money. Fuck whatever happens to your wife and daughter." I was getting sick of this guy. "Why is that, Bentley? Why can't Nicki have her own money? She easier to control when she's broke?"

He held up his hands. "Okay, let's back up. I insulted you about the money. I apologize. We must find Nicki. Priority one."

"I'm serious, Bentley. If it's not to keep her submissive, why be so stingy?"

"You want to get into this now?"

128

"In the spirit of cooperation, yes. Now's good for me." I couldn't believe the guy forgot about the rainy-day cash in the safe deposit box.

And I wasn't about to remind him.

HE DRUMMED HIS FINGERS on the table until he saw me watching.

"Okay, look," he said. "I buy Nicki all of what she needs, and most of what she wants. And provide an adequate discretionary allowance. But she can't handle large sums of money. Something slips, you know, in her psychology."

"Give me a for-instance."

"Okay. Sure." His eyes flicked up. "She received credit cards in the mail I didn't know about. High-limit. Pretty soon we started getting encyclopedias—complete sets—delivered to our front door. She'd been buying them up on eBay. And some rather nice grandfather clocks."

"You don't like grandfather clocks?"

"How many does one house need?"

"What does Nicki say, when you ask her about the books and clocks?"

"She cries."

"But does she remember? I mean, is she really placing the orders, or is someone gaslighting her? Like you, for instance, or Haley."

"She remembers. Like remembering a dream, she says."

"Like sleep-shopping."

HE LAUGHED AND LEANED back with his hands behind his head. I'm no body-language expert, but I suspect it felt good to unload.

"Did she tell you how we met, Ted?"

I had things to do, but he didn't wait for an answer.

"I was in my early twenties," he said. "Twenty-three, because I'd just earned my business degree. I'd have graduated sooner, but I changed my major twice. Some buddies and I drove a Volvo wagon with a million miles on the clock down to Pompano Beach for a week of sun and debauchery."

"How did that work out for you?"

"Not great. I had a healthy fear of skin cancer, and wasn't much of a carouser."

"So what were you doing here?"

"A question I asked myself ere too many days had passed."

"How many days are going to pass before you get to the point?"

If he abridged his story because of my comment, I couldn't see how.

"I was loafing on the pier one morning," he said, "rather bored, and I happened on a library right across the street. Now, I love to read, and the idea of browsing a library on a boys-go-crazy vacation struck me as oddly perverse. A guilty pleasure if you will."

"A young renegade."

HE IGNORED MY INTERRUPTION.

"So I strolled in, sand on my flip-flops, towel around my neck, wearing a desert hat and these wild surfer shorts—peach-and-green orchids—and there, sitting in an overstuffed chair, reading a book by the window, the light blessing her face like a Dutch painting, was the prettiest girl I'd ever shared the same plane of existence with."

A real poet. "Spoiler alert," I said. "You married her."

"Not so fast, Ted. I asked her where to find the biographies and she dragged me to the reference desk where I could ask for myself. A while later, she let me sit and read with her, and before long I discovered she was a local. So I asked her to show me around the city."

"And the rest," I said, "is history."

"Funny you mention history, because that was her thing that day. Not dancing, or beachcombing, or shopping. Not swimming or clubbing. She wanted to cruise museums and climb the old lighthouse."

"Something wrong with museums?"

"No, but atypical for a twenty-year-old girl, right? She was giving me clues, even then, that things in that pretty little head weren't—like Cody says—within tolerances."

"Because she liked museums? And a lighthouse?"

"Other things too, Ted. Little things. Like the book she was reading when I first met her. What do you think it was about?"

I didn't guess.

"Hypnotism," he said. "She was reading about hypnotism."

"And why is that significant?"

"When I asked her, she said she was walking in a dream. I thought we were flirting, trying to be interesting and quirky. I didn't know that over the years she'd just get worse. Especially after Haley was born. I just didn't know." He looked down and a glint brightened his eyes. "And even if I'd seen into the future, I wouldn't have changed a thing." He shook his head and smiled. "She was just too exquisite, as she sat there bathed in crystalline light. And you know something, Ted? I still find her exquisite. Just exquisite."

I nodded, but kept my mouth shut. I knew exactly what he meant.

"Please," he said. "Let's find her."

43 Cody lives

IT'S TRUE NICKI HADN'T wanted Bentley involved. But now that she'd gone missing, the rules had changed.

So I left him in the virtual space and went to my rental for the case documents.

ANOTHER BLISTERING DAY IN south Florida. When I opened the rental door to grab the papers, the inferno blasted me.

"Mr. Danger!"

There. Two stories up, Cody squatted by a dish antenna among a web of supports and cabling.

"Cody," I said.

"Hey, you guys finished?"

"Taking a break."

"Signal good?"

I shrugged. "Just like being there."

He gave me a short salute and a yellow-handled tool slipped from his vest and bounced on the roof ledge. When he grabbed for it, his heel skidded, his butt clipped the ledge, and just like that, he was falling. His hand snagged a cable loop, which tautened and snapped, and his plunge continued.

"Oh, shit." We both said it.

Then he landed in the big bushes with the shiny leaves.

When I got to him he was laughing. "I hope you recorded that, bruh."

"Anything broken?"

He untangled from the shrubbery and crawled onto the sidewalk. The dropped ratchet lay nearby. He slid it into a vest pocket, staggered to his feet, and, like every human being who ever rose from a fall, brushed himself off.

"The worst part," he said, "is I need to go back up. It's loose now, for sure."

"Where's your ladder?"

"Roof access is inside." He limped toward the door.

"And you're not hurt?"

"Nah. I'm okay." He stopped and pulled a moue. "Well, I'm hurt that Mr. Vavul thinks I'd fuck his teenybopper daughter."

"You heard that?"

"I hear everything that goes on in that room." He tapped the device in his ear. "Although Mr. Vavul doesn't need to know that, right Mr. Danger?"

"I'm not great at keeping secrets."

He shrugged. "Whatever."

INSIDE, CODY TOOK A left down a narrow hallway. I walked into the conference room and found it smaller. The virtual half had vanished behind a wall of dead monitors.

"Bentley?" I said.

Silence.

I stepped into the hallway and yelled for Cody.

He appeared around the corner. "Problem?"

"Blank screens in there. No audio."

CODY GLANCED BEHIND ONE of the TVs. Rapped it with his knuckles. Then harder, with his fist. Always worth a try.

"It's the feed from the roof," he said.

"Will this take long? Should I wait?"

He looked at me for a beat, then crumpled into the closest chair. His mouth twisted down and his face paled. He gulped.

"You okay?"

"I don't know." He swiped at the sweat beads on his forehead. "Shit, I could've broke my neck, you know? Lost the feed, blinked out."

"A little existential moment here."

"Seeing those blank screens kind of spoke to me."

I waved a hand toward the video wall. "Pretty amazing

technology, though. Like Bentley was in the room with us."

He gave me a strange look. His color was returning. "You're kidding, right? This is Stone Age." He launched into a lecture on holograms, avatars, VR, robots, AI, and singularities until my eyes glazed over. I bit back a yawn that broke through anyway.

"So how long to fix this setup?" I said.

He stood and rolled his head on his neck. "Depends on what I find. A reconnect would only take a minute, but if I need a part ..." He wandered off.

I LEFT. MAYBE I wouldn't share Nicki's secrets with her husband after all. My gut still said that wherever Nicki might be, she was there voluntarily.

We'd hear from her when she was ready, and not before.

44 Ho ho ho

THE HYPNOTIST INSPIRED ME with confidence. She looked serious. Somber. Like she meant business.

And nothing artsy-creepy about her office. No rainbow suncatchers or magic crystals. Not one *You Are Special* poster. Even the building was right. Neither low-rent shabby nor upscale snooty.

Okay, I was being evaluative. And defensive. And dilatory. My experience with hypnotists to date had left me leery.

WHEN I HAD DROPPED off the juvie-nudie rag with Rytt, she told me the hypnotist's name—a Ms. Lucille Cruiset—and gave her a five-star review.

"Navi and I love her," she said. "She's helped clients remember details that flat-out solved cases for us."

I was standing in front of Rytt's desk. The window glare behind her stung my eyes.

"She just puts them under?" I said. "And that's that?"

"She's calm and she's smart," Rytt said. "And she's on your side. Talk to her for five seconds and you know she can help you, even before the abracadabra."

"So how did she help? With a client, I mean."

"You're nervous about seeing her, aren't you?"

"I'm not saying. You'll call me a pussy again."

Her pursed lips hid her smile. Almost. "Sit down, Ted. You're ready to bolt."

I sat in her visitor's chair.

SHE PULLED HER CHAIR next to mine. Nice move. Affable. I'd have to remember it.

135

"We had a client," she said, "an older widow, whose son lived with her. She planned to sell her house, move to a cheaper place she'd found. The son was against it. They argued. Then the late husband's handgun went missing."

"The son took it."

"She thought so. She hired us to find out what he was up to. Well, Navi let the son chat her up at a bar. They drank. He told her he didn't want his mother to move because she'd live in a more dangerous area and ultimately wouldn't save much money. Et cetera. Navi decided he was a good guy having a legitimate disagreement with his mother."

"And the hypnotist? Lucy ..."

"Lucille. Lucille Cruiset."

"Lucille."

"We convinced our client to see her. In a single session, we found out where the handgun was, which was a huge relief to the client. Who also seemed less anxious. More trusting toward her son. Of course it helped when she realized he didn't have the gun."

"So, happy ending."

Rytt nodded. "She paid our bill and we never heard from her again."

"Where was the gun?"

"Oh, she'd rented a storage unit so she could de-clutter her house for prospective buyers. She forgot she stuck the gun in a box of Christmas decorations."

"Ho ho ho," I said.

"And speaking of Christmas," she said, "you have a present for me?"

"Sure. Angels."

SHE DREW BACK BEFORE taking the book from my hand.

"The guy my client wants to find," I said, "is inside the back cover, standing with the girl."

Starting at the front, she turned each page deliberately, pausing to examine each picture.

"Inside the back cover," I said.

She held up her hand. "Where were these taken?"

I glanced at the two-page spread she was viewing. "I don't know." I edged my chair closer. "No, wait a minute. Keep going."

She turned the pages and the generic setting became real. A place I'd visited.

And in the last photo, those shapes on the horizon—there, in the distance behind Haley and her big naked buddy—were no longer random shadows. They were specific contours and structures: Key Biscayne and the Rickenbacker Causeway.

The pictures had been taken on Virginia Key Beach.

I SAID IT OUT loud. "These pictures were taken on Virginia Key Beach."

Rytt nodded. "The nude beach."

"On Virginia Key?"

"Yes, on Virginia Key. Didn't you know about that?"

I shook my head.

"Ted, everybody knows there used to be a nude beach on Virginia Key."

"Used to be?"

"Yes. After the segregated beach closed."

I remembered the *colored only* sign in the Derish-and-Maddy packet. *What other answers will I find in there if I just take the goddamn time to look?*

Rytt found the publisher's name—Kolaca—on the back page of the comb-bound booklet, and verified the man to track down—Ronnie Panko. She'd done a preliminary web search and found the address obsolete.

"Of course, if you run across the guy in the picture with Haley, find out who he is too." I was joking.

She ignored my sarcasm. "Of course."

"Thanks, Rytt. I owe you."

"You'll get the bill."

45 Toxin and tears

LUCILLE CRUISET'S OFFICE WAS in an older one-story complex, stucco, in a warm color that whispered *umber*, on what passes for a shady street in Miami. I dumped the rental in a semi-shaded spot off Dixie Highway, across from a neighborhood park. Two tween girls in neon helmets stood straddling their bicycles near the park entrance, their backs dappled with sunshine, not in a hurry to go anywhere.

Good for them.

I FOUND THE RIGHT door and stepped inside. No reception area, just a single large room burnished with sunlight softened by curtained windows along two walls.

Across the room, a slender woman in a tweedy jacket sat at a blond wooden desk, writing on a legal pad with a yellow pencil. Not a single computer screen in sight.

SHE STOOD WHEN I closed the door. "You must be Ted Danger." Her hair was umber too. Friendly eyes, but she didn't smile.

"That's right," I said.

"I'm Lucille Cruiset. I'll be with you in a minute."

As she returned a file to an oak cabinet, I surveyed the room. Two bookcases, books in no apparent order. Faded throw rugs over practical carpeting. Upholstered chairs in quiet colors—they looked comfortable—and a sofa with a low back and one big pillow. A scuffed coffee table with a box of tissues. The decade might have been any in the past half century.

She crossed the room and shook my hand. "Call me Lucille or Ms. Cruiset, as you prefer."

"And I'm Ted."

HER EYES WERE ODDLY asymmetrical, with irises like storm clouds clearing on a bright afternoon, pupils big and deep. And circling each pale iris, a border as black as the pupil itself, making the whites burn whiter.

It was hard to look away.

"Where do you want me, Lucille?"

"Wherever you choose."

I feinted for the sofa but settled into a comfy chair. We sat more or less facing each other across the coffee table.

Her nose was crooked, a vertical crease in the tip. Unblemished skin with fine lines around her eyes and mouth— a mouth neither full nor thin, and without a trace of a smile.

"Rytt says you need help with a case involving photos of nude children."

My eyes were drawn back to hers and I felt half hypnotized already. *This woman can help me. Thank you, Rytt.*

"That's right," I said. And I told her about Nicki and the photo of Haley on the nude beach. About Derish and how he had made me see Hope when Maddy walked in.

"Derish Flin," she said. "And Madam Fernando."

"You've heard of them."

"He's notorious. In fact, so is she."

"Ever since he hypnotized me, he's got me in his grip. He made me see Hope, like I said, but then, two or three days later, he put me under by phone, and sent me to a specific spot on Virginia Key—I'm not sure how I found it, he'd given me a post-hypnotic suggestion"—and then the words were pouring out, tripping over themselves—"and this guy there, his name was Ted too, which was no coincidence, probably, I don't know, and then things started changing with all the—"

"Slow down, Ted. We're in no hurry."

So I took a breath, and held it. And when I exhaled, something toxic and heavy flowed out, leaving me weightless. I looked at Lucille and tried to talk but my throat had closed up and suddenly I was crying.

Where the fuck did this come from?

With the tip of her pencil, Lucille pushed the box of tissues my way.

I TOOK ONE AND wiped my face. "Sorry. I don't know what just happened."

"Breathe, Ted. Keep going."

I breathed. "I don't know what's real and what isn't. On Virginia Key, the causeway vanished. It was just open water. Then Key Biscayne bulged right over it. The air changed."

"How do you account for that?"

"A dream. Hallucinations. Illusions. Derish is making me see things. Do things. Even before that, I met a ... Never mind."

"Tell me, Ted. Whatever it is."

"I met a talking monkey. Ape. He wrote me a note. *Help me*, it said. I mean, really? Even if he was half human? Or is it all Derish? Derish in my head."

SHE WROTE ON HER pad. Looked up. Tapped the pencil eraser to her front teeth. "Tell me more about your investigation."

So I told her about Wally and Reva; about José María and Yesi; about Bentley and Cody; about the Axelrods—Jenny and Hardy and their bundle of joy, Boyce; and Slaven and Bustamante. And about Kolaca Publications and Ronnie Panko. Somewhere in my rant I mentioned Tru, and Hope, and even my mother. Don't ask why. And finally, trying to be clever, to flirt a little, I told her about a certain hypnotist I recently met. A hypnotist named Lucille who never smiled.

She set her pad on the table.

"DO YOU WANT TO know why I don't smile, Ted?"

"Yes."

"Because I don't want to."

"Fair enough."

"Also because I was beaten many years ago, upon my face." *Oh shit.* "I'm sorry," I said.

"Of course you are." She picked up the legal pad and held it in front of her. "I was walking and a group of young men called out to me. Saying they wished to have sex with me. Whistling also. This was downtown."

"You don't have to tell me this."

"One of them objected because I did not smile. He disapproved. *You should acknowledge someone who pays you a compliment*, he explained to me."

I kept silent.

"To punish me, they knocked me to the ground and kicked my face with their shoes."

Her eyes were dry.

SILENCE IN THE ROOM. No devices hummed. No clock ticked. Outside, no traffic passed. No children played.

"What do you want from me, Ted?"

My shoulders relaxed. "Okay. Derish and Maddy hold the key to this case. I want to interview them without Derish putting me under with a hypnotic trigger."

"That's what you want?"

"Yes. I want to be free of Derish's power. Right now, I can't even talk to him on the phone." Out of nowhere I was burning with rage, or humiliation. "He's dug his hooks in me. They're sharp, and they're deep, and I want them out."

"All right, Ted. Relax. I can do that."

THE WARM DEPTH OF her gray eyes revealed the sorrow I'd overlooked before. But there was power there too. Power she would unleash on my behalf.

A shiver coursed through every nerve. "I believe you, Lucille."

46 Derish dethroned

SHE TOLD ME TO get comfortable.

"You will fall into a state of relaxation similar to sleep," she said, "but in this unique state you will be able to speak easily and move freely. Is this clear to you?"

"Yes."

She told me to look at a spot on the ceiling until my eyes got tired. When I closed my eyes, I didn't feel like opening them again, and she took me deeper into trance. But this time I could remember the whole process.

"As I ask you to recall previous suggestions made to you under hypnosis, you will do so easily, and safely, as if you are watching a video in a relaxing environment. And all such suggestions are now defunct and disabled. Is this clear to you?"

"Yes."

"Then you can now recall everything Derish Flin has ever said to you regardless of your level of trance at the time."

As simply as that, the doors in my mind flew open, and I remembered.

The first day I'd met Derish, he'd hypnotized me while we waited for Maddy. During that session, he'd blocked the sting of my sunburn, and then cycled me to near consciousness and back into trance, over and over, deeper each time. Then he set the hook.

"And just as you are now in a deep state of relaxation," he said, "you will fall into an even deeper state when you hear me say the words *virgin birth* to you and only you."

He'd reinforced his suggestions by telling me they would grow stronger each day when I ate my first meal. *What a louse!*

LUCILLE MADE SHORT WORK of Derish's post-hypnotic suggestions, dismantling the breakfast reinforcement and removing the *virgin birth* trigger to the trance state.

"And," she said, "any attempt by Derish Flin to hypnotize you by any means is self-canceling and ineffective, forever and in perpetuity. Is this clear to you?"

"Yes."

"Resisting his power is now easy, because there is nothing to struggle against. His influence no longer exists."

She walked me through my phone session with Flin, outside the gas station, during which he'd directed me to Virginia Key. I was surprised to remember that at one point he'd turned the phone over to Maddy. She's the one who told me who I would meet. Unfortunately, she didn't explain a bit of it. "Keep your mind open, Ted," she'd said. "Watch and learn."

WE KEPT AT IT for a while. Lucille instructed my subconscious mind to scan for relevant patterns and to bring them directly to light for evaluation, bypassing cryptic filters like nebulous dreams and guesses.

It worked instantly, and the meaning of my Haulover beach daydream—the distant lands rising from the sea, the ancient ancestors—became clear. My landmass vision told me the shapes in Haley's photo were land. Key Biscayne. And my forebears whispered what I'd begun to suspect. That the girl in Haley's photo was not Haley at all, but her mother, Nicki.

Or even Grandma Reva.

LUCILLE APPLIED HER OWN back door into my subconscious—a hand on my arm and the phrase *please down deep*—for future tune-ups. Then she brought me out of it, suggesting I'd feel refreshed and fully alert, and I did.

"Derish Flin can't touch you now," she said. "That's what you wanted."

"Right."

"And I gave your subconscious a nudge, to help with your

investigation."

"Thanks. It's working."

"Officially we're done." She didn't stand up. So I didn't either.

"But I have advice for you," she said, "if you want it."

I didn't hesitate. "I want it."

47 Please down deep

LUCILLE LEANED BACK IN her chair, the picture of quiet confidence.

"I'm a psychologist as well as a hypnotist. And I can tell you, Ted. You need to see someone. A psychologist of your own. You have issues."

"Like what?" I said.

She scanned her notepad. "I believe you have serious detachment issues. You sabotaged your relationship with Hope, just as you neared a permanent commitment. You've distanced yourself from Tru. There's something going on there. And you might have mommy issues too."

"That's it? I cheated on Hope and lost her, so I have issues? Anyway, we hardly talked about Hope. Or Tru. I barely mentioned my mother."

"You need to talk about her. And about Hope and Tru."

"Hope was a long time ago."

"I'm talking about right now, Ted. You have issues today. You're disengaged. As if you see life as a form of fiction."

"Shakespeare said life's a stage and we're all players."

"Yes, you're a player, so to speak. Your relationships with women are fleeting and shallow."

"But often pleasant."

"And often not. Your head is off-kilter when it comes to women."

"Ouch. I've got *off-kilter-itis*?"

"And you minimize your pathology with jokes. No, Ted. I would need more time with you to posit a diagnosis."

"So, I need to figure out how to relate to women."

"Yes," she said. "Unfortunately, that statement is true for

most of the male population."

"So I'm pathological, but also, you might say, within normal tolerances."

"Possibly not. You see the world as a screenplay, as a type of entertainment. You don't see real people in real crises."

"Maybe we're all poorly drawn characters in a poorly plotted book," I said, "and our author hasn't made us self-aware enough to know it."

"You know, when you talk like that you denigrate and belittle the people all around you."

"How do you figure?"

"You're saying their pain isn't real. My pain isn't real. This"—she raked a hand near her face—"isn't real. The blows, the bones, the broken nerves, it never happened. Just a tale told by an idiot, signifying—"

"Look, I told you I'm sorry I brought it up."

"Not me, Ted. I'm not talking about me. I'm talking about the girls in the pictures. They're real children, innocents being exploited, displayed as sexual playthings, toys of arousal. And you know the iceberg goes deep. These very children or others like them are used and abused, physically, sexually, and psychologically, here and around the world every day, every hour. In pain and damaged, in body and soul, thousands of children sold, literally, into slavery and desperation. People suffer, Ted. They die. And you treat it like an intellectual exercise, a who-dun-it, a cozy Agatha Christie."

"I have feelings. Empathy. I'm not a psychopath."

"I'm not presuming a diagnosis. I'm advising you to get the work done. Take the time. Do it right."

"Why don't you just fix me with hypnotism?"

"That's a throwaway line. Flip and inauthentic."

"Real people can be flip."

"You're getting tired of this conversation, aren't you? It's too much work. It's not providing the easy answers you want."

"You're reading my mind."

"Life overwhelms you. It's too complex. You procrastinate.

You've carried around that Derish-and-Maddy envelope since yesterday and barely looked at it. Maybe it's depression, bipolar disorder, borderline personality. Fear of failure, or success. Get the work done, Ted."

I held up my hands. "Okay, after I wrap up this case. Till then, are you sure you don't have a quick fix for me?"

SHE SHOOK HER HEAD but gave me something anyway.

"Okay, Ted. One more. You felt overwhelmed this morning until Yesi fed you coffee, two pills, and a magic elixir. Then life made sense."

"Right."

"And you've had these feelings before. Both extremes."

"Sure. Sometimes all I can do is crawl into bed and sleep. The waking world is thick and sticky and opaque. It saps my strength to breathe it, to move in it, to try to see through it."

"But not always."

"No. Other times, it's obvious that if you want to do something, you simply take the necessary steps. Reality is right there in front of you, crystal clear and available to manipulate in whatever way works. What could be more self-evident?"

"So, it might be manic-depression, or lord knows. But I can give you a temporary fix, if you want one. It's a neat trick. And it's not too much work, so you'll like that."

"Yes, please."

So she touched my arm and said the magic words, *Please down deep*, and please-down-deep I went. Then she helped me remember four times when life made sense, when I felt alive and motivated. We distilled that feeling into tiny imaginary capsules in infinite supply hidden inside my fingertips and toes. Clenching my toes would pop the capsules and flood my body with relief. For ubermojo, I could flex my fingers as well.

She woke me up, and I remembered everything.

LUCILLE WAS A GODDESS, for sure, powerful and wise, and I considered asking her to lunch, but something stopped me.

A goddess?

Is that how I view women? Either celestial goddesses or earthly playthings? She'd cut close to the bone, and I needed to slink away and lick my wounds.

I rose to leave and she said, "Good luck, Ted." She shook my hand. "It's been ..."

"It's been what?"

Her lips drew back, baring oversize teeth with long canines. "... interesting," she snarled.

I stifled the urge to growl back. Halfway to my rental I figured it out.

Damn. Lucille Cruiset had smiled at me.

48 Minus eleven years old

THE DAY WAS HOT, but drier than yesterday, and the rental was scorching inside. I left the windows up to bake in the gifts Lucille Cruiset had granted.

The kids on bikes had moved on, leaving the park serene and green. A bead of sweat stung my eye.

I started the rental and lowered the windows. On my way to Dixie Highway, I drove past Lucille's building, her windows blank, nothing inside revealed. She didn't pull the curtain back and wave goodbye like my mother did when I left for school.

My mother. Something in my head I need to check out? What about the other women in my life? Like Hope. Tru. Lucille.

Navi and Rytt. Jenny. Maddy. Nicki. Haley.

Then Hope again. My mother. Again.

And Tru. Again and again.

I clenched my toes and serenity flowed and flooded my body and mind. Calm. *If I have problems, I can address them. That's how life works.*

Current problems: One, starving. Two, packet from Derish and Maddy largely unexplored.

So I bought lunch—Diet Coke and a grilled chicken salad— at a drive-thru near the university. Cruised Coral Gables to the north until I found a wide spot by the road where I could dine under giant banyans and study my documents unmolested.

THE FIRST SHEAF OF papers gave me the scoop on Virginia Key. In the 1940s (I learned), before the Rickenbacker Causeway existed, Dade County established a blacks-only beach on Virginia Key. Over time, as segregation eased and a sewage

149

plant encroached, the beach saw fewer families, but new habitués took their place: gays and nudists. Then in the early 1980s, the city of Miami took over the beach, mostly ignoring anti-nudity laws until the mid-1980s, not long before closing the beach altogether.

And the beach remained closed for another twenty years.

I believed the nude photo of Haley was taken on Virginia Key around 1984, at the latest, just before the nudists were finally run off. Making Haley about, say, minus eleven years old at the time.

So the young woman in the photo was not Haley at all.

Unless you believe in time travel. Which, on Virginia Key, is not much of a stretch.

I FINISHED MY SALAD and sucked down my drink till the straw *schlurp*ed.

The boulevard where I'd pulled over was shadowed by banyan trees and various stone structures. Arches and arbors. Picturesque. A wedding party had moved in, and a broad blond guy in a gray tuxedo hiked over to my rental.

"How you doing?" he said. His scalp gleamed through his buzz cut. "Say, we're going to take wedding photos. Under the arbors, all around."

"Nice spot for it."

"Sure is. Would you mind moving your vehicle, so it's not in the shots?"

"No."

He tilted his head. "No? You won't move it?"

"No, I wouldn't mind."

He gave me a look and went back to his party, who were setting up under gnarly banyans near a stone column. I was behind the photographer for this series, so I didn't scram.

IN THE WEDDING PARTY, the men's identical tuxedos left the groom incognito.

The women were a different story. The bridesmaids wore

wine-red knee-length poufs that left the bride unmistakable in a full-length gown that ebbed and flowed like heavy cream.

Also, she was the only woman visibly pregnant.

My newly awakened subconscious told me to ponder mothers and their children.

My mother and me.

Jenny and her stepson Boyce.

Reva and Nicki.

Unnamed bride and unborn infant.

Kendria and her suckling child.

And, of course, Nicki and Haley. The eye of the storm.

But I'd learned. *People are not always what they seem.*

THE PHOTOGRAPHER FINISHED THE banyan shots and began to organize the next *mise en scène*, so I started the rental and took off.

Enough of mothers. Time to visit a father and son.

49 Nearsighted lechers

WHEN I WALKED INTO the camera shop, Jeter was sitting on a stool watching the Flagler Street traffic pass him by. Customer population holding steady at zero.

"Pop's in the back," Jeter said. "I'll get him."

I had interrupted Pop's afternoon siesta, for sure. The clues: a dazed look, a puffy face, and an awesome yawn that tugged at my own jaw.

He squinted. "Ed Danger," he said.

"It's Ted."

"What I said. You track down your nekkid man yet?"

"Getting there. Look at this."

We took our positions, me on my wobbly stool again. I slid the *Nature Beach Angels* booklet onto the scoured glass and spun it to face them.

Pop turned a page and ran a hand over it. "This is run-of-the-mill copy paper."

"And the pictures?"

"Land Camera." He turned another page.

"And where were these taken?" I said.

"Don't know," he said. "Jeter?"

"Not Haulover. Too much vegetation. Haulover's more urban. Collins Avenue, city all around."

POP TURNED ANOTHER PAGE.

"What if I said Virginia Key?" I said.

"Don't know," Jeter said. "Pop?"

"Virginia Key, you say?"

I pointed. "Here. Key Biscayne in the background. And here's the Rickenbacker."

Pop removed his glasses, swabbed them with his purple rag, and propped them low on his nose. "May be."

I flipped to the last page, inside the back cover. "Here it is again. Recognize this one?"

MY NEWLY AWAKENED SUBCONSCIOUS was screaming something I couldn't make out.

Jeter ran his finger across the photo. "This fuzz could be Key Biscayne. And that'd be the Rickenbacker, all right."

"Let me eyeball the rest of these pictures, Ted," Pop said. "I believe I can—"

"Hold it." I put my hand on his wrist. "We're missing something. Something about this picture."

HALEY, OR WHOEVER SHE was, stood grinning at us, hand on jutted hip, her other arm snaked around the man next to her. His hand on her neck in a possessive gesture. Controlling. Or ... protective?

"What is it?" Pop said.

"Something obvious. But I don't know what it is."

"Well, then," Jeter said. "How do you know we missed it?"

"Good question, son," Pop said.

"Thanks, Pop," Jeter said.

"I saw a hypnotist this morning. She cranked up my subconscious, and it says we're missing something."

"Ted, you're thinking too hard," Pop said. "Let's take a gander at these other pictures and it'll come to you."

SO WE LOOKED AT the pages we'd skipped. Found no clues.

"Shot with the same camera," Pop said. "Least nothing says otherwise."

He left the back cover open. Haley, if that's who she was, wore not a scrap of clothing, yet my eyes kept scanning for something I could see but not recognize.

"Your conscience telling you anything?" Pop said.

I didn't bother correcting him. "No."

"How's about we look at the original again? Maybe it'll steer us right."

I SET THE ORIGINAL next to the copy in the booklet.

The three of us leaned over the two photos like nearsighted lechers with naughty French postcards.

"So maybe it's not the same picture," Pop said.

"Like a game," Jeter said. "Find ten things different."

Pop gave up first. He leaned back and pushed his glasses a millimeter higher. "Ted, why did you come back here?"

I wasn't sure. But then I was. "To show you that the picture was taken from Virginia Key. And to ask why the hell you didn't tell me, the last time we talked, that Virginia Key had a notorious nude beach for years. And everybody in Miami knows it."

"Well, who told you that?"

"Friend of mine. Private detective here in Miami."

"First off," Pop said, "your friend's wrong. Virginia Key's just a little spit of sand where maybe you watched the dolphin show, and maybe you smelled the sewer plant, but I guaran-goddamn-tee you, you can live your live-long life in these parts and never hear a peep about any nudie beach out there. And I'm the living proof."

"You tell him, Pop."

"And second off, why aren't you running down your culprits and clues instead of complaining to an old man about something you got no right to complain about. See item one."

"Pop's got a point," Jeter said.

I was outnumbered, and duly chastised. Time to run down my culprits and clues.

50 Uneasy bliss

SLAVEN AND BUSTAMANTE'S NEW home base was half an hour to the west, in Fontainebleau. My GPS proposed the Dolphin Expressway, but I stuck with Eighth Street to gain pondering time. And concluded that my conversation with Pop and Jeter was just another random crumb in a universe filled with random crumbs. They tumble briefly through our experience, skewed and out of focus. Then vanish into the void of eternity, forever beyond our fleeting moment of existence.

Essentially meaningless.

Like life itself, in the scheme of things.

Essentially meaningless.

So tired. A nap would be nice.

A long nap. So ... tired.

DAMN IT.

It's embarrassing how fast I crash into that low-grade despondency. *Lucille, you're on to something. I need to get my head examined.* Or more iron in my diet.

I curled my toes tight, and gripped the wheel. Imaginary capsules popped in my digits, and serenity surged through my body. Amazing stuff.

AT AN UPSCALE STRIP mall, I wheeled my rental into the lot and parked near a shop whose name I couldn't pronounce. Too many apostrophes. Extreme close-ups filled the windows. Young faces, in the throes of uneasy bliss or tranquil pain—I get those two mixed up.

I didn't check out the merchandise.

A NARROW STAIRCASE BETWEEN the mystery shop and a nail salon ushered me to the second floor, and the private-eye digs of Slaven and Bustamante.

The suite was quiet, the air chilled. As I closed the door behind me, Navi strolled from her office and met me in the reception area.

"Ted," she said. "We must stop meeting like this."

"What other way should we meet, Navi?"

She shook my hand, her fingers like ice. "I'm certain I cannot imagine." Her smile thawed the air. "Rytt's out investigating. Has she called you?"

I told her she hadn't, and she sat me down at a conference table by a picture window with tinted glass. Offered me coffee from one of those single-serve machines.

"Has she found anything?" I said.

"She wasn't sure, when last we spoke. Perhaps."

"Tell me about it."

"I don't wish to misrepresent her findings." She gave me my coffee in a thick ceramic mug. "Why don't you call her?"

A BOATING CHANNEL FLOWED outside the window, a stone's throw away. And beyond the water, a well-groomed neighborhood that looked like a nice place to come home to.

"What's that river?" I said.

"Canal," she said. "The Tamiami. Not the same—how do you say, *cachet*?—as Biscayne Bay, but a water view even so."

From our cool and silent chamber, we watched a powerboat pass through the sun shimmer, east to west. No sound penetrated the smoky glass.

Like watching TV at zero volume.

"I have work," Navi said. "Call Rytt." She entered her office and closed the door halfway.

And I was alone again, Aunt Jolene.

MY CALL WENT TO Rytt's voice mail. I told her where I was and that I'd hang around a while.

Time to get busy.

The conference table was small and oval, mid-range quality. But Slaven and Bustamante had splurged on the chairs. Warm microfiber, nicely padded. Good lumbar support, and half a dozen adjustments. Too bad they didn't give massages.

The envelope from Derish and Maddy sat on the table in front of me. While I played with my chair, my subconscious delivered a message, in the voice of Lucille Cruiset.

Maybe it's fear of failure. Maybe it's fear of success. You keep finding reasons to put it off.

Point taken, Lucille.

I opened the envelope.

51 The Astral Eye

A THREE-PAGE ARTICLE from a rag called the *Astral Eye Almanac* described a paranormal vortex along the east coast of Florida, near Miami. The author cited aural and visual anomalies, temporal disturbances, and other weirdness from Dinner Key to the grounds of Vizcaya to—there it was—Virginia Key.

Shoddy graphics and a typewriter font hurt the document's credibility. But the part about Virginia Key—wow. Over the years, beachgoers reported that Bear Cut, which separates Virginia Key from Key Biscayne, briefly narrowed or disappeared entirely when viewed from a certain stretch of beach. Talk about déjà vu.

The first reports occurred well before construction of the Rickenbacker Causeway. Later reports stated the causeway itself vanished and reappeared. Changes in the quality of light and air accompanied these visual phenomena.

Skeptics shrugged off the so-called paranormal episodes, noting that a simple fog masking Key Biscayne or the causeway would also change the air and light.

Harder to dismiss were reports dating from the times of the conquistadors regarding a tribe of ape-like humanoids that appeared on the key when the other aberrations were in full swing. One account referenced a tribal leader who called himself *I-Who-Travel* or *The-One-of-Words*.

Primary witnesses, however, had often been using psychotropic substances, or had experienced the phenomena at the borders of sleep, adding to skepticism about the accounts.

In counterpoint, the author argued—not too shabbily—that the workaday brain tends to reject the inexplicable, while a mind in a relaxed or enhanced state is more open to accepting the reality before it.

HEAVY STUFF.

"Ted, stop that." Navi stood in her office doorway, arms crossed beneath her pert and perky breasts. Sorry, that last observation was irrelevant. But, hey. You know?

"Stop what?"

"Kicking the leg of the table."

"Oh." I stopped.

"What is it that agitates you?"

"This article. About a vortex on Virginia Key."

"Vortex. Like the tornado?"

"Yeah, except a vortex of paranormal activity."

"Many things have occurred on Virginia Key over the years. But paranormal?"

"You're a skeptic."

"Who wrote this article? What are her credentials? Or his."

"A man wrote it. Hold on." I flipped to the first page, the one with the crude graphic of the Florida coast being targeted by ... well, yes, it did look like a tornado. But instead of cars and cows and trees spinning out of it, it was ringed with question marks of various sizes. Clever.

And there, across the bottom, the author's name. Fred Madison.

"Fred Madison."

Navi shook her head.

"Look," I said. "It's just a rag and I never heard of this guy either, but this stuff happened to me, exactly like he says."

She arched an eyebrow. "I'm going back into my office now. The paperwork to operate this business is *ridículo*."

"Hire some help."

"Of course. And go into the red each month from the expense."

"Navi, I appreciate your help. You'll be paid in full."

She uncrossed her arms. "Stop kicking the table, Ted. It

sounds like a headboard that bangs to the wall during hatred sex, and I find it distracting."

She returned to her office, leaving the door half closed. Or half opened.

Hatred sex?

52 Paths of destruction

ODDLY ENOUGH, THE NEXT packet of articles from the Derish-and-Maddy envelope was also about vortexes. But physical ones. Tornadoes.

Articles from 1983 editions of Miami and Fort Lauderdale newspapers described a swarm of nasty twisters that tore through south Florida in March of '83 from Pompano Beach to Biscayne Bay.

Oh shit.

I caught myself kicking the table again and stood up to stop it. I paced the room with the articles in my hand, studying the timelines and paths of destruction. According to one report, a tornado actually passed through downtown Miami before slashing its way across Biscayne Bay, where it appeared to fade. But it had only paused to catch its breath. It rallied, and zeroed in on—you guessed it—Virginia Key.

1983. My brain was churning. Spinning the pieces, forcing them together. Pop swore the picture was from thirty years ago, roughly when the nude beach on Virginia Key had been shut down.

But Haley hadn't even been born yet. She was over a decade from existence.

THE PREGNANT BRIDE IN the Coral Gables wedding pictures, mother of the unborn. I wondered why I was thinking of her.

Ted, it's your subconscious. I can help you out with this.

Fantastic.

Start with the picture Nicki gave you. At the time it was taken, Haley wasn't born yet, right?

Right.

She's not in the picture yet. So to speak.

Ha ha.

And the pregnant bride. Her baby is not in her pictures either. But the mother is.

Gotcha. The picture is the mother, not the child.

Right.

The picture on the beach. It's Haley's mother. It's Nicki.

There you go. And that's why you didn't recognize Haley from her picture when she showed up at El Toro.

But Nicki is not the same girl, remember? She changed. That's what Reva said.

How old was Nicki in 1983, Ted?

Let me think. She was born in, uh …

1970.

How did you remember that?

I remember pretty much everything. So in 1983, Nicki would have been …

Thirteen. And the girl in the picture looks like a thirteen-year-old. But why couldn't I figure this out on my own, without this subconscious bullshit?

Good question. Probably a side effect of too much hypnotism.

Great.

I'D HACKED MY WAY through most of the documents in the envelope. In the last remaining packet, I found copies of Dade County adoption records. Wallace Albert Landis and Reva Joan Landis adopting Nicole LaFuze. Paper-clipped to the adoption decree was a note—fine-point pencil on steno paper. I heard Maddy's voice in the precise lettering.

TED, THIS IS A copy of the original adoption order ostensibly lost during a file transfer in the 1980s. On the register, also attached, the decree ID contains transposed numbers, a plausible error, further insulating the truth from casual exposure. Strategies like these helped us isolate Nicki from the people and events in her past that place her in danger. We've kept all relevant paperwork in a safe place, accessible if events demand. We're all getting older now, and maybe it's time for the truth to come out. We're trusting you to do the right thing, Ted. Especially for Nicki.

Maddy and Derish

53 Woe and entropy

LONG CONCEALED IN A dark cavern of fear, at last the reclusive truth staggered toward the sun. In a manner of speaking.

I still couldn't identify the man in the picture, which is what I'd been hired to do. But did it matter now? Nicki wanted to know for only one reason. To find out what he was doing with her daughter Haley. But I believed the girl in the picture wasn't Haley at all.

Or if it is, somebody's got some 'splaining to do.

RYTT CALLED WHILE I was in the PI office washroom, warming my hands under the hot water. A chichi basket of rolled terry towels provided for clients' hand-drying needs.

I flicked the water off my fingers.

"Hey, Rytt," I said.

"Ted, I found the guy."

"Spanky? Planky?" That didn't sound right.

"Panko, Ted. Ronnie Panko."

"Yeah, I knew that."

"Like the crumbs. If you want him, come get him."

"What? Where are you?"

I exited the bathroom. Navi watched from her doorway.

Rytt told me she'd followed a lead to an independent book printer near Hialeah where Panko worked as a sales rep—officially at least. Rumors implied he handled other jobs.

"Like what?"

"My source wasn't specific," she said. "Look, Panko could take off at any time. I don't want him to spot me and connect me to my source. So get your butt moving. I'll fill you in when you get here."

She gave me the address and signed off.

"What happened?" Navi said.

"She found him." I shoved my papers into the envelope. "She wants me there in a hurry."

"Is there a problem? Do I need to—" Her cell buzzed and she checked the display. "Never mind. It's Rytt."

THIS TIME I WAS in a hurry, so I let my GPS choose the route. Up the Palmetto Expressway for ten minutes, then east for twenty on 932. Fast food, strip malls, and used cars. Closer to my target, the landscape got grittier. Loans, lawyers, and guns.

My target address was near the main drag but you couldn't get there from here, to coin a phrase, because a massive railyard overpass cut off the cross streets. But my GPS was up to the job and zig-zagged me to my destination, a broad building on a dusty industrial street hard against the tracks.

Discreet signage displayed the name. Gribler Press.

The building's three-tone paint job—shades of tan—was in good shape. Separating the structure from the street was a single row of ten parking spaces. Rytt's car filled none of them.

SHE HAD PARALLEL PARKED her ride, an older Sable, near a retail store with Spanish signs in the windows. I dumped my wheels at the crumbled concrete base of a warped metal framework that might have had a purpose once, but now looked like a monument to woe and entropy. I hoofed it to the Sable.

Rytt leaned over and popped the door. "You see Gribler Press?"

I dropped into the passenger seat. "I see it."

"Ronnie went in the door on the left. Up the ramp to the porch with the awning."

"When was that?"

Her notebook was black with a ribbon bookmark, like a Bible. "Forty-three minutes ago."

"How'd you find him?"

"My source told me he worked here, as a fixer, so I staked

out the front. He showed up twenty minutes later."

"Don't you love it when that happens?"

She shrugged.

"Is there another way out?"

"Don't know, Ted. There's no street behind the building, just railroad tracks. So I couldn't drive back there. And I forgot my hobo disguise."

"Fair enough," I said. "What kind of place is this, exactly?"

"They specialize in books for self-publishing writers. And one-offs under their own imprint. Paranormal romance. Erotica. Whatever's hot."

"How do you know all this?"

"I called Navi. We've been online."

"So, erotica. Like pictures? Magazines?"

"More like novels. And collections. Anthologies."

"Not like *Nature Beach Angels*."

"Doubtful. That was homemade, in my opinion."

WE STARED AT THE building. The door didn't open.

"Which car is his?" I said.

"That sedan. The Lincoln."

The car was big, and old, and low to the ground, as if the springs gave up years ago. A repulsive shade of yellow with a whiff of pink, a touch of rust, and a ton of dust.

"Describe him for me. Panko."

She checked her notes. "White, average height, no glasses. Auburn hair combed back, a little spiky, wearing—"

"Wearing a black T-shirt with a silver chain and a linen blazer, right?"

She looked up. "That's right."

I pointed. "There he is."

54   Well-dressed death

RONNIE PANKO.

He approached his heap with his blazer draped across his forearm, a can of Dr Pepper sweating in his hand, and a tabloid under his elbow. His free hand dug around in his pocket and came out with keys.

"He's all yours, Ted. How do you want to play it?"

Ronnie slid a key into the car door. I guess his remote locks were broken. Or his Lincoln was too old for those gizmos.

"I'll follow him," I said.

"You want backup?"

I slipped out of the car and turned my face to prevent eye contact with my target. "No thanks, Rytt." I slammed the door and hustled to my rental.

Ronnie was already backing out, wheels cranked, kicking up dust. He squealed away toward 932 and I peeled out behind him.

Discreetly, of course.

AFTER THE JACKRABBIT START, we traveled west at a sedate pace, then hung a right and cruised north on a through street whose name I missed. He swung the Lincoln into a burgers-and-fries drive-thru, so I parked at a taco place across the street where I could watch and wait.

After two minutes the smells alone clogged my arteries.

When Ronnie's land yacht lurched onto the right-of-way, the low-speed chase was on again. We trekked north, turned twice, and made every light. Just when I thought he'd get wise, he wheeled into a funeral chapel and docked in a shady spot near a low plastered wall.

I didn't see a stakeout spot so I circled the block to ponder my next move. When I reached the funeral home again, Ronnie was still behind the wheel, cramming his craw with french fries.

Those things'll kill you, Ronnie.

What the heck. I chose the direct approach, and swung into the parking lot. By the time I found my own shady spot, Ronnie had donned his blazer and was sauntering to the chapel entrance, brushing his hands together.

He nearly wiped his greasy hands on his pants.

I followed him to the entrance alcove, caught the glass door as it closed behind him, slipped inside, and hung back.

A SLACK-FACED WOMAN in a charcoal suit spoke to Ronnie. I heard the name *Stoneburner*. Then Ronnie looked at his hands, detoured down the hall, and stepped through a door marked MEN.

The woman padded my way. "Name of the deceased?" A smoker's voice, somber and phlegmy.

"Uh, Stoneburner?"

She led me to a lectern by a wide doorway. A felt letterboard listed the schedule of events.

"You may sign the book here," she said. "Electronically."

"Thank you." I poised my fingers over the keys and she drifted toward the main entrance. A greeter, I guess. Like at that discount mart, but more funereal—or not.

IN THE VIEWING ROOM, alone with the loved one. Three-piece suit. Every hair in place. Tight-lipped and stoic about the whole being-deceased deal.

"Hey."

I jumped. Ronnie had come in while I was busy viewing.

"Hey, Ronnie."

"Sorry, do I know you?"

"Let's sit."

"Sure," he said.

I conjured the *Nature Beach Angels* booklet from under

my jacket and flipped it open. The images of sunny young nudity clashed with the chill presence of well-dressed death.

Ronnie leaned away. "Where did you get that?" He glanced around the room. Still just the three of us.

"You peddled them all over the state. And I picked one up."

"Put that away."

"Sure. But first look at this guy right here." I pointed to the object of my search.

His eyes darted away and back again. Twice. "I don't know him. And for the record, I deny everything."

"You recognize him. And I can prove you distributed this document."

He stood. "I'm leaving. I don't—"

"Ronnie, before you walk away, understand this. If you don't tell me what I want to know, I will report this to your supervisors at Gribler Press. How will they react knowing you're responsible for distributing this kind of material?"

HE TILTED HIS HEAD as if I were a rare species, *Homo stupido*. "You're clueless, aren't you?"

"Okay. That tells me about Gribler Press. You're not concerned, because they print stuff just like this. And worse."

"Do you have any idea who you're dealing with? Any idea?"

Did he really just say that? "Well, other than Ronnie Panko, kiddie pornographer, not really. Enlighten me."

"That's not—" He shook his head. "I'm gone. Your threats don't scare me."

"Okay, buh-bye. I'll just wait here for Mr. Stoneburner's family and friends, and ask them what I'm asking you."

He glanced at the exit. "I shouldn't talk to you, but I can't trust you not to be stupid. Let's get out of here. I'll go first."

"Don't disappear on me, Ronnie. I know where you work. I know where you live." Not really, but he didn't know that.

"Give me one minute. Then go to your car. Where are you parked?"

I told him.

"Okay," he said. "Follow me in your vehicle. I'm in the Lincoln."

"Where to?"

"Not far. There's an out-of-the-way park. Nobody I know ever goes there."

"You like to watch the little girls on the swings?"

He started to laugh but seemed to remember where he was. "One minute. I don't want anybody to see us together."

I nodded. "Ditto."

55   The Queen of the Snow

AFTER THIRTY SECONDS I got bored, and I didn't trust Ronnie not to run off. So I left Mr. Stoneburner with his coiffed hair and dapper suit and strolled out to the lot. Ronnie sat behind the wheel of his Lincoln.

He didn't look my way.

I FOLLOWED HIM TO the park, and it was like he said. Off-street parking, more or less hidden by a curve in the drive, a hedgerow, and a wooden park sign. No teeter-totters, slides, or swing sets—not that kind of place. Found another shady spot for the rental—my lucky day—and a minute later Panko clambered into my passenger seat and slammed the door.

Right away he tried to take control. "Okay, spill it. Who are you, and why are you busting my balls?"

"Cards on the table," I said. "Ted Danger, PI. The mother of the young woman in the picture hired me to track down the man posing with her. That's the primary goal."

"So you're not after me. Or Gribler Press. You're not working for the cops."

"I told you who I work for."

"I'm going to wise you up." He made a frowny face. "You're wading into deep shit here."

I opened the back of the *Nature Beach Angels* booklet. "Tell me about the guy in the picture. You recognized him."

He closed his eyes and touched his temples. The picture of cogitation. Squirmed, took a last look over his shoulder, sucked in a breath, and dove in.

"He's the son of the single most vicious drug pusher ever to fuck up our fair state. La Reina de la Nieve."

NOT THE ANSWER I expected. Or wanted to hear.

"The Queen of the Snow," I said.

"No doubt. Nellmary LaFuze, she called herself. Her son is Jack LaFuze—the guy in the picture."

At last I had a name. And a pedigree. I could work with that. "Any idea where I can find this guy LaFuze?"

"Nobody knows. A twister sucked him up on Virginia Key back in the nineteen hundreds and he never came down. Could be chasing munchkin tang all over Emerald City."

He laughed at his own wit, so I did too—positive feedback—and kept feeding him questions.

"How do you know all this?"

He angled my direction and leaned on the door. Getting comfortable. "Jack was a regular at the Virginia Key nudie beach. Had plenty of money, from Queen Momma's rackets, I guess. But the truth is, he didn't give a shit about the family business. In fact, he was a little"—he spun a finger at his ear— "slow in the head. Me, I was just a kid trying to make a dollar. Got the idea of taking Polaroids, you know, of the nudists, and selling them for a couple bucks each."

"Posed or candid?"

He shrugged. "Both. Sometimes they'd smile for the camera. Buy the picture as a souvenir. Sometimes I just shot people having fun in the sun."

"Especially the little girls." I winked to keep him talking, but he didn't need encouragement.

"Not especially. But yeah. The female form is way more attractive than the male, after all. It's nature."

I must not have agreed fast enough.

"No, really," he said. "Look at art. Advertising. It's obvious. Women are more photogenic."

He nodded and I nodded back. *Keep talking, Ronnie.*

"And it's a no-brainer," he said, "that younger is prettier, right? A lot younger—now that's the forbidden fruit. Sweet, but hard to come by. Which raises its value. Basic economics. Nothing pervy about it."

"You've got your rationalizations lined up nice and neat."

"Who doesn't?"

ENOUGH SOCIOLOGY 101. I steered him back to history class.

"How do you know so much about Jack LaFuze?"

"I took a lot of pictures, like I said, and Jack was a fan of little girls. But not in a bad way. He was like a kid himself. He'd buy my leftovers, and him and his daughter would put these scrapbooks together. So I made him a deal. I'd provide the content, and he'd build me a book. That's how *Nature Beach Angels* was born."

"You mentioned his daughter," I said.

"Yeah. Cute little thing. Real sassy. Well, you can see in the picture. That's her."

MAYBE I SHOULD HAVE been more surprised. But it made sense. Almost. "The girl in the picture is the daughter of Jack LaFuze? The granddaughter of Nellmary LaFuze, La Reina de la Nieve?"

"That is precisely correct," Ronnie said. "Ding-ding-ding, we have a winner. And the girl's mother definitely did *not* do what you said. Hire you to find Jack. No way."

"Why do you say that?"

"Because the girl's mother, Jack's wife, she died a long time before Jack disappeared."

"How long before?"

"Years. Months. I don't remember."

"But you're sure she died?"

"Sure I'm sure," he said. "Her mother-in-law blew her up."

"Blew her up?"

"Blew. Her. Up."

Good lord. What was I getting into?

56   The dirt on Gribler

THE WHOLE THING SEEMED bizarre and implausible. Like I'd beamed into a weird new world of randomness and surprise. "The whole thing seems bizarre and implausible."

"Hey, man," Ronnie said. "You can't make this shit up."

I shook my head. "Nellmary? Jack's mother killed his wife?"

"Nellmary wanted her boy all to herself." He winked, the magnanimous authority enlightening the humble halfwit. "Jack freaked out. Told me she damn near murdered his kid too."

"The girl? The one in the picture?"

"Yep."

"What was her name?"

"Nicole," he said. "Nicole LaFuze. Jack called her Nicki."

Damn.

DAMN DAMN DAMN.

"Nicki LaFuze," I said. "What happened to her?"

"She was on the beach with Jack when the twister hit. I think she got ... that thingamabob." He slapped his head.

"Concussion?"

"No. Like a blackout. Coma. Could of been amnesia. Rumor went around, the Feds moved her to witness protection. Anyhow, she was gone."

"Why would she need witness protection?"

"She knew things. Or she could of been a target for a vendetta, because of La Reina's whole evil-deeds lifestyle. Look, I don't know. It wasn't a big deal."

"Not a big deal? Granddaughter of the Snow Queen? Father ripped from her side by a twister on a nude beach?

174

Coma? Amnesia? Witness protection? It had to be a huge story."

"Nah. La Reina kept a low profile as far as John Q. Public was concerned. This was before all the social media crap and 24-hour news. It was a long time ago."

"So if it's all ancient history, why do I need to tread so carefully? Why do you say I don't know who I'm dealing with?"

"Well, sure, La Reina's long gone, and I quit selling the *Angel* books. But there's still drug traffic and, let's say, edgier mags and stuff. You know, with models who aren't technically eighteen yet."

"What does that have to do with me?"

"The people who run things, they don't like strangers asking questions. There's lots of money passing through lots of pockets. The hint of a threat, and they deal with it."

"And how do you fit in, Ronnie? You back in the underage photo business, on a bigger scale?"

"Look, you got your answer about the guy in the picture. Leave the rest alone. It's nothing to do with you. Nothing."

HE HAD A POINT. But he didn't know when to stop talking.

"Anyway, there's lots worse things going on in the world."

Okay, Ronnie was back to self-justifying. Maybe I could string him along and find out what was really going on. *Hell, can't hurt to ask, right? I mean, what could go wrong? Ha ha.*

"Who's Stoneburner?" I said. "Hit man? Enforcer?"

He squinted at me. I figured our conversation was over. But the guy loved to hear himself talk. "Hell, no. He was a numbers guy. Stroked out at his desk."

"Numbers guy. Accountant? Or the numbers racket?"

"Cash flow, that stuff."

"What was he to you? Why were you at the viewing?"

"Getting my name on the roster, you know? Showing respect."

"So you're both part of an organized crime ring? Through Gribler Press?"

"Look, you don't need to know all this." He glanced around and sucked air through his teeth. "I've said too much already."

No kidding.

I OPENED MY PALMS. No threat. "Just a few more questions, Ronnie. You've piqued my curiosity."

"And by the way, people call me Ron these days."

"You got it, Ron. So how is Gribler Press linked to organized crime?"

"Christ, when you put it like that ..."

"How should I put it?"

"Listen. People struggle. Jobs are hard to find, and if you get one, it doesn't pay diddly. Especially if you're not entirely legal. If you don't have the Social Security, the paperwork."

"A Social Security number."

"That's right. So the ladies in the family, they can help out. Especially the *chicas* and *mamacitas* who want, like, a modeling career."

"PORNOGRAPHY," I SAID.

"No. No. Not necessarily."

"Not necessarily."

"Right. There's this whole market for, you know, art layouts. Hard copy."

"Hard-core?"

"No, hard *copy*. Ink on paper. People collect it. Young models, sure, but no sex. Scenario work, you know?"

"So hard copy. Like magazines."

"Yeah. Online stuff scares people. There's a record somewhere that never goes away. One wrong click, there's a knock at your door."

"But if you're caught with pictures, that's evidence too."

"Sure. And that's why there's limits, like I said, with the kids. No sex. And the scenes look old, you know? Old-fashioned furniture. Typewriters and record players. Box TVs with rabbit ears. And they print this disclaimer. Says the pictures are historical, and profits go to fight child exploitation. Give the perverts deniability."

"This is sleazy. I feel dirty just talking about it."

"It's not that bad. People get exploited all around the world, right? But we give these families a fighting chance. The right model can earn enough to make a difference. Buy Dad a car, improve his job prospects."

"So organized crime money is like a family benefit. It provides a social good."

"You betcha. That money gets spent right here, goes hand to hand. That's the multiplier effect, and it lifts the whole neighborhood."

His answers sounded rehearsed. Come on. *Multiplier effect?*

57 Life is messy

WE'D BEEN TALKING A long time, and not a man, woman, or child had entered the park. Or left it, which is what I felt like doing.

"Okay," I said. "You guys are saints."

"Sometimes, yeah. Believe it or not."

"And these kids. Where do you take their pictures? You don't wait for a nice day and haul them to a nude beach."

"No, we've got a studio right there at the plant. With old-timey props like I told you about."

"And that's it. Nudie shots. Innocent stuff. The family's paid, the economy booms. Sweetness and light, happily ever after. No touching, no trauma, no sexual slavery."

"No, nothing like that. That's not what I deal with."

"But someone does."

"Look, I'm not responsible for everything that happens in this world."

"Like what?"

Panko pulled a black cocktail napkin from a blazer pocket and wiped his face. "Life's messy. Situations don't have easy answers."

"Situations?"

"Well, a girl might not have anybody paying attention. The dad splits. Mom gives up. Whatever. Maybe it's just kids raising kids."

"But your bosses at Gribler—they find out and step in."

"Or maybe the home life's bad. Stepdad's abusing the girl, renting her out."

"So what do you do about it?"

"Maybe nothing. You can't fix everything."

"But sometimes ..."

"Sometimes the girl gets a new life," he said. "A new home."

"You're not talking adoption."

He turned in his seat, checking the view out the back window.

NOTHING TO SEE.

"New life, like I said. Earns money. It's a real win-win."

"What's your role in this, Ron?"

He shook his head. "Nothing. Unless the stepdad makes waves. Then I explain things. With a financial incentive."

"And if he doesn't make nice?"

"Somebody with a different incentive comes by," he said. "I don't see stepdad around anymore."

"He moves to a nicer neighborhood?"

"Guy like that, the world's better off without him, right?"

"He's a bad pimp," I said. "Inadequate ROI."

He leaned back and looked down at me. "Don't overthink things, my friend."

"Ronnie, I doubt we'll ever be friends."

He didn't answer.

"These girls with new lives," I said. "They just vanish? No questions?"

"They're not the cheerleaders who somebody's going to notice they're gone. Half of them never went to school at all. Not in the U.S. of A. anyhow. They fall through the cracks."

"And their disappearance doesn't make a ripple?"

He pointed his chin at me. "And the cool thing is, we got people in county records who clean things up for us."

What a gasbag. If I kept asking, he'd keep answering.

BUT THEN NICKI CALLED.

She wasn't missing anymore.

58 Tranquility for Nicki

ME: "HOLD ON, NICKI."

Ronnie: "So are we done?"

Me: "Give me your number, Ron. And here, take mine."

Ronnie: "Jesus! Don't call me. We never met. We never talked."

Me: "Call me if there's anything else I should know."

Ronnie: "Jesus! I don't even know you."

Me: "Call me."

Ronnie: "Jesus!"

He got out and slammed the door. Three times harder than he strictly needed to.

But he'd taken my card.

"YOU STILL THERE, NICKI?"

"How are you, Ted?"

While grown-up Nicki spoke to me on the phone, little-girl Nicki grinned up at me *au naturel* from *Nature Beach Angels*. I closed the booklet and tossed it behind the seat.

"Listen, Nicki. Are you all right?"

"I feel very good. How do you feel?"

"Never mind me. We've been worried about you. Where are you? Where have you been? What have you been—"

"Go easy, Ted. I've just spent two days at my tranquility spa and you're taking the glow off."

"Well, I wouldn't want to de-glow your tranquility."

"Is that sarcasm, Mr. Danger?"

RONNIE PANKO'S MASSIVE LINCOLN blew past my rental, shaking the sheet metal. The behemoth leaned into the turn, tires squalling, and exited stage right. Taking Ronnie out of my life for, I hoped, a very long time.

"I'm being serious now, Nicki. Are you really okay?"

"I'm at Mom and Dad's, with Haley. Although she's not here right now."

"In Pompano? In Florida?"

"Pompano Beach. That's in Florida."

"You flew down?"

"Of course."

"Is Bentley with you?"

"Bentley?"

"Your husband, Bentley."

"Why would Bentley be here?"

"Have you called him? Does he know you're all right? He's been worried about you, Nicki."

"Well, he can stop worrying. You can all stop worrying. I simply needed a break, that's all. I couldn't stop thinking about everything, all alone in that big empty house. Everyone left me. Bentley. Haley. Even you." Her voice rose. "Why do I have to be alone? I'm married, I have a child. And I paid you a lot of money. But everyone left. So why shouldn't I leave too? I needed—"

"All right, Nicki. You're fine now. Tranquil, right? And I want to talk to you about the case. I've made progress."

"The case."

"I'll be up later today. I'm in Miami now."

"I'm in Pompano. Pompano Beach, Florida."

"Gotcha. Nicki, can I talk to Wally?"

"One moment, please."

One moment, please?

I held on for a while, but no one came to the phone. So I cut the call, fired up the rental, and steered east toward I-95.

Nicki spoke the truth the first day I met her.

She's a little bit crazy.

59 Incognito hypnotist

NEAR THE I-95 NORTH ramp for Pompano Beach, I stopped for fuel, a restroom, a pack of salted cashews, and a cold Diet Coke, in that order.

I wasn't far from Derish and Maddy's motel hideout. Before I got back on the road, I found the Rey-Day in my *Called Numbers* list and autodialed. *Call me Mr. Gadget.* The clerk put me through.

"Hello, this is James."

"Derish, it's Ted."

"Ted. Maddy told me you called the night we checked in."

"Yet you didn't scurry off to another hideout."

"Running's a nuisance. I don't much like it."

"I'd like to talk with you and Maddy about Nicki Vavul. Little Nicki Landis, you called her. I've learned things."

"Like what?"

Where to start? "Does the name LaFuze mean anything to you?"

"Oh boy. Okay. But just you and me. Not Madeline."

"Why's that, Derish? Maybe both of you should be there."

"Maybe not, Ted. Anywho, she's out to dinner."

"Alone?"

"We're too conspicuous as a couple. When she gets back, it's my turn. Meet me at the shopping center down the block. The old mall. We can talk there."

"How is it people don't recognize you two?"

"Madeline can change her appearance quite radically," he said. "I mean very, very radically. She always could."

"What about you?"

"Ted, let's talk in person."

"I don't want you messing with my head, Derish."

He laughed, and I didn't like the sound of it.

THE SALTED CASHEWS I'D wolfed down with a Diet Coke had curbed my appetite. Or so I thought, until I strolled into the second-floor food court through a piquant smog of cinnamon rolls, pretzels, and by-the-slice pizza melting into chaos behind steamed glass.

Derish hadn't arrived, so I waited in a white plastic chair at a white plastic table.

This could be any mall in America. The smells and the sights. The people, dressed in just about anything.

Take the guy coming up the escalator. MIAMI on his aqua baseball cap. Aviator shades. Strappy sandals. Thin legs. Drawstring shorts. Sunshine-yellow T-shirt with blue waves and a three-nut palm tree.

He kept coming my way, as if he were going to greet me.

"Hello, Ted," he greeted me.

"Derish. I didn't recognize you."

"Thank god. I'd hate to be wearing this vapid costume for nothing."

"You want to talk and eat?"

He scanned the food court and pursed his lips. "Not here. There's an Irish pub downstairs. How about a Guinness, with bangers and mash?"

I SKIPPED THE GUINNESS, but the bangers were smashing. We tucked right in.

"So you're not afraid to be seen with me now," I said.

"I'm tired of hiding out. I'd like to get this behind us."

"Get what behind you?"

"I wish I had the documents I put together for you. The envelope. That would explain a lot."

"About Virginia Key. The '83 tornadoes. The adoption."

His Guinness stopped halfway to his mouth. "How do you know about that?"

"I'm a trained investigator, Derish."

"Seriously, tell me how you know about that."

"Why didn't you want me to see the envelope earlier, Derish?"

He spoke the code words to put me under. Nothing happened.

"Answer the question," I said.

He removed his aviators, looked into my eyes, and said, distinctly, "Virgin birth."

Nothing happened. Again.

60 Maddy's secret

DERISH RAISED HIS GLASS and drank deep. When he lowered his beer, he was smiling. He dabbed his lips with a napkin.

"I underestimated you, Ted." He slipped his glasses back on. "You've made progress on the case, and neutralized my post-hypnotic trigger. That's a rarity, I assure you. But as for your question, you've got it wrong. Exactly backward."

"In what way?"

"I'm not the one who wanted to keep the envelope from you." He drank again, without the napkin-dabbing.

"It was Maddy?"

A dollop of creamy Guinness burnished his upper lip. He licked it off. "Think about the first time you showed up at our house, Ted. Who invited you in, when you said you were investigating Nicki Landis?"

"Well, you did. But you didn't tell me anything."

"Maddy and I are in this together. She had to agree the time was right."

"But the note in the packet. Maddy's note. It explained about the adoption."

He shook his head. "I wrote that."

"It was signed *Maddy and Derish*."

As he leaned forward, his glasses caught the neon shamrock over the bar. "The point is, we've kept too many secrets for too many years."

"Like what?"

He answered with silence.

"Why so cagey, Derish? Either you want me to know or you don't. Let's hear it."

He took off his hat and glasses, and ran a hand through his

hair. "It started ... well, let's start on Virginia Key."

"The nude beach."

"Yes, yes, the nude beach. But you know, in those days, nudists weren't the only so-called reprobates on Virginia Key. There was another group."

"Beatniks? Hippies looking for a paranormal trip?"

"Good guess, but no. I'm talking about gays."

HE STARED AT HIS glass with half-closed eyes. "I used to hang out there."

"What's your point?"

"Not a lot of people know this, Ted. Among the general public. But I'm gay."

"I'm no expert, but that seems unlikely to me."

"I don't act gay? How should I behave?"

"No, not that. It's Maddy. She told me about all the women you've been with. It's the great heartache of her life."

"That's a distortion, Ted. If anything, the opposite is true. It's Maddy who's been with ... numerous partners. Men."

"That seems even more unlikely."

"It's an act. You think I'm in disguise tonight?" He drained the last of his Guinness. The foam slid down the glass. "Maddy wears a disguise every day of her life."

"I don't know your motive, Derish, but you're lying to me."

He flashed a neon-green smile. "You know, I used to run into Maddy on Virginia Key. Before we were a couple. Before she became Madam Fernando, in fact."

"She's a nudist?"

"You could say that. She was also researching Virginia Key's paranormal manifestations."

"Now, that seems plausible."

"Ted, everything I'm telling you tonight, plausible or not, is the god's honest truth."

THE WAITER BROUGHT DERISH'S second beer and my first. Why not? I took a pull and knew I'd made the right choice.

"Your narrative isn't holding up, Derish. Nothing that's happened up to this point supports what you're telling me now. It's too random."

"Real life's not always like a well-plotted novel."

"Well, it should be," I said.

He shrugged. We drank.

"Look," he said. "You came into possession of the packet somehow. About Virginia Key, the tornadoes, the adoption."

"Yes."

"So you read the *Astral Eye* article about the paranormal phenomena."

"Yes. The phenomena that exactly matched what I saw the day you sent me to Virginia Key. Which tells me they were post-hypnotic suggestions you planted, based on the article."

DERISH WAS SHAKING HIS head again.

"I sent you there because Maddy asked me to. Virginia Key is the key, so to speak. Extraordinary things can happen there. Events that trigger far-reaching consequences."

"Like what happened to Nicki."

"Of course. And do you remember who wrote it? The *Astral Eye* article?"

"Hang on." A quaff of Guinness gave me time to think. My god, that's real beer. It could be its own food group. Okay. Navi and I had talked about the author ... a president's name.

MADISON.

"Madison," I said. "Fred Madison."

"That's right. Fred Madison wrote the article Maddy Fernando wanted you to read."

"So what?"

"Fred Madison. Madeline Fernando. They're the same person, Ted. Maddy Fernando identifies as a woman these days, but genetically, she's a man."

"What?"

He didn't answer. And he wasn't smiling.

61 Just one thing

"DERISH," I SAID. "MADDY Fernando is not a man."

"I met her on the gay beach at Virginia Key." He slid his fingers around his beer glass. "Believe me, she's a man."

"But what's your point? Why are you telling me this?"

"For the same reason Maddy sent you to Virginia Key."

"And that is?"

He downed the dregs of his second Guinness. I'd barely dented my first.

"Things are not what they look like, Ted." He covered his mouth and belched. "And people are not who they seem."

I pushed my beer away.

"You're not going to finish that?" he said.

"No." I called the Rey-Day again and asked for James Dare's room.

MADDY ANSWERED AFTER THREE rings. "Hello, Ted."

"Hello, Fred."

Derish crossed his arms.

"No one calls me that anymore," Maddy said.

"I can't believe you lied to me. You're a fraud."

Derish stood and walked away.

"You're with Derish. Let me talk to him."

"No. That's not how I found out." The lie came easily.

"I can tell you're lying, Ted. That's the truth. Put Derish on the phone."

Derish disappeared into a restrooms alcove.

"He's not here. Believe me or don't."

"Be that way," she said. "What else have you found out?"

"I know what happened with the storm. The tornado. And

the adoption."

"Then you know everything. Or you think you do."

"Tell me how the adoption worked," I said. "Why are you in danger now?" Silence. "Maddy?"

"It's complicated," she said. "I had a friend who knew someone in county records. Reva and I were friends too. We met when she was a nurse at Two Saints, and I was an on-call psychologist. In fact, we dated for a while. Until I understood why my dates with women were so unsatisfying. And before she met Wally. And had Terry."

"Terry?"

She didn't answer.

"Don't stop now," I said.

"This is dangerous. For Derish and me. We'd rather you figure it out on your own."

"Time for the truth, Maddy."

"What happened to *Fred*?"

"You're more of a *Maddy* to me."

"Ha! So we're friends again?"

"I don't know," I said. Then, "Yes, friends."

"Then let me talk to Derish."

"Okay, we're at the pub. But he's in the restroom."

"Pub? Let me guess. He's drinking Chivas, rocks."

"Nope."

"Guinness then."

DERISH RETURNED WIPING HIS hands on his shorts.

"Here he is," I said.

He shook his head, but sat and took the phone.

"Hi, Fred," he said.

Maddy: [loud, unclear]

Derish: "Okay, Maddy. Sorry."

Maddy: [quieter]

Derish: "Just two. But I might finish Ted's, if he doesn't get busy."

Maddy: [long response]

Derish: "I just believed it was time."

Maddy: [unclear]

Derish: "Okay, Maddy."

Maddy: [unclear]

Derish: "Okay."

He cut the connection.

"You hung up? I had more questions."

"I'm leaving."

"Hold it," I said. "Tell me what happened with Nicki. I mean, she's traumatized, her dad's dead, her grandma sells cocaine and kills people. Then what?"

"Let me talk with Maddy. We'll call you."

"Okay, but give me something. Help me out here, Derish."

"Really? You're asking?" He leaned back, his hands behind his head. "Oh, sure. Five minutes ago you were calling me a liar. *That seems unlikely to me*, you said."

"Well, it really isn't very likely, is it? That Madam Fernando is a man? Even if it's true."

"When this is finished, come spend an evening with us." A sudden motion, and he was in my space. "Perhaps we can validate the particular gender of each one of us. And sexual orientation too."

I leaned back. "That seems unlikely to me," I said.

HE LAUGHED AND STOOD. "You're a funny guy, Ted."

"Come on. One thing. Please."

"Okay. Nicki was suffering, but not physically. You know firsthand that hypnotism can calm a physical irritation." He stretched. "So why can't it sooth a pain that's strictly mental?"

"Give me a few more details."

But he was already walking away. "That seems unlikely to me," he said.

62 They've got Haley

MY GUINNESS WAS GETTING warm. I drank and ruminated.

The key, according to Derish, is that no one is who they seem. Maddy, for sure, but who else? All the signs say Nicki.

Maybe tonight was the right time to brace Nicki about her past.

But it was definitely the right time to visit the men's room. So I did. My phone rang as I was washing up. As usual.

"Ted, it's Wally."

"Yeah, I'm headed up there," I said. "I got delayed."

I propped the phone on my shoulder while I dried my hands with cloth-like paper towels. I poached a few to toss into my rental.

"Wally? You still there?"

"You cocksucker," he said.

"What? Did you just—"

"I told you to get out. Go back home. I told you everything was okay. But you wouldn't leave it alone."

I RETURNED TO THE booth and found the waiter hovering.

"Did you want anything else?" he said.

"Hold on, Wally," I said. "Just the check, please."

He disappeared to wherever servers go when you ask for the check.

"What's going on, Wally?" I slid into the booth and picked up my Guinness. Not much left. I set it down.

"She's gone," Wally said. "They've got her."

"Somebody's got Nicki?"

"Haley, asshole. They took Haley."

"What? Who took her?"

"Ah, shit. A friend of mine. Or used to be a friend."

"Who? Why? Where'd he take her?"

"He's been following you, Ted. Were you talking to Ron Panko today?"

"Shit." My turn to say it. "Yeah, Ronnie and I had a heart-to-heart."

"Well, hell. I tried to tell you. You wouldn't listen, you had to rile people up. You got too close."

"Back up. Who's been following me? Besides you, I mean."

"Me?"

"Couple of days after I got here. I lost you in a parking garage."

"Okay, I'm bush league. But this guy knows his stuff. Once he picked you up, you didn't have a clue."

"Who is this guy, Wally? Why was he following me?"

"I've known him a long time. Sort of a criminal."

"Sort of."

"Shit. He's pretty high in the organization, matter of fact. Pablo DePriest. They call him Papa. Not a bad guy, really, at first. Well, I take that back. He's always been bad. But over the years, he's got deeper into it. I don't like it, but I owe him."

"For what?"

"For Nicki. When Reva and me got her, he made sure the paperwork wasn't a problem."

"So what's this DePriest want with Haley? What's his next move?"

"I don't know, Ted. Why didn't you leave it alone?"

"Okay, chew me out later. Right now we need to find Haley. You call the police?"

"Hell, no. These guys, you rat them out to the police, it's a death warrant."

"So what the hell are we supposed to do? Let them keep Haley?"

"It's you they want, Ted. They want you gone. Out of the state, out of their hair. Haley's just leverage."

"So they'll contact me?"

"Yeah, I'm pretty damn sure they'll contact you."

"How? How will they do it?"

"Any way they want. They know where you're staying, who you been talking to. They have your phone number."

"How do they have my number?"

"I gave it to them when they called—when Haley called. Christ, they made her call us herself. She's just a kid, Ted. And she's scared. You've got to tell these people you're not a threat. The sooner you deal with it, the sooner we'll get Haley back."

"Did they leave a number?"

"*Leave a number?* Hell, no, they didn't leave a number."

"Okay, okay." Jesus. Haley. Fuck fuck fuck. "Okay. Tell me about this guy, Papa DePriest. Who is he, exactly?"

SILENCE ON THE CELL. I waited.

"Okay. I met Pablo back when I was lifeguarding and he was a kid on the rescue squad. His crew would come to the beach for accidents or demonstrations or whatever. He was—"

"Political demonstrations? Protesters?"

"No, no. Public service stuff. You know, teach the tourists how to not drown. He was good at it. A show-off."

"Got it."

"He was young, like I said, but he knew people all over town. Never-met-a-stranger kind of guy. Knew the angles. All the rules and how to break them. Eventually got booted from the squad—between runs he'd fool around with these flirty beach girls. Show them his equipment in the back of the ambulance, if you know what I mean."

"So he's on duty when he's doing this?"

"Oh yeah, sure. But the thing is, these little vixens didn't necessarily have the ID, you know? Showing they were legal for the goings-on behind closed doors."

"Ambulance doors."

"Bingo."

"He's a rapist," I said.

63 Dire straits

THE WAITER DELIVERED MY check in a leatherette folder and didn't leave. When I stayed focused on the call, he drifted off.

"Not entirely," Wally said. "It was consensual."

"Got it. Statutory only. Nice. So what's he into now, this Papa?"

"Girls. He's got contacts all over south Florida. Knows the immigrant situation in five counties."

"The immigrant situation," I said.

"He's built up this organization, benevolent society, that helps people out. Legit charity work. But first it needs information about who needs help."

"Vulnerable families? Unaccompanied minors? Like that?"

"He knows who he can recruit. You know, it's the oldest profession, Ted. These families, they're in dire straits."

"Jesus, I've heard this story before, from Panko. The daughters can raise the family's standard of living, or leave an abuse situation, and live a life of glamour in the sex trade. Win-win."

"Hey, I'm not defending it. But it happens. Somebody's going to do it."

"Come to Papa, child. A better life awaits."

"Might be truer than you think, Ted. Silver-spooners like us don't know what their lives are like."

"And what do you owe this guy again?"

"He's got a network for processing the girls he relocates. I mean, he was just getting started back when we got Nicki. He helped make sure the paperwork went through clean. Got us to the top of the list, I guess. Whatever he did, it worked. Nicki's ours. If we keep a low profile, everything's fine. Then you come along asking questions, and people start looking too close. Ergo, shit hits fan."

ERGO? "WHAT COULD HAPPEN, Wally? No one's coming to take your baby. She's a grown woman with a kid of her own. It's over."

"Don't be stupid, Ted. What happened with Nicki was just the beginning. Matter of fact, it might of started the whole ballgame. You know, false records. Covered tracks."

"Disappearances. Human trafficking."

"Ah shit. Don't say that. But yeah. We start talking about who did what, and for who—and when I say *for who*, I mean for me and Reva and Nicki—hell, that's the original camel's nose under the tent flap. We let that cat out of the bag, we're asking for payback."

"Like Haley."

"Like Haley," he said.

"All right. Jeez, I better get off the phone, in case they call. Look, I'm coming to see you and Reva. I'll want everything you've got on Pablo DePriest. Even if it has nothing to do with Haley or his recruitment business."

"Well, there is one other thing."

"What's that?"

"He has a coffee business on the side. Illegal beans from Cuba."

"Good coffee?"

"Sure is. Reva gave you a cup the day you got here."

"I could use it right now."

"I'll have her start a pot."

"And one other thing, Wally."

"What's that?"

"When this is over, I want to know the truth, the whole truth, and nothing but the truth about what happened with Nicki."

64 Soledad vanished

THE INSTANT I ENDED the call, the waiter was back with a crystal-clear cup of steaming coffee and a silver creamer.

"We're closing pretty soon," he said. "I just ... I overheard your conversation. Is everything all right?"

"Not really." I dealt cash onto the check. "Keep the change. I'll get out of your hair."

"Wait. Here's coffee, if you want it. No charge."

"Irish coffee?"

"Just coffee." He sat opposite me in the booth.

I sipped. *Strong brew.*

"Like I said. I heard you on the phone."

I added cream.

"My girlfriend's little sister," he said. "She had a friend from Cuba, who just ... vanished. Like she never existed."

"When was that?"

"Last year. About this time."

"Around here?"

He nodded. "Her name was ... Her name is Soledad."

"Soledad."

"So are you investigating, like, girls disappearing?"

"Not exactly," I said. "But I'm learning things."

WHEN THE YOUNG WOMAN with the confident stride approached the table, I pegged her as the manager. Her striking green eyes made her a natural to run an Irish pub.

"Hi, I'm Kelly. Is everything all right here?" She glanced sideways at the waiter.

Kelly. Sure, why not? "Fine," I said. "Excellent coffee."

She looked at each of us. No one said anything.

"I'm glad you like it," she said. "I hope you come back and see us."

"Of course."

Kelly returned to the front of the pub.

The waiter scribbled on an order slip. "My number. Call, if you can."

IT WAS DARK. I climbed into my rental, but before heading off, I called Rytt.

"Hello, Ted."

"Bad news, Rytt."

"Say it."

"Someone's been tailing me, and saw me with Panko. They grabbed Haley, apparently to stop the investigation."

She drew a long breath. "Okay. What do you need from us?"

"I don't know yet. But if they're after me, you could be in their sights too."

"Who are we talking about, Ted? Who's doing this?"

SO I TOLD HER what I knew, that a criminal outfit in Miami—a gang that targeted vulnerable women and girls, particularly immigrants, for everything from nudie pics to full-blown abduction and prostitution—was tied to a record-fixing racket at the local level. And the whole dirty business started when my client, called Nicki LaFuze at the time, had been left alone and terrorized after her father—who happened to be the estranged son of the Snow Queen, a ruthless cocaine importer—was ripped from her arms by a stray tornado that blasted the nude beach on Virginia Key, and Reva and Wally Landis had solicited the help of their friend Papa DePriest to put the fix in for Nicki's adoption.

And I gave her the players' names. Ronnie Panko she already knew—jack-of-all-trades at Gribler Press, a facility that published soft-core kiddie books, with an on-site studio to shoot the content. And Pablo DePriest, a gang bigwig and founder of a charity racket that sniffed out exploitable prey in impoverished communities. The only other name I had was Stoneburner, the late numbers guy for the criminal enterprise.

AFTER TELLING HER THAT, I realized how little I really knew.

"So what's next, Ted?"

"You guys watch your backs. I'll buzz up to Pompano and see what Wally can tell me. And track down Haley."

Papers shuffled on the phone. "Ted, Navi dug up a home address for Ronnie Panko. Your problems started when you followed him from Gribler. Maybe he knows where they took Haley."

"Yeah, maybe. He's low-level, so he could be out of the loop. I bet he's in hot water himself for talking to me."

"Oh, I don't doubt that." She told me he lived in the Palminole Apartments, unit 24.

"Nice neighborhood?"

"Middle-class, I think. Hold on." I held on. "Okay. Here's the map. It's on the river."

"The canal?"

"No," she said. "The Miami River."

"So, upscale neighborhood."

"Hmm. Looking at the street view now. It's okay. No cars up on blocks."

"That's a video feed? Is it live?"

"It's a mapping program, Ted. Maps. With street-level images."

"Okay, it's not a live feed."

"Christ, Ted."

65 Nobody home

THE HUNK-A-JUNK LINCOLN SKULKED in slot 24, jaundiced in the Palminole security lights.

So Ronnie's at home.

With guest parking scarce, I grabbed a spot at a nearby plaza and hiked back. A big green rock that turned out to be a coconut propped open the card-controlled door to Ronnie's building.

Excellent.

A languid elevator brought me to the second floor. First door on the left. 24.

When I knocked, the door receded in the jamb. Another tap, and it popped open a half inch. The doorknob didn't turn.

I nudged with my foot.

"Ron, it's Ted." I smiled for any neighbors at peepholes, and stepped in. "Your door was open. You all right?"

No answer. The place felt empty. I checked the half-bath in the hallway. Neat but dusty. Then the master with its rumpled bed and jumbled closet. Next, the main bath. Pitted chrome and a wet-towel funk. A smaller bedroom held a pressboard desk and an exercise bike with a missing pedal.

Ronnie wasn't home.

No blood spatter. No soap message on the mirror. No envelope centered on the mantle under a spotlight, with *Ted Danger* inscribed on the front.

But my subconscious nudged me to the bedroom dresser.

RONNIE'S WALLET AND CELL phone. Lying there abandoned. Where would a guy go without his wallet and cell? To the trash bin? He'd be back by now.

And why was the apartment door locked but not latched? I checked it over. The button lock was engaged. A deadbolt and security chain, both open. On a hook near the doorframe hung a keychain with a Lincoln logo. One key fit the apartment door perfectly.

So, okay. Maybe Ronnie would return in two minutes with a logical story. I could wait. Snoop around. Not much of a plan.

Meanwhile, Haley's in a bad place, with bad people. Right now.

And I need to find her. Right now.

I need to get moving. Right now.

PANIC HIT ME HARD, burning my chest, flaming through every extremity. Any decision could be the wrong one. No way to know. Indecision and futility turned my bones into anchors. I needed to sit. Maybe lie down.

But I clenched my toes and fingertips, and popped the fantasy capsules planted there. Ice-cold rationality supplanted the heat, counterbalanced the crippling weight.

Relief.

But in a deeper place—disgust. This artificial calm, this child's game of *let's pretend*. A crutch for an invalid.

Damn it. Enough agonizing self-appraisal. It's a pain in the ass. So I weighed the information I had and chose my actions.

I'll rifle Ronnie's drawers for clues. Then hotfoot to Pompano to grill Wally Landis. If the kidnappers call, I'll alter my steps accordingly.

It was a plan.

THEN MY PHONE RANG and everything changed.

66 Get us out of here

I DIDN'T RECOGNIZE THE calling number.

"This is Ted Danger."

"Thank god." Rustling noises.

"What? Speak up."

"I can't. They might be listening."

"Who is this?"

"It's Ron. Ron Panko."

"Ronnie. I need to talk to you. Pablo DePriest has kidnapped my client's fifteen-year-old daughter Haley."

"Shit, man, I know all that. Except how old she is."

"Do you know where they took her?"

"Fuck yes. She's right here with me, for fuck's sake. At Gribler Press. You got to get us out of here."

ON THE PHONE, HARSH whispers.

Ronnie: "All right. Shut up, will you?"

Me: "Who's that?"

Ronnie: "It's her, asshole. She's telling me to keep it down before they hear us."

Me: "It's Haley? Let me talk to her."

Ronnie: "You can talk when you come and get us, man. This is your fucking fault. They know I talked to you, and now I'm in deep shit."

Me: "Ronnie, let me talk to Haley."

Ronnie: "After you save us. I told you."

Me: "Put her on now, if you want my help."

Ronnie: "Jesus. Here."

Haley: "Ted. Ted, they kidnapped me right on the sidewalk. Call the police. Call somebody. This guy's a creep. Hey! Stop—"

Me: "Are you all right, Haley? Haley!"

Ronnie: "Don't call the fucking police. Just get us out of here until things cool off. If the fucking cops show up, there's no fucking turning back. It won't end until somebody's dead, and I don't fucking want it to be me. Or your niece, of course."

Me: "Watch your language, Ronnie."

Ronnie: "You are fucking shitting me, right?"

Me: "No. Is Haley all right?"

Ronnie: "She's peachy, Uncle Ted. But she won't be much longer. These assholes specialize in making girls disappear, you know, and not in a good way."

Me: [to myself: *Not in a good way?*] "Where exactly are you?"

Ronnie: "Gribler Press, I told you. They got us locked in the studio they use for the, you know, the girl pictures."

Me: "What do they plan to do with you?"

Ronnie: "Fuck! I don't know, man. That's why you got to come now. How soon can you get here?"

Me: "All right. How far is it from your place?"

Ronnie: "From my place?"

Me: "Yes. I came here looking for you."

Ronnie: "You're inside? Inside my fucking apartment?"

Me: "Yes."

Ronnie: "I *told* those assholes you have to slam the door."

Me: "This is where they grabbed you?"

Ronnie: "Yeah. Wouldn't even let me take my wallet. Or my cell. Hey, can you bring my cell? And my wallet?"

Me: "Yeah. I guess so."

Ronnie: "And listen, I know exactly how much cash is in my wallet. Don't get greedy."

Me: "Jesus, Ronnie."

Ronnie: "Yeah, okay, fuck that. Just get me out of here. *Us,* I mean. What? What are you—"

Me: "What?"

Haley: "Ted, I was listening on the way here. They're going to keep us locked up until daytime, when it gets light. So nobody'll notice."

Me: "Notice what?"

Haley: "Loading a truck in the middle of the night. Putting us in a truck. At the dock thing."

Me: "The dock?"

Haley: "When it gets light. The dock for trucks."

Me: "The loading dock?"

Haley: "Yes."

Me: "Wait a minute. They let you keep your phone?"

Haley: "No. They took it. This is an old phone with a cord. It has a wheel on the front with holes. This place is wack."

Me: "Hang in there, Haley. I'm coming. Let me talk to Ronnie again."

Ronnie: "Bring my knuckle-duster, Uncle Ted."

Me: "Whose phone are you using, Ronnie?"

Ronnie: "These assholes got this closet with these old props. So the pictures look like the olden days, like we talked about. Takes the curse off it."

Me: "And there's a phone in there?"

Ronnie: "Yeah. And I found where to plug it in. Painted over. About shit when I punched through and got a dial tone. It's an old rotary. Your niece here acts like she never seen one. Never stuck her finger in a phone hole. Like a phone virgin."

Me: "That's not even funny. And she's not my—never mind. Just stay away from Haley."

Ronnie: "She might need protection."

Me: "I'm going to ask her when I get there, and she better give me the right answer or I'm going to fuck you up."

Ronnie: "Chill, man. We're freaking out here. Come and get us already."

Me: "How many people are guarding you, and where are they?"

Ronnie: "Two guys grabbed me and tossed me in here. Two different guys grabbed your niece."

Me: "Different guys."

Ronnie: "Yeah, I seen all four assholes. Two of them

dumped your niece in here twenty minutes after me."

Me: "So, at least four bad guys."

Ronnie: "We don't know who's coming or going."

Me: "Okay. I'm on my way."

Ronnie: "Bring my phone, will you? It's—"

Me: "Got it. And your wallet."

Ronnie: "And my knuckles. They're in the drawer by the bed. Uh, just ignore the other stuff in there."

Me: "Okay, here they ... oh, gross."

Ronnie: "Don't look at that."

Me: "That's not something you can unsee."

Ronnie: "You find the knuckles?"

Me: "Okay. Yeah. I'm on my way. And, hey, Ronnie?"

Ronnie: "Yeah?"

Me: "Just ... just stay away from Haley."

67 Danger in the dark

JUST BEFORE THE BLOW landed, I felt the danger.

AS I WAS LEAVING Panko's digs, my head was already at Gribler Press, planning strategies. I'd skipped the slo-mo elevator and hustled down the stairs, exited at the coconut, and turned left on the pebbled path that skirted the river and wound back to the street. I was poking the screen on Ronnie's phone, hoping to reveal an amazing clue and solve everything.

Rustling from behind, like an alligator ambush. My hair bristled. But the predator was human.

The pain was brief. Then darkness.

THE DARKNESS RESOLVED INTO a tight space tinged with red. Vibrating, humming, bouncing. Hard fabric below, flat and rough. Metal above, smooth, but here's a ridge. Another bounce and oh my head. Oh my head.

I was on my back, my legs wedged to the side, knees bent. I found leverage and untwisted. Now I saw the source of the red cast. Light seeped in from the taillight fixtures.

Taillights. The trunk of a car.

Another jolt and the car swept right. I braced myself, and the coarse floor gripped me like Velcro. The car straightened and the whine of the wheels glissed upward. Faster.

My hands and legs were free.

I found the quick-release handle, and longed to pull it and escape. But I preferred not to roll down the highway at sixty miles an hour, limbs flapping. *Pop the deck for a quick look-see?* Probably piss off whoever was in the cabin when, *ping-ping*, the TRUNK AJAR light came on.

Time passed. Wheels hummed.

Brainstorm.

Find a tire iron, smash a taillight assembly, stick my hand through the hole, and use one-handed sign language to request help ... if I knew any sign language at all, and the car behind me was full of deaf SWAT cops.

Or let this play out. Cooperate, and hope my cooperation leads to Haley's freedom.

Another jolt, bounce, bump. A whack to the head. I touched it where it hurt most. *Okay. Nothing wet or mushy.*

Time passed. Wheels hummed.

HALEY HAD SAID THEY'D move her after daylight. I tried to see through the taillight assembly. Still nighttime? Not sure, but yeah. No trace of daylight.

Long straight stretches, more turns. Pauses, like rolling through stop signs. A subtle drop and the tire noise changed. Crunching. Slowing. A man's voice, muffled. And the car rolled to a stop.

The engine died. No traffic sounds. No roil of surf.

Profound silence. Was my adventure over? Maybe I should have taken the risk, popped the trunk, when I had the chance.

If this is the end, what are my last thoughts?

Predictably, I suppose, I thought of my mother.

And of Hope too, and how I had betrayed her.

And Tru, who I would never see again.

And Haley, of course. What had I dragged the poor kid into?

And then I said, "Fuck that, Ted. You're not dying tonight. Not without a fight."

The latch released with a *thunk* and the lid popped up. Stars filled the sky.

TWO GUYS. OKAY.

"Talking to yourself, Ted?"

He was short and husky, with a face like a shovel. Broad

forehead and a chin with a blunted point. Same expression as a shovel too.

"I guess," I said. "Too much carbon monoxide in here."

"Hop out."

I got out slowly. *Let them think I'm impaired.*

A hunk of moon. Not full, but beaming. Roadway white with moonglow, scrubby landscape sketched in chalk and charcoal.

Dust under my feet. Damp in the air.

We'd left the city lights behind. *Everglades.*

"What did you hit me with?" I said.

"We got a message for you."

"First tell me about Haley. Where is she? Will you let her go, now that you've got me?"

He turned to his silent companion, who was taller, younger. Big eyes, mouth-breather. Creased forehead. A worried guy. Or deep thinker.

Nah.

"Rusty can do that, Ted," shovel-face said. "Go ahead, Rusty. Tell Ted here about Haley."

Young Rusty stepped in with a sucker punch to my gut. My legs crumpled and I went down. Tried to inhale.

"Now tell him where she is. That was your next question. Right, Ted?"

His kick snapped something in my nose.

"Now tell him if we'll let her go."

He swung a foot, and if his goal was gonads, he struck out. But I moaned as if he'd hit a homerun—or one strike and two balls.

"Now, as I said, we got a message for you. Stop snooping. Go home. Then we'll see about getting your girl Haley back to her momma, good as new."

Rusty's brow was smooth. As if his attack had calmed his nerves. "Maybe better than new," he said. "There's plenty we can teach her."

"Shut up," shovel-face said. He gazed at the desolation all

around. Space and silence. Then he nodded. "Have a nice walk." He turned and left me in the dirt.

"Wait." It hurt to talk. "At least give me a ride." *Breathe.* "Back to town."

"I don't think so, Ted." He stopped by the car door. Moonlight flashed off the screen in his hand. "And we'll just keep this too."

It was the cell I was carrying when they jumped me.

But the joke was on them.

It was Ronnie's.

68 Little blue pills

THE EVENING WAS BALMY, and as the big sedan's taillights dwindled in the distance—a Chevy Impala, if I had to guess—I felt like napping by the roadside to recover from my beating. But a gust of mosquitoes found me and my mental forecast called for scattered alligators. The Impala's brake lights flared and vanished less than a mile away, where gravel met pavement.

I started hiking in that direction. East? I guessed that Rusty and shovel-face had driven me west until the paved roads ended, then another stretch toward the Everglades to execute their thump-and-dump.

As I limped toward civilization, I checked my cell phone. The one Rusty and shovel-face failed to find, no doubt because I'd hidden it so cleverly by putting it in my pocket. The battery was strong. I just had to decide who to call.

A bar of coverage would help too.

Street numbers in Miami indicate your location relative to downtown, and when I finally reached solid pavement, the signs confirmed my suspicion. I wasn't far from the old Axelrod homestead. And my phone delivered the good news. Two full bars of signal strength.

So I scrolled through my numbers and made the call.

THE PHONE RANG A long time.

"Hello?"

"Jenny? It's Ted Danger."

"Ted, why are you ... What time is it?"

"Late. Early. I need your help."

"You sound funny."

209

"Yeah, my nose. Listen, Jenny. I'm not far from your place." I gave her the cross streets. "I was dumped out here, and I've got to get to Miami ASAP. Before daylight."

"That's ... you've got a few hours."

"But I don't have a car. Can you pick me up? Right now?"

"What's happened?"

"I'll tell you in the car. Jenny, it's important. And urgent. Believe me."

A pause. Then, "I'll be right there."

I KEPT WALKING, CUTTING the distance, and ten minutes later there she was in her old Taurus sedan, rolling to a stop next to me. And god bless her, she hadn't even stopped to drag a comb through her hair.

Neither had Boyce, who stared from the front seat.

"Thanks for coming, Jenny."

"Jesus, Ted, you're a mess."

I headed for the back but Boyce jumped out and held the front door for me. So I slid in. The seat was warm, but I shook off the shoeburyness.

"You too, Boyce," I said. "Thanks for coming."

He slid into the back seat, cloaked in darkness.

Jenny executed a perfect Y turn, and gunned the car back the way it had come.

"He's a light sleeper," she said.

"Does he have his learner's permit yet?"

She laughed, showing teeth.

"What what," Boyce said. *He's laughing?*

"Tell me what happened, Ted."

I told her. The nutshell version. "So I need to borrow your car. Just swing by your place so you and Boyce can get out and I'll be on my way."

"Ted. If the cops see you behind the wheel like that, they'll arrest you on general principles."

My shirt was a war zone. In the visor mirror, my face was no better.

AT JENNY'S PLACE, I stumbled from the car. My head ached, my face throbbed, and I needed to puke. Boyce swooped in and kept me upright. He hauled me toward the house but I took a detour and vomited in the bushes. My gut clenched again but nothing came up. The spasm passed. I felt better.

After I gargled with cinnamon mouthwash in the bathroom, Jenny sat me down at the kitchen table. She brushed off my jacket and hung it on a dinette chair. My bloody shirt went into the sink. She worked on my face with a hand towel and warm soapy water. Boyce had disappeared but he came back with an armful of T-shirts.

I could tell I was bouncing back when I noticed Jenny hadn't changed out of her bedclothes. Her simple night dress— aqua, maybe turquoise—covered her shoulders and showed not a hint of cleavage. But the sheer fabric played tantalizing 3D contours of her free-range breasts as they bobbled and swayed with every move.

I caught Boyce watching too. *Was I behaving like an animal? Or was he behaving like a human being?*

JENNY MUST HAVE NOTICED, because she left the kitchen without a word and returned with a ratty robe over her jams. She dropped a few pills into my palm. Blue pills. Oval.

"Tell me this isn't for ED, Jenny."

"Don't flatter yourself. It's Adderall. Take a couple now and keep the rest for later."

SO I AMPED UP, pulled on a maroon *Kiss My Paniscus* T-shirt, slipped into my sport jacket, and gave Jenny a smooch that started out quick and brotherly. Then it slowed down and got interesting.

She pushed me away and squeezed her keys into my palm. Boyce had disappeared again.

"Thanks, Jenny," I said. "Say goodbye to Boyce for me."

I jumped into the Taurus and barreled toward Miami.

69   Boy a man

JENNY'S TAURUS HAD A portable GPS unit stuck to the windshield with a suction cup.

Traffic was light at oh-dark-hundred, and I managed to program the GPS without crashing.

After dragging me around a handful of local streets, the GPS swung me onto 821. I goosed the gas and the old Taurus didn't disappoint. It leapt northward, pressing me into the seatback, and I was on my way to Miami.

IN SPITE OF EVERYTHING, I felt myself grinning, aware of how much I loved driving alone, at night, nothing in my way, fuel gauge near F. And not a person in the world knew exactly where I was. It was a glimpse into the mystic solitude we knew before birth, that would enfold us after death.

Or maybe I was just high on amphetamines.

In any case, my sense of aloneness was so deep that when two black bonobo eyes glowered at me in the rearview mirror, I screamed like a little girl.

The Taurus drifted but I lurched it back into its lane.

"Jesus Christ, Boyce."

"What."

"*What* is right, buddy. What the fuck."

He stared. My eyes flicked to the road and back.

"What the fuck, Boyce."

"Boy help," he said.

HE SPOKE SO RARELY his voice creeped me out.

"Jesus, thanks, Boy, but this is going to be dangerous. And we're not just blundering in there guns blazing. We might need to use stealth, you know? It means we've got to be quiet, Boy. Very quiet. Not make a sound. Do you know how to be quiet?"

I risked looking over my shoulder. His eyes remained forward, unblinking. *Is he even breathing?* I checked the road again.

"Boyce, listen to me. Can. You. Be. Very. Quiet."

This time when I glanced back the corner of his mouth was twitching in that quirky grin he'd inherited from Hardy.

"Jesus. I get it. Okay. You can be quiet."

"Boy fight, too."

He wasn't grinning anymore.

SO I TOLD HIM what to expect when we got there, which worried me for two reasons. One, I didn't know how much he understood. And two, I didn't have much to tell him. My plan was generic—analyze the situation and take the optimal steps to extract Haley before daylight. Ronnie Panko I was less keen on helping, but I owed him for pointing me toward Haley.

We reached the halfway mark and I considered calling Slaven and Bustamante for backup. Then my phone rang. *Now what?*

"Ted Danger."

"Ted, it's Jenny. I can't find Boy."

"Jenny. You say you can't find Boy?" I glanced at the mirror. Boyce shook his head.

"I locked the doors after you left," she said. "I thought he was inside."

"But he wasn't."

"No. I couldn't sleep. I went to his room. Ted, I'm worried."

"You're worried about Boy." I spoke into the phone but I was talking to Boyce. "It's for you," I told him.

HE CROSSED HIS ARMS and stared out the window.

"He doesn't want to talk to you," I said.

"He's with you?"

"Yes. He stowed away. Scared the shit out of me."

"Bring him back," she said.

"You know there's no time, Jenny."

"He's not ... He's just a boy."

I didn't have an answer for that.

"If there was someplace you could drop him off," she said, "or ..."

"Where. The zoo?"

A strangled laugh. "Sure, take him to the zoo. Right. And if he likes it, tomorrow you can take him to the circus."

"Funny, Jenny."

"Ah shit, Ted. Let me talk to him."

I kept my eyes on the road and offered Boyce my phone. "She needs to talk to you."

After a moment he took it. "What," he said.

She talked for a mile or two, her voice a thin reverberation. First loud, then quieter.

Then silent.

Boyce spoke: "Boy a man."

He handed me the phone.

"Jenny?"

"Keep him safe," she said, her voice flat.

She cut the connection.

Boyce said nothing.

My NEXT CALL WAS outgoing, to Rytt Slaven. My night for waking up women I'd slept with.

Me: "Rytt, I'm getting a premonition about this."

Rytt: "Call the police, Ted."

Me: "Not yet. I might have better luck on my own."

Boy: "What."

Me: "Right. And with my partner, Boyce. And you, if you'll do it."

Rytt: "Who's Boyce?"

Me: "A big ape I picked up south of Miami. For muscle."

Boy: [shakes his head]

Rytt: "Call the police, Ted."

Me: "These goons I'm up against. They may have influence with the police."

Rytt: "They can't stop a nine-one-one call. And it's on record."

Me: "It may come to that. Look, you've got contacts. People in power, who you trust."

Rytt: "Well. Yes, it's possible. It's likely."

Me: "How about this? Get over there as a witness. Officially I'm telling you that I'm bracing an informant tonight. Or this morning. Ronnie Panko. Who asked me to meet him at Gribler Press. That's all true. And I've asked you to observe. If things escalate, call nine-one-one."

Rytt: "I don't know."

Me: "That's not an answer, Rytt. Say no, right now, and go back to sleep. Or drag your ass out of bed and haul it over to Gribler Press."

Rytt: "Such a he-man. You make a girl swoon."

Me: "Yes or no, Rytt."

Rytt: "Fuck it. I'll be there. And I'll add it to your bill."

70 No man's land

WE PARKED NEXT TO a gas station/convenience store on 49th, or 932 (or 103rd—don't ask). Boy waited in the Taurus while I chatted with the clerk. English was not his first language.

I told him I'd driven too long and needed coffee and a stroll before moving on.

"I believe you have been hurt," he said.

I'd forgotten about my face. "Yes, I have a medical appointment at my destination."

"And where is your destination?"

"Not much farther, but I was dozing. Will my vehicle be all right in your lot while I walk? It's a Ford Taurus."

"You are too much worried, my friend," he said. Which meant *yes*, I decided, so I went out and got Boy.

I forgot my coffee.

IN A LONG-BILLED cap, gray hoodie, sunglasses, and harem pants, he could pass for one hundred percent *Homo sapiens*. Especially if you ignored his feet, long and hairy, with toes like sausages.

We hiked up 49th until it elevated for the railway overpass. Then we angled down into no man's land where a retaining wall cut off the cross streets. We hopped the wall (clambered, in my case) and landed at the dead end of our target street. A few doors down, Gribler Press stretched between a single row of parking spaces in front and a vast expanse of rail lines in its backyard.

When we crossed in front of the building—two guys strolling in the wee hours—no alarms went off. No flashlights in our faces, no laser dots on our chests.

In the center parking spot sat a Chevy Impala. Gray. With my DNA and jacket fibers in the trunk, I'd be willing to bet.

WE FOUND RYTT HUNKERED down on a concrete block in the shadow of a dumpster. She stood and gave Boyce the eye.

"You weren't kidding," she said. "This one's got muscle."

"Keep your voice down," I said. "Rytt, Boyce. Boyce, Rytt."

"Hello, Boyce." Rytt held out her hand.

Boyce looked at her eyes and kept his hands in his hoodie.

"Boyce," I said. "Say hello to Rytt."

His nostrils flared. "Talk later."

"Oh my," she said. She lowered her hand.

"Are you ready, Boyce?" I said.

He lifted the corner of his mouth. *Guess that's a yes.*

"You boys do your thing. I'll be watching from here."

"Did you bring your gun?"

"Yes. My little one."

"And your phone?"

"Of course. When should I call nine-one-one?"

"You'll know."

ALTHOUGH DAWN WAS HOURS away, streetlamps and security lights washed a pale glow over the scene. It was not a dark night.

Nor was it stormy, for that matter, and no shots suddenly rang out.

A tangle of greenery at the corner of the Gribler tract gave cover for a nocturnal reconnoiter. We knelt and watched the building.

Boyce touched my arm. "Ted stay. Boy go. Boy go up."

He went.

71 Shadows in the night

I PULLED OUT MY PHONE and found the number Ronnie had called from. It rang eight times.

"Hello?" A whisper.

"Haley?"

"Ted?"

"Yes. We're outside. Are you okay?"

"We're still locked in."

"What's happening? What took you so long to answer?"

"We had the phone wrapped up in these ... things. To keep it quiet. Scarves and feathery things and these little, like nighties. For pictures, I guess. It's ... god, Ted, get me out of here."

"Where's Ronnie?"

"He's asleep."

"Asleep?" *Asleep?*

"He knew where they keep pills in here. In a drawer. To help the ... to help everybody relax when they need to. He's scared. That's how he's dealing with it."

I could relate. "Who else is in the building, Haley?"

"I think two guys. There were two old guys before. Then we heard people talking, and now it's these other two guys. One of them is kind of old. But not old-old."

"So, two guys. The old one, is his face like a shovel?"

"What?"

"Is he short, with a wide forehead and a little pointy chin?"

"He took me to the bathroom. His head's like a big acorn."

"Acorn-head. Okay, good. So what's the layout inside?"

"The what?"

"Layout. Where things are."

"Okay. There's this canopy bed by the wall. It's pink with frilly edges. And there's a cabinet—"

"Hold on. The building layout. Rooms and hallways."

"I don't know all that."

"You're in the studio now, right? So, that's near the front? The back?"

"The middle, toward the back. There's a hallway behind a sitting place, before the machines, and you turn and it's the second door, or maybe there's another one."

BOYCE PUT HIS BIG paw on my shoulder and I almost screamed again.

"Hold on," I told Haley.

"No door on roof," Boyce said. Panting, his eyes bright.

"So there's no way in from the roof?"

"No door on roof."

"Haley, where do you think these guys hang out in there?"

"When the guy took me to the bathroom, the other one was sitting in like an office near the front door."

"Like an office."

"It had glass walls, that didn't go all the way down."

"Okay. I want to separate these guys. Do they have a regular schedule to check on you?"

"I don't know. That acorn-head guy came when I pounded the door. He's a creep."

"A creep."

"He held my arm the whole way to the bathroom and I know he was listening when I peed."

BOYCE KEPT STILL, HIS breathing now silent.

"Soon," I told him.

He nodded.

"Haley, we're coming in. Leave the phone on so I can hear what happens, and call acorn-head again."

"What about the guy who's asleep? Ronnie?"

"Um, let me talk to him."

"Hold on." Clacks and rustling. Her voice in the background. Then in my ear again. "He's not waking up."

"Okay, fuck it. I mean, forget it. If he wakes up, tell him we're coming. To stay out of our way."

"Okay."

"Call acorn-head."

"What should I say?"

"Anything. Just get him away from the entrance."

"Anything."

"Well, don't tell him we're here."

"Right, Ted. Like I'd do that."

"And hide the phone, but leave the line open."

BOYCE RAISED AN EYEBROW.

"Ready?" I said.

He showed me his teeth.

"I'm going to the door," I said. "You stay to the side, out of sight."

A knocking noise from the phone. Pounding.

Haley's voice: "Hey. Hey, somebody!"

Pause.

Haley: "Hey, can somebody come in here?"

More knocking.

Haley: "Can someb—"

A man's voice, indistinct.

Haley: [quieter] "He's here, Ted. He's unlocking the—"

Rustling sounds.

Man's voice: "Who are you talking to?"

Haley: "Him. I'm trying to take a nap and he won't stop snoring."

I stopped listening and raced for the factory. With Boyce my silent shadow.

72 Assault on Gribler

I LEAPT UP THE concrete steps and skidded to the door under the awning. Wrenched the doorknob. Locked. So much for taking them by surprise.

I smoothed my lapels and knocked. Firmly.

On the phone, Haley and acorn-head—it was shovel-face, I knew the voice—continued their muffled dialog.

I knocked again.

The door opened enough to reveal a big slice of face. The wide eyes, the attitude. The altitude. It was the tall young thug, Rusty.

"What are you doing here?" he said. "You're supposed to be getting out of town."

"I'm trying, believe me. But I need my cell phone. It's got my travel documents on it. And credit cards."

"Credit cards?" His brow was furrowed again.

"You know, it's all ones and zeros," I said. "Digital. Give me my phone and I'm out of here."

"How did you find me?"

"My phone, Rusty. The GPS chip. They've all got them now." I didn't know if that was true, but I saw it on a TV show. "Don't you keep up with the technology?"

"Your phone's in your hand."

"Borrowed this one from a friend." I held it out and he opened the door a bit farther. "Look, if—"

"Hold it. Didn't I just beat the bejesus out of you?"

I shrugged. "It didn't take, I guess. No worries. Happens to the best of us."

"I can fix that," he said. He looked over my shoulder. "You alone?"

I smiled my smarmiest. "Just me and my monkey."

"Funny guy. But not for long."

WHEN HE OPENED THE door, I stepped back and said, "Okay, Boyce." Rusty said "What?" and Boyce moved in and swung a shoulder and his arm followed in a big arc. His hand was a blur that clipped Rusty above the ear. Rusty staggered and went down, but didn't stay. He tucked and rolled and sprang back up, his face bloody but beaming, eyes and teeth gleaming.

"It's on, dude!" he said. "Come at me!"

While Boyce kept Rusty busy, I plunged deeper into the factory. Office space to the left and easel displays on the right. Ahead, a lectern facing three rows of folding chairs.

The sitting place.

Beyond the sitting place, the shop floor. *The machines.*

And in between, an alcove. Which I guessed would open to the studio hallway.

My assumption was confirmed when acorn-head popped into the alcove. One look at me—and at Rusty getting pummeled behind me—and he made an *oh-shit* face, U-turned, and disappeared the way he came.

I took the straight-line route—vaulting a bench, skewing the chairs, and toppling the lectern—and got to the alcove in time to see acorn-head twist a set of keys in the lock three doors down, slam through the doorway, and vanish inside. The door had nearly closed when I got to it and kicked with everything I had, smacking it with the flat of my shoe. It flew open with no resistance and I tumbled into the room. And plunged—gracelessly, I admit—onto the floor.

Unlike young Rusty, I did not tuck, roll, and rise up again.

ACROSS THE ROOM, ACORN-HEAD struck a tough-guy pose with one arm around Haley, gripping her above the elbow, while she stood tight-lipped and rigid, trapped in his grasp. In his other hand he held a Western pistol I didn't recognize. It had a plasticized look, and the colors were too primary.

I lifted myself on one elbow. "Come at me, dude."

"Stay down and no one's going to get shot." He shifted the gun between me and Haley. It moved twitchily, as if it had no mass.

"That gun's not going to shoot anybody," Haley said.

"Shut up."

"It's a toy. Cowgirls and Indians."

He tossed it across the room, where it bounced off a plush bear with big black eyes and clattered to the floor.

When I looked back, he was drawing something sleek and slender from his pocket. He wrapped his fist around it and rested his thumb on a silver nodge along the side.

"This," he said, "is not a toy."

He nudged the nodge, and *snick*, a blade flashed, four inches long, closing in on Haley's bare wrist.

I held out a hand. "Be careful with that."

He toggled the switch, retract and thrust. The cutting edge pressed Haley's skin.

"Careful," I said.

"You're right. I wouldn't want to slice her arm open."

He raised the knife to her neck. She closed her eyes and moaned.

"I get it. You're in charge. Just put that away."

"Shut up."

RONNIE GROANED AND STRETCHED on the little bed with the pink canopy and we all looked his way. I considered rushing acorn-head but from my position on the floor he could have filleted Haley into ten paper dolls before I got my feet under me.

However, just because I was impotent (so to speak) didn't mean Boyce was too.

73 Bad news for Boyce

I DIDN'T KNOW WHY Boy chose that particular moment to explode into the room, and I didn't much care. I was just glad to see him.

Acorn-head wasn't. He did an honest-to-god double-take and Boyce was on him, ripping him away from Haley. Boyce fought in silence, without human words or animal cries. Ignoring the flailing knife, he lifted acorn-head by the biceps, flung him to the threadbare carpet, and pounced, slapping and bashing with that same shoulder-rolling maneuver he'd used on Rusty.

The knife hit the carpet and bounced my way and I snagged it, keeping my fingers away from the bloody blade. The weight surprised me. Heavy. I slid the switch and the blade pulsed into the handle.

Nice.

But the blood on the blade worried me.

Haley skirted the tussle on the floor and reached to help me up.

"Come on, Ted. I want to leave now."

A shadow fell across her face and a blast clapped my ears like a blow. Gunshot. I pulled Haley to the floor as Boyce tumbled off acorn-head and lay still.

THE MAN WITH THE gun was talking but I heard nothing but shrieking, like the breedle of a smoke alarm with fresh batteries.

He must have been seventy years old and four hundred pounds, with a face—or what I could see of it behind the beefy slabs of flesh that encased his big round head—that had seen it all and was disgusted by it.

His movements were slow but deliberate. He gestured with his gun, a nine, and in a strangely high voice for a guy that big, told Haley and me to sit on the bed. At least I heard "on the bed" through the din in my ears. The rest I interpolated, using my finely honed detective skills.

So we bypassed acorn-head moaning on the floor, and sat on the canopy bed. I had to scoot Ronnie's legs over. Acorn-head said "Oh, god" and sat up. The shooter walked over to Boy and held his semi-automatic to his head.

And said, "Bang."

Acorn-head said, "Where's my knife?" and I resisted the urge to look at the ceiling and whistle. He patted the floor and began searching under things.

"Look, you guys have made your point," I said. "We're done here. Let's all go home and forget this ever happened."

THE BIG-GUTTED THUG with the gun pulled two kids' chairs from a game table. With a wheeze and a grunt, he squatted on both, settling in like a king on his throne, his legs splayed, claiming his space.

"Yeah, well," he said, "you should have thought of that a week ago."

"Anyway," I said, "the cops could be here soon." I twisted a fingertip in my ear. "That was a loud gunshot."

He nodded. "Hell, I couldn't resist pluggin' that rascal." His laugh trilled in alto range. "And there's no outside walls in this room. Somebody'd have to be right by the building to even hear the shot, and recognize it. And they'd need a reason to get involved. Huh! What are the odds of that?"

Pretty damn good, in actual fact, but I didn't say so. "Still, the sooner you let us leave, the sooner you can clean up the, uh, crime scene and get back to business as usual. We're obviously no longer a threat."

His deep-set eyes narrowed further. "Nobody's going anywhere."

74 Save those tears

ACORN-HEAD WAS ON his knees, peering under the bedskirt. He stuck his head up. "At least not until the truck gets here."

"What truck?" I said.

"The truck of tears, man. The truck of sorrows. And you'll ride that sucker to the end of the line."

"Shut up, Buzz," the gunman said.

So acorn-head had a name. Buzz.

"Why should I?" he said. "I want to see him sweat, after he sicced his monkey on me."

"He's not my monkey."

"Whose monkey is he?"

"He's a federal agent," I said. "It's a new GMO program."

"GMO?"

"Genetically Modified Organism."

Buzz grinned. "So I beat the shit out of a bionic man."

THE GUNMAN WHEEZED AND the chairs creaked beneath him. "Not the way I seen it. More like that GMO-rang-a-tang beat the shit out of you right up till I shot him in the back."

"Ah, hell, Lacy."

"No names."

"What? You said mine."

"Yeah, well, you're more expendable than me."

"Fuck you." Buzz looked him in the eye. "Lacy."

"Goodbye, Buzz." Lacy leveled the gun at Buzz's big forehead. "Bang," he said.

Buzz shook his head. "Christ, don't do that."

HALEY LEANED AGAINST ME. Her quiet sobs trembled the bed.

Lacy curled his lip. "Don't cry, honey," he said. "Save those tears for later. You'll need 'em."

He laughed and something popped and creaked. I thought his chairs were collapsing. Until a pungence breached my nose and seared my throat.

Haley coughed.

"Enough of this," he said. "Buzz, tie these two up and lock them in again. I gotta take a screaming shit."

"That's gross," Haley said.

"You don't know gross, my child. But you're gonna find out."

"Back off," I said.

"Or what? You gonna ride to the rescue?"

Buzz was tying my hands behind my back with a feather boa. *This is a first.*

"Maybe," I said.

"Maybe? Maybe you were laying on the floor when I come in and little girly-girl was helping you up."

Buzz finished my bonds and started on Haley's.

"At least he wasn't asleep," he mumbled.

Lacy: "What's that you say?"

Me: "Were you sleeping, Lacy? Napping instead of supervising?"

Lacy: "Thought these greenhorns could handle things. Truth is, I can't hardly take these all-nighters anymore."

Me: "So who else is here, besides you and Buzz and Rusty?"

Buzz: "Nobody."

Lacy: "Buzz, you are stupider than a sack of stupid."

Buzz: "What?"

Lacy: "Jesus, next you'll tell them about the secret tunnel under the bookcase."

Buzz: "Secret tunnel?"

Lacy: "Come on. I'm gonna pop a hemorrhoid if I don't get to the crapper lickety-split. And I don't trust you in here with these nosy parkers."

On their way out, Lacy, with a delicate anal squeak, released another smidge of gas, and Haley said "Yuck."

The door slammed behind them.

With a jangle of keys, the deadbolt hammered into the jamb.

75 You can say Girl

HALEY WAS STARING AT Boyce, who lay on his side on a throw rug. Knees drawn up, eyes closed, and jaw slack, with a glimmer of teeth. A slick of blood gleamed on his shoulder and snaked through the creases of his neck.

"Is he going to be all right?" Haley said.

"There." I pulled my hands free and tossed the boa aside.

"How'd you do that?"

"I turned my wrists sideways when Buzz was tying them," I told her. "That gave me slack."

I got busy on the half-assed knots binding Haley. *You're a sorry excuse for a villain, Buzz.*

Boyce coughed and his chest rumbled.

"Who is that guy?" Haley said. "Is he going to be all right? He really saved me from that sharp knife."

"His name's Boyce," I said. "They call him Boy. He's—" *What is he?* "He's helping me with the case."

"Kind of cute, isn't he?"

I glanced up from my work. He did have a sweet face.

"If you say so." I untied the last knot.

She pulled her hands free and massaged her wrists. "Thanks. Is he going to be all right?"

Okay, she was going to keep asking until I answered. The words *I'm sure he'll be fine* popped into my head but I bit them back. She hated being patronized.

"I don't know," I said. "He's been shot."

"I know that. I was there, remember?"

BOYCE'S WOUND TURNED OUT to be a left-shoulder through-and-through that oozed blood from both sides. His forearm—same

229

side—bled from a knife wound. Haley ransacked the dresser and brought towels and washcloths for compresses. I secured them with the boas Buzz tied our wrists with. It looked like an amateur job because it was.

Haley had found pajama bottoms, and she looped them around Boyce's neck to support his arm. As she tied the final knot, he opened the big dark marbles of his eyes and stared into her face. She spoke to him, quiet and calm, and adjusted his sling.

He reached out with his good hand and touched her cheek. She didn't flinch.

His lips moved and her neck blossomed cherry red.

"What did you say?" she said.

"Pretty." The corner of his mouth twitched.

Haley leapt to her feet and hurried to the bookcase along the wall.

"Come on, Ted. Help me move this." Her face pulsed in scarlet.

"What? Why?"

"The secret passage. To get out."

"Haley, there is no secret passage," I said. "Lacy was being sarcastic. See, he was mocking Buzz's willingness to provide us with information that would be against their best interest for us to—"

"Cripes, Ted! I know that! But we've got to check, don't we?"

BEFORE I COULD MOVE, Boyce staggered to his feet and shuffled to the bookcase.

"Boy help," he said.

The two of them slid the bookcase along the wall to expose the floor beneath it. They didn't need my help. It was a kid's bookcase, after all.

And of course there was no secret tunnel. I swallowed an *I told you so.*

"Sorry," Boy said. "No way out."

"Oh, that's okay," she said. "Thanks for helping me, Boy. That's your name, right? Boy?"

Boy thumped his chest with his good hand. "Boyce," he said. "You say Boy. I like."

She smiled. "Okay. Boy. I'm Haley." She touched her chest, near her heart. "You can say Girl. I like."

"Girl," he said. He placed his big hand over hers. Too close to second base for my personal comfort level.

"My god, you two, stop it," I said.

They both turned my way and said, "What." Then looked at each other and laughed.

Christ. What next?

Ronnie moaned on the bed, answering my question. I'd forgotten about him.

And then, sirens.

"THANK GOD," HALEY SAID. "The cops. It's finally over."

"Hold on," I said. "The bad guys can hear the sirens too. They might get desperate. Take hostages."

Ronnie, dragged out of dreamland, sat up on his elbows. "What should we do?"

"What you mean *we*, kemosabe?" I said.

He stared at me with wide eyes. "Hey, wait a minute. I'm a victim here too. I got kidnapped too, right? And who found the phone and called you to rescue your niece? And who kept her safe until you—"

"Bullpoop," Haley said. "You took pills and passed out. When Buzzkill pulled a knife on me, Boy's the one who saved me."

Ronnie seemed to notice Boy for the first time.

"What the fuck," he said.

Boy growled deep in his throat. His upper lip quivered.

"What the fuck," Ronnie said again.

"What," Boy said. "What fuck."

"What the fuck!" Ronnie said.

THE SIRENS GREW LOUDER.

"Ronnie," I said. "Pay attention. Help yourself out here."

"What do you mean?"

"You're part of the gang behind all this. Not just the sleazy kiddie pics, which are bad enough, but the whole deal. Human trafficking, child prostitution, murder."

He shook his head. "I never."

"You're an accessory, and the whole gang's going down. We know enough of the players now, and they're going to start rolling over. You need to catch the wave early, while your testimony's still valuable."

"They'll kill me."

"Could be they were going to anyway. From their point of view, the whole thing started to unravel when you spilled your guts to me. Help us out and maybe you'll get witness protection. Relocation. A new identity."

"You promise?"

"No, but I'll put in a word. I owe you for helping me find Haley."

"And if you don't help us," Haley said, "I'll tell them that thing you did before Ted and Boy got here."

"We don't need to talk about that now," he said.

"What?" I said. "Haley, what did he do?"

She shook her head. "I need a Z-Pak just to say it out loud."

"Hey, tell me more about the witness protection program," Ronnie said. "How does that work, anyway?"

"Haley," I said.

"Not now, Ted," she said. "We need to make a plan, right?"

76 Rescue at Gribler

WE SHOVED BLANKETS UNDER the bedspread to look like Ronnie was still there. Haley and I sat on the bed with our hands behind our backs, and Boy lay down on the floor. My fist gripped Buzz's automatic knife, thumb on the trigger.

"Ronnie, grab something to use as a club and wait behind the door in case the wrong person comes through."

"Wrong person?"

"Someone who's not a cop."

"Oh, right." He ran around picking things up and putting them back. Dolls. Stuffed animals. A plastic beach pail.

"What a dope," Haley said.

"Hey, I'm—"

"Quiet," I said. "Someone's coming."

FOOTSTEPS, RUNNING, GETTING LOUDER. Then a jangling at the door. Someone in a hurry, fumbling with keys. Ronnie picked up a classic spin-n-ride toy and lugged it across the room. Sit-n-puke, we called them. Christ. That was wrong on so many levels. But at least it was heavy.

Snap of the deadbolt and the door opened.

Buzz. With a gun. A black semi-automatic. Not a toy.

"The *wrong person*," I said.

"What?" Buzz said.

Ronnie didn't take the hint.

Buzz's gaze landed on Boy. "Who wrapped up the monkey?"

"Did it himself," I said.

"With one hand?"

"With his feet," I said. "Prehensile."

233

"What?"

"In case the *wrong person* comes through the door," I enunciated.

"What? Never mind. The cops—"

HE NEVER FINISHED HIS sentence. He glanced over his shoulder, reacting, I think, to the rasp of steel bearings in a big steel ring as Ronnie got the message at last and swung the whirl-n-hurl at Buzz's head.

Not an ideal weapon. Imprecise. Rounded edges. Not designed for aerodynamic finesse, or power multiplied by leverage.

But it was heavy. And even if it didn't annihilate Buzz, it ruined his aim. The two shots he squeezed off left Haley, Boy, and me unscathed. I leapt across the space between us while he tripped over the spin-n-spew entangling his shins. He got his feet under him but stepped on the spin seat and pitched forward as I tackled from behind. Ronnie was wailing as I crashed on top of Buzz, whose chest cushioned my fall with a *whumpf*. I wrapped my hand around the semi-automatic clenched in his fist.

A croak leaked from his throat and he didn't move. I straddled his back, held his knife to his ear with my free hand, and slid the switch.

THE BLADE DEPLOYED WITH a snap I knew he'd recognize.

"Drop the gun," I said.

"*Kk kk*," he said.

"I'm shot," Ronnie said. "I'm shot."

"Drop the gun." Louder this time.

"I ... can't."

Okay, I had his finger pinned in the trigger guard and wouldn't ease up. As long as I held the slide, the gun wouldn't fire.

Buzz got his breath back. "Ow, man, you're breaking my finger."

Ronnie: "I'm shot. I'm shot in the foot."

Buzz: "You broke a couple ribs too."

Me: "Drop the gun."

Buzz: "I can't! You speak English? Ow."

Ronnie: "Oh god, I'm shot. I. Am. Shot."

Then Haley was there. She knelt beside me with her knees on Buzz's forearm.

"Ow, that hurts," he said.

"Good," she said. "Ted, let go of the gun so Buzz-hole can let go of the gun."

"Ow, god, hurry up. Ow."

Ronnie: "I'm shot."

Me: "Buzz, I'm going to let go, and if you do anything but let go of the gun, I will cut you with your own knife."

Buzz: "Ow-ow-ow. Okay. Ow."

Me: "Haley, when we let go of the gun, take it to the bed. Don't touch the trigger. Don't point it at anybody."

Haley: "Thanks for telling me that, Ted. I was going to skip around and look down the gun hole to count the bullets."

Ronnie: "Am I shot?"

Buzz: "Get off my arm. Ow."

Me: "Okay, Buzz. When I let go, you let go."

Buzz: "Fuck yes. I agree. Fuck."

Haley: "Hey, watch your fucking language. Right, Ted?"

I eased my grip on the gun and felt it slip away.

Haley: "Got it."

She ran back to the bed.

Me: "Don't run with a gun in your hand!"

Ronnie: "You know what? Maybe I'm not shot."

Officer: "Police! Nobody move."

77 In the wind

NOBODY MOVED.

The officer, a broad-shouldered bronze-skinned woman with gelled hair and tinted glasses, held her weapon in a two-handed grip. As she scanned the room, I imagined what she was seeing. A teenage girl on a canopy bed with a semi-automatic pistol. A man with a knife straddling another man on the floor. A third man balancing on one leg and holding his foot. And a hairy guy with a bloody shoulder passed out on a rug, his arm wrapped in pajama bottoms. Plus dolls, toys, kids' furniture—including a frilly pink bed—and a scattering of pastel feather boas.

Officer: "What the fuck."

Buzz: "Ow. He cracked my ribs. Get him off me."

Me: "This guy had a gun."

Haley: "I took it away from him."

Officer: "You took it away from him?"

Ronnie: "I don't think I'm shot after all. The bullet just went through my shoe."

Officer: "Shut up."

Ronnie: "I understand, officer."

Haley, Me, and Buzz: [all talking at once]

Officer: "Everybody shut up. You, girl. Slide away from the gun. Hands where I can see them."

Haley: [slides] "Okay. But Boy needs an ambulance. Boyce. He got shot. He was helping."

Officer: "Soon."

Haley: "Okay."

Officer: [to me] "You. Toss the knife, easy, toward the wall."

Me: "Okay."

Buzz: "Close it first, okay?"

Me: "Okay." [retracts blade]

Officer: "Jesus! Just obey my lawful order if you don't want to get shot!"

Me: "Sorry." [tosses knife]

Officer: "Nice knife, though."

Buzz: "Thanks, Ted."

Me: "Shut up, Buzz."

Officer: "Now. Any other weapons I should know about?"

Ronnie: "Over there. I mean, it's not exactly a weapon. But when that guy came in with a gun, I hit him with that sit-n-shit."

Officer: "I didn't know they made those anymore."

Ronnie: "It's an old one. We just use it for ... oh, never mind."

Second officer: [enters with weapon drawn, looks around] "What the fuck."

WITH EVERYTHING THAT HAD happened, I couldn't believe it was still dark outside.

More police showed up, including plainclothes investigators, and they got the good guys sorted from the bad.

Ronnie was the problem child. He tried to paint himself as a good guy, pointing out that, after all, he (1) was kidnapped—a victim just like Haley, (2) helped with Haley's rescue by notifying me of her whereabouts, and (3) protected us from a man with a gun, armed with only a child's spin-and-vomit toy. He also agreed to help the cops mine his phone for evidence—the phone I had delivered to him earlier, in the studio, along with his wallet. He said I could hang onto his brass knuckles.

The cops took him away. Buzz and Rusty too.

BOY WAS WEAK FROM blood loss. Paramedics started a drip—saline, I suppose, spiked with antibiotics—and transported him to a clinic near his home, where I learned Jenny Axelrod had arranged with Boy's doctor—pediatrician? vet?—for emergency treatment.

Lacy, the giant gunman with gut issues, was in the wind, although his vehicle was found parked nearby. In the living quarters where he'd slept that night, the restroom smelled of fresh fecal matter and one brave tec claimed the toilet seat was still warm.

A swarm of officers—from multiple forces, based on their uniforms—had cleared the building, and the mood swung from high anxiety to business as usual as investigators collected evidence and discussed jurisdiction.

Haley stuck with me, and I didn't blame her.

78 Going hunting

A SOFT-SPOKEN GUY on the young side of middle age with a gold badge and a wrinkled suit—Jacomet, he said his name was—had parked Haley and me in an office near the main entrance. Then he'd answered his cell, frowned at what he was hearing, and charged out of the room, telling us over his shoulder to stick around.

And that's where Rytt caught up with us.

"So you guys are all right," she said.

"Yeah," I said. "It's good you called the cops when you did."

"And you must be Haley. I'm Rytt."

Rytt grabbed a chair next to Haley and at a signal I couldn't see they leaned together and hugged. Haley started crying. She seemed fine before that, but who knows?

WHILE RYTT RUBBED HALEY'S back, I told her what Buzz said about the truck of tears coming for us today.

"What does that mean, *truck of tears*?"

Haley lifted her head. "He called it the *truck of sorrows*."

"That can't be good," I said.

"Are the cops watching for it?" Rytt said.

"More or less. They've moved the obvious police vehicles off the street. But no one thinks it's really coming."

"Did the truck guys get tipped off?"

"Probably." I told her about the heavy-duty bad guy, Lacy. Still at large, so to speak. "He would have called and warned them."

Rytt told me what happened on her end. How she heard the initial shot and called nine-one-one. And notified trusted contacts, to bring the situation to light before anyone buried it.

She also called Navi, who showed up promptly to kick ass and take names.

As RYTT TALKED, HALEY fell asleep in her arms. Poor kid. I'd be exhausted too—except I'd choked down another Adderall. Bam. *I could bench press a four-hundred-pound pedophile and not break a sweat.* A message from my subconscious. *Find Lacy. A seventy-year-old obese man doesn't get far on foot.* Chemicals percolating in my blood said *Get moving!*

"Rytt, can you stay with Haley?"

"Where are you going?"

"If the detective comes back—Jacomet—"

"I know him," she said. "Marvin. Marv Jacomet."

"Tell him I went to the john."

"Where are you really going?"

"Hunting," I said. "For big game."

79   Secret passage

THE FACTORY FLOOR WAS deserted. I nodded to a bored-looking street cop leaning against the wall near a side exit. He nodded back and stretched and I kept moving. The print operation wasn't huge, and I found the small living quarters in the north corner, in the back. The door was open.

Lacy's napping place.

I put my hands in my pockets and stepped inside.

A sharp-edged fluorescent fixture cast a cold hue over the room.

A rumpled single bed, with sheets the color of despair, sagged along one dark-paneled wall. Smooth pale brick defined the remaining walls, from the floor up to four feet, where bubbling plaster—chartreuse, I'd call it—stretched to the dusty ceiling.

At right angles to the bed stood a worn dresser trimmed with a pale doily, upon which sat, like garage sale rejects, an electric clock, an incandescent lamp, and a chipped ashtray. A galvanized table clad in metal strap and angle iron supported a tower of appliances—a compact refrigerator, a microwave, and, balanced on top, a hotplate with a tangled cord. Convenient but precarious.

Dominating the next wall, a six-foot bookshelf with little on the shelves. Plastic flatware, a blanket, a stack of thin towels.

Scuffed concrete floor, with a greasy rag rug by the bed.

Lastly, a door into a narrow bathroom with a sink that hadn't glistened in thirty years, a big commode with a black split seat, and a dank shower with a crusty curtain.

Nowhere for Lacy to hide. The police already looked.

But we've got to check, don't we? My subconscious again,

in Haley's voice this time. *We've got to check.*

She said it just before she and Boy moved the studio bookshelf.

My subconscious switched to Lacy's tenor. *Jesus, next you'll tell them about the secret tunnel under the bookcase.*

I studied the arc of scratches on the floor.

Could Lacy have been that stupid? Or was he just showing off?

THE BOOKCASE SWUNG OUT freely to reveal a four-foot access door—not under the bookcase, but in the wall behind it—with a recessed lever. Ronnie's brass knuckles were still in my jacket so I slipped my fingers through the rings. Not much of a weapon against a gun, but it's all I had, and I doubted Lacy would be lurking like a plus-size boogieman.

The handle swiveled down with smooth resistance and the door swung inward on silent hinges. The concrete floor advanced into darkness.

No sounds. No smells. No premonitions.

I ducked sideways and, before stepping through, noticed two canvas straps the right height for pulling the bookcase to the wall. But I wasn't concerned with covering my tracks. Plus, until I could find a light switch—or a flashlight, or a lantern, or a flaming torch in a wall sconce—I needed the light.

I stepped across the threshold.

80   Into the abyss

THE LONG SPACE PARALLELED the bathroom wall on my right. My eyes adjusted, and dusty pipe and conduit faded into view. Junction boxes and meters and valves. As I advanced, the concrete floor changed to metal grate, rusted but feeling secure.

Ahead, the grate fell away to nothingness. I edged closer and peered down into a rectangle of darkness. A rung-ladder, red with rust except where feet and hands had worn the metal smooth, extended downward and dissolved into blackness.

But not total blackness.

A pumpkin down there. It disappeared when I looked straight at it, but faded in when I shifted my eyes.

I gripped the edge of the grate and swung onto the ladder. Looked down. My night vision sharpened.

Not a pumpkin.

A big round head.

And a big round body attached to it. And neither one moving.

I descended.

LACY HAD APPARENTLY ARRIVED at the bottom faster than he expected. Maybe he slipped from the ladder, or misread the distance and stepped into empty space.

Maybe he had a heart attack.

Maybe he was pushed.

Maybe it's all a dream and now I wake up.

THE END

OKAY, ENOUGH OF THAT.

I leaned my face close to Lacy's and held my breath.

Not a trace of respiration, not a sound, not a stirring. I rested my ear on his massive chest, which neither rose nor fell. Not a hint of a murmur nor a flutter of a beat. His fingers were cold, with no pulse in his pulpous wrist.

Darkness all around, the only light leaching from the rectangle of murk above.

Where had Lacy been headed? I turned a slow three-sixty. Concrete block walls on three sides, but in the fourth direction, under the bedroom, nothingness. Shifting my eyes revealed no details in the inky void.

A voice in my head: *Don't go there.* So I didn't.

Next step. Inform the police.

And with Lacy dead, the truck of sorrows might still be on its way to Gribler Press.

IN THE DARKNESS, THE opening bars of a song—something about an *eye, and the sky.* I looked up. Nothing looked back.

The music repeated. A ringtone, from beneath the cooling corpse. Which I could not budge.

I braced myself to grip the folds in his shirt but the fabric was too tight. I dug my fingers under his neck and pulled. No joy.

Eye, and the sky. Definitely.

New strategy. I wrapped both hands around his wrist and tugged, but his arm remained pinned. I yanked. Nothing. I planted a foot on his torso and heaved. Put my back into it.

He belched, I screamed (but in a manly timbre, to be sure), and his arm shifted, revealing a glow leaking from the edge of a face-down cell phone.

I wrenched the phone from under him, cringing as the screen scraped the floor. The music ended with a critical tone and a blinding message. *One missed call.*

81 Ted's charade

DETECTIVE MARVIN JACOMET DIDN'T smile when I slipped back into the office where he'd told Haley and me to wait. He was pacing the far side of the room holding his cell to his ear.

"Yes, sir," he said. "That's right, sir."

His rubber-soled shoes traced a silent path on the linoleum.

Haley cut her eyes in my direction and Rytt shook her head. They were sitting where I'd left them. I took my seat.

"Where have you been, Ted?" Rytt said.

Jacomet swiveled our way, eyebrows up. "Yes, sir," he said. "I will."

"I tracked down Lacy," I told Rytt.

"Yes, sir," Jacomet said. He slipped his phone into a jacket pocket.

"The fat guy?" Rytt said.

Jacomet shot me a glare. "Don't run off like that. This is a complicated scene, and you have no official capacity here."

"I found Lacy," I said.

"The fat man?"

"Deceased at the bottom of a rung-ladder."

"The evil bastard who shot Boy," Haley said.

Speak of the devil and he shall appear. In this case, as a quiver in my pocket and the *eye and the sky.* His ringtone interrupted our conversation.

"What's that?" Jacomet said.

"*I, in disguise,*" Rytt said. "Right?"

"What's that mean?" Haley said.

"Lacy's phone," I said. "I can do his voice."

Jacomet blinked. Nodded. "Do it."

I LOOKED AT THE screen and saw my problem. I didn't know how to answer the damn thing. Haley *tsk*ed and reached over and swiped. Easy.

The best defense is a good offense, to coin a phrase, so I stretched my neck and squealed, "What the hell. Can't a man crap in peace?"

Jacomet moved into my space to listen in. But nobody replied. Until someone did.

"You are calling me about the furniture, Mr. Flan." A man's voice, obscured behind a layer of white noise like blowing wind, rolling tires, and rumbling engine.

"No, you called me," I said.

"You are calling me before, Mr. Flan," the man said. "About the furniture. Two pieces, you say, for the transportation." A clipped inflection in his voice. Unfamiliar.

"It's all good," I said. Jacomet scowled and I shrugged.

"This Mr. Flan?"

"Who the fuck else?" I said. "Look, that fucking roach wagon gave me the bloody runs, and I'm not in the mood to chat. Just get your ass in here. What's your ETA?"

"ETA?" Jacomet mouthed.

"ETA?" the phone voice said.

"What time you gonna get here?"

Silence. Maybe I blew it.

"Just get your ass in here," I said again.

No one answered.

82 Exotic

NAVI GAVE HALEY AND me a lift to the gas station in her little Asian coupe—Haley sitting sideways in the back—then she took off. No one had towed Jenny's Taurus. And parked next to it, backed in, was Wally's tangerine mini-ride, tinged a weary brown under the mercury-vapor lamp buzzing above it. And there was Wally behind the wheel, his gaunt face haunting the shadows.

When he saw Haley, he unfolded from his go-kart, and she crossed the lot and reached for him. He wrapped her in his big arms and they didn't seem to say much.

It's rude to stare. Okay.

So I crossed my arms and leaned on a post and looked away, noticing how the morning sky bled blue over the night—a silent duel at dawn, day versus dark, with dark fated to melt away into vanishing shadows. Traffic building, most drivers still running with headlights, their illuminations fading as the advancing sun made its power known.

Headlights burning yellow, white, or blue, revealing each vehicle's rank on the technology spectrum. Two extremes. An exotic supercar, sleek, low, and wine red, with beams like blue lasers, leapt into the lot and stopped dead by the entrance doors. And not long after, a ramshackle moving van—nearly an antique, the cargo space bulging over the cab, with two yellow headlights, one flickering—lurched over the apron and rocked to a halt by the gas pumps.

SOMETHING ABOUT THIS TIME of day, black sky blurring to blue, streetlights blinking off, made me want to crawl into bed for a while and come back later. Behind me, the buzzing stopped, and when I turned, the security light had shut down, fading behind the fogged lens.

Wally and Haley stood apart now, Haley touching Wally's forearm, talking. He shook his head, looked down, and wiped a hand across his face.

I yawned until my jawbone popped. "Hey, you two! I'm getting coffee. Want anything?"

They didn't.

I MET THE GUY from the exotic as he exited the store. He looked too young for a car that ended in *ghini* or *gatti*.

"That yours?" I said.

He grinned but didn't stop to chat. "For the next twenty minutes," he said.

I watched as he disappeared behind the high-gloss near-horizontal windshield. The engine started with a precision rumble. He waited while the driver from the decrepit van walked across the lot behind him. The van driver looked down, pulling cash from a wallet chained to his belt.

I held the door for the van driver. He was two decades older than the kid in the supercar, with a slack face and coveralls that smelled like sour milk. The door closed behind him and I waited in the morning zephyrs to clear my lungs. The block lettering on the van read *Moving experts, Furniture and Goods* with no phone number or web address. A movement in the cab caught my eye. Another laborer, at first glance. But he sat tall in the seat, with a righteous expression—a slender guy, dark hair and eyes—and my mind said, *He's the supervisor, the boss.*

Just my subconscious making assumptions.

THE DOOR OPENED BEHIND me and the van driver stepped out, toting a pastry bag and two coffees. Sticks of jerky sprouted from his pocket like a dead bouquet with the flowers lopped off.

I stepped into the chill of the store. A fragrance of fresh coffee, stale donuts, and lingering BO. The coffee called to me, but a sudden twinge sent me hustling to the restrooms in the back.

Not to put too fine a point on it, I was sitting with my pants down, half dozing, when someone called my name. I pulled myself together, washed up, and heard it again.

Haley's voice.

I opened the door with a paper towel and dropped it behind me. Haley stood by the magazine rack near the entrance, scanning the store. The restroom door clicked shut and she spun in my direction.

"Ted. Ted, we've got to stop Grandpa!"

83 Hunk of iron

THE TAURUS FIRED RIGHT up and even laid rubber across the parking lot. Haley pointed me left, east, and I cut the wheel and opened her up. The old sedan wasn't a precision-tuned supercar, but by god it was an honest hunk of American iron, not some computerized go-kart, and it would haul us from point A to point B without any bullshit.

Except for one thing. *Where is point B?*

"All right," I said. "What happened?"

"Grandpa saw that old moving truck."

"The moving van? It said, uh, *Furniture and something* on the side?"

Oh shit. *Furniture.* The truck-of-tears guy on Lacy's phone. He wanted to confirm the furniture transport. Two pieces. Must have meant Haley and Ronnie.

"The truck of tears," I said.

"The truck of sorrows," Haley said. "Maybe they're going to the printing place after all."

"Maybe."

We were fast approaching the last turnoff before the road elevated to span the tracks. I pulled the Taurus to the shoulder. If the truck was headed for Gribler Press, it would have taken a right and then skirted a couple of blocks to the printing plant.

"I don't see them," I said. "They knew I wasn't Lacy. And if I'm wrong, the cops at Gribler can handle it."

"Good," Haley said. "I don't want to go near that place."

"But check the cross streets as we go by. For the moving van, or Wally's car."

I eased back onto 49th.

"What color was the van?" Haley said.

250

"It was a pale ... greenish gray? Brownish? Kind of misty."

"If you say so."

I drove the Taurus at a crawl, and we scanned the side streets as the pavement rose. Nothing.

"Now what?" Haley said.

I NAILED THE PEDAL to the floor.

"We'll head this way," I said. "Try to catch them."

The railway overpass gave us a good view.

"Ted, is that—"

"I see him. Maybe."

Far ahead, where details faded in the haze, a glint of neon orange. Turning left.

Sparse traffic, the road mostly ours. I spurred the Taurus onward.

THEN I BACKED OFF.

"Ted, don't slow down."

"Wait a minute, Haley. You're safe now. We need to hang back. Let the police deal with it."

"We can't tell the cops where they are if we lose them, Ted." She banged her fist on the dashboard. "Get this piece of poop moving!"

"Jesus, Haley." She had a point. I mashed the pedal, and the Taurus leapt ahead. Closing the gap, but not fast enough. "Where exactly did he turn?"

"At the red thing way up there. Like a big sign, or—"

"I don't see it. Look, it's time to let the cops know."

She already had her phone out, whipping her fingers across the screen.

"Wait a minute," I said. "Where'd you get your phone? I thought the guys who grabbed you took it."

She didn't look up. "They did. But when the police guy—"

"Jacomet."

"—took us to that office room, my phone was laying on a thing behind the desk. When he went out I put it in my pocket."

251

"It could be evidence."

She gave me a blank look.

"Okay. You calling nine-one-one?"

"Looking at the map first."

"Hold on." I dug out Jacomet's card and passed it to Haley without slowing down. "Call Jacomet. He'll know what we're talking about."

THE CALL WENT THROUGH faster than I expected.

"Hi," she said. "It's Haley. I talked to you before."

His answer sounded terse.

"My grandpa is following the truck. The one that was coming to get me? And me and Ted are following my grandpa."

She listened.

"We're in the car now," she said, "following my grandpa. He's following the truck. It's like an old moving van."

She nodded. "He wants to talk to you, Ted."

I held her phone in my right hand and drove with my left as I updated Jacomet. He didn't sound happy.

"Are you certain this is the van we want?" he said. "What did Mr. Landis tell you?"

"He talked to Haley," I said. "Let me ask her."

I asked her.

"We were talking and he was staring at that truck," she said. "At the gas pumps. Then he said *I can't believe it.*"

"What else?"

I was holding the phone toward her so Jacomet could hear.

"This is where he turned," she said. "That red building."

"What?"

"Ted, grandpa turned left at this street. Go left. Left!"

I hit my signal, slammed the brakes, and skidded into the turn from the through lane, across the path of a looming minivan. Cutting it close. Luckily, the driver wasn't on the phone like I was and hit his brakes in time. His face was three big circles. Two eyes and a mouth.

Mine must have looked the same to him.

84 Drive faster

THE TAURUS SLEWED OUT of the turn, but I'd dropped the phone. Haley found it under my seat.

"Be careful," she said. "I don't want to scratch it."

"Christ, Haley. I ... Yeah, okay, sure."

"—going on?" Jacomet was saying.

"We're headed, uh, north. What's the street, Haley?"

"There's a sign." She tracked it as we flew by. "It said twenty-seven."

"Twenty-seven," I said.

"Just twenty-seven?" Jacomet said.

"Just twenty-seven?" I said.

"We're going too fast. There's another one. Slow down."

I slowed.

"Okay. It says N, W, twenty-seven, A, V."

"Northwest Twenty-Seventh Avenue," I said.

"I heard her," Jacomet said. "Are you still behind the truck?"

"Haley, do you see the truck? Or your Granddad?"

She raised against her seatbelt. "The road curves a little. Go faster."

I went faster. "Jacomet, you still there?" No answer. "Hello?"

"Hold on," he said.

I blew past two motorbikes and a Honda Civic.

"I've got a map," Jacomet said, "and dispatch is on the line. Tell me why you think this is the truck we're looking for."

"Haley? What did your granddad say before he followed the truck?"

"He said *You stay with Ted.*"

253

"What did he say *about the truck*?"

"He said I should tell you the priest is in the truck, and you'd know what he meant."

The signal ahead turned yellow, then red. A car and a pickup blocked the northbound lanes. The left turn lane was wide open, so I swerved into it.

"Why are you turning?" Haley said.

Cross traffic cleared. "I'm not." I ran the red and veered into a through lane.

"I didn't get that," Jacomet said.

"I'm not turning," I said.

"No, *about the truck*."

"Haley," I said. "Could he have said DePriest? It's a name. Dee. Priest."

"I guess."

"So DePriest was driving the van," Jacomet said.

"No," I said. "He was riding shotgun. Waiting in the cab."

"Why would DePriest ride in the transport truck? He's a big cheese."

"Could be he had something personal in mind for Ronnie Panko. Who the hell knows?"

"And how does the truck of tears just happen to refuel at a gas station where you and Wally are people-watching?"

"A rhetorical question and a moot point. That truck could be filled with prisoners and slaves, and you can help us track it down, or not." I pressed the accelerator and scanned the lanes ahead.

"Okay, Danger," Jacomet said. "Give me a description of the truck and the Landis vehicle. We'll find them. You can back off."

JACOMET STAYED ON THE line while Haley and I gave him what we could. But we didn't back off.

"Ted," Haley said. "There's a truck up there."

"Where?"

"Way past the McDonald's."

"You see Wally's car behind it?"

"No."

The truck's color was vague, its shape ambiguous.

"Jacomet, we might have eyes on the truck," I said. No answer. "Jacomet."

"Yeah, I'm here."

"We see the truck ahead. I'm going to catch it."

"Don't kill yourself, Danger. Or Haley. That's an order."

85 Brush-off

I LOCKED ONTO THE suspect truck, dodged traffic, and blew another red light, earning me a honk or two. In my focus on the road ahead, I failed to notice the nondescript exit sweeping off to the right. And the little orange car trailing in the smoky exhaust of a dilapidated moving van.

BUT HALEY AND I both looked straight ahead. Our suspect truck grew larger as the gap narrowed. Larger and less likely. We pulled next to it at a railroad crossing where an endless train rambled by. Bad news. This was not the truck we were looking for. It was a plumber's van. Wrong shape and size. The color just as ugly, though.

"False alarm," I told Jacomet.

He grunted.

"Look," I said. "Have your suspects told you where the van was going next?"

"Nobody's passing out schedules. But I'd say it's headed north. Orlando, or Jacksonville, then Atlanta and points beyond. Or along the coast—Savannah to Charleston."

The passing railcars had picked up speed, and beat a hypnotic rhythm of wheels on steel. The last time I'd slept was ... when? I focused on Jacomet's words to make sense of them.

"So they told you Atlanta or Charleston," I said.

"Not explicitly. That's based on intelligence gathered prior to last night's events."

"So where's the van now?" I said. "Exactly. Your best guess."

"I'd say they fueled up and headed for I-95 North or the Florida Turnpike. There's ... It looks like a ramp off Twenty-

Seventh Avenue that ... Hold on. Where are you right now, Ted?"

So I was *Ted* now, not *Danger*. "Still on Twenty-Seventh. Stopped at a train crossing."

"Yeah, I hear it. Okay, let me check the map. You're ... Hold on, Ted. Wait a minute."

I held on. The train cars kept coming. Haley asked me what Jacomet said, so I gave her the gist.

"We should have caught up to Wally and the van before this," I told her. "They must have turned off."

"So now what?"

I TRIED TO ASSESS our mess but my brain was fried. Then Jacomet was back.

"Ted, thanks for the tips. You can definitely back off. Take Haley home. Rest up. We'll be in touch."

"What happened? Did you find them?"

"Stay back and let us do our job. We'll talk later."

"Wait. What about I-95 or the Turnpike? A ramp off Twenty-Seventh, right?"

"Keep safe, Ted." He was gone.

"What did he say, Ted?"

I handed her the phone. "He brushed us off. Something happened."

"What? To Grandpa?"

"I don't know. He said there's a ramp off Twenty-Seventh. Leads to I-95 North or the Florida Turnpike. Can you find it on your phone map?"

She was already looking. "Okay. Here's the train crossing. We're right here."

CL-CLACK CL-CLACK CL-CLACK. CAR after car after car. And no caboose in sight. I closed my eyes and kept them that way.

"What are we looking for?" Haley said. "Ninety-five?"

It took a moment for her question to register. "I-95 or the Florida Turnpike," I said. "They run north, like to Georgia."

"Okay. Here's ninety-five. Here's ... It says *Florida's Turnpike.*"

"Sounds right."

"Okay. Here's the curve-off place from twenty-seven. We went right past it. Go back, Ted. U-turn."

I forced my eyes open as the caboose passed by. The gates lifted. We crossed the tracks, pulled a U-turn, and headed back.

"How far?" I said.

"Get in the left lane. I don't know if we can get on it from here."

"Yeah, okay. You're right. No access from this side."

"Can you turn anyway?"

"The median's too high."

"There's a gap up there," she said.

"That's a crosswalk."

"Well, I don't see anybody cross-walking it."

I SLOWED TO HANG a left.

"Wait," Haley said. "Cops."

A police black-and-white screamed our way in the oncoming lane, full lights and siren. It veered onto the exit Haley and I wanted.

"Ted, is that for Grandpa?"

"Could be in a hurry for donuts."

A deadpan look. "Follow that cop."

86 Crash

WE TURNED LEFT AT the crosswalk without incident, unless you count the dirty look from a guy in a northbound pickup. I powered the Taurus up the exit and merged onto Florida 9. According to Haley's map, we would hit a tangle of ramps up ahead where Florida 9 splices into I-95 and the Turnpike.

We never got that far.

IN SPITE OF THE morning sun through the windshield, I could pick out the accident details.

The scene looked fresh. No ambulance or fire equipment yet. The moving van lay on its side near the road, in a wide grassy area that stretched to a stand of low trees and brush. Wally's car was pulled over farther ahead, but we didn't see Wally. On this side of the van, a police cruiser blocked the right lane, lights flashing. A heavyweight cop stood nearby, directing traffic into the left lane. Closer to the wreck, another cruiser, both doors open.

I PULLED OVER BEFORE we got close enough to deal with the cop.

"Stay in the car, Haley," I said.

She squinted in the sun. "Okay, Ted."

I took two steps and turned around. "I mean it. You've been through enough. Stay here until I get back."

She shaded her eyes. "I'll be fine."

"If anybody messes with you, scream. Honk the horn."

"Go find Grandpa, Ted."

I got my badge out, not that it means much, and headed for the accident scene.

259

A SLENDER ARM, BARE and tan, rested on the driver's sill of a Volvo wagon in the break-down lane. Glossy plum fingernails tapped a rhythm on the mirror. The arm was attached to a woman in a floral sundress. When I paused by the window, the nails stopped tapping, but music in the car kept playing. Lyrics in a language I didn't recognize.

I flashed her my badge.

"You a cop?"

"Detective. Did you see what happened?"

"May I?" She reached for my badge and I handed it over.

A canine head, bear-size and drizzling ropes of drool, emerged from the back window with a show of teeth and a bark like a thunderclap. I stepped back.

"Mars!" she said. "Mind your manners."

The big guy, Mars, turned around once in the backseat, rocking the Volvo, and lay down.

"I saw it happen," she said. "That little twee car cut off the truck, and the truck swerved and tilted. Then it swerved the other way and jostled off the road and fell over. And the back door popped open."

"Did you see—"

"Can you take my name and contact me later? I need to get Mars to school." She was staring through the windshield, shading her eyes.

"If you could wait a—"

"Holy Moses," she said. "It's people."

87 Here be alligators

WITH THE MOVING VAN on its side, the vertical doors in the rear became horizontal. The bottom door rested on the grass like a ramp.

Two women emerged duckwalking from the truck, followed by a third on hands and knees, bloodied and bowed. Their dusty faces blinked in the daylight. All three stood and lurched across the grassy berm, hotfooting it for the trees and scrub fifty feet away.

Fifty feet away, where a girl ran, dashing, leaping onto the chain-link fence separating the right-of-way from the trees, a girl in dusky shorts and tank top, black hair flying, sockless in gray sneakers that might once have been white, reaching the top, tumbling over in a tangle of long legs and dark locks, losing a shoe that bounced into the weeds, flashing a pale arch and grimy heel as she fled into the landscape.

Then sirens, lots of them, closing fast, as a caravan of responders barreled down the far side of Route 9, a big engine in front, its nose diving as it slowed for the U-turn. And more cruisers, and an ambulance or two, all running hot, lights and sirens, approaching from behind. Mars started barking and I said "Someone will get to you" to the woman with the plum fingernails, and I sprinted for the chunk of fence where the girl with one shoe had vanished into the brush.

IT TOOK ME LONGER than her to scale the fence—the pop of a seam, a quick slash of pain—and I levered myself over the top and fell, twisting an ankle. I tested my weight on it, ignored the twinge, and ran again, not sure where I was going.

Just away from the highway.

Twists and turns through the pathless wood revealed not a glimpse of the girl. I stopped to listen. My breath rasped. Behind, sirens. Fewer now, and buffered by trees and distance. Above, breeze through branches. Bird chatter. My breathing quieted. Ahead, to the left, rustling. I stepped in that direction.

A scream, sharp and shrill. Cut off in an instant.

I advanced, footsteps damped by the forest floor.

BUT NOT REALLY A forest, I learned, as I glimpsed the dapple of water through the trees. A lake, with its far side not far at all. And there, skirting the wooded area, was the girl with one shoe, looking tatty and small as she stumbled forward in the grip of the tall man from the moving van—the man with the long forehead, now dashed with blood, the thinning hair in tonicked disarray, and the dapper salt-and-pepper Van Dyke. He clenched her arm at the elbow, dragging her along the shoreline toward a network of streets and homes near the lake's south end. She held a hand to her face.

I STEPPED FROM THE shadows into the morning sun.

"DePriest," I said. "DePriest!"

He spun, his arm around the girl's neck, her head at a bad angle. His black eyes raked across the woods and then met mine.

"It is you," he said. "If I had my blade I would cut you for what you have done."

"It's over, Papa," I said. "The woods are crawling with cops. Helicopters are coming."

"You lie, fool. Go back to wherever you came, and perhaps I release the girl unharmed." He leaned back, lifting her to her toes. Her face darkened.

"She'll slow you down, DePriest." I took a step toward him.

"Stop," he said, "or I disjoin the head like the *gallina*."

"You're strangling her."

His nostrils flared. "*¡Cállate, cabrón!* Do not dare to—"

Two pops from the highway, *pop pop*, muted but

unmistakable. Gunfire.

DePriest glared and the words formed on my lips, *They're coming for you, Papa, they're closing in*, but I bit them back. I sensed he would snap the girl's neck without a qualm, if only to humble me. So I waited. Said nothing.

This is how Ted Danger reacts in a crisis? By waiting?

It was the right decision, this time.

DePriest spat, took three paces to the lake, and thrust the girl into the water, where she stumbled and fell and churned away from him.

"Here be alligators," DePriest said. "Perhaps you can remove *la perrita dulce* from their waters before they dine on her *cuerpecito sabroso*." He laughed as the child thrashed and gagged. "Or leave her to the alligators and come to me, *idiota*, and I will dissect you with only *las uñas y dientes*."

When I didn't take the bait, he lifted his chin, hissed in my direction, and took off. I considered giving chase, but my ankle was throbbing. And the girl—the sweet puppy, DePriest had called her—didn't deserve to be alligator chow, right?

Besides, DePriest probably *could* dissect me with his teeth and nails.

SO I WADED INTO the lake as the girl splashed and choked and dog-paddled. I didn't see any alligators. But in Florida waters lurk beasts of nightmares. And the surface definitely rippled, very near us. Maybe just the wind.

Or a school of piranhas.

I grabbed the girl's bony shoulders. "Stand. It's shallow."

She stood but bared her teeth. "*No me toque.*"

"Got it. Don't touch you." I turned and slogged for dry land. "But *cuidado*. Watch for alligators."

"Alligators?"

"That's right," I said. "Uh, *los cocodrilos*."

"I come with you," she said. "*Espera.*"

She beat me to shore.

88 Me llamo Marisol

"MY NAME IS TED," I told her.

The morning was warm, but her thin frame shivered under her sopping tank top. I took off my sport jacket, which had stayed above the waterline, mostly, and draped it over her shoulders. She didn't run, but she looked like she wanted to.

She slipped her arms through the jacket and pushed the sleeves to her elbows.

"What's your name," I said. "*Tu llama.*"

"*Nombre,*" she said. "*Me llamo Marisol.*"

"Marisol? Wait. Do they call you Sol? Soledad? A middle name? A nickname?"

She frowned. "My name is Marisol."

"Okay, Marisol. Let's go to the ambulance. *Vamos a la ambulancia. Al doctor.*"

"The truck is there." She touched her throat. "*El camión de las lágrimas.* It is evil."

"The evil man is gone. The evil man went there." I pointed toward the homes. "*Allí fue el hombre malo.*"

We looked in the direction DePriest had fled. Didn't see him.

"The ambulance is this way," I said. "And the police, the detectives. They can help you get back to your family. *Tu familia.*"

"Okay." She walked beside me in her bare feet, her other shoe lost in the lake muck, hands deep in my jacket pockets. "You are police?"

"No, I'm a private detective."

When we entered the woods, Marisol promptly stepped into a patch of spiky pods and let out a wail. The little bastards

264

were scattered all over.

So I scooped her up and hauled her out of there. She weighed nearly nothing and the extra pressure on my ankle seemed, bizarrely, to sooth it.

She hid her face and sobbed.

A COMPACT STAND OF trees—soft-needle pines—provided a sheltered place to stop. I lowered Marisol onto a cushion of mulchy plant stuff and squatted beside her.

She wiped her face with the back of her hand. Her cheek bore the mark of DePriest, where he had smacked her into silence. "Why you stop?"

"The gunshots," I said. "You know, *pop pop*. The gun."

"I hear no gun," she said.

"No. No more gunshots. Let's wait a few minutes to make sure."

She scooted away. "I no wait with you."

"Fair enough," I said. "I'll go ahead, and see if it's safe. You wait here. It's not far. *Muy cerca. Usted puede, um, esperar. Esperar aquí.*"

She nodded. "I am very hungry."

"Soon. Just wait here."

I left her leaning against a tree trunk, picking at her feet.

THE CHAIN-LINK FENCE emerged from the trees, with the grass margin and highway just beyond. Firefighters, police, paramedics, civilians, victims. Giving help or getting it. No one taking cover.

A cop I'd seen at Gribler was crossing the open grass.

"Officer," I said. "Excuse me."

Her hand drifted toward her sidearm. "Step forward."

I did it. "I'm a private detective. And I found a girl from the truck who crossed the fence. She's okay, but she's hungry and barefoot and she stepped in nettles."

"Where is she?"

"Waiting in the trees. I'll bring her out, if it's safe."

The officer nodded. "There's an opening in the fence, that way." She pointed.

"So the gunfire's over."

"Seems to be, yeah," she said. "The perp in the truck got off a couple shots before he gave it up."

"Anybody hurt?"

"One civilian," she said.

Oh, shit. Wally. "An older gentleman? Tall, slender?"

"You'll need to speak with the detectives."

"And listen," I said. "The other perp, the one in charge. We saw him on the far side of the trees, by the lake. Headed for the houses."

She reached for her radio.

MARISOL WAS GONE.

This is the right place. Here's the flat spot where she sat.

"Marisol. Marisol!"

I turned three hundred and sixty degrees, slowly. And there she was.

"I hide," she said.

"Good. We can go now."

She didn't move.

"I can carry you," I said.

She stepped back. "*No me toque.* Please. I follow."

ON THE WAY SHE told me about a girl called Soledad.

89 Good news bad news

THE COP MET US at the fence, along with a paramedic and a Latina woman from a social services organization whose name I didn't catch. The Latina spoke to Marisol *en español* and I understood roughly *nada*.

"She's hungry," I told the woman. I made sure the paramedic heard me too.

The social worker glanced my way, said "Of course," and I was dismissed.

Marisol touched my arm. "*Espere, señor* Ted."

She handed me my sport jacket and I shrugged it on. She looked away.

The paramedic wrapped a big green blanket around the kid, making her look smaller and more tragic.

THE COP LED ME to a makeshift interview space in the shade of a fire engine. Plainclothes cops were questioning witnesses and coordinating activity with the uniforms. In the center of the storm, Marvin Jacomet.

He shook his head. "It's you."

"Funny, that's what DePriest said when I showed up."

"Not so funny. Where exactly did you see DePriest?"

I pointed. "Other side of the trees, by the lake. He had a hostage, Marisol—she's with a paramedic over thataway—and when he heard the shots, he shoved her in the water and vamoosed."

"Show me." He opened his tablet to an overhead view.

"About here. He was wearing a charcoal shirt with silver collar tips, and khakis. And he ran toward this street."

"When?"

"Like I said, when the shots were fired."

Jacomet keyed his radio and mobilized his forces. I slipped away and headed back to the Taurus. A helicopter buzzed low, kicked up a grit storm, and angled toward the lake, its clamor shouting my name.

IT WAS LIKE A good news/bad news joke, but it wasn't funny. Not at first.

Bad news: *I don't see Haley in the car. God, will this morning ever end?*

Good news: *There she is, stretched out in the back. Poor kid must be exhausted.*

Bad news: *What the hell! Is that blood on her shirt? Oh, Jesus. The cop said a civilian was hurt in the gunfire.*

Good news: *No way! If she'd been shot, paramedics would have rushed her to the hospital.*

Bad news: *But that's definitely blood, and she's definitely unconscious. Haley!* "Haley!"

Good news: *She's waking up. She was just asleep.*

I swung the back door wide and squatted by the opening. "Haley, what happened? Are you hurt?"

"Ted," she said. "Grandpa got shot."

SHE STARTED CRYING AND I tried to get up but thumped my head on the Taurus roofline and pitched forward, banging my shins on the sill. Which jolted me back up.

At which point I whacked my head again. And fell onto my wounded shins.

"Ow, fuck," I said.

Haley giggled. "Watch your language, Ted."

"Not funny," I said, but she only laughed harder. My chest loosened and I laughed too, until my gut hurt and my eyes overflowed. Fatigue, relief, hysteria. Haley scooted over, and I climbed in. And finally got a grip.

THE TAURUS WINDOWS STOOD wide open, and breezes dried my face. Lake water in my pants smelled swampy.

Haley hiccupped.

"Tell me what happened," I said.

"I got out to find Grandpa, after you left me all by myself."

"Before the shooting or after?"

"Before."

"I told you to wait in the car."

"I saw you go over the fence after that girl."

"You should have stayed in the car, Haley."

"Do you want to hear this or not?" She crossed her arms.

"Okay. I want to hear it."

"Well, the cops told me to stay back, but I kept going when they weren't looking."

"Jesus. You kept going."

"I looked all over. And then I heard him yelling. He was yelling in the truck window. Like he climbed the front part, and he was going in. And then bang. Like a gun sound."

"A shot. Two shots."

"I don't know. Grandpa fell and landed on the dirt. I helped him get up and run, but he fell down again and people came and took him on a carrier. The truck man put his gun down and climbed out. Everybody pointed their guns but nobody shot him. An ambulance lady said I was okay, it was just Grandpa's blood, so I came back to the car and fell asleep."

Incredible. "I wonder how Wally's doing."

"Ambulance lady said she'd seen worse."

THE SUN WASN'T IN our eyes anymore. Clouds had moved in. With rain. Hard rain.

We scrambled to close the windows, but everything inside steamed up. Through the fogged windshield, figures dashed across the scene, arms folded over their heads. The air in the Taurus percolated with the splattering drone of rain on the roof and the wet-metal smell of blood, sweat, and exhaustion.

My god, what a morning.

90 Tell me everything

I DON'T REMEMBER MUCH about the trip to Wally and Reva's place until I parked in the rutted drive and Haley and I dragged ourselves into the house.

Nicki and Reva were all over Haley, bloody shirt and all, and they wanted to know exactly what happened to Wally. Haley told the story while I listened from the sofa with my eyes closed. When I woke up later, I was still on the sofa, but flat on my back with my shoes off and a blanket over me.

It was dark.

A TRAPEZOID OF MOONLIGHT painted the floor between the sofa and rocking chair, illuminating the toes of two shabby slippers that fifty years ago might have been fuzzy. Reva was sitting motionless in the dark.

Then the rocker creaked. "You're awake," she said.

"Forty percent." I tried to sit up and nearly made it.

"I should thank you for returning Haley to us, but you endangered her life. She might have been the one shot."

I couldn't deny it. "What time is it?"

"Nighttime. Morning. Sometimes I don't sleep."

"How is Wally?"

"The old fool," she said.

"How is he?"

"Don't get old, Ted. You get helpless. Useless. Everything hurts. Life loses whatever meaning it once had. You wish you'd never been born."

"How is Wally?" I couldn't see her expression in the dark, but her head shook slowly.

"Bad news about Wally," she said. "He missed his chance

to go out a hero. He'll survive."

"That's harsh, Reva." My empty stomach let out a moan. *Feed me.*

"The old fool."

"You said that. Um, Reva, do you have any food in the house?"

She sighed. "Sure, Ted. There's pudding cups. Tapioca mostly, and vanilla. Cottage cheese, the low-fat kind. We like to mix it with applesauce. Chicken broth—low sodium. And saltines. Potato bread. It makes good toast, with oleo. Might be some coconut yogurt left. Or lemon. Help yourself."

"Maybe later." Was she jerking my chain? She was a morose old lady, for sure, but with a sense of humor. "Now it's time to tell me about Nicki. The adoption. Everything."

She didn't speak. I thought she'd dozed off.

A snuffle in the darkness. Then another. She was crying. "Did you ever lose a child, Ted? A daughter?"

OUT OF NOWHERE, HEAT and sadness flowed through me. *Odd. Must be empathy for Reva.*

"No," I said. My voice echoed in my ears.

91 Her name was Terry

REVA TOOK A SHAKY breath. "We didn't have children—Wally and me—until we were in our thirties. We were selfish. Too much in love with loving each other. You know, Wally was quite the man. The strapping lifeguard. Fit. And physical." She cleared her throat. "But you want to know about Nicki."

"Take your time, Reva."

"Eventually, our fires of youth cooled, and we had a baby. A girl. Theresa Nicole Landis. We called her Terry."

"Not Nicki? From Nicole?"

"We called her Terry," she said. "I loved her. Wally loved her. Fiercely. Nothing could harm our Terry. Nothing. The power of our love kept her safe. She grew up strong, invincible."

"And talented," I said.

"Yes. She painted. That was her in the photograph I showed you. The morning you arrived."

"I remember. She's right-handed."

"Wally taught her all he knew. In the water, she was like a sleek ocean mammal. A dolphin. A mermaid. Strong and autonomous."

"Autonomous," I said.

Silence settled in and stayed a while.

HER WORDS CAME QUICKLY then, as if she couldn't bear to hear them. "There came a storm in nineteen and eighty-one. A hurricane. It was August. We survived the winds and the rain and the surge. But afterward, the ocean was agitated. Unsettled on the surface, and underneath ..."

"Underneath?" I said.

"Unpredictable. Treacherous. Everybody knew, *stay out of*

272

the water. Wally knew. I knew. And Terry knew. She *knew*. We were safe. We had survived."

The window was a picture of night, but in a lighter shade. Illusion, or was dawn coming?

"But someone didn't know," she said. "A tourist. From your state, Ted. Ohio. Why does someone from Ohio come to Florida in August, Ted? Why?"

"Tell me what happened, Reva."

"Terry was a strong swimmer. And she loved her dad. Revered him. So there she was, on the beach with friends, walking the shoreline after the storm, safe and alive, when this woman from Ohio gets into trouble. She'd gone out too far, and the ocean had her."

"Terry," I said. "Your daughter. She went into the water."

"Just like that. Terry went into the water. I wasn't there. Wally wasn't there. We didn't need to be with her every moment, Ted. She was smart, she was strong. She was with her friends. She was fourteen, and she wasn't my little girl anymore. My baby. I could see the lovely strong woman she would become. She was fourteen, Ted. Fourteen."

She leaned forward and her face materialized in the moonlight. An apparition. A specter with blind eyes peering wide at what I could not imagine.

"Fourteen," she said, her voice rising, lilting, "and into the cauldron she cast herself to save the life of a foolish stranger."

She sat back and was silent.

"A brave girl," I said.

Her voice flattened. "Her friends told us she got sucked under quickly."

Jesus. How do you respond to that?

"As if the sea were angry that she would challenge it so casually," she said. "And like the great shark taking its prey, it wrenched her down to silence and death."

She took a breath, slow and deep.

"At least I hope it was like that. Fast, like turning off a

light. Young and alive one moment, in the thrill of the rescue. Then gone in an instant. A terrible instant, but blessedly brief. And then nothingness."

"They never recovered her body?"

"No one ever saw her again, Ted. But I knew she was gone. Wally though, he's another story. He drives to the beach, and sits, and watches. Watching the girls, he says. But somewhere deep, he's watching for her. He's watching for Terry to step out of the surf and walk across the sand, smiling that smile. Asking if he's proud."

Finally her voice broke.

"Asking if her daddy is proud of his brave little girl."

SHE DIDN'T SAY ANYTHING for a while and I didn't hear her crying. Maybe she was all cried out.

"What about the tourist?" I said.

"The ocean spit her out. Safe as houses. Terry's friends told her what happened, and she claimed she saw nothing. Had to rush off, hurry back to Ohio. Or Iowa. I don't ... It doesn't matter. She left and no one knew her name and no one ever will, and Terry was dead."

"I'm sorry."

"I was dead too, in a way. There's still a dead spot, right here."

I'd closed my eyes again, and her story erased the small dark living room. The sea roiled before my eyes, under a scouring sky, its ancient song in my ears.

My head drooped and I forced it up. But I let my eyes rest a while longer.

"Then what?" I said. "Now tell me about Nicki."

MY VOICE SOUNDED DISTANT. I was fading. I cracked my eyes and a whisper of daylight had crept into the room.

"Nicki saved me, Ted," she said. "She saved the part of me that hadn't died."

"What happened?"

I wanted to know but my eyes shut down and the ocean whispered my name.

"That's Wally's story to tell," she might have said, but the patterns in her words eluded me, and the sirens of the sea held sway.

I MUST HAVE SLEPT two or three more hours. For a total of ... well, once around the clock—the analog kind, if you remember those—and then some. Reva's chair was empty, and a tepid daylight replaced the darkness. A sleeping vibe to the house.

I didn't leave a note. If they wanted me, they knew my number.

The pieces were coming together, and I needed solitude, to ponder my next moves. So I hopped into the Taurus and headed for El Toro to plan the denouement.

With one crucial stop along the way, at my favorite café on Atlantic Boulevard, where I devoured three days of calories in one sitting. A sublime experience, except for the tang of body odor polluting the breakfast aromas. I sniffed, and I myself was ground zero.

A lot had happened since my last shower.

A whack on the head, a ride in a trunk, a beating.

A knife fight, a rescue, a descent into darkness.

A high-speed chase, a gangster face-off.

And a plunge through a pond of (alleged) alligators and (potential) piranhas.

Just another day in the life of Ted Danger, Private Eye.

MY FEAST LEFT ME satiated.

And awake and alert, thanks to double-digit sleep at Reva's and a quart of coffee with breakfast. And, not much later, a hot shower and fresh clothes in my room at El Toro.

A life-is-good morning. Even when Ronnie Panko's brass knuckles turned up missing—*probably lying at the bottom of Alligator Lake*—my day was looking up.

Until I asked Kendria Spitler the gender of her baby.

92 *Ted castigated*

IN EL TORO'S COURTYARD, Kendria Spitler's baby slept in a high-tech stroller with black hardware. A canopy top and mesh sides protected the kid from the hit-or-miss sun and the warm Florida gusts that stirred the pool waters. Kendria, in a modest cover-up with narrow stripes, lounged by the stroller on a towel-covered chaise. I hadn't seen her since the drama in my room the night Haley arrived.

"Hi, Kendria," I said. "How's the baby."

"Ted," she said. "Ted Danger. The baby's ... the baby is fine."

"Boy or girl? I never got a chance to ask." I eased into an open chaise next to Kendria. "May I join you?"

She closed the book she was reading, a lime-green paperback with a palm tree on the cover. "No you may not. You're a bit creepy for me."

"Sorry. I'll—"

"Never mind. Stay where you are. I was just going in."

SHE STOOD AND FOLDED her towel. "I need to feed the baby soon, and sometimes"—her eyes narrowed—"I feel people gawking if I do it out here."

"Look, Kendria. I don't mean to be creepy. Let me know what I've done and I'll make it right."

She tucked her book into a stroller pocket. "Maybe you're a great guy, but I'm uneasy with you around my baby. So, no questions, no answers. I'm trusting my intuition, and I'm asking you to respect that."

I held up my hands. "Of course," I said. "I just—"

"Don't tell me *I just*. This isn't a discussion! Not everybody has to ... never mind."

As she pushed the stroller away, the sea breeze folded the stripes of her wispy cover-up into odd moiré patterns. She turned and caught me staring. Jesus. I looked away, my face burning.

What the hell!

Voices chattered in my head. *What's her problem? You were just being friendly. If she wasn't in the mood to talk, she could have said so without the attack!*

And the opposing view. *What, the tough-guy detective gets butthurt when someone doesn't want to chat? Poor baby! Don't be so thin-skinned, for god's sake. Man up!*

I BROODED BY THE pool, craving the solitude of my room but choosing to stay clear of Kendria.

A nice day, which ticked me off—*thunder would suit me better*—and the spiral descended. Across the courtyard, José María rolled a vacuum cleaner down the walk and carried a small appliance with a dangling cord. He nodded and I waved but didn't speak. He was a known smartass, and I wasn't in the mood.

I pulled out my phone and called Tru.

She can be a smartass too, but with her I didn't mind.

93 Mother Teresa on a unicorn

HER VOICE ON THE phone felt like home.

"Tru," I said. "How are things in Dayton?"

"Boring, Ted. Nobody calls, nobody knocks. I've even organized your bookshelf."

"By title, author, or subject?"

"By color," she said. "How's the case coming?"

I told her.

TRU'S A GOOD LISTENER. Asks good questions. But she got quiet when I told her about Terry.

"Tru? Still there?"

"Must have been hard on Reva," she said. "Losing her child like that."

"I guess."

"I mean, can you imagine?"

Didn't Reva ask me the same thing? "No, I'm lucky not to have kids. Too much potential for pain."

"I hope you don't mean it, Ted. That's bye-bye to the human race, if people think that way."

"I'm just one guy who's not cut out to be a dad. It's not extinction."

Her voice softened. "You might be a good father."

"You think? Moms creep out when I'm around their kids. I'm the anti-father." I told her about my run-in with Kendria.

"That really bothers you, doesn't it?"

"Well, yeah. Where was she coming from? Does she see something I can't see myself? And the hypnotist, Lucille Cruiset. She told me to get my head examined. And Reva, says you get old, you wish you'd never been born. Jeez, is that what

278

it boils down to? Life's a bitch and then you don't die?"

"Ted, how much vacation time do I have?"

"What?"

"Listen to me, Ted. That woman who didn't want you near her baby—maybe the dirtbag daddy has your eyes. Who knows? You skeeve her out and she's got to listen to her gut, the hell with your delicate sensibilities. Stop obsessing. Get back to the case. Figure out what to do next. Right now."

But I wouldn't drop it. "And the girl from the truck. Marisol. She was afraid of me."

"Duh! That kid just escaped from the terror van! Used and abused by every man she ever met. And you expect her to treat you like Christ the Savior in a Superman suit?"

"Well, when you put it that way."

"What other way makes sense, Ted?"

"No, it makes sense. She was afraid. But still, she ..."

"She what?"

"She wasn't who I thought she was."

"What? Who did you think she was, Ted? Little Anastasia?"

THAT MADE ME LAUGH.

"Yeah, that'd make a better story. But no, seriously. The other night a waiter overheard me talking to Wally about missing girls, and he told me about this Latina girl. Soledad. And when Marisol ran for the fence, I thought, *that's her. It's Soledad. And I'm going to save her.* As if life's a big puzzle and all the pieces snap together and make sense."

"Yeah," she said, "like a bad novel, when everything's this amazing coincidence."

"But listen. When she said her name was Marisol, I asked if people called her Sol, or Soledad, and she said no. Later, though, she told me there *was* a girl named Soledad."

"In the moving van?"

"No. Another place, before that. She got sick and they took her away."

"So we don't know her situation," she said. "Soledad's."

"No. But I still thought I could save her. Is that crazy?"

"Yes, Ted, that's crazy. It's crazy to think you can save every child. It's crazy to think every mom will love you, and beg you to hold her baby. Your job puts you in all kinds of sordid situations and you can't expect everyone to treat you like Mother Teresa on a unicorn with rainbow farts."

"All right. Enough talk therapy," I said. "What did you say about vacation time?"

"You feel any better, Ted? Tell me the truth."

"Yes. I feel better."

"Good, because here's my sad story. I'm going crazy here. It's damp and gray. I'm bored, and my skin is starving for tropical sunshine."

"Vitamin D?"

"Well, Jason and I aren't exactly getting along."

"Gee, that's too bad."

"Right. So what am I saying, Ted? You going to make me beg?"

"TRU, COULD YOU COME to Florida and help me wrap up the case? I could use a fresh pair of eyes on—"

"Talked me into it. I'll forward the phone, hang a sign on the door, and hop a jet south."

A small plane passed overhead pulling a message in block letters. I couldn't read it from my angle. And it didn't matter.

"Call me with your flight info," I said.

"Okay. Hold on. Um, got it."

"What?"

"Confirmed. I'll be there tomorrow." She gave me her ETA. "And while I'm down there, we need to talk."

We need to talk?

And just when I was feeling better, too.

94 Fill me in

NOTES AND CHARTS AND doodles. Over the next three hours I filled half a legal pad with known facts, gut feelings, checklists, and mind maps. Planned my next steps. One task I kept putting off finally rose to the top and I made the call.

"Hey, Jenny. It's Ted."

"Ted. About time you called. I miss my car."

"Of course," I said. "How's Boyce?"

"The doc released him. His arm's in a sling, but he's home."

"He did good, Jenny."

"I know. But he's … he seems depressed."

THE LITTLE PULSE OF pleasure in my chest surprised me. *Misery loves company.*

"There's a lot of that going around," I said. "Believe me."

"Would you … Do you want to talk to him?"

"Sure. Put him on."

I waited, and didn't mind. The ocean breeze, on the warm side of comfortable, staggered through my room at El Toro and rustled my pages.

"He doesn't want to talk," she said.

"That's okay. He's a man of action, not words."

"Man of action? He doesn't know what he is."

"Who does, Jenny? Like I said, lot of that going around."

"He needs a girlfriend."

"I don't doubt it. You should have seen him flirting with my client's daughter Haley. Awkward to watch, but cute."

"Okay, he's going upstairs. I've embarrassed him."

"Typical stepmom," I said.

"Right. Typical."

281

I HEARD THE SMILE in her voice.

"So, Ted, when are you bringing my car back?"

"Is tomorrow okay? My associate, Gertrude Hart, is coming to town and she can drive my rental to your place and pick me up."

"Why don't you come down early? You can wow me with your latest triumphs. Fill me in, so to speak."

"I don't know about that, Jenny. You and I can get pretty, uh, volatile when we're together."

"Whatever can you mean, Ted?"

"I mean, blood where there shouldn't be any, and a nasty pain I never want to suffer again."

"What doesn't kill you makes you stronger, Mr. Danger."

"I'm strong enough, then."

"Coward."

"That's as may be. But look, if you really want to know about the whole deal with the photograph and all—"

"Yes. I do."

"Okay. I've got an idea to wrap things up. I'm going to get all the players together on Virginia Key. That's the eye of the storm. And I'd love you and Boy to come."

"You mean like a picnic?"

"Sure, a picnic."

"Count us in. I'd love a break from this place. And, Ted?"

"Yeah?"

"I need my car."

"Tomorrow, Jenny."

"Put gas in it too."

"Sure."

"Fill 'er up, big boy."

"Yes, ma'am."

Yikes.

95 Wake up the dogs

PROPPED UP IN A hospital bed, Wally still wore that defiant go-to-hell look. But it was sixty percent more intense with a ripe hematoma swamping his left eye.

"What happened to your face, Wally?" I said.

"Ted!" Tru said. "That's rude."

Wally waved his hand. "Got banged up falling off the truck cab." He gave Tru a smile, but his damaged face made it a leer. "Who's this?" he said.

"Wally, this is Trudy Hart, my associate, just down from Dayton. Tru, Wally Landis, crime-fighter."

Wally snorted and touched his side. "Don't make me laugh, gumshoe. I been shot, you know."

"How bad?"

"Could be worse. Nicked my ... well, never you mind."

"Are you in much pain?" Tru said.

"I'm okay, thanks for asking," he said. "Say, girl. How old are you, if you don't mind telling an old man?"

"Why do you want to know?"

"Wally's a connoisseur of the female form," I said. "He ogles by the shore all day."

"I can answer for myself, Danger." He turned his attention to Tru. "I'm a people-watcher, and I won't deny it. Old habit from my lifeguard days. But something about you tickles my curiosity. We haven't met before, have we? Your face ..."

TRU SHOOK HER HEAD. "I don't see how that's possible."

"Really, Wally?" I said. *"Haven't we met somewhere before? What next? Do you come here often? What's your sign?"*

Wally cocked his head at me and said nothing.

Tru was more vocal. "Honestly, Ted. You can be a real asshole sometimes."

"She makes a lot of sense," Wally said.

"All right, all right. Listen, Wally, you feel up to talking?"

"What about?"

"About the past. About Nicki."

He looked out the window.

"Do you want me to leave?" Tru said.

When he turned back, his eyes were glistening. "Stay." His lips twisted. "If you leave me alone with this smartass bastard, I might beat the tar out of him."

THE ROOM WAS CRAMPED—not like the ones on TV, where the family, in-laws, and classmates from grades one through infinity can visit, with a buffet lunch and a brass band.

But Tru found a low stool that she rolled to Wally's bedside, where she sat and promptly took his hand. Incredible.

I leaned back in a cushioned chair. It fell open into a cot.

"What do you want to know, Ted?" Wally said.

I folded the cot back into a chair, but it collapsed into a crooked ottoman. Tru stared and Wally shook his head.

"Okay, then," I said. I perched on the chair from hell and pulled out my notebook. "First I'll tell you what Reva said."

"Reva's a fine gal," Wally said. "But her memory gets iffy."

"She told me you sit and watch the ocean, Wally. Like the first day I met you."

"Guilty as charged."

"And she told me what the ocean took from you. Took and never gave back."

HE SQUEEZED TRU'S HAND. "Terry," he said.

"Yes," I said. "Terry."

"Reva told you she never came back, did she?"

I nodded, and his expression warmed, with a melancholy glow behind his eyes.

"Wait," I said. "She survived?"

"They never found her body," he said. "She could be alive somewhere."

"But she never came back to you."

"Well, Ted, that's true, in a way. But then there's Nicki." The smile in his eyes came out of hiding.

"I asked Reva about Nicki," I said. "She said it's your story to tell."

He looked down. "For a long time, we haven't talked about it. Too dangerous. Might still be."

HIS LIPS THINNED AND a muscle flexed in his jaw.

"Life's dangerous," I said. "Maybe it's time to come clean. For Nicki."

He turned to Tru. "What do you think? Is it better to let sleeping dogs lie?"

She blinked. "Secrets have their purpose. But a time comes when the truth needs to be told." She looked me in the eye. "Too many secrets between parents and their children, for too long ... It's not right."

No one spoke. A phone rang down the hall and someone answered it.

Light glinted in Tru's eyes. Then she smiled at Wally. "Wake up the sleeping dogs," she said, "and risk the bite."

Wally closed his eyes and nodded.

A chime sounded somewhere, its meaning a mystery.

"All right." He looked at the ceiling and breathed deep. "Let me tell you about Nicki."

96 It can't be her

"I DIDN'T KNOW WHAT to expect," Wally said. "Beach patrol called me at home, my day off. They needed help. Tornado'd touched down on Virginia Key, and people were banged up. I knew about the nudists out there, and that made it worse, in my mind—being naked in a tornado."

"When was this?" I said.

"This was 1983. In March. We still lived in Miami, and—"

"So Terry was gone two years by then."

"Not quite," he said. "We weren't over it, but we'd gone numb. Accepting misery as the normal state of things."

"You didn't expect her to walk out of the surf anymore."

"Can't say, Ted. Sometimes I still think she might." He took a breath or two. "That particular day, Reva was at the hospital, Two Saints. But she had me working in Terry's old room. Turning it into a sewing room. I was replacing an outlet. We hadn't really changed anything since ..."

Tru got Wally back on track. "What did you do when you got the call?"

"Well, I hauled ass to Virginia Key. Had this '73 Harvester with a window that slipped down when you hit a bump, on the passenger side. We had rain on and off that day, and I was worried about the window. Crazy, right?"

"What did you find when you got there?" I said.

"Not a lot of carnage, thank god. The sand was smoothed over, like the footprints were leveled off. And the ocean had a slow-motion look. Like the calm before the storm, only this time, afterwards."

"What about Nicki?"

"Didn't see her at first. Clumps of people here and there,

commiserating. Paramedics working on injuries. Couple guys buzzing around on four-wheelers. And I thought about Terry, and the storm that killed her. I mean, here were all these survivors. Why couldn't she have survived too?"

NOBODY ANSWERED HIS QUESTION.

"Anyway, there was no time to dwell on it. I looked for somebody in charge, make myself useful, and then ... then I needed help myself."

"What happened?" Tru said.

"My heart slammed around in my chest and my breath stuck in my throat. There was a girl. Could have sworn it was Terry. She was sitting on the sand with a towel around her, facing the sea, and there was something about the tilt of her head, her shoulders, the way she tucked her knees up and hugged them."

"It was Nicki, right?" I said.

"I got closer and she didn't look up. I couldn't see her face and I'm thinking, *it can't be her*, but still. Crazy things happen. Maybe she had what's-it-called, amnesia, and she's been with a foster family, or ... I don't know what. But I got closer and she turned and I saw her face and I saw the tears and I asked her if she was all right and she looked at me and said *My daddy*. First words she ever spoke to me. *My daddy*, she said. *I lost my daddy*. And I swear my heart just about cracked in two."

"Jesus," Tru said.

WALLY RAN HIS FINGERS under his eyes. Wiped his hands on the sheets.

"Yeah," he said. "Jesus."

"So you knew by then she wasn't Terry," I said.

"When she looked at me and said *My daddy*, it was like it didn't matter. A bigger thing was going on. Like the more I knew she *wasn't* Terry, the more she really *was*, in a crazy way. Like something between us made our paths cross, pulled us together."

Tru nodded as if she knew what the hell he meant. My face must not have shown the same encouragement.

"Does that sound a little off base to you, Ted?" Wally said. "A grown man feeling that way?"

"Maybe," I said. "This case has me sensitive to stuff like that."

Tru shook her head. "Come on, Ted. Haven't you ever felt a connection like that? Maybe to a girl you know, who's not a relative?"

"Well, Ronnie Panko kept calling Haley my niece," I said. "And she's not a relative."

"But does she feel like a niece to you?" Tru said.

"No, not really. Maybe."

"So you've never met anyone and thought, *Hey, you know what? She could almost be my daughter.*" She looked at each of my eyes. Left, right, left, right, et cetera.

A shiver crept across my shoulders.

"What does this have to do with Nicki?" I said. "Can we get back to that, Tru? Okay with you, Wally?"

BUT WALLY WAS STARING at Tru. His eyes narrowed. "My god. That's why your face is familiar. I do believe—"

Tru shook her head and Wally laughed.

"Hey, Ted," he said. "How's your scalp feeling? Your noggin. The old coconut."

"What?"

"Been hit over the head with anything lately?"

"Well, yeah," I said. "When I got kidnapped and thrown in the back of a Chevy. But what's—"

"Nothing, Ted," Tru said. "Forget it. Wally, let's get back to your story."

He ran a finger and thumb across his lips and winked at Tru. "Okay. Now, where was I?"

97 Smooth operator

WALLY TOLD US THE girl didn't seem badly hurt, but he got her to a paramedic for first aid and a ride to the hospital. "The paramedic," he said. "I've told you about him. It was Pablo DePriest."

"Were you worried about him examining the girl?" I said. "It was Nicki, right?"

"Yeah," he said. "No, I wasn't worried. Pablo wasn't into child sex, that I was aware of. He'd flirt around with the teenage girls, the older ones, mostly, and maybe take it too far once in a while, but he didn't force anything, far as I know, and he didn't mess with the real young ones."

"Quite the gentleman," Tru said.

Wally ignored the sarcasm. "I suppose so, like you might call Don Juan a gentleman. More like a smooth operator." He closed his eyes and touched his forehead wound. "Where was I?"

"Virginia Key," I said. "DePriest and Nicki."

"Okay. She told us her name was Nicole LaFuze—Nicki— and her dad was Jack LaFuze, and she'd lost him in the storm. Pablo asked me if I realized who we had in the wagon. Jack LaFuze was the son of the Snow Queen, Nellmary LaFuze, the Queen of Cocaine in Miami. That made Nicki her granddaughter."

SO FAR, WALLY'S STORY tallied with Ronnie Panko's.

"So how did you and Reva end up with Nicki?" I said.

"Well, day of the storm, we didn't know what happened to Nicki's dad. But nobody saw him after the twister hit, so as time went by, it seemed like as not he was dead. And that day on

Virginia Key, Nicki latched onto me like somebody she could trust, and wanted me to ride to the hospital with her. Most victims got transported to Mercy, but I convinced Pablo to take us to Two Saints."

"Where your wife was working," Tru said.

"Yeah. When I walked in with Nicki she turned white as this sheet. Fell against the wall and near fainted. I mean, it was pitiful, because I knew how she felt. But it was funny too."

"So Reva thought the girl was Terry," Tru said. "Right?"

"More I got to know Nicki," he said, "the more I knew she wasn't the tough and fearless girl our Terry had been. But I could imagine how Terry might have changed, if she'd survived being swallowed up by the ocean. Maybe she'd have been just like Nicki. A little scared and mixed up. A girl who needs her mom and dad more than she used to."

"So when Reva saw her the first time," Tru said, "did she think it was Terry?"

"God, yes. Bowled her over. But she was like me. When she realized it wasn't Terry, it didn't matter."

"How did you come to adopt her, then?" I said.

He pursed his lips. "I'm worn out, but I'll give you the gist. Turned out Jack LaFuze was gone, like I said. Death by tornado. He'd split from his momma, the drug queen, because she'd murdered his wife, Nicki's mother. They say she wanted Nicki dead too."

I played dumb. "Nicki's mother died?"

"Yeah. Didn't I tell you? Her dad was all she had, till the twister got him."

"And this Snow Queen, she had Nicki's mother killed?"

"The Snow Queen was crazy. Psycho. What's the word? When you don't feel somebody's pain?"

"Psychopath," I said.

"I already said psycho."

"Sociopath," Tru said.

"That's it," he said. "And paranoid too. Except people really were out to get her. She killed people like bugs. Other gangsters. Cops. Employees she got bored with. She didn't care. The streets of Miami flowed red."

NOT THE LOW-PROFILE picture I got from Panko.

"The story I heard eventually," Wally said, "was she wanted Jack in her drug business. But he was a little simpleminded, for one thing. That's a whole 'nother story I'm too tired to tell. And second, the violence put him off. Then the car bomb killed his wife. Sheer luck Nicki wasn't in the car too. After that, Jack had nothing to do with Nellmary."

"And she stopped gunning for Nicki?" Tru said.

"About that time, the old Snow Queen's evil ways came back to haunt her. Everybody wanted her dead. Suppliers, police, her own people. She was too unstable. Vola-tile."

"What's your point?" I said.

"Point is, she was a marked woman. Near bought the farm a couple times here in Miami. Finally hightailed it to god-knows-where. Six months later, she was dead. Somewhere in South America."

"She had her own problems," Tru said.

"Exactly right."

"So you were able to adopt her," I said. "Nicki."

Wally leaned back and closed his eyes. "Well, it wasn't that simple. But Reva had a friend from college. Guy friend. This was before she got her nursing degree. Turned out he was the psychologist who came into Two Saints and worked with Nicki right after she was admitted."

HIS VOICE WEAKENED. WORDS came more slowly. "Fred Madison was his name, and ... she and Fred were an item at one time ... before I came along and put an end to that."

"Madam Fernando," I said.

He didn't react.

I leaned in. "Madam Fernando."

98 Proof of concept

WALLY TWITCHED AND OPENED his eyes. "To make a long story longer," he said, "Fred—"

"Madam Fernando," I said.

"Right. But he was still Fred back then. Fred Madison. He had connections with the county records folks, and a soft spot for Reva. He knew she needed someone like Nicki in her life, after Terry drowned. Fred was always, you know, sensitive about what people needed."

"Intuitive," Tru said.

"Yeah, intuition. So he told us what he'd do, to slide the paperwork through. Camouflage Nicki's tie to the Snow Queen—you know, a misspelling here and there, a folder stuck in the wrong drawer." He shrugged. "In case someone came looking for a revenge kill or whatever. And *Vi-ola*, Reva and I would have a daughter again."

"*Voilà*," Tru said.

"I don't understand what that has to do with Papa DePriest and Gribler Press," I said. "What's the connection?"

Wally sighed. "I'm tired. Can we talk later?"

"Sure," I said, "but give me the short version. Get it off your chest, Wally."

"Okay." He ran a hand across his mouth. "Fred couldn't make it work."

"Why not?"

He shrugged his good shoulder. "Files were moving to computer programs or some shit. Backups and duplicate records. Fred's connections couldn't control it."

"So what happened?"

"I made the mistake of telling Pablo. How we tried to

grease the skids on the adoption, and hide Nicki's past, and it didn't work. He was very interested. Wanted the who, what, where, when, and why. And *how*, especially."

"So what? What did he do with the information?"

"Everything. He knew how to find the right people in the right places. How to win them over to his way of thinking."

"How did he know that? And why would he care, anyway?"

"Pablo was a bright guy. Saw the potential. He knew plenty of people who needed their records, let's say, revised a little. Dates changed. Histories cleaned up. And they would owe him. Nicki was a trial run."

"A test case," Tru said.

"Proof of concept," I said.

Wally nodded. "He kept things small and simpatico, at first. Like he was helping people abused by the system. Humanitarian stuff. He used soft soap and bribery to get the records changed. Cutting the red tape, for the little guy."

"Magnanimous," I said.

"Time went by, he sweetened his carrots and sharpened his sticks. Dirtier changes, but they paid better. Over the years, he's built up his own network in jurisdictions all around here."

"And that worries you?"

"Sure. He's got friends in low places and high. And he won't let anybody threaten his seat on the throne. You found out firsthand, Ted. And so did Haley."

"His operation's blown now," I said. "He's on the run."

"You don't know Pablo. He never forgets, and he never forgives. As long as he's alive, we watch our backs."

"Tell me more about how—"

"Uncle," he said.

"What?"

"Uncle. Enough." His eyes closed again. "Let an old man rest."

"What happened with Nicki?" I said. "Just—"

"Ted," Tru said. "Let an old man rest."

WALLY SMILED BUT DIDN'T open his eyes.

"Derish Flin," he said.

"What? What about Derish Flin?"

"Derish Flin happened to Nicki," he said. "Talk to Flin. Now go."

"Okay, but first—"

"You heard the man. Out."

A NURSE NO BIGGER than Tru but two generations older had marched in and barked the order. She wore violet scrubs and carried an electronic clipboard. It looked complicated.

She sidled up to Wally, who was suddenly bright-eyed.

"You two may step out," she said, "while I tend to Mr. Landis."

"Wally," I said. "Do you know this woman?"

He winked at her. "Don't worry. This lovely lady's not a gangster. Although she does have a sadistic streak."

"Don't start with me," she said.

99 Shut up and listen

LEAVING WALLY TO FLIRT with his nurse, we navigated half a dozen corridors to get to the parking garage. I wrangled the Taurus down a tight ramp and steered into blinding late-morning sunshine. The day wasn't blistering yet, but it was hot.

Wally had said *Talk to Flin*. And I intended to. But first things first.

"That fucking Wally," I said.

"So he likes to chat women up," Tru said. "Who cares?"

"I'm not talking about that." I gave her the address of the lot where my rental was towed the night I got shanghaied, and she keyed it in. "I'm talking about this case. The job Nicki Vavul hired me to do."

"Find the man in the photograph."

"Exactly. And who was the first person I showed the picture to? The first damn person."

"Um, you went to the Landis house to show it to Reva."

"But she's blind, and she sent me to the beach. And then who did I show the picture to, the very first day I arrived in Miami? The first goddamn morning."

"Wally Landis."

"Wally Landis. Kindly old gent. Still has an eye for the ladies. How precious. Doesn't know a thing about the people in the picture. Dirty marks on clean paper, he says."

"Dirty marks?"

"I ask him about nude beaches and he sends me to Haulover. A total waste. He had to know the photo was from Virginia Key, that it was Jack LaFuze with his daughter Nicki LaFuze—or should I say Wally's daughter, Nicki Landis?"

"He'd seen the picture before?" Tru said.

295

"Well, I haven't figured out the whole—whatchamacallit—history of who had the picture, and when."

"Provenance."

"Yeah. But Wally knew it was the same girl he met on Virginia Key, day of the tornado."

"But he didn't know you. You show up out of the blue—"

"He knew I was coming. He knew Nicki hired me."

"Sure, and you show up and—"

"He could have at least—"

"Ted, shut up and listen for one minute."

I SHUT UP AND listened.

"Look," she said. "You show up waving this picture in his face, and he's supposed to trust you, a stranger, with a secret he's held for fifty years, that could destroy his family."

"More like thirty years. So he lies, I go chasing all over south Florida, and his granddaughter ends up kidnapped by child pornographers and white slavers."

"He couldn't have predicted that."

"And his big family secret? His part in the genesis of the whole vile enterprise. He was there at the beginning, and he knew what it had grown into. But he kept silent. That makes your sweet old man an accessory to the most heinous crimes you can imagine. Rationalize that, if you can."

She didn't answer. The GPS voice guided us one turn closer.

I turned the fan up another notch.

"He had a reason," Tru said. "He wanted to protect Nicki from the consequences if people found out who she was—the granddaughter of a murderous psycho drug queen."

"And that justifies all of Papa DePriest's atrocities over the last thirty years?"

"I didn't say that. I just mean Wally wants to keep his daughter safe. He loves her, Ted. That's powerful."

"If you say so."

"I do say so. You think I'm wrong?"

"Jesus, how the hell would I know?" My tone was too harsh. Tru sat stiff in her seat, biting her lip and staring straight ahead. But I couldn't believe she was defending the old fart.

AFTER I RANSOMED MY vehicle, spending more of Nicki's cash, we drove separately to Jenny's place—Tru in the rental, me in the Taurus. Along the way we stopped twice. Once to fuel up the Taurus and once to grab subs and Diet Cokes at a franchise on South Dixie, near Leisure City.

I'd proposed an epicurean lunch at the Sea Knight Brazier but Tru declined the butter-and-garlic experience. At the sub shop I ordered meatballs and pepper jack on a cheesy roll. Tru chose the whole-wheat veggie with baked chips. We agreed to split a cookie, but she insisted on chocolate chip, while I held out for oatmeal raisin. To break the stalemate we skipped dessert entirely, probably the wiser choice.

If only all of life's decisions were so simple.

100 Boy meets girl

OUR CARS WERE OVENS, so we opened the windows and stood by the doors to vent the heat.

I scanned the parking lots on both sides of the street. Vehicles pulled in and out, and zipped by on Dixie, flashing sub-tropical fire off metal and glass.

Nothing suspicious.

"Tru, did you notice anything strange, driving down here?"

"Like what?"

"Like somebody behind you? The same car, before we filled the tank, and after?"

"Like an old truck with refugees spilling out the back?"

"Sure."

She shook her head. "Let's go, Ted."

"Seriously, Tru. DePriest is out there."

"Running for his life."

"Stay on your toes." I touched her shoulder. "I don't want you hurt."

"Ted, you really do care."

"Of course. Don't ever doubt it."

She looked at me and climbed into the rental.

No one followed us to Jenny Axelrod's—as far as I could tell.

WE WERE SITTING IN her front room—too small to call a living room—where I'd first met Boyce. I wanted to toss the Taurus keys to Jenny and bolt, but she'd invited us in for iced tea, and I couldn't say no. Not after I'd sought her help in the dead of night and kept her car indefinitely—not to mention getting her stepson shot. Or the sexual weirdness she and I had shared.

Jenny served the tea in ice-cold mismatched glasses.

"How's Boyce?" I said.

"Quieter," she said, "since his private-eye adventure. But he was always quiet."

"How is he physically?"

"Good. The doctor gave him a sling he wears when he wants to show off."

"I heard he saved a girl's life," Tru said. She was curious as hell about Boyce, I could tell, but too polite to ask indelicate questions.

"The little girl in the picture," Jenny said. "Right?"

"No, it doesn't look that way," I said. "We're pretty sure it was her mother in the picture. Nicki."

"Her mother? Didn't the mother hire you?"

"Yes."

"And she didn't remember getting the picture taken? Stark naked with the man on the beach?"

I shrugged. "We don't have all the answers yet."

TRU SUCKED IN HER breath.

One second the base of the stairway had been empty space. The next it was filled with bonobo. Bonobo in cutoff sweats, a sling, and nothing else. Bonobo with eyes fixed on Tru.

"Boyce," Jenny said. "Ted's come for a visit. He brought our car."

"Ted I know," Boy said. His nostrils flared. "Who is woman?"

Tru breathed deep.

"I'M GLAD THEY'RE GONE, Ted," Jenny said. "I need to talk to someone about Boyce, and you're elected."

Boyce had taken Tru for a grounds tour, a circumstance I wasn't entirely comfortable with, but he was my comrade-in-arms, who had saved my life and Haley's and been wounded twice in the process. So I had to trust him. But I hadn't let them go without a stern word.

"Boyce, I expect you to be a gentleman in Tru's company," I'd said.

"That's right, Boy," Jenny said. "Be nice."

Boy thumped his chest with his undamaged arm. "Boy good," he said.

His lip twitched.

Tru surprised me by smiling sweetly before she and Boy walked off. I'd expected quick blowback for implying she couldn't take care of herself.

But no, she just smiled sweetly.

101 Jenny's Boy problem

JENNY WAS SMILING TOO. "Alone at last."

And I was tempted to wipe the smile off her face. To overwrite our awkward sexual history with something more luscious, and less ludicrous.

"Don't leer at me like that, Ted. Unless you mean it."

"Right," I said. "If Boyce and Tru weren't around ..."

She nodded. "Sure. And if you weren't gay."

"Well, about that ..."

"Never mind, Ted. Look, I need to talk to you about Boy."

"Right. He seems to be healing fast."

"Physically. But he's different. He's a different ... person."

"What's he doing?"

"He seems ... introspective."

"Good for him," I said. "*The unexamined life isn't worth it*, somebody smart once said."

"Yeah. *Know about yourself.* I've heard that. But for Boyce, I'm not so sure it's a great idea."

THE ICED TEA HAD no sweetness. I liked it.

"What happens when he examines his life?" she said. "He's not a child anymore, and he knows it, especially after Miami. But what does adulthood mean for him? A tribe and a mate? A wife and a family? Can you imagine the uproar?"

"Is Tru safe with him?"

"Well, I think that's up to Tru. But you see the problem. You know him better than anyone, and even you shudder to think about it—Boyce with your associate. So what does he do? Move to the jungle and live like a fricking animal? He'll always be a freak in this world, Ted. And he's beginning to realize it."

Tru and Boyce hadn't been gone long, but I was getting antsy. "Boyce is unique, Jenny. So no, he'll never fit in, because there's nobody else like him. He's just got to live with that."

"I don't know if he can, Ted."

"You think he'd harm himself? Suicide?"

"Yes. I don't know. How do you know what someone like Boyce will do?"

"You don't. And we just sent him through the ruins with my girl."

"She's not a girl, Ted."

"Associate. Friend. Whatever. She's in a deserted barn with a guy who is not only the spawn of Hardy *Hard-On* Axelrod but also half bonobo, a tribe whose favorite hobby is hair-trigger sex."

"Dial it back, Ted. For one thing, the females dominate bonobo culture, so that puts Tru in charge. And Boyce is no Hardy. Stop worrying."

"Then what should I be doing, Jenny? What do you want from me?"

"Be a friend to Boyce. A father figure. He likes you. He trusts you. You don't treat him like a monkey. Or a freak."

"I live a thousand miles away. But we could be pen pals. Trade postcards on holidays and fruitcakes at Christmas. Would that help?"

She stood, took my glass, and walked away with a stiff back, disappearing into the kitchen.

"Hey, I wasn't done with that," I said, and she muttered something like *asshole*.

I CROSSED TO THE front window and scanned the property. No sign of Tru and Boyce. *Where are they?*

Jenny's footsteps approached but I didn't turn around.

"Okay, maybe I was asking too much," she said. "You used me when you needed sex, when you needed a ride in the middle of the night, when you needed your wounds treated, when you needed a car for three days, when you needed my boy to get shot and stabbed on a dirty factory floor—whatever you need, I give and you take. But when I ask you to show concern for my son, to be a friend to him, to help save his life, that's too much to ask. You turn into a smartass."

"That's revisionist history," I said. I turned to face her. "I needed sex? You jumped me when I was asleep, and the episode ended badly for me, as you may recall. I needed your boy? Boyce was a stowaway. I never asked him to come and didn't want him. As for the ride and the use of the car, okay, they had value."

I pulled a roll of Nicki's hundreds out of my pocket. "How much do you want?"

"I don't want your money, Ted," she said. "Wait a minute. Yes I do."

She took the cash, peeled off a few bills, eyeballed what was left, and took a few more.

"And I also want to know why you're being such a jerk." She sounded more curious than angry.

I'd been sore without knowing why, but I got over it. It helped that she took the money.

"Hell, I don't know," I said. "I just don't feel like anybody's father figure. I never had kids, and I've got too many issues I don't want to pass on to another generation."

A HOT BREEZE REACHED my neck and I turned. Tru and Boyce stood in the open doorway. Closer than when they left, and I wasn't happy with their body language. Or with the blush staining Tru's cheeks. Boy's expression gave away nothing.

"Jenny, thanks for the tea and the use of your car," I said. "We have an interview with Derish Flin and we need to get moving. Goodbye, Boy."

Our abrupt departure was rude, and I knew it, but the tiny house was closing in on me.

102   That feels good

AFTER DRIVING JENNY'S LOW-SLUNG loose-jointed Taurus for too long, I relished every moment behind the wheel of my rented SUV. Firm ride, taut steering, and a good view of the road ahead. The case in Florida was winding down, and it felt right to be driving the vehicle I started with. Like things coming into balance. *Or is that a weird thought to have, a little obsessive-compulsive?*

Or is it weird to think it's weird, a little neurotic?

Fuck it.

I gave Tru our Coco Brisa destination and she programmed the GPS for the home of Derish Flin, hypnotist, and Madam Fernando, whatever she was—spiritualist, confessor, seer. Transgender aficionado of psychic phenomena.

THE ROUTE FELT DIFFERENT in the sunshine. It seemed a thousand years since the GPS in Jenny's Taurus had led me along these roads in darkness. The night of the backseat bonobo. Boyce.

"So," I said. "What did you and Boyce talk about?" I kept my face forward, watching the road.

"He doesn't talk much," Tru said. "A man of few words."

"A man? Is that how you see him?"

"A man of few words, Ted. It's an expression."

"Yeah, I know. It's just that his stepmom's worried about him. His existential crisis or whatnot."

"Well, if anybody's entitled to an existential crisis, it's Boyce."

"Right," I said. "So now she wants me to be his mentor. A father figure."

"I heard what you told her. You're not father material."

"But on the other hand, the kid saved my ass at Gribler. I owe him."

"Well, I've gotta tell you, Ted. A father figure is not his priority right now. Wrong gender."

"He wants a mate. Is that what you're saying?"

"Or just a hookup," she said.

"Did he say so? Did he make a pass? Or what?"

Tru angled an AC vent toward her face. "Mmm. That feels good."

"I hope that's not your answer."

She laughed. "Let a girl have her secrets, Ted."

"Yeah, that's fine. But tell me what happened."

"He's an odd guy. Awkward, like an adolescent boy, but he's got this wild quality. Animal magnetism."

"Not too magnetic, I hope."

"Well, a lady likes to be appreciated."

"Dammit, Tru."

"What?"

"Never mind."

"What, Ted?"

"Don't think I didn't notice, when you two got back to the house."

"Notice what?"

"How close you stood. Your face was flushed."

"It's hot outside and we'd been walking. So I was glowing, all right?"

"That's all?"

"I'm going to get pissed in a minute, Ted. I don't need your judgment. And for your information, I'm not into sex with animals. Of course, Boy's only half animal, so I could meet him halfway—in the middle, so to speak."

She's joking, right? Pulling my chain. "So, be honest," I said. "Can I tell Jenny that Boy isn't really depressed, he's just horny?"

"Why can't he be both?" she said. "Like, *hey, I might die a virgin.* Wouldn't that depress you, no sex for the rest of your days on earth?"

"Make life a lot simpler."

"Sure, you say that now, in the afterglow."

I GLANCED SIDEWAYS AT her. "What does that mean?"

"Boyce's momma was drooling all over you the second she answered the door."

"Step-momma," I said.

"And she was keen to get Boy and me out of the house."

"Nothing like—wait. Nothing like that happened."

"And now suddenly, coincidentally," she said, "you're hypersensitive about who's hooking up with whom."

"Jenny and I were just talking. About Boyce. That's the truth. Not that it's any of your business."

"If you say so."

"And I don't mean to pry into your affairs," I said. "I just want you to use good judgment."

"Good judgment."

"About guys."

"You want me to use good judgment about guys," she said. "And why is that?"

"Because you're a valuable employee, and I don't want some crazy drama to distract you from your job."

"And I'd need family leave to raise my brood of bono-babies."

"Tru, get serious for a minute. You really are a valuable employee."

"Employee?"

"Well, I care about you personally, too. I don't want you hurt."

"Ain't that sweet?" She crossed her arms. "You'll make a jim-dandy daddy someday."

I didn't have a reply for that, and she didn't elaborate.

103 Fruit and booze on ice

I PARKED ON THE street in front of the house.

"It's a nice place," Tru said.

"Not as nice as the first time I was here," I said.

"What do you mean?"

"I don't know. The sky's not as blue."

"Ted, you're not making sense."

"I know it," I said. "Let's go in."

DERISH OPENED THE DOOR in slo-mo. Dramatically. Dressed in slacks the color of warm oatmeal, loafers without socks, and a silky polo in a pearly shade of deep blue.

"Ted," he said. "Back for more, I see."

"Do your worst, Flin." I made sure to smile when I said it.

"And this is?"

"This is Trudy Hart," I said. "My associate. Tru, this is Derish Flin, whom I've told you about. Don't look directly into his eyes. I mean it."

She extended her hand.

"Oh, and avoid shaking his hand."

"Pleased to meet you," she said. She looked directly into his eyes and shook his hand. Nothing happened.

"There," he said. "No harm done. You see, Ted? I can control it when I want to."

"When you want to," I said.

He winked at Tru. "Come in," he said. *"Take the Dare!"*

WE SAT IN THE Florida room, where I'd first met with Derish. The big windows and french doors showcased the manicured grounds and pristine pool, and the ceiling rippled with

307

reflected sunlight.

Derish served us sangria over ice, splashing it into heavy tumblers from a swervy carafe.

Tru took a sip. "What's in this?"

"You like?" Derish said. "It's mostly fruit. And booze. Wait. Should I check your ID?"

"Where's Maddy?" I said.

"Meditating," he said. "Or planning a dramatic entrance. Who knows?" He sipped noisily. "Lots of vitamins in fruit, you know."

I opened my notebook and clicked lead into the tip of my drafting pencil.

Tru smirked.

"Don't start with me," I said. "Technology's overrated."

Derish settled into his recliner.

"And Ted's an old soul," Maddy said, sweeping into the room. "I knew it the first time I saw him."

SHE WORE A SHAPELESS gown of fluid hues, in patterns shifting from familiar to forgotten. She kissed Derish's cheek and I smiled. The beauty of her face had faded not a whit. I stood and reached for her but she turned to Tru and stopped dead, the colors of her vestment falling into stillness.

"Maddy," I said, "this is—"

She showed me her palm. Her billowed sleeve pooled at her elbow and her bangles rested on her forearm.

"This is Tru," she said. "I knew you would not remain separated for long, Ted, and I told you as much the first time we met."

"Yeah, maybe," I said. "Tru, this is Madam Fernando."

Tru stood and Maddy air-kissed her cheeks.

"Tru," Maddy said. "I feel we have much to say to each other. Shall we retire and leave these two to their schemes and strategies?"

"Of course," Tru said.

"Hang on, Maddy," I said. "Don't I get a hug?"

SHE SMILED AT ME and I felt ... it's crazy, but I felt her aura wrap me up in warmth and wellbeing. Then she and Tru exited stage right, hand in hand.

"Don't be offended, Ted," Derish said. "She's still a little shy around you, since you learned about Fred Madison."

"What?"

"That she didn't want to hug you. Don't be offended."

"I'm not. She gave me a psychic hug. It was way better."

His eyebrows ticced up. "She did?"

"You didn't feel it?"

"No, it's pretty targeted, usually," he said. "Although she has a shotgun mode she can apply when she so chooses."

"So you know what I'm talking about."

"Oh, sure. That's how Maddy gets what she wants. Stuns you with her bliss ray."

"Like when you hypnotize people."

"Yeah, but no. Similar results, but my method is less cooperative and more, shall we say, coercive."

"Yikes."

"Perhaps. But between the pair of us, we get the job done."

"Speaking of which," I said, "let's talk about Nicki."

104 Bruised and abandoned

MY SANGRIA WAS GONE. Nothing left but melting ice and a limp slice of orange. Derish noticed.

"Want a refill, Ted?" He made no move to rise from his recliner.

"No. I only want one thing now. Tell me what happened to Nicki."

Derish stood and stretched and crossed to the wall of windows. His shoulders rose and fell. "Maddy still isn't sure this is the right course to take. To revive what's been buried."

I stayed silent.

"That's why she left the room. One reason, anyway."

With his back turned, I couldn't read his expression. This time, his silence outlasted mine.

"Look," I said. "Wally's told me most of it already. Plus I've learned things on my own. It's all coming out."

"What exactly do you think you know?"

I TOOK A STAB at it.

"Okay," I said. "Nicki's father was Jack LaFuze, the simpleminded nudist who took young Nicki to Virginia Key to frolic with all the naked people. He was the son of the Snow Queen, Nicki's grandmother, the murderous drug queenpin of Miami. A tornado on Virginia Key took Jack out, literally, and left Nicki alone on the beach, bruised and abandoned, to be rescued by Wally Landis and Pablo DePriest, and subsequently adopted by Wally and his wife Reva. But not without the further help of Señor DePriest, who coordinated a bit of document shuffling in the county records office, all with the best of intentions, of course. Namely, to make sure Wally and

Reva ended up with Nicki, and to sever her connection with the nightmare world of her grandmother."

Derish nodded. "Not a bad summary. Nothing disgraceful about any of that."

"Until, from those innocent origins, Papa DePriest builds a massive criminal enterprise."

"Yeah. That bastard."

"His days are numbered," I said.

"Maybe." He rested his forehead on his fingertips.

I waited.

When he spoke, he didn't look up. "All right, Ted. What do you want to know. Let's be done with it."

I scanned my notes. "What happened with Nicki, after she was adopted? Why can't she recognize herself in the picture with Jack? And why doesn't she know her own father?"

Derish nodded. "That's my doing," he said. "I did that."

105 Whatever you need

WIELDING HIS GOLDEN TONGS with aplomb, Derish delivered two cubes from a spherical ice bucket to his tumbler. Added an ample dram of sangria and a slice of orange. Quaffed quickly, and topped his drink again—his third or fourth since we arrived, but he seemed unimpaired.

"I hardly know where to start," he said. He wandered from the bar to the windows, glanced over the grounds, and finally returned to his chair. The whining servo tilted him back.

"Nicki's adopted by Wally and Reva," I said. "Start there."

"Okay, Nicki's in a loving home, a stable environment, et cetera, et cetera, et cetera."

"But."

"But, she's traumatized. Her father brutally ripped from her side. Her mother murdered. Her grandmother, as you put it, a nightmare. And now she's living with strangers."

"So you hypnotized her?"

"Slow down, Ted. Remember, at that time, *Maddy's* working with Nicki. Talk therapy, and sending her those bliss rays of hers. Or *his*, I suppose. She was still more Fred than Madeline back then, at least in public."

"But it doesn't take? The therapy?"

"No. Reva and Wally keep slipping, calling her Terry. Which reminds her that she's an outsider. Plus, she—"

"So Maddy recommends hypnotism," I said.

"The funny thing is, it's Nicki who brings it up, in therapy. Nicki blurts out—to paraphrase what Maddy told me, of course—*Terry's the one they want, not me. Just hypnotize me to stop remembering my old mom and dad. Make me Terry.*"

"Jesus. Is that even ethical?"

312

"Ha! Good question." He sipped his drink and licked his lips. "No, probably not."

"Or legal."

"You know, the legality of the whole situation was on shaky ground already."

"Okay. What next?"

"Well, Maddy didn't like the idea, but she told Reva and Wally about it. It had a certain elegance. A symmetry. And then the Snow Queen survived a couple of assassination attempts, and she was back in the news. Scared the dickens out of Nicki—and the adults too, for that matter."

"So they finally did it."

"Maddy tried. But she wasn't convinced it was right, and that's one reason she failed, in my opinion. And she's not really a hypnotist."

"So she called on you? A stage hypnotist?"

HE HELD UP HIS non-drinking hand.

"It was Nicki again. Her dad, Jack, had taken her to see my act at one of the colleges around here. Apparently I impressed the girl deeply, and in her hour of need, she believed only Derish Flin could help her."

"So you did it."

"Maddy can be persuasive. Very persuasive. Still, it took a while. They told me the whole story. How the sea had—"

"Wait. How well did you know Maddy by then?"

"I'd seen her on Virginia Key, as I told you before, but we hadn't met formally. Not until she and Reva contacted me because of Nicki's insistence."

"This is all pretty incredible," I said.

"Yes, I thought so too. Where was I, Ted?"

"The sea had done something."

"Yes. Stolen Terry and then given them Nicki. And now Nicki was freaking out, and wanted to assume the role of their original child."

"Like I said. You did it."

"Well, they'd already moved from Miami to Pompano Beach by this time, to get Nicki away from places where people knew her. They'd cut her hair, and darkened it a shade or two."

"Closer to Terry's hair color?"

"Yes, but they were already pretty close. Sandy blond."

"Tell me what happened, Derish."

"I did it. I talked with her first, for a long time. And with Wally and Reva. It was a personal challenge for me, you know? Not like helping someone to stop smoking. But to change one person into another."

"Playing god, in a way."

"In a way. But not imposing my will forcibly. *Do it my way or burn in hell forever*. More like a god that gives you what you need."

"God, that makes you sound like a bona fide megalomaniac."

HIS FACE BEAMED. "YES it does, doesn't it? But trust me, Ted, I didn't go into it lightly. And I didn't simply put her under and tell her she was Terry, either."

"But that's what they wanted. Right?"

"I was worried it would be too much. That her mind would rebel in unpredictable ways."

"So how did you do it?"

"I left the door open. I told her she could remember events from Terry's life as her own memories, if she wished. But that her name was still Nicki—which was Terry's middle name, after all—and she could also remember her own history, if she chose to. Or let it fade if she felt comfortable with that."

"So instead of changing her outright," I said, "you left doors open to both identities. Which did fuck her up, to some extent."

"Look, Ted. I'd never done anything like this before. I couldn't predict the long-term effects."

"So you covered your ass by framing it as her free choice, not your divine command."

"If you say so. But I honestly wanted to give her a way back, if it became necessary."

"So Nicki LaFuze became Terry Landis," I said, "except she kept the name Nicki. And for the next thirty years, no one caught on. That seems unlikely."

I DRAINED THE MELT from my tumbler. Derish got up and poured me another good slug and I didn't stop him.

"When you put it that way," he said, "it does seem unlikely. But it wasn't thirty years, just like that." He snapped his fingers. "It was one single day. And then another day. And then another—another day in the life of Nicki Landis. With new memories to push Nicki LaFuze further into the background."

"Except that she would show up in Nicki Landis's oddball impulses."

"Well," he said, "what exactly are you talking about?"

"Her obsession with the past. Feeling lost. Disappearing. Spending money on bizarre things she doesn't need. The day we met she told me she was a little bit crazy."

He pursed his lips and frowned as if trying to look reflective.

But he just looked drunk.

106 Secrets can hurt

TRU AND MADDY RETURNED from wherever they'd been, and I was glad to see them. They sat on the sofa and Derish used the opportunity to change the subject.

Derish: "What have you two been up to?"

Maddy: "Just talking about the men in our lives."

Me: "Nothing bad, I hope."

Tru: "I wouldn't say that." [turns to Maddy] "Would you?"

Maddy: "I agree."

They didn't elaborate.

"Maddy," I said. "Derish was telling me about Nicki taking Terry's place, as Wally and Reva's daughter. It seems incredible that they could get away with it for thirty years."

"It does, doesn't it?"

"Is there more to it? Now's the time to let the truth out. All of it. For Nicki."

MADDY LOOKED AT DERISH. "He doesn't want me to tell you," she said. "For my protection, mostly. And it's really not important as far as Nicki is concerned."

"Tell me," I said. "If it doesn't need to go any further, it won't."

She sighed. "Once or twice I got a call from Reva. Things had been going well for them. She was happy. Nicki was happy. Wally was ... Well, Wally was Wally." She rattled the bangles on her wrist. "But one time a record got kicked back from the school system because Nicki's ID triggered an error."

"What did you do?"

"A bad thing, I'm afraid. I called Pablo DePriest. I felt dirty, but at the time I rationalized that I was shielding Wally and

Reva. Going to DePriest myself so they wouldn't have to."

"What did you ask DePriest to do?"

"Nothing. I just told him the problem, and he made it go away. No more questions from the school."

"So it's fair to say that not only did DePriest build his criminal empire based on the original manipulation of Nicki's records, but you also maintained contact with him over the years, and benefited from his illegal services."

"Ted," Derish said. "That's a very negative spin to put on Maddy's rather kindhearted objectives."

"Thank you, Derish," she said. "But I won't be ingenuous. I must take responsibility for my actions, and their results."

"You were protecting an innocent girl," he said. "A girl who was happy being the only Landis daughter, eager to leave Nicki LaFuze behind forever." He picked up his tumbler but only dross and dregs remained. "Until Ted Danger came along, anyway."

"No," I said. "I didn't precipitate this. It was the picture. The nude picture Haley brought home from Wally and Reva's."

"That damn picture," Derish said.

Tru yawned. "So how did Haley end up with the picture in the first place?"

"That's one thing I've been waiting to hear, Derish," I said. "Tell us how Haley got that picture."

He shrugged. "I do not know, Ted. I do not know."

I BELIEVED HIM.

"Ted, what are you going to do?" Maddy said. "If you divulge this information to Nicki, she may not take it well."

Tru nodded. "She could come unglued."

"Not my concern. She hired me to find the man in the picture, and I found him. She deserves her money's worth, even if it hurts."

"I know you better than that," Tru said. "You won't hurt Nicki if you can help it."

"No, and here's how we can soften the blow. We'll have a

picnic for Nicki, on Virginia Key. Upbeat. Non-threatening. Lots of people, so she doesn't feel singled out."

"Like who?" Derish said.

"Definitely you and Maddy," I said. "I'd want Wally and Reva there too, and Bentley and Haley. My private-eye partners in crime, Slaven and Bustamante. And Pop and Jeter from the camera store, and José María and his sister Yesi from El Toro. The more the merrier."

"What about Jenny and Boyce?" Tru said.

"Yeah, Jenny already said they'd come."

"You'll be taking Nicki full circle," Maddy said. "Back to where it started."

"And I want you and Derish to help smooth the way," I said. "Derish, can you help her remember without freaking her out?"

"I believe I can." He yawned and shook his head. "I wish I were more convinced that this is the right course to take. The right thing for everyone."

"The *right thing* sounds simple," Maddy said. "But it can be elusive. Nicki's not the only vulnerable party here, you know." The grim look she gave Tru meant something, but I didn't know what.

"One thing's for sure," I said. "This old secret has hurt her. It's time for the truth to come out about her father."

TRU MADE A LOW sound in her throat. When I looked up, she was staring at me.

"What's wrong?" I said.

She looked down at her hands and shook her head. "It's just ... what you said. About the secret, hurting her. And the truth coming out. About her father."

I waited for more, but it didn't come.

She stood and strode to the big french doors and fumbled with the handles. The doors didn't open.

"Where are you going, Tru?" I said.

She kept her back to us.

"Want to take a swim?" Derish said. "We can find you a suit. Not a problem. Or you can go without, if you like. Our privacy's pretty good here. Barring the random drone."

Tru's shoulders tensed and she didn't answer.

"Tru," I said. "What is it?"

Derish looked at Maddy. "Was it something I said?"

MADDY CROSSED TO THE doors and opened them and Tru escaped without a backward look. Maddy glared at us. "Secrets can hurt," she said. She followed Tru around the pool, angling toward the gazebo, leaving the doors open behind her.

Florida heat poured in. Humid, with a bite of chlorine.

I looked at Derish and he shrugged.

What just happened?

107 Not bootylicious?

EARLY MORNING, EL TORO. Jacomet and I crossed paths in the parking lot.

I was inbound—balancing two extra-large coffees and locking my rental—and he was heading out—hustling into his midsize Buick. We spoke a dozen words and he skidded off, his front wheels throwing sand.

Tru's towel spilled over a chaise by the pool, but she had disappeared. As I crossed to her ground-level room, the door opened and she stepped out, eyes wide.

"Ted, I was ready to send a search party. Gimme that coffee."

WE SAT BY THE pool and sipped. The coffee was still hot, and damn good. Loads better than El Toro's watery bean juice.

"I saw Jacomet in the lot," I said. "He was in a rush to get away."

"He got nervous when I caught him peaking down my swimsuit."

"That doesn't sound like Jacomet."

"I might have encouraged him a little. He thought I was a kid at first. Your daughter."

"What was he doing here?"

A breeze rustled the palms. "He didn't tell you?"

"He said he dropped off my stuff with my cute assistant."

"*Cute*? Not bootylicious?"

"He was in a hurry."

Tru re-lidded her cup. "Thanks for the coffee, Ted. If you touch it, I'll rip your arm off. Wait here."

She sauntered to her room and returned with my badge.

320

"Here. Jacomet says you left this at the crash scene with a woman and her doggo. And to stop playing peace officer."

"That's all?"

She smoothed her towel and sat. Examined her coffee from all sides. "He said he's single. Divorced. We flirted. He got flustered and ran off. Claimed he was late for an interview with Wally and Reva." She watched me over the rim of her cup.

There was more to say, I felt certain. But no one said it.

108   Never odd or even

THERE SHOULD HAVE BEEN magic in the air on Virginia Key that day. A sense of the phenomenological. The phantasmagoric. A day to reveal secrets, to waken nightmares.

But I wasn't feeling it. An ordinary day, the white-glare sky bleaching the seascape. The beach was only sand, bland and mussy, strewn with tired seaweed. Tepid waters lapped the shore with neither threat nor promise, and farther out, languid swells peaked and vanished, painting broken bands of foam to parallel the far horizon. A horizon hazy and dim, but fading upward to pallor, blending into commonplace clouds, too few to block the sun.

WE'D STAKED OUR CLAIM to a wide stretch of beach near a tumble of rocks jutting into the water. Behind us, toward the parking lot, stood a grove of trees—palms mixed with leafier specimens. And near the trees, a concrete table, long and listing, a faded canopy canted over one end.

By squinting seaward from our sandy nook, we could see to our right the dusky silhouette of Key Biscayne. And skimming between Key Biscayne and Virginia Key, the Rickenbacker Causeway, glinting with the traffic it bore across Bear Cut.

WHEN TRU AND I got there just after noon, Pop had already arrived. He sat at the table in a white terry robe next to a red cooler filled, I found out later, with bottled water and cream-cheese-and-olive sandwiches on rye. He'd snagged the only shady seat, but the earth turns and shadows would surely grow.

In the surf, a thin balding man staggered through elbow-high swells.

"Where's Jeter today?" I asked Pop. "Minding the store?"

"Store's closed a couple hours," he said. "And Jeter's in the drink already."

I looked again. "That's Jeter?"

"Left the rug at home," Pop said.

As we talked, private eyes Slaven and Bustamante showed up in modest beach wraps carrying between them a basket of wines, cheeses, and breads of various configurations. Wally and Reva arrived with Nicki and Haley, followed by Jenny and her stepson Boyce, who made a stir in his beefcake muscle shirt and dinosaur board shorts. I lost track of who brought what, but the table was filling with coolers and boxes and baskets. Good smells in the air.

Then came Bentley, straight from the airport, in a mulberry golf shirt, nice chinos, and loafers. He carried a transparent to-go box of airport food for one.

"I hope you have something to drink," he said, and Navi Bustamante said "Fear not," and lifted a bottle of wine by the neck from an insulated foil bag.

His gaze lingered on the bottle, and on Navi too, for no longer than was appropriate—she had shed her cover-up, revealing the lean Latina tidbits below—before he joined his wife, daughter, and in-laws dispensing more prosaic beverages in the shade of the canopy. Jeter, back from his ocean excursion, examined a lavish fruit basket, and commented to no one in particular, "No melon, no lemon," prompting Haley to tell him to "Sit on a potato pan, Otis," to which he replied, shaking his head, "Madam, I'm Adam." Bentley squinted at Jeter with an odd smile, and looked away.

Maddy and Derish, elegant as ever, even in beachwear and schlepping a red thermos and a platter of cling-wrapped brownies, arrived at the same time as José María and Yesi, and that was everyone.

Everyone I was expecting.

109 Time to tell Nicki

WE ATE THE FOOD, drank the drinks. We floated on ocean swells, waded in the surf. Even Bentley shed his loafers and got his feet wet.

A weight pressed my shoulders down, my arms, a force unseen, pushing. A weight, but also a source of power, a ballast of calm, making me stronger. The time was right to tell Nicki what she wanted to know.

Nicki might have sensed it too. She called me over to sit with her while Bentley and Haley walked the shore. Breezes through the grove dappled sunlight on her face, which revealed not a single line of tension.

"Ted, thanks for today. Being here with my parents, and Haley, and Ben—it's nice." She brushed a tangle of hair behind her ear and it blew across her face again. She left it there. "And all these people ..."

"They all helped," I said. "One way or another."

"So you solved it." It wasn't a question. "You know who the man is. In the picture with Haley."

MADDY AND DERISH STROLLED oceanside, nearing the rocks.

"Remember that couple, Nicki? I introduced you earlier."

"Yes. Her name's Maddy. Madam Fernando. She's a mind reader."

"More like a spiritualist. A therapist too."

"And he's the hypnotist. Derish Flin."

"You know him?"

"He's rather famous."

"Have you ever met them before today?"

"I don't think so."

324

"When you were young. Your dad took you to see Derish's act."

She shook her head.

"Think. Derish Flin. Madam Fernando. Fred Madison?"

Her eyelids flickered. "I don't have to remember."

"What do you mean, Nicki?"

"What? I don't know." She squeezed her hands together.

"Relax, Nicki," I said. "You're among friends."

"Right now I'm not so sure about that."

"You're fine. Hang in there."

THEIR SHADOWS TRAILING BEHIND, Maddy and Derish returned from their walk.

"Can you two sit a while?" I said. "Nicki wants to know about the man in the picture. And I think it's time."

They eased into canvas chairs facing Nicki. Maddy smiled and must have launched a bliss ray because we all leaned forward and Nicki's hands came to rest on her thighs.

Derish held out his palm and Nicki placed her hand in his.

"We've met before," he said. "When you were very young."

"I don't remember," she said.

"You're going to remember things today that you've forgotten for a long time," he said. "And that's as it should be. You're calm and relaxed and among friends. And as you remember, you will remain calm, relaxed, and protected. Do you understand?"

"Yes."

HE TOUCHED HER FOREHEAD and spoke into her ear. She closed her eyes and her muscles seemed to liquefy. As she swayed, Derish caught her shoulder.

"Go easy," Maddy said. "Don't push it."

He grinned. "Me? Push it?"

Bentley cleared his throat. He and Haley were back.

"What's going on?" he said. "What's wrong with Nicki?"

Derish waved a hand. "Post-hypnotic trigger. From thirty

years ago and still works perfectly. She's in a state of deep relaxation. Hypnosis."

"I'm not entirely comfortable with that," Bentley said. "You need to snap her out of it."

HALEY TOOK HER FATHER'S arm. "Dad, this is for Mom."

I met his eyes and nodded. He stepped back.

"Nicki," Derish said, "although deeply relaxed, you can easily respond to my questions. Do you understand?"

"Yes."

"Soon I'm going to count backward from five to one and you will awake refreshed and relaxed. You will remember everything that happened while you were hypnotized. Do you understand?"

"Yes."

"In fact, you will find your memory is better than ever before, and you can easily recall many happy moments in your life, and experience the joy and happiness appropriate to those memories. Do you understand?"

"Yes."

"Also, sad and unhappy events from your past—memories perhaps you chose to leave behind until now—will be more available to you, to remember gradually and peacefully. And as you reveal these memories to yourself, feelings of sorrow may be appropriate. That's for you to decide. You will remember that these events exist only in the past—far from the here and now, where you are surrounded by people who love and care about you—and that you are a strong and resilient adult who calmly assimilates forgotten memories, happy or sad, with confidence and serenity. Do you understand everything I've just told you?"

"Yes."

Derish turned to Maddy and she nodded. He winked.

"Now as I count down from five to one," Derish began, and he went through the whole mumbo jumbo to bring Nicki back.

I HELD MY BREATH as she opened her eyes and squinted and smiled.

"How do you feel?" Derish said.

"Good. Fine."

"Do you remember what I said while you were hypnotized?"

"Of course."

"Do you have any questions?"

"No." Her head tilted. "Wait. Didn't you ..."

Derish leaned in. "Yes?"

"Didn't you used to have more hair?"

He opened his mouth but nothing came out. A splash of red blotched his cheeks. *Derish Flin, blushing. That's my girl!*

Nicki laughed and I heard panic behind it. *Or am I projecting?*

She touched Maddy's arm. "You were nice. I remember that."

Maddy nodded and patted Nicki's hand.

"Nicki," I said. "Are you ready to talk about the picture?"

110 Girl in the picture

NICKI LOOKED AROUND AND didn't answer. The audience for our little drama had grown.

Rytt and Navi had settled in the shade on a blanket with a sweeping spiral design. Bentley and Haley hovered a few steps behind Nicki, Haley leaning on her dad. Wally and Reva huddled at the end of the table, not far from Jenny and Jeter, who perched on either side of Pop, who himself was keeping Rytt and Navi under close surveillance. And who could blame him? José María and Yesi approached from the strand to the north, and Navi called Yesi to join her and Rytt. José María closed in on Jenny and got a cold glare from Jeter. *Hmm.* Yesi and Navi sat cross-legged chatting in Spanish. Then Tru and Boyce strolled onto the beach from a trail through the vegetation. They were holding hands but let go when they saw us watching.

Shakespeare's line popped into my head, about the world being a stage and people making entrances and exits. In this scene, just entrances.

I REPEATED NICKI'S CUE. "Are you ready to talk about the picture?"

This time, she picked it up. "With everybody watching?"

"In the open air," I said. "No more secrets."

"Even Haley?"

Haley's mouth twitched. "Mom, I've been online since I was six. *And* I was kidnapped by perverts. An old picture from a nude beach won't ruin me."

Nicki bit her lip. "Okay. I'm ready."

EARLIER, I'D STOWED THE envelope on the table under a carry-on-size suitcase someone had used for picnic supplies. The case looked familiar, but it seemed irrelevant at the time.

I slid the photo from the envelope.

"Nicki, one reason I brought you to Virginia Key today was because of this picture. It was taken on this stretch of beach."

She held the photo with her fingertips.

"Look at this part of the image," I said. "This smudge is Key Biscayne. And this faint line—it's the Rickenbacker."

She gazed across the water. Held the picture at arm's length. Drew it closer. Inched it out. "It lines up. You're right."

I nodded.

"But ... this isn't a nude beach, is it? So why are the man and Haley—" She shook her head. "Why are the people in the picture naked?"

"It used to be," I said.

"What?"

"It used to be a nude beach. Long ago."

The muscles in her shoulders tensed. "Ted, who is the man in the picture? The man with ..."

"You don't recognize him?"

"No, of course not," she said. "Of course not." Her lips drew back and her nostrils flared. "Why do you think I hired—"

HER FACE FROZE AND then went soft. She checked the photo again.

"He looks familiar," she said. "Maybe I ... No. No, I don't know him. I don't *think* I know him. I ..." A muscle jumped in her neck.

"Do something for me, Nicki," I said. "Will you?"

She tore her eyes from the picture. "What, Ted?" Her voice was a whisper.

"Stand up," I said. "And Haley, will you step over here?"

Nicki stood in slow motion. I positioned Haley to her left.

Haley was barefoot, in a white two-piece with lacy trim, string ties at her hips. Nicki stood a head taller in chunky sandals with thin straps. She wore a cover-up that sheathed her body from breast to thigh in a subtle tropical pattern.

"Nicki, can you take off your wrap?"

"What?"

"Your cover-up. Take it off."

She looked at me and raised her chin.

Bentley cleared his throat. "Ted, is this really—"

I held up my hand. "Please."

NICKI UNTUCKED A FOLD, and the layers peeled away, revealing a modest black bikini with a mesh décolletage that exposed more than it hid. But cleavage wasn't my mission of the moment.

I looked lower, and found what I wanted. The final proof. A glance at Haley confirmed it.

"Nicki," I said. "Haley has four moles on her stomach. They form a curve from her left, um, from here, down to her navel." A wave of my hand traced the arc.

Jeter and José María leaned in for a better view. We all did.

Haley parked her fists on her hips and pooched out her stomach. "Take a picture. It'll last longer."

I turned back to Nicki. "You've got a few moles too."

She looked down. The navel-gazers redirected their attention.

"But yours make a different pattern," I said. "They form a triangle around your navel, pointing downward."

"Yes," she said. "Sometimes Bentley likes to—"

"Ahem," Bentley said. "TMI, Nicki. Please."

Someone laughed, but Nicki didn't.

SHE LOOKED UP AT me with eyes so vulnerable, so fragile and exposed, that I wanted to stop. To spare her what came next.

"What is it, Ted?" Her voice was small. "What does it mean?"

"Look closely at the picture, Nicki," I said. "Tell me what you see."

"What am I looking for, Ted?" Her eyes glistened, and she

blinked. *She knows*, I thought. *Or is beginning to.*

"Look at the moles," I said. "The pattern on the girl's stomach." I swallowed the lump growing in my throat and choked on the next words. "The triangle."

NICKI STUDIED THE PHOTO, and no one spoke. The beach held a silence as old as the earth.

She shook her head, and the tears pooling in her eyes spilled over. They rolled down her cheeks and dropped from her chin.

Then she raised her eyes and straightened. Her gaze swept the beach, near and far, resting on no one.

And one halting step at a time, she began to walk to the sea.

Bentley broke the silence. "Should we stop her?"

But she slowed on her own, halfway to the water. Another half step. And another.

And she stopped.

111 Vortex

I COULDN'T LOOK AWAY. And the more I focused on Nicki, the more everything changed around her, like optical illusions you see when you stare at a single point. The sand and sky and trees and ocean dimmed and rippled at the edges of my vision, and when I turned to look, they were still there, but with features lost or added, borders pinched or pulled.

A murmur in the air. Pop said, "What's she pointing at?"

Nicki stood motionless, her arm extended seaward. And the color-shifted sky revealed what couldn't be there. A swirl of ashen cloud resolving into a tip, a tip in the center of a vortex that thickened and swung and dropped, and slashed the ocean swells, spinning, spuming, turning, churning—

And a resonance, deep and dark and basso low, a black pulse, felt more than heard, a clutch in the gullet, a clinch in the gonads. I slapped my eyes shut and shook my head to clear the visions in my mind.

And when I looked again, unreality still ruled, but the sky was blank and silent. A screenful of static on a cosmic TV. The vortex had vanished—for me, at least.

But what are Nicki's visions?

She remained upright, gazing at the sky, until she whirled and swayed and staggered three steps away from the sea, and then, as if slammed from behind, her body jolted and arched and she tumbled into the sand and lay trembling, curled in a protective ball, one breast bared where her halter had twisted beneath her.

She seemed oblivious to every eye, every gaze, and I wondered what in the holy hell had flung her to the earth like a puppet with severed strings.

BENTLEY AND DERISH SNAPPED out of it first, and arrived by her side at the same time.

"Nicki." Bentley touched her shoulder. Squeezed it. He turned to Derish. "She can't hear me. This is your fault."

"Nicki," Derish said. He sat on his haunches in front of her. "Listen to my voice. You're safe now."

Maddy took my hand. "Come on, Ted. She trusts you. And those two aren't helping."

What can I do that her own husband and a master hypnotist can't?

MADDY LED ME ACROSS the sand.

"Nicki," I said. "It's Ted. Ted Danger."

Derish shook his head. "Leave her to me. I've got this."

"I'm her husband," Bentley said.

"She needs space," Maddy said.

Nicki rolled onto her back and sat up. She scanned the beach in both directions, blind to the four of us huddled around her, it seemed, and everyone else. She looked down at her bare breast and touched the nipple, and then removed the bikini top entirely and tossed it aside. It landed in front of Bentley. He held it out to her, but he might have been the shadow of the ghost of the invisible man for all the response she gave him.

A moan escaped from Nicki's throat. She hugged her knees, and cried.

AS THE SKY CLEARED, a hazy shadow fell across Nicki's face. It was Wally, holding open a blanket.

"Here," he said. "Let's get you covered up." He wrapped the blanket around her shoulders and over her knees. "Are you hurt?"

She looked up at him and sobbed. The tremble in her chin broke my heart.

"My daddy," she said. "I lost my daddy."

112 Secret of the suitcase

WE BACKED OFF TO give them space, so I don't know what passed between Wally and Nicki. The breeze and surf shrouded their words.

Nicki laughed at something Wally said, and he groaned and plunked his ass down next to her. He retrieved her halter, and she knocked the sand from the cups and slipped the blanket off her shoulders. This was no time to stare but I couldn't look away from her slender back and the fluid ridges of her spine and scapulae as she worked her double-jointed sorcery and *Vi-ola*, as Wally would say, her top was secure.

AN HOUR LATER, THE party was all but over.

Rytt and Navi had been the first to leave, followed by Pop and Jeter, with José María and Yesi right behind. Next to exit were Derish and Maddy, but not before Derish took me aside and revealed the special ingredient in Maddy's brownies—and no, it wasn't love—that might have opened our minds to the oddities we'd experienced that day on Virginia Key.

Well, that explained a lot.

Jenny Axelrod shook the sand out of her blanket and collected her things, but couldn't find Boyce. He'd wandered off again with Tru, which I wasn't happy about, but I was too burnt-out to muster much trepidation.

And Jenny didn't look worried, either. She spread her blanket over the sand again, stretched out, and promptly fell asleep.

AS NICKI RECALLED LONG-BURIED odds and ends about her childhood—and shared them with her family and me around

334

the beach table—the disquiet that had haunted her every word and gesture seemed to melt away. She glowed with calm.

The case, I believed, was over. Another triumph for Ted Danger, Private Eye.

But one detail nagged at me. "Nicki, I don't understand where Haley got the photograph she brought home from Wally and Reva's."

Haley looked up at the mention of her name. "I don't know anything about that."

"It was in here," Nicki said. She lifted a small suitcase from the sand and put it on the table.

"I recognize it," I said. "Haley had it with her when she showed up at El Toro."

"Yes," Nicki said. "And she used it when she visited my parents."

"But how did the picture get in there?" I said. "Where did it come from?"

NICKI STUDIED THE OCEAN as if the waves held the answer. I followed her gaze. Nothing but sea and sky.

Her fingers brushed the case and she smiled. "This was mine. My little suitcase. From when I was Nicki LaFuze."

"Yours?"

"When Haley took it to see my parents, the picture was already inside. I'd hidden it in a secret pocket in the back. A very long time ago. I'd forgotten until today." The muscles in her jaw tensed and released. "And now I remember. I put other ... things in there too. Documents."

"Are they still there? Right now?" I spun the case and thumbed the latches, popping the clips.

Nicki slapped her hand on the lid. "I don't know."

"Let's take a look-see."

"They're private, Ted."

"More private than you and your dad naked?"

Her head snapped back as if I'd punched her.

"Ted," Bentley said.

"Okay, I'm sorry, Nicki. That was a stupid thing to say."

"Yes, it was," she said, "and yes, more private than that."

"Right," I said. "Okay." I snicked the latches closed. Reluctantly. "We'll leave it for now. Although I've gotta tell you, my curiosity is killing me."

NICKI SET THE SUITCASE at her feet. "Maybe I'll tell you about it someday. But not today."

"Fair enough. But I don't see how the suitcase traveled from your old life with Jack LaFuze to your new one with Wally and Reva. You didn't carry it around with you at the nude beach, did you, full of secret documents?"

Wally cleared his throat. "I can answer that. Right after she came to live with us, Nicki needed a few things from before. She and her dad had an apartment in Homestead, and Pablo helped me track it down before it got cleaned out. We broke in one night and grabbed a bunch of Nicki's stuff."

"Including the suitcase."

"Yeah. And when Nicki got married, she took it with her."

So that explained everything. Except whatever the hell was tucked away in that secret pocket. Could be a faded treasure map to the lost LaFuze fortune—dusty coffers bursting with jewels and gold ingots.

Or maybe I'd been reading too much bad fiction.

Nicki was crying again, so I didn't push it.

113 Ape-men

THEN IT WAS REALLY over, almost. After final hugs and tears, Nicki made her exit, toting her mysterious suitcase, with Haley and Bentley by her side, Wally and Reva plodding behind.

The new and improved Nicki Vavul. At peace, and projecting an aura of calm. No longer *a little crazy*. Maybe.

Time will tell.

AND THEN I HAD the beach table all to myself, and I sat and stared across the endless ocean. Nobody around but Jenny on her blanket in the sand, propped on her elbows, eyes to the sea. The sun was descending behind us, tired of lighting the day.

I closed my eyes and listened to the wind, and the ocean. Birds in the distance. Until the sounds lost their meanings. I lowered my chin to my chest, and sighed, and slept.

"TED. WAKE UP."

I opened my eyes, got my bearings. Tru stood holding her elbows, scanning the landscape. Jenny was gone, her blanket left behind.

"Where's Jenny?" I said.

"This is weird." Tru brushed sand from the bench and sat.

"Now what?" I looked around.

"I don't see the bridge, and that other island. Key Biscayne. It's all connected."

Just that quickly, I saw it too.

THE RICKENBACKER CAUSEWAY. GONE.

"Not again," I said.

"What's going on, Ted?"

"Power of suggestion. Maddy's brownies. Hypnosis. I don't know."

"Maddy's brownies?"

"How many did you eat?"

"None," she said. "Well, a bite. It tasted funny."

I looked across the water. "If it's an illusion, it's a damn good one."

"I don't like this. Are we going to be okay?"

I knocked my knuckles on the tabletop. *Ouch.* "This is solid. Real. The visions we're seeing, they're known phenomena. Virginia Key is a mystery spot. Things get warped, but they snap back."

"I wish we could just go."

"Me too. But where's Jenny?"

"She's looking for Boyce," she said.

"Wasn't he with you?"

She shook her head. "We were walking, headed back. Then the air changed and the path looked different."

"Different how?"

"Gone. But we heard the ocean so we kept going and then Boyce froze, and his eyes got wide and his nose was twitching like crazy. I asked him what was wrong and he turned around real slow and pointed."

"At what?"

"Rocks and shrubs. A fold in the landscape."

"Rocks and shrubs."

"Then he said *They come*, and I said *Who?* and he didn't answer."

"Just rocks and bushes?"

"Well, you know, nature stuff. Trees and those sand dune things."

"But no *they*, as in *they come*."

She squeezed her eyes closed. "I don't know. Maybe. Dark shapes. Shadows moving in the breeze. Or maybe ..."

"Maybe what?"

SHE LOOKED AT ME, lips tight.

"What, Tru? Animals? People?" She didn't answer. "Teens on trail bikes? Dudes in dune buggies?" I kept guessing. "Aliens from Alpha Centauri? Angels from the astral plane?"

"Screw you, Ted," she said.

"I've had it with this place," I said. "It's messing with my head."

"Ape-men, all right? They were ape-men. Like Boyce."

"Jesus. Ape-men like Boyce."

"But different," she said. "I didn't get a good look."

"Like a tribe?"

"Yeah, maybe."

So the legendary ape-men of Virginia Key are back again.

And just when it couldn't get any crazier, Papa DePriest shows up.

AT THE BEACH, YOU naturally face the ocean. Lost in the rhythm of swells and breakers, breakers and surf, surf and sand.

The ebb and flow had masked the sounds of his approach.

"Do not get up," he said. Gripped in his fist was a double-barrel derringer.

Tru and I did not get up.

"Good Lord," I said. "Papa DePriest. What the hell are you doing here?"

He had found clean clothes and ditched the moustache and goatee. His hair gleamed with pomade.

Looking awfully dapper for a man on the lam.

"I have come to kill you, *cabrón*, for the troubles you have caused with your meddling."

"It's over, Papa," I said.

"Exactly the words you spoke when last we met. And yet, it was not over then, nor is it over now."

"Everybody's onto you. Friends disown you. Allies shun you. Run while you can. An attack on us today will only seal your fate."

My words did not appear to terrify him to the extent I'd hoped.

"No, this attack will seal *your* fate," he said. "In a most literal way." And he smiled.

I resisted the impulse to smile back. Over his shoulder, from the sub-tropical thicket, a loping figure emerged, with long arms and dark eyes, wearing dinosaur board shorts.

"HOW DID YOU FIND me, DePriest?" I said.

"You wish to delay your imminent doom," he said. "You are

a fool and a coward." He bared his teeth and raised his little *pistola*. "You think I have lost? No. Many people respect me and do my bidding. They know that Papa will not relinquish the power so easily, not for a fool of a gringo as you. My *compadres* have reported to me your every feeble action, while I expand my influence daily and far into the future. And after I kill you, and take from you this lovely child, I will—"

"I'm not a child." Tru's voice betrayed no emotion.

DePriest studied her with narrowed eyes. "So you are not. Perhaps it is better that—"

I never found out what he had in mind, because his head snapped to the side as he caught sight of Boyce bounding across the sand, closing the gap, but still too far to do us any good. And Tru and I, blocked by the concrete table, couldn't make a move on DePriest.

"What in the fuck?" DePriest said.

He raised his derringer in Boyce's direction. Boyce came no closer, but did not retreat. He stuck his elbows out and began to hop and spin, with vocalizations like "oo-oo, ah-ah."

DePriest lowered his gun. "Some fool has dressed that *mono* in clothing."

"He's a valuable specimen," I said. "My colleague here is a linguist, and she's taught him over two thousand English words and phrases."

"Exactly how valuable is this specimen?"

Tru caught on fast. "He's insured for a quarter million dollars."

DePriest pursed his lips. "I will take you both. Call him to us."

"Very well." She stood. "Boy! Momma say come. Come now."

BOYCE STOPPED SPINNING. HE looked at Tru and tilted his head. His mouth hung open, wide and pink, his fat tongue lolling.

What a ham.

"Momma say come. Come now." Tru opened her arms

wide, then touched her chest. "Come now!"

I bit my lips to keep from giggling.

Boyce said "Oo-oo ah-ah" and shuffled across the sand, knees bent, knuckles dragging. Above his gaping mouth, his eyes narrowed in warning. *Don't laugh.* And that was all it took. I felt it boil up and tried to throttle it, but the chortle erupted in my throat. DePriest looked at me and I faked a cough and said "I'm all right—choked on saliva," and he spat and said "*Que payaso*" and when he turned back it was too late.

EYES BRIGHT, TEETH BARED, Boyce stood tall before DePriest, wrapped a big paw around his gun hand and pushed it straight down. DePriest swung with his free arm but Boy swatted it away just as the derringer fired with a pop like a cherry bomb.

Tru looked at me. "Was that a—"

Then the other barrel fired, and DePriest screamed, and I thought it was all over.

It wasn't.

115   DePriest DePantsed

DEPRIEST ROARED AND HOPPED on one foot, gripping his knee, dropping the derringer into the sand. He kicked off his loafers, stripped off his pants, and—ignoring Tru and me—inspected his wound, a bloody slash down one shin.

Right. Ignoring Tru and me.

What the hell? After all his crimes, threats, and insults, does he really think I won't kick his ass just because he got nicked by a bullet? I came around the table to let him have it, to play gringo bingo on his head, by god, but Boyce's big hairy arm blocked me.

"What the hell, Boyce," I said, but he gave me that twitchy half smirk of his, sidled in close to DePriest, and grabbed his pants.

"Oo-oo, ah-ah," he said, and darted off, serpentine style.

WHEN DEPRIEST SAW HIS trousers blowing in the wind behind a scampering orangutan, or whatever he thought his nemesis was, his wound seemed forgotten. He sprinted after Boyce, who had paused near the water to don DePriest's pants over his board shorts. He'd pulled on one leg when Papa got too close, charging full tilt. Boy screeched like a monkey, leaned right, feinted left, and galloped off again, leaving DePriest pinwheeling into the surf until he found his balance, spun, and raced after Boy again, boxers billowing.

Three times DePriest came within a bonobo hair of grabbing Boyce. Until Boyce disappeared through a break in the vegetation, with DePriest one stride behind.

Leaves quivered, and over the surf we heard a faint thrashing. Then, fainter still, another noise. A yelp.

And then, nothing.

Tru broke the silence. "What the fuck just happened?"

My thoughts exactly.

AFTER A WHILE I got tired of waiting around and started searching for DePriest's gun. No luck.

Then Boyce came back.

116 No mate for Boy

HE STRODE ACROSS THE sand with his head high, back straight. DePriest's trousers no longer dragging behind him, but neatly folded across a muscled forearm. He presented them as if they were a gift.

"Pants of man," he said.

"What am I supposed to do with those, Boyce?" I said.

"Ted, take them," Tru said.

"Man not need."

"What happened to him, Boy?" I said. "To DePriest."

He shook his head. "Man not need."

I laid the pants on the table. "Are we going to find a body in the vegetation over there?"

"Man not there," he said. "Man not here."

"Where is he, then?"

"Other place. Far."

"What other place? Where?"

Boyce stood motionless. I couldn't read his expression.

"Boyce," Tru said. "Before, when we were walking. Where did you go when we saw the ... others?"

"They come," he said. "They want Boy."

"It's the tribe, isn't it," I said. "The proto-humans that people have spotted around here for hundreds of years."

"Proto-humans?" Tru said. "Living in Miami? How is that possible?"

"Not from now," Boy said.

"Not from now on?" she said. "They're leaving?"

He didn't answer. I looked for the Rickenbacker, but still couldn't see it. Only a mist that seemed to be both moving and frozen solid at the same time, like an unsettling psychotogenic

345

phantasmagoria. Or the walls when you're drunk.

"They want Boy. Need Boy. Boy go."

IT WAS THE LONGEST speech I'd ever heard him make.

"When will you come back, Boyce?" I said.

He didn't answer.

"I've got to tell you," I said, "I was sure glad to see you pop out of those trees when DePriest had us at gunpoint. You saved my life, and you saved Tru."

"My hero," Tru said. She was smiling.

The corner of his mouth twitched upward.

"And that whole *oo-oo ah-ah* thing," I said. "Pure genius."

His half smirk mutated into a snarl. *Time to change the subject.*

"How did you know we needed help?" I said.

"Boy not know."

"You just happened to be strolling back at that moment?"

His throat muscles rippled. "Boy—" he said. He blinked and looked away.

"What is it?" I said. "Tell us."

"Boy say goodbye."

Tru moved in and took his hand in both of hers. "You're not coming back?"

"Here," he said, "Boy is ... freak."

"But—"

"Here, no mate for Boy." He gazed into Tru's eyes.

"Good point," I said.

"Ted," Tru said.

"There," he said, "many mates."

"Awesome," I said.

"Ted!"

"I go," he said. "I teach."

"Teach what?" she said.

"I teach talk."

She wiped her eye with the back of her hand. "You should stay."

"Look, Tru," I said. "Let me translate. Boy's a hero to us, sure. But to most people, he's, uh, an oddity. As much as we like him—love him, even—he's saying he'll never fit in with modern humans. On the other hand, with the tribe he found, he'll be a leader, a visionary. He'll teach them language skills and he'll have his choice of the females."

"You talk good," he said. "You come too."

I shook my head. "Forget it. I'd steal all your women."

"Ted, you're not at all funny," Tru said.

BOY LIFTED HIS FACE and his nostrils quivered. "Boy go. Say goodbye now. Goodbye to Tru. Goodbye to Jenny. My Jenny-Mother."

"And to Ted," Tru said. "Say goodbye to Ted."

He looked at me with flat eyes. "Ted," he said. "Not so much."

I laughed and clapped him on the shoulder. He clapped me back and turned to Tru.

"Goodbye to Tru," he said, and clapped her on the shoulder.

"Oh, no you don't," she said, and pulled him in. "Don't look, Ted."

Their hug escalated into lip-lock territory.

I coughed. "So, Boy. Have you said goodbye to Jenny yet?"

They broke their clinch and I was glad to see it.

"Where Jenny-Mother?" he said.

"I don't know. She went searching for you."

He looked down at his feet. "Tell her love. Boy love."

"We'll tell her," Tru said.

BOY TURNED AND TOOK three steps toward the trees and stopped. Tru put her hand on my arm and shook her head. He turned, facing us, his expression blank. But his big dark eyes were wet.

"Ted," he said.

"Yes? What is it?"

I couldn't believe the tough guy was crying.

"Don't forget," he said. "Don't forget Boy."

At that moment I realized I'd never see him again. "I won't forget you, son," I said. "I could never forget you."

I took a step in his direction, but he spun and hightailed it across the sand.

I FELT MYSELF TEARING up a little.

Jesus. And Tru was crying again too.

"You called him *son*," she said.

"Did I? I guess if I ever have kids, I'd want them to be brave and honest, like Boyce."

She looked away. "What about me, Ted?"

"No," I said. "I really hope your kids are nothing like Boyce." I grinned. She didn't.

"That's not what I meant."

"What did you mean?"

"Okay, Ted," she said. "What I ... need to tell you ..."

As Boyce reached the trees, a figure appeared from the path in the vegetation. A woman in a swimsuit, a towel around her hips.

"Tru," I said. "Look. It's Jenny."

They didn't talk long. Jenny hugged him, but his arms hung at his sides. Just that quickly, she let him go and started our way as Boyce vanished into the trees. Neither one looked back.

"That was a quick goodbye," I said.

"He had to hurry," Tru said. "Things are ... changing."

I looked toward Key Biscayne, and the causeway faded in, out, and back in. A thinness in the air, a tang of internal combustion. The verdure where Boyce had disappeared seemed paler, threadier.

And the gap he had passed through was gone.

JENNY'S CHEEKS WERE WET but she was smiling.

"You holding up all right?" I said.

She nodded. "Tru, Boyce really liked you. It meant a lot to him, how you treated him like a regular guy."

They gravitated toward each other and hugged, and tears flowed.

"I feel bad for you," Tru said. "You'll miss him."

Jenny wiped her face with her towel. "I'm terrible, I know. But it's a relief he's gone. I love that kid, but he lived a tortured life here, and I couldn't help him." She planted her heels and stretched and I swear I heard sinews popping. "God," she said. "I want to act out, you know? I feel thirty pounds lighter and twenty years younger."

"And you look great," I said.

She grinned. "What should we do about that?"

"Anything we want," I said. "We're both single, no kids, nothing to hold us back or stand in our way."

HER GRIN FADED AND she glanced over at Tru, who was still crying. I felt bad about flirting with Jenny while Tru was still in pain.

"Hey," I said. "He'll be all right, Tru. He's found a place where he's—"

"Shut up, Ted," Jenny said. She put an arm around Tru's shoulders and leaned in. "You haven't told him yet?"

TRU'S BROW CREASED. "YOU know?"

Jenny sighed. "Everybody knows, hon."

"How? How can everybody know?"

"Wally figured it out, and he told Reva and she told Maddy, who claimed to know all along, and pretty soon everybody knew. Today we were all talking about how clueless you-know-who is."

Tru sniffed and laughed and nodded. "Clueless," she said.

"Not a good trait for a detective." Jenny grinned and cut her eyes in my direction.

"What are you two talking about?" I said.

Tru looked at Jenny. "Should I?"

Jenny gave me the once-over. "I don't know. I don't know if he's worth it."

Tru bit her lip. "What the fuck. We'd better sit down for this."

118 Spoils of war

So WE SAT AGAIN at the concrete table, me on one side, and Tru and Jenny on the other. And smack dab in the center of our triangle, Papa DePriest's crisply folded *pantalones*.

"We don't need these," Jenny said. "Whose are they, anyway?" She slid a hand under the pants and picked them up.

"Papa DePriest's," I said.

"Uh oh," she said. "There's something in these pants, and no smartass remarks from you, Ted Danger."

I put on an innocent face. "Don't be absurd."

Jenny unfolded the pants. "Eureka, look what I found."

A brass chain snaked from a belt loop to a buttoned pocket. Jenny popped the button and slid out a leather wallet, embossed, and a ring of keys with a black fob.

She glanced around the beach. "Somebody tell me why we have Papa DePriest's pants."

"What's that design on the billfold?" Tru said.

"It's that Japanese kitten," Jenny said. "You know."

"That's surreal," I said.

JENNY LOOKED AT ME. "That's surreal? *That's* surreal? After everything else that's been—" She shook her head. "Just tell me what these trousers are doing here."

So we told her about DePriest and his derringer, and how both barrels had fired as Boyce disarmed him, wounding DePriest, who removed his pants, which Boyce stole, inciting DePriest's pursuit and ultimate relocation to another time or place or, for lack of a better word, dimension, from which he was not expected to return. Oh, and Boyce's return of the pants, which he delivered just before he said his final goodbyes and he

351

himself vanished into the place we cannot explain.

"All right," Jenny said. "That's cleared up. And I hereby claim this loot."

"What?"

"Spoils of war. Boy captured it from the bad guy, and what was Boy's is now mine."

"Jenny, you can't just—"

"Woo-hoo. What kind of car do I get?"

She snapped the keys off the chain and pointed the fob at the parking lot. A robust double-tap blasted from the other side of the trees.

"Not too wimpy," she said. "Could be a truck. Don't wait up, kids." She took off.

"Wait a minute, Jenny," I said. "Come on, Tru. We've got to stop her."

"That broad's crazier than Nicki," she said.

THE HORN SOUNDED AGAIN and guided us to a nondescript sedan in the truck-of-tears color, but grayer. Or greener.

Jenny stood by the passenger door pressing fob buttons. The trunk popped, lights flashed, and the horn played *La Cucaracha*. Nice. She reached for the door handle.

"Wait, Jenny," I said. "You're not seriously taking that car, right?"

"You're funny, Ted. No, I'm not going to drive around in a wanted fugitive's car. I don't have a death wish. But there might be goodies inside."

"Hold on," I said. "No fingerprints."

She opened the door with the corner of her towel.

119   Blackmail

WE SAT AT THE beach table in a triangle, like before, but more spread out. Each with our own prize, booty we'd retrieved from DePriest's car before we wiped it down and locked it up.

Jenny's object of plunder: a pale blue suitcase, hard-sided and scuffed.

Tru's: a canvas bag with frayed seams.

And mine: a deep aluminum briefcase. Locked. But I found the key on DePriest's keyring.

I OPENED THE LID.

First, two flash drives and a stack of CDs with cryptic labels. And stapled documents of dates, names, and numbers, and symbols I couldn't make sense of.

Then, half a dozen folders of business documents: invoices, purchase orders, and contracts. Hotel and travel receipts. More dates and coded entries.

A notebook, pocket-sized and leather bound, with columns of data it would take a cryptographer to decipher.

And at the bottom of the case, a fat interoffice envelope with a string-and-button closure. The contents: a photograph album, long and black, with worn edges.

Inside, there they were again. Naked kids. All with adults this time. But not smiling into the camera on a sunny nude beach. Not posing with quaint props and old toys, feather boas and plastic six-shooters.

I TURNED EACH LEAF with care. Till now, I knew intellectually we were dealing with these kinds of images, situations, and people. But it had all felt abstract.

It didn't anymore.

STILLNESS ALL AROUND. TRU and Jenny no longer rifled DePriest's things.

"Ted," Tru said. "What are you looking at?"

"It's the DePriest blackmail collection. The men in these photographs can probably help DePriest. Or could once."

"Bigwigs," Tru said.

"Or little wigs in key positions."

Jenny leaned over. "Oh my god." She pointed to a pulpy guy with hairy shoulders. "I recognize that moron. Hardy and I had to deal with him over some zoning bullshit. I remember he had these weird—"

"Put those away, Ted," Tru said. "Let's hand them over to the police."

I kept turning pages. The shock was wearing off.

We *Homo sapiens* are a nasty piece of work, no doubt about it.

"Ted," Jenny said. "Did you hear what Tru said?"

I reached the last page. A prepubescent boy and girl stood in their dirty socks while a man in his underpants squatted between them, cupping their buttocks.

Bad stuff, for sure. But not the worst in the stack.

"Yes," I said. "I heard her. And no, these materials are not going to the police. Not yet, by god. We don't know if some of these lowlifes are cops themselves. This shit's got to stop."

"So what do we do?" Tru said.

"I don't know."

THEN I DID.

"Slaven and Bustamante," I said. "They can take everything, and make sure it doesn't get buried. Make copies. Bring in the media."

"Could be media guys diddling kids in these pictures," Tru said.

I closed the back cover. "Could be anybody."

NOBODY SPOKE. THE BREEZE ruffled the papers. I squared everything up and put it back in the case.

"Uncle," Tru said.

"Uncle?"

"Like Wally says. I give up. I'm tired of being here." She wiped a hand across her face. "I feel grimy, inside and out. I want to go home."

120   Raining again

IT WAS RAINING WHEN we landed in Dayton. A warm rain. Steady and resolute. Cleansing.

While Tru liberated her car from long-term parking, I babysat our bags in the loading zone outside the arrival gates. Humid air, scented with earthworms, wafted under the high canopy and slipped into my clothes. An intimate welcome.

It wasn't Miami, but it was home.

MIAMI. I WAS GLAD to be out of there.

The DePriest materials we'd left with Rytt and Navi yielded new revelations by the hour, and it wasn't all blackmail stuff. The drives and disks and folders opened floodgates of hard intel that would keep cops and prosecutors busy for months to come, exterminating deep-rooted trafficking and child exploitation operations all over Florida, nearly as fast as new ones would pop up to replace them.

Progress, I guess.

TRU PULLED UP WITH the car, and I loaded the bags and climbed in. Five minutes later we merged onto I-75 South, downtown ahead of us.

"It's good to be back," Tru said.

"You said it. But I miss the ocean already."

The rain dwindled to heavy mist. Tru slowed the wipers to intermittent.

"Will we need to go back to Florida?" she said. "For depositions or whatever?"

"It's possible. Rytt and Navi will be answering a lot of questions, for sure. We may be out of it."

AFTER I'D CALLED RYTT and told her what we'd found in DePriest's car, things happened quickly. We worked out a scenario that placed DePriest's goodies directly into Slaven and Bustamante's possession, without intermediaries. Our script omitted messy details about metaphysical phenomena, human/bonobo genetics, and the Cocaine Queen's granddaughter naked in a tornado thirty years ago.

"BUT WHAT DO THEY get out of it?" Tru said. "Rytt and Navi. Who's paying for their time?"

"Nicki," I said. "She felt responsible—since it started with her, and her parents covered it up for so long."

"And Bentley's okay with Nicki spending the money?"

"It doesn't matter what Bentley thinks. Something in Nicki's little suitcase—some kind of document—it changed everything."

"What was it?"

"She won't tell me. But she's not Bentley's poor relation anymore."

TRU SIGNALED LEFT AND passed an old Buick Electra sauntering in the slow lane. Then she signaled right and accelerated through the mist—which was turning into rain again—leaving the Electra behind.

"All those innocent kids," she said.

"It's tough," I said. "But what we did, it'll help, some."

"What haunts me is, where the hell are the parents? Why don't they protect their children?"

"Maybe they're dead. Or crushed by their lives, by their work, and they don't have anything left for their kids."

"Then they should find a different job," she said.

"They might have to take what they can get, just to survive."

"I suppose so." She didn't sound convinced.

"Maybe they were abused themselves," I said, "and don't know how to be decent parents."

A long minute passed as another mile sluiced under our wheels.

"And then ..." Her voice was faint behind the tire hiss and the motor hum, the wind, the rain, and the broken beat of the wiper blades.

"Then?" I said.

She took three breaths. Deep ones.

121 Good parenting

"SOME PEOPLE MIGHT BE parents and not even know it," Tru said.

I laughed. "Only the dads."

She wasn't laughing. "Ted, do you ever think you might have a child somewhere? A son you don't know about? Or ... a daughter?"

"Nah. If I got a woman pregnant, she'd tell me. Why wouldn't she?"

"There might be a reason."

"Well, yeah. If I lied about my name, and disappeared. But I've never done that."

"Maybe she knows how to find you, but she doesn't want to."

"Why would—"

"Maybe she's angry because you cheated on her when she needed you most."

"Wait a—"

"Maybe she was pregnant with your baby and afraid of how you'd react. And when she finally got the nerve to tell you, she found you in bed with another woman."

HOT IN THE CAR. Too hot. The humidity was drowning me. I pointed a dash vent at my face.

"That's a lot of maybes, Tru," I said.

"What if Hope was pregnant when she left you, Ted?"

"She would have told me."

"Why do you think she was acting different? Why did things change between you two?"

My heart was banging in my chest.

"How old would he be, Ted? If Hope had your son? Or your daughter. How old would she be, right now?"

"I don't know," I said. "I don't know. Let me think."

"My age, Ted."

"Could be." I looked at her face and saw what I'd missed before.

The steel in her gaze, the set of her jaw: Hope.

The warmth behind the toughness: Mom.

The smartass expression lurking in the eyes: I'd seen it in the mirror often enough.

"Yeah, your age," I said. "That'd be about right."

"Not *about* right, Ted. Exactly right. *Exactly*."

THE VIEW THROUGH THE windshield was blurred, and I blamed the brine that stung my eyes. But no, the rain had taken a violent turn, slapping the glass.

"Turn up the wipers, Tru."

"I can see just fine."

"Do it for me. I want to see where we're going."

A flick of her hand and the wiper beat quickened. "Is that a metaphor, Ted? It's dopey."

I shrugged. "And for god's sake turn your lights on."

"I told you, I can see fine." Her lips made a tight line.

"That's important," I said. "But perhaps, Grasshopper, it's equally important for others to see you."

"Stop it." She fired up the headlights, signaled right, and merged into the exit lane.

"Where're we going?" I said.

"I can't drive," she said. "I'm shaking like a ... I don't know what."

Her knuckles white on the wheel, she drove in silence, finally swinging in at a cluster of midscale bars and restaurants.

She parked near a Mexican-themed cantina, shut down the engine, and rested her head on the steering wheel.

Rain pummeled the roof.

I touched her shoulder. "Why didn't you tell me before?"

She didn't look up. "Why didn't you go after Hope?"

I didn't have an answer she'd like. "We've talked about that already."

"But things are different now," she said. "Between you and me." She raised her head and looked me in the eye. "Aren't they, Ted?"

I HELD HER GAZE and felt a sudden serenity. As if Madam Fernando had beamed her magical bliss rays across the miles, just for us. Rays of love and approval. And bliss, of course.

"Let's talk about it over fajitas, *mija*," I said. I tipped my head toward the cantina. "Start with warm chips and hot salsa."

She fixed me with a look of undisguised evaluation.

Thinking it over.

"Extra guacamole," I said. "And ice-cold *cervezas*."

Her eyes narrowed. Then she nodded. "Now that's what I call good parenting."

She shot me half a smile and the rain slackened to nearly nothing, almost like cause and effect. And who's to say it wasn't?

Stranger things have happened. That's for damn sure.

THE HOSTESS, A SLIGHT Latina with gleaming hair and a placid smile, seemed too young for the job.

Maybe the restaurant's a family business. Everybody with a part to play, even the kids.

"Just the two of you today?" she said.

Tru looked up at me. I offered my arm and she took it.

"Yep," she said. "Just me and my dad."

AT OUR TABLE BY the window, the hostess delivered our menus and turned away. But not before I read the name on her gleaming ID tag. In a few seconds I started breathing again.

Tru leaned over and touched my hand.

"I saw it too," she said.

Soledad.

Epilogue

NEAR THE END OF our meal, she leaves for the restroom and I sit alone amid the ruins of our fajitas and flan and I try to conjure the solitude I've borne for too many years.

It's gone.

BEFORE THE DOOR CLOSES behind us, the girl, Soledad, pushes it open and follows us out.

"Excuse me. This is yours." She offers me a clamshell carry-out box.

"We didn't have leftovers," I say.

Tru shakes her head, agreeing.

"It's for you." The girl presses it into my hands.

"Are you sure?" I move to open it.

Her hand flies to the lid. "No, not here." Her eyes shift to Tru, then she turns and re-enters the restaurant.

I stare at the box.

"Shall I call the bomb squad?" Tru says.

"Nah. Let's risk it."

IN THE CAR, I set the box on the floor and fasten my seatbelt.

Tru puts the key in the ignition but doesn't twist it. "I don't think I can wait, Ted."

"Me neither."

I pick up the box. It isn't heavy. Snap open the tabs. Crack the lid just enough to see what— No. Close it.

"What is it, Ted?"

"I must be crazy."

"What's in there?"

I peek again. Close the lid.

"Ted, you look pale. What's going on?"
I shake my head and hand her the box.
She opens it and removes the contents.
"What the hell? Is this yours?"

IT'S FIVE SIZES too big, but she slips it over her fingers. Punches my shoulder.
"Well, Dad?"
"It's Ronnie Panko's," I say. "Ronnie Panko's brass knuckles."

Made in the USA
Monee, IL
08 July 2021

73121812R00215